In her debut novel, **A NEST OF SNAKES**, *Deborah Levison boldly tackles a tough and timely subject: private school abuse. Part thriller, part courtroom drama, this gripping story is told in searing prose that propels the reader forward, right up to the last, jarring page.*
—Gary M. Krebs, author of Little Miss of Darke County: The Origins of Annie Oakley

A NEST OF SNAKES *is a massive leap from Deborah Levison's* **THE CRATE**, *which was an incredible true crime read. Its gut punch immediacy and emotional heft entrances the reader in a thriller that follows a sympathetic character who survived a horrific trauma in a boy's school. The jagged road that leads to a staggering climax propels the story forward like a rocket through a barbed wire gauntlet of emotionally-wrought drama, thrills, and deep characters that refuse to let go. A story both timely and powerful, Levison's strong writing should be one of the fall's most talked about novels.*
—David Simms, author of Dark Muse and Fear the Reaper

Levison delivers a harrowing story of one man's fight for justice as he confronts the demons from his past. Haunting, suspenseful, and beautifully written, **A NEST OF SNAKES** *is a disturbing look into abuses of power by those we trust the most.*
—Anne K. Howard, author of the award-winning true crime story, His Garden: Conversations with a Serial Killer

Brendan Cortland is a broken man. Broken by abuse as a child at an exclusive boarding school and the shame he felt. But in Deborah Levison's skillfully told novel, Brendan finds his path to redemption, first by tracking abusers online, and finally by going public and accusing his own tormentors. Heartfelt and horrifying, **A NEST OF SNAKES** *is a story that must be told, and remembered.*
—James R Benn, author of the Billy Boyle WWII mystery series

A NEST OF SNAKES

A NOVEL BY

DEBORAH LEVISON

WILDBLUE
PRESS

WildBluePress.com

A NEST OF SNAKES published by:
WILDBLUE PRESS
P.O. Box 102440
Denver, Colorado 80250

ISBN 978-1-957288-40-6 Hardcover
ISBN 978-1-957288-39-0 Trade Paperback
ISBN 978-1-957288-38-3 eBook

Interior Formatting by Elijah Toten
www.totencreative.com

A
NEST OF
SNAKES

PROLOGUE

Brendan's shoulders ached as he wielded the machete, slicing through the thick, leathery skin of a viper as it reared up at him from the nest. After that came another, and another. Bloody and seething, the snakes continued to hiss and strike even as the blade flashed. Slithering black mass became gory red mess as he shredded each muscular serpent into strips, hacking away for what seemed like hours. At last, the heap of raw meat lay still at his feet. His knife clattered onto the stone floor of the cave as Brendan doubled over, eyes closed and hands braced on his knees, chest heaving with exertion.

He didn't notice the last of the vipers coiled on a ledge of the cave wall, mere inches from his face.

PART ONE

2015

CHAPTER ONE

The buzzing alarm clock jolted Brendan awake. He lay there shuddering for a few seconds as his ragged breathing slowed, the pillow beneath his cheek drenched with sweat, the duvet tangled at his feet. He swung his legs to the floor and ran a hand through his damp, stringy hair.

Eight o'clock. Like every other morning, Brendan didn't have to be anywhere in particular, and the empty hours to fill before his Wednesday afternoon appointment loomed long. It took less than five seconds to find a blank page and jot words in his journal. *Snakes, again*, he scribbled. Like every other morning, he forced himself out of bed. Under no circumstances was he allowed to sleep away the day, his doctor advised.

Brendan shuffled to the office across from his bedroom and sank into his leather chair to open a laptop, one of a few on his desk. He'd spent solitary hours and years staring at monitors.

He clicked on a message board, commenting and posting with a temporary IP address he changed after each use, using a series of encrypted gateways and firewalls that rendered him virtually untraceable. All his data was saved in an "air-gapped" computer—one that had never been connected to the Internet and was therefore unhackable.

Over time, he'd amassed hundreds of files representing the four types of online predator he hunted: Occasional Users, who were almost invisible and tough to catch because they didn't download the obscene, illegal images they viewed in cyberspace; Collectors, who, as the name suggested, collected images but didn't interact much in chats; and Distributors, who shared illegal content and offered technical advice on how to avoid being caught.

Eventually, they all tripped up. One guy posted a photo of his own daughter's birthday party—innocent six-year-olds running through a sprinkler with the house number easily spotted in the background. That one was a no-brainer. At first, when Brendan began hunting these deviants, he'd settled for exposing a guy, shaming him, and threatening to out him to his spouse or parents or employer as a pedophile. After a while, though, Brendan realized he could do better: he could gather enough evidence to tip off the local authorities, which was exactly what he'd done to individuals in Turkey, Indonesia, France, and around the United States. On his information, several of the pervs had been arrested and convicted. Through one of his hubs, he'd helped bring down a human trafficking ring. Not all that different from what the Feds were doing these days with online stings, maybe, but Brendan had been at it longer, had formed friendships, had all the time in the world to devote to it, and his IT skills were fantastic.

This morning the chat rooms were quiet, as he predicted; things didn't heat up until nightfall. That's when the vermin crawled out from under the rocks to begin posting, after dinner, after their unwitting families went to sleep. That's when Brendan did his best hunting: in the dark.

Behind his screens, he could be anyone. A hunter. A vigilante. A defender of children from those who would exploit them.

Slumped on the marble bench in the shower, Brendan let a half hour's-worth of hot water wash over him. He donned the ironed shirt and pants Irma had laid out on his chair, then went downstairs for the single cup of decaffeinated coffee Irma had brewed. He could hear her puttering nearby as he hoisted himself onto a kitchen stool and steered his gaze outside.

Rain pelted the window, soaking the early spring grass and bright green shoots. It fell in sheets from the slate shingles of the gazebo and bent the delicate stalks of the season's first daffodils, darkening the mulch in the flower beds to glistening black. The scent would be sweetly sharp, Brendan thought, trying halfheartedly to recall the feel of rain. Or snow, or wind, or sunshine, for that matter. When had he last ventured out into the world long enough to be touched by the elements? Irma did the grocery shopping and other errands. Anything else Brendan needed or wanted, any of the myriad electronics and gadgets and bizarre bric-a-brac that filled the rooms of his life, could be ordered online and delivered. His general concierge physician received a handsome monthly retainer should a house call be necessary. Even the short trip across his village of Summer's Pond to Greenwich proper for his weekly therapy session, from garage to garage, could be managed without stepping out of doors.

Dr. Aldrich had been pleased when Brendan agreed to get his driver's license decades earlier. "It's a big leap, Brendan," he'd said, nodding approval. "The first of many more on your path to independence." But when it came time to register inside the crowded motor vehicle department, Brendan had frozen, skewered by the stares of strangers; flushed and panting, he'd stumbled back to the parking lot. These days the groundskeeper, Tomasz—Irma's son—drove him back and forth to appointments. Brendan remained locked inside his compound and inside his own head.

"*Dzień dobry*," Irma said, bustling in to rinse the coffeepot, her coarse gray hair swept off her too-wide forehead and woven into a braid. Her hairstyle hadn't changed in the thirty years she'd been the family housekeeper. "You would like egg and toast today?" She played the game well. Brendan ate two slices of wheat toast and two soft-boiled eggs every day.

"Thunderstorms this evening," she continued, her Polish accent heavy. She set breakfast on the table, careful not to brush against Brendan's arm. As usual, her face—eyes, nose, lips couched between the broad forehead and even broader chin—showed little expression. "I make soup for supper. Fish chowder, the creamy kind you like?"

Brendan lifted a shoulder, still staring out the window.

"And dessert, of course. We celebrate." She paused for a beat, in case he answered. "All right then. I go to market. I'm back before you leave for appointment." Irma buttoned her trench coat, lifted her purse and umbrella from the hook in the butler's pantry, and let herself quietly out the back door.

A few minutes later, Brendan ate a spoonful of runny egg. A yellow droplet of yolk fell on the single blossom Irma had plucked to decorate his plate, a token for his special day.

At two o'clock, right on time, Brendan pushed open a door left ajar a crack to indicate Dr. Aldrich's readiness for an appointment. In all these years, Brendan had only to wait on a handful of occasions outside a closed door, as Dr. Aldrich insisted on punctuality.

"Come in, Brendan. Have a seat," the man said now, composed and reserved as always. "How are you?"

Brendan clutched his jacket and folded his six-foot build into the overstuffed chair across from the doctor's. He glanced around the home office at the familiar yellowing diplomas, awards, and certificates as if to assure himself he'd be in good hands. He knew the credentials by heart: Bachelor of Science, University of Virginia. Doctor of Medicine, Columbia University. Residency at Johns Hopkins University. Board certified by the American Board of Psychiatry and Neurology. Licensed to practice in New York, New Jersey, and Connecticut. Voted "Distinguished Mental Health Practitioner of the Year" three years in a row.

"Okay."

Dr. Aldrich nodded. "How has your week been?"

Brendan shrugged ever so slightly.

"You took your meds?"

A nod.

"Still journaling?"

Another nod.

"Have you been on the treadmill?"

"Once or twice."

"Good." Dr. Aldrich studied him from behind rimless glasses, seeing what he always saw: the unkempt, dull blond hair, shot through with gray and sorely in need of a cut. Grizzled stubble on a doughy face like a pincushion; a plain beige crew neck and khakis clinging to a flabby frame; translucent skin and sad, furtive green eyes under dark brows, framed by unusually thick, black lashes. When Brendan first started coming for therapy, he'd been an extraordinary young man—*that Cortland boy! Like a movie star,* people exclaimed—but now, over twenty years later, he sagged. Middle-aged and forlorn.

"You're following the rest of your routine?"

"Nine hours of sleep a night. No naps."

"And the dreams?"

Brendan's gaze skittered sideways, toward the window. Yes, he'd had the dream again. He muttered something.

Outside and to the right, on the busy Greenwich, Connecticut street, Range Rovers and luxury sedans streamed past on an avenue lined with trendy retailers, boutiques, cafés, and upscale design shops. A woman, probably a nanny, pushed a plastic-covered stroller down the sidewalk. A little girl skipped ahead in pink rain boots, holding a Disney princess umbrella.

"Louder, please," said the doctor.

Brendan cleared his throat. "Last night," he whispered, watching the ruffled umbrella bob out of sight. He thought about his dream. Chopping up a nest of snakes wasn't new. That, and a dozen similar nightmares, were all variations on a common theme: Brendan battling hordes of malicious predators, amphibian to mammalian, and any weapon he found to protect himself from attack proved impotent. This familiar reptilian scene would prompt another arched eyebrow by his therapist. He swallowed.

"The snakes."

Dr. Aldrich reached to turn the dial of a small device on his desk. The sweetness of wind chimes tinkled through the office. "Go on."

"Vipers."

Dr. Aldrich folded his hands together.

"A nest of them. I was trapped, in a cave this time. I had a knife but I dropped it." Brendan trembled with the brimming memory. Beads of perspiration racked together on his upper lip, an abacus of pure terror.

"We're counting," the doctor reminded him. "And *one*, and *two*…"

Yes. *One*, Brendan recited silently, with a long breath in and out from deep in the bellows of his lungs. *Two*, another breath, and slowly his toes unclenched. *Three*, the relaxation spread upward. He forced himself to continue describing details aloud as his breathing blanketed the fear.

Glancing at his notes, Dr. Aldrich nodded. "It's been a few weeks since the last one. The longest gap in a three-decade span, I think. I'd been hopeful that maybe, just maybe, they'd stopped for good? Well, we'll keep working on it. Let's continue."

Brendan exhaled slowly, listening to the soothing chimes, and calmed enough to answer the doctor's next questions. "I haven't had a drink since last week. No sugar for three days. I will tonight, though, because there'll be cake," he added.

For the first time in the session, Dr. Aldrich smiled. "Ah, right! Happy birthday, Brendan. Forty-seven, yes? Any word today?"

"Mom left a voicemail. She said she'd try again later."

"And from Zac?"

"No."

"I see." Dr. Aldrich smoothed his white goatee. "Well, I wish you a healthy and successful year. As I've often said, you are stronger than you think. You'd be surprised at what you can reclaim."

Before Brendan could formulate an answer, a knock sounded. Dr. Aldrich excused himself and rose to answer, careful to open the door only a hair, just enough to speak in hushed tones with the person on the other side.

After a minute, he sank back into his chair, contemplating his patient. "You should know that I've decided to rent out space across the hall, starting at the beginning of the month," he said. "I've explained your situation to the new tenant. She's an attorney. We will do our best to prevent it… but there will be a possibility of your running into her as you come and go."

Brendan stared straight ahead.

"That is, until you're ready to meet her," Dr. Aldrich added.

"Why would I want to do that?" Brendan didn't raise his eyes, leveling his gaze instead on the psychiatrist's argyle vest.

Dr. Aldrich's voice was calm. "Because, Brendan, this attorney might like to represent you. In a lawsuit."

Silence.

Finally: "How do you feel about that?"

Brendan gazed out the window once more. A young couple huddled together in the downpour and hurried across the intersection, laughing. How did he feel? He'd lost so much of his life. Never held a job. Despised by his ex-wife. Hadn't been outside the walls of his seven-thousand-square-foot prison, or seen his son, in years. The closest thing he had to a friend was a therapist; his family, a maid and a groundskeeper. The very thought of having to interact with strangers nearly loosened his bowels.

By the time Tomasz backed the town car out of the psychiatrist's garage with Brendan hunkered in the rear seat, the deluge had slowed to a drizzle.

Irma stacked the mail in its usual spot on the kitchen island. Mostly financial statements, always ignored.

Large, brightly-colored envelopes rested under the regular bills. Brendan tore them open. "Best wishes from Barnaby Investment Partners" and "Happiest of birthdays from your friends at Mercedes-Benz." The local realtor sent regards. Brendan rifled through the letters again, looking for childish penmanship. There was none.

He left the pile on the counter. Irma would arrange the greeting cards on the fireplace mantel, he knew, and leave them on display for a few weeks before discreetly tossing them into the trash.

Brendan wandered out of the kitchen to survey his kingdom. In what once had been a gracefully-appointed living room, priceless antiques now stood alongside model trains and pinball machines. Here, a modern Edra chair shaped like a gerbera daisy; there, a sixteenth-century cast-iron loom. Stacks of vintage Superman comic books covered the top of a gorgeous Restoration Hardware table. Lucite stands enclosing autographed sneakers—once owned by basketball players, judging from the size of them—lined the hallway. Fine art and vintage posters hung on the walls above them. A Giovanni Manozzi cherub contemplated Campari bitter in the neighboring frame.

Down the hall, a gleaming grand piano claimed the center of the music room. Besides the original wing chairs and credenza containing sheet music, tiered racks now exhibited instruments of every variety: electric, brass, timpani. A didgeridoo, calabash rattles. Records and CDs were stacked on the floor between twin speakers as tall as Brendan himself and powerful enough to regale the neighborhood. Across from them, life-sized wax mannequins presided over the bespoke orchestra.

French doors opened to another room that at one time had been a prized library. It adjoined the more manly study Kenneth, Brendan's father, had once kept for himself; but this soft space had belonged to his wife, the cocoon where she curled in a recliner with a glamor magazine while expensive editions of Brontë, Dickens, and Tolstoy languished on the shelves. It was the single room on the main floor into which Brendan hadn't crammed his garish toys. Its décor remained unaltered, Dr. Aldrich interpreted, because Brendan hoped Eliza Cortland would return one day to reclaim it.

Across the foyer, a last entrance remained: to the den. Brendan glanced inside, past the fireplace and camelback sofa to the sole occupant of the room.

"Hello," he mumbled.

A pair of small, black eyes met his. Like all Brendan's impulsive acquisitions, this one hadn't maintained his interest for long after its arrival at the mansion in Summer's Pond.

Brendan wheezed up the stairs to the landing and looked outside. The last birthday party at the house had been a decade earlier: A circus theme, replete with jugglers on stilts and ponies and dancing poodles in a striped tent just below the window. Perfect for a two-year-old. Zac had toddled around with a cupcake cradled in his palms and a first lick of frosting smeared on his lip, until a wild-eyed clown cackled in his ear. Zac shrieked and dropped the cupcake. Brendan remembered wanting to scoop him up and make it better, to breathe in the sweet, untainted scent of his son. But he'd hesitated, feeling useless, knowing he didn't have the capability to comfort his boy, not trusting his own arms to do the holding. He stood there until Zac's mom swooped over to console him and led him back to the draped dessert table with a backward glance of scorn.

Since then, birthday festivities had paled. Brendan's own childhood friends hadn't called or texted in years. Even the thinking-of-you notes signed, "Best always, Shawn," disappeared as Brendan's world compressed to nothingness.

Outside, the rain pattered intermittently while a pale disk of sunlight glowed from behind the clouds. The turquoise pool shimmered, bordered by damp flagstone and sculpted boxwood in planters, perfectly maintained though no one used it. And there was beefy Tomasz with a wheelbarrow and chainsaw as usual, on his way to tend to the far quadrant, an isolated, overgrown area of the property far from the main house.

Brendan continued up the stairs to his suite of rooms. A cell phone lay on the desk in his office. No texts, just two missed calls from an unknown name. No reason to bother with the voicemails—probably spam. He lifted the device to his ear.

"Brendan?"

"Hello. Can I... can I speak with him?"

"It's the middle of the day on a weekday. He's at school."

Idiot, Brendan chided himself. *Of course.* "Later, maybe?"

"He's very busy this week. Playoffs start this weekend."

"Well, it's… you know, it's my birthday, so I thought…"

"Oh. Right." The woman's voice on the other end sounded aggrieved. "He's got hockey practice until eight-thirty. He'll call you after pick up."

In the background, a deep male voice: "Who are you talking to?"

Brendan cleared his throat and continued. "He has a phone, right? Couldn't I just have his number?"

"We've discussed this before. Not a good idea." And she disconnected.

Brendan returned the phone to his desk and turned toward the closet. A six-numeral sequence unlocked a safe, a familiar pattern he'd spun and clicked countless times. When the heavy metal door swung open, Brendan stared at the contents for a few moments: gold bars, which long ago were a sound investment and might be again. A wad of cash in case of an emergency. Manila envelopes of documents—copies of wills, deeds, trusts. Divorce papers. And, lying on top of it all, a Bren Ten semi-automatic pistol.

The gun felt solid and heavy in Brendan's palm. Yet again, he thought how very easy it would be to point it at his temple and be done with it, instead of fighting the chokehold on his throat that made him want to weep. He thought of the laughing couple walking arm in arm, and the little girl stomping in puddles with her pink boots.

Dr. Aldrich's voice echoed in his ear, the same words ricocheting for years. *"You have the strength."* Brendan knew what that meant: venturing outside his safe space. Interacting in the real world, with real people. Baring his neck to their teeth and talons.

And at today's appointment, some new words: *"She can represent you in a lawsuit."*

How many times had Dr. Aldrich encouraged Brendan to consider filing charges? "For justice," he'd said. "Compensation. Closure." He stopped suggesting it when it became apparent that Brendan wouldn't be able to handle the public nature of a trial. Now the psychiatrist had broached the subject again, as if a lawsuit had materialized anyway.

Straightening his arms, Brendan pointed the gun at the wall with both hands the way he'd seen it done in movies, and squinted through one eye. He conjured targets, hideous faces he once knew, and pretended to fire, blasting them into red-oblivion.

"Bang," he said, under his breath. Now *that* would be closure. But his arms dropped limply. He slid the pistol back into the safe and spun the dial.

A lawsuit? Brendan had long ago begun to pursue his own justice from behind his computer screens. The kind that would dispense a very different outcome.

With a sigh, he pushed aside the air-gapped computer and powered up another, his everyday laptop. On that one, his homepage loaded quickly to his ex-wife's favorite social media site and populated with her family's photos: boating near the Florida Keys, spring skiing in Beaver Creek. A lifestyle Brendan helped finance, even though her second husband had plenty of money.

A new set of pictures popped up: the blonde mother and three blond children, flanked by a tall, chiseled man, awash in the orange of a Santorini sunset. Their beauty and their happiness seemed to transcend the screen.

The sheer *normalness* of their expressions contrasted sharply with Brendan's life. The realization engulfed him. He pressed PRINT and the image spat from his printer. He clicked his mouse again and again as sheets of paper fluttered to the floor. He'd been robbed of his family, and all around him the image of a robber smiled, smug.

It was so unfair. All of it. So monumentally, grotesquely unfair.

Brendan stood abruptly, sending his chair rolling backward to collide with the wall. For a moment, the room seemed to dip sideways. As if on fast forward, the events of the past flashed through his mind on warp speed, culminating in the gaping, yawning emptiness of today. He looked down, surprised to see his fingers gripping the handle of the sliding glass door that led to a stone balcony overlooking the pool. With growing astonishment, he pulled open the door and watched his own foot step outside.

Stepping onto his balcony was dizzying and for one petrifying moment, Brendan thought he'd topple over the railing and onto the flagstone three stories below. "One," he rasped aloud, "two, three," until he could pull himself upright open-eyed. As the vertigo receded, he became incrementally aware of the outside world surrounding him: Raindrops splattering onto his cheeks. Birds twittering and squirrels chittering from high branches beyond the gardens. A tangy smell of wetness. He leaned on the cold stone, feeling the unfamiliar roughness under his palms, and gazed around with growing wonder.

"*NIE!*" Irma screamed from behind him, flinging herself out the sliding door so suddenly that Brendan very nearly fell despite himself. Alarmed, the woman grasped his sleeve and yanked him back toward the safety of the house, latching the glass door after him. She leaned against its frame and clutched her chest as her eyes swept the room, taking in the images of his ex-wife all over the floor. She turned to Brendan accusingly.

"I wasn't going to jump," he whispered, standing uncertainly in the middle of the room, surrounded by the printed faces scattered across the carpet. A captive audience.

"Then why you go out there?"

"I just want… to be normal. I have to prove that I can be normal."

CHAPTER TWO

Those few seconds outside in the rain didn't dissolve thickly-laid fear, nor did they transform Brendan entirely. But something in him had shifted. Something subtle, on so deep a cellular level that at first he hadn't recognized or even registered it. But there it was all the same. For the first time in over a decade he'd felt the faintest glimmer of optimism, a determination to succeed outside his fortress. He wrote in his journal: *Went outdoors today. And didn't self-destruct! Maybe there's hope...*

That evening, when Brendan trudged downstairs for dinner, Irma gestured toward the formal dining table. It had stood untouched for many days—three hundred and sixty-four, to be exact—but this annual commemoration, at least, warranted the fuss. She'd unwrapped the fine bone china from wisps of tissue in the sideboard, retrieved a crystal water goblet from the mahogany breakfront, and set a bouquet of tulip buds into a gold-etched vase.

Over the decades Irma had spent working in the Cortland mansion, the finery it housed—heirlooms from generations ago—felt like extensions of herself. Not Brendan's array of ridiculous Internet purchases, of course, but the valuables, the treasured things. She lifted them from shelves and out of drawers to dust and polish and care for as tenderly as if they were living flesh. Her most loving caresses were reserved for the objects that filled her world, not the people.

Now, as Brendan slouched at the head of the table, Irma approached cradling a Royal Copenhagen tureen that cost half of an average worker's annual salary. The aroma of chowder wafted to her nostrils. Despite the other ingredients in the soup, the parsley, the paprika, the cod, the cream, all she smelled were potatoes. Potatoes sickened her.

Nothing dug up her memories like the aroma of potatoes—memories hearkening back to her adolescence in Lesc, a rural village in eastern Poland at its border with Belarus, back when her parents were alive, long before she'd come to the New Country.

Those innocent days were a blur now, a faint recollection of hide-and-seek in sweet grasses taller than her head, grasses that bordered her father's crops. Except for one night in December of 1955 when Irma was fifteen years old. The violence of that night was not a blur. All these years later the memory remained sharp as a needle.

Forcing her mind back to the present, Irma ladled a bowl of steaming chowder from the tureen and sliced into a loaf of artisan bread, releasing its fragrant breath.

Brendan ate slowly, savoring the nuances of her rich cooking. He downed three bowls of chowder, mopping up the last delicious drops with the crusts. When it came time for dessert, a decadent, buttery, flourless torte lit with one small birthday candle, he mumbled thanks to Irma before blowing out the flame. She blinked, caught off guard for the second time that day.

Two days passed before Brendan mustered his courage again. This time, the conscious intention of going outside, once he decided to do it, filled him with trepidation. He was numb in the way only someone traumatized could be, someone paralyzed by guilt. *Don't know if I can do this,* he wrote. *Trying.* His footsteps echoed through the marble foyer over Thursday and Friday as he forced himself closer and closer to the front door. Finally, on Saturday morning, Brendan found himself outside in a slant of bright sunshine.

Rounding the corner from the guesthouse path onto the cobbled drive a half hour later, Irma came upon him standing on the threshold, as white and still as the two marbled pillars framing him on the porte-cochère. She nearly dropped her purse.

On Sunday, alone for most of the day, Brendan left the house yet again, so single-mindedly that he forgot to take his meds for the third day in a row. Despite a pounding heart and legs that quivered bonelessly, he pushed one foot in front of the other all the way to the road. The distance seemed interminable, as if he'd survived a catastrophic accident and needed to learn to walk again.

Past the high hedges, at the point where his private drive intersected with Whelk Lane, Brendan stopped. Just beyond the coarse shrubbery lining the road lay the sparkling vista of Long Island Sound, closer and more glorious than he'd experienced in years—the perspective from the main deck of a cruise as opposed to an upper cabin window like those of his living room or his parents' master bedroom a floor above. Brendan soaked in the panorama of billowing white sails and gulls wheeling in a cloudless sky. How could he have shut out all this beauty for so long? Just then two women appeared, jogging around the bend on the far side of the road.

"Morning," they called out in unison as they passed by.

Strangled with panic, Brendan reeled and lurched back toward the safety of the house. He drew the heavy drapes and cowered in bed for the rest of the day, clasping his journal in a shaking hand, inking pages with expletives of self-loathing.

That night another dream came: He bobbed in the middle of a sea at dusk, alone for miles, clutching a spear in his fist. The horizon glimmered in pinks and purples, as pretty a scene as his mind could conjure. Suddenly, a gunmetal triangle rose up from the mirk to cut the surface, followed by another and another. The fins circled closer, until razor teeth sank into his ankles and pulled him under. The spear slipped from his grasp and spiraled into the depths.

When he woke up, he couldn't breathe.

Despite the terror of the previous hours, when Irma poured his coffee on Monday morning the hard little seed of hope poked at Brendan again. He imagined Dr. Aldrich's voice. *"Think what you've accomplished,"* he'd say at the next appointment, sounding proud. *"See? You have the strength."* A wave of embarrassment followed the thought. Here he was, a grown man, anticipating his doctor's praise just for going outdoors.

He asked Irma to accompany him across the road so he could feel the water. She walked beside him, careful to maintain a few inches between them as Brendan couldn't stand to be touched.

The two-minute walk from the house to the shore stretched tenfold as Brendan hesitated at the edge of the sand, reluctant to continue. At long last, they stood in the surf. He leaned down and dipped a hand into the chilly water. When he straightened, he looked at Irma with a faint smile, leaving her speechless.

She couldn't remember the last time she'd seen any expression on his face. Except despair.

Dr. William Aldrich wiped the last few crumbs of a ham sandwich from his goatee. Another week had passed, and now another working lunch at his desk, dictating notes from his morning sessions. He scrawled, *Likely bipolar* in the folder of a young lady. Yesterday she'd breezed into the office wreathed in smiles, eager to describe her school and friends and the fine arts degree she wanted to earn. Today she'd returned, morose, slapping down a few charcoal drawings from her portfolio before scrunching them up and tossing them into the trashcan.

One minute to two. Dr. Aldrich's phone dinged with a new notification: *"Congratulations, you won!"* Confetti showered the screen around the green digits 6-7-0, meaning six hundred and seventy dollars had been transferred to his account. He welcomed the payout on yesterday's wager favoring Aloof Balloon in the upcoming Guineas races in the United Kingdom. The gray Thoroughbred had performed well at Gulfstream and Dubai. Dr. Aldrich longed to sit back, pour over the stats, see how things were shaping up for Churchill Downs, but instead he flicked off the volume. He had the afternoon to slog through still, hours more listening to the monotonous drone of insecurities and neuroses and the drivel of his privileged clientele.

Opening the most recent folder labeled "Brendan R. Cortland, b. 1968," Dr. Aldrich frowned. Only a few sheets of paper rested inside; his part-time secretary had stored sister files, completed decades earlier and inches thick, in the basement. He wrote the date, April 8, 2015, below the previous week's entry, in which he'd simply scrawled "N/C" for "no change." N/Cs filled columns as far as his eye could see.

"Hello," he said, replacing his pen in its spot on his blotter. He glanced up behind rimless glasses as his patient entered, clutching his jacket as usual. The same lank hair, the same soulful green eyes, the same colorless outfit stretched over the bulge of a gut.

The cell phone buzzed once again with the results of another bet. Dr. Aldrich glanced down. A sad face shook its head from side to side, dissolving into a red minus fifteen hundred. *Goddamn.* He needed to get back to the stats, give them his full attention, recoup his losses. He couldn't afford to lose another penny this month. He clenched his fists in his lap and glared at the glowing screen.

"Doctor."

Across from the desk in the overstuffed chair sat Brendan, his lips twitching upward ever so slightly, just enough to reconfigure the flatness of his face. It took several seconds for Dr. Aldrich to notice the change.

"You look different," he commented, forcing his eyes from the phone and peering at his patient. "Has something happened since your birthday? Is there something you'd like to tell me?"

Brendan nodded and licked his dry lips. "Yes," he whispered.

"Remarkable," Dr. Aldrich muttered under his breath, furiously filling his pages, his racing bets forgotten. *Patient maintains eye contact,* he wrote, *and displays deepening facial expression with increased inflection in voice. Demeanor cannot be termed normal as of yet but may be characterized as blunted... a marked improvement from the flat affect seen to date.*

The phone vibrated again, but Dr. Aldrich ignored it as he continued to take notes while Brendan spoke. *Patient continues to whisper but shows clear signs of engagement. Discussion during regular session notes several separate attempts initiated by patient to conquer agoraphobia, including the day after another severe anxiety dream, the reporting of which did not necessitate relaxation technique. Patient reports increased interaction with household staff.*

Shaking his head, the doctor laid down his pen. Scientific literature reported spontaneous recovery from catatonia associated with schizophrenia, but many of those cases involved patients who'd been catatonic for days or weeks. Of course, Brendan hadn't been catatonic in the true sense, certainly not for years or decades.

The illness Brendan suffered since beginning therapy ebbed and waned. A spate of symptoms had appeared on the heels of his father's death, and then again when his mother moved to Italy. During the course of Brendan's marriage he felt overwhelmed with anxiety, especially after failed attempts to succeed in business, financial comfort notwithstanding. Soon came night terrors. Brendan reported the sporadic sensation of "losing time," but not enough to substantiate dissociative disorder. Dr. Aldrich was reluctant to make the narrow and dogmatic diagnosis of schizophrenia.

Holding off on prescribing benzodiazepines or electroconvulsive shock therapy, he'd written in his earliest notes. *Patient's thinking is not disorganized.* There was no evidence of delusions or hallucinations, and Brendan's early echolalia and verbigeration, the repeating or echoing of words or nonsense syllables, had disappeared quickly. With the birth of his son and subsequent divorce, though, Brendan had become increasingly depressed and apathetic, a state that deepened over the years to something resembling catatonia. His condition became more like a chronic, major depressive episode characterized by inexplicable feelings of melancholia and worthlessness.

Dr. Aldrich suspected abuse, of course. The dreams, especially of snakes, were obvious enough; even a lay person could interpret them. But the doctor wondered if there was something more that his patient had yet to reveal. Something that hadn't surfaced under hypnosis, an additional wellspring of trauma that perhaps Brendan hadn't disclosed to anyone anywhere, not even in his journal.

Regardless, the talk therapy and journaling and antidepressants seemed to keep him functioning at least well enough to attend weekly sessions, even if he skulked along the hallway to the back door with his face burrowed in his jacket collar until he reached the safety of the garage and his waiting car. Dr. Aldrich often suspected that the man had chosen him only for the location of his private home office on Chatwick Road near the corner of Greenwich Avenue. Isolated access. Lush shrubbery and a high fence separating the charming Victorian from the suite of professional offices next door. The doctor did his best to make sure there was little possibility of Brendan crossing paths with another patient or with his wife, Leslie.

Now, he contemplated the small yet medically significant spontaneous improvement he saw in the person across from him. Would he sustain it, or revert back to his clinical depression? "Brendan, can you tell me exactly what happened and how you were feeling on your birthday, just before you opened the sliding door to the balcony?"

"Sad."

"Not angry?" Dr. Aldrich left the rest unspoken. Both of them knew Brendan had yet to express anger.

Brendan glanced toward the front window, remembering the little girl in the rain boots, and shrugged slightly. "No, just sad. With this feeling that something was ending, like I'd come to the edge of a cliff and had to decide which way to go."

"So you stepped out on the balcony, imagining you were on a cliff. And you wanted to jump off and end it all?"

"No... the opposite. I wanted to... see the valley beyond the cliff, to prove I could... survive the view." His fists, balled in his lap, relaxed. "It was my birthday and I didn't even get a text or card from Zac. I'm afraid he thinks that I'm... you know, damaged. Crazy. I don't want another year to go by like that. At first it was awful, but then it felt like snow melting away after winter. Instead of black and white I could see color for the first time."

"Remarkable," Dr. Aldrich repeated. He looked up from his chart as Brendan stood to leave. "Brendan, I'd like you to take this. Have a look when you're ready." He held out a folded pamphlet.

"What is it?" Brendan asked, turning it over.

"It's about the lawyer I mentioned. You don't have to agree to anything right away. Just think about it."

Brendan shook his head. "I've already told you... I don't know if I could."

"I think you can," Dr. Aldrich said.

Alone in his bedroom that evening, Brendan stared at the brochure. The face of one Dylan James, Esq., stared back. This woman, Dylan James, Esq., handled civil suits in a variety of personal injury matters, helping all sorts of people who had been harmed. Dylan James, Esq., had an Ivy League education. Dylan James, Esq., had worked at a leading firm on a precedent-setting verdict in a high-profile case years earlier, one Brendan remembered reading about in the newspaper. Dylan James, Esq., had kind-looking eyes. Eyes that seemed, the longer Brendan stared at them, able to understand everything.

As the days passed, Brendan feasted hungrily on the landscape around him. He strolled his little stretch of shoreline at dawn, before the earliest of joggers appeared, and again at night, alone in the moonlight, drinking in the salt air, mesmerized by the rhythmic rush at his feet. He meandered for hours on his sunlit garden paths, tracing his fingers along rough bark and jagged leaf, pausing to listen, to smell. He dug out an old horticulture book of his mother's and carried it around his grounds to match trees and blooms and fruits to those on the faded pages.

When Tomasz next pulled into the garage on Chatwick Road and lumbered around to open the rear door, Brendan surprised him. For all these years, he'd ducked from the town car to the entrance of the house. Now, he turned to step outside. Along the hedging, someone had planted shrubs Brendan recognized from his book as common lilac. Bending down to the profusion of purple to catch the scent, he glimpsed a young woman lifting a carton from atop a row of packing boxes lining the edge of the walkway. She met his eyes with a soft smile before disappearing behind the house. He waited a minute to see if she would return, but she didn't.

Dylan James tucked a handful of her freshly-printed leaflets into an acrylic holder at the edge of her new glass desk, alongside a little tray of business cards, and wiped a fleck of dust off her keyboard. Her office was coming together nicely. It looked professional yet inviting, modern yet intimate. She caught her reflection in her lamp, elongated in the curving chrome shade, and searched there for the image of the flourishing professional she longed to be: confident, knowledgeable, adventurous, eager to make an impact on the world. Eager for justice.

But instead of gazing into the crystal ball of the future, all she could see were shadows of the past. She'd already failed and lost everything. She drew a deep breath. She wasn't sure if she could ever put that past behind her.

On Sunday afternoon, Brendan once again found himself opening an unused door and stepping through. This time, he ended up not on his balcony or front porch but inside a pristine, porcelain-floored garage, slotted for four vehicles but occupied only by three—an old, oversized Cadillac, the town car Tomasz chauffeured, and Kenneth Cortland's vintage two-seater Mercedes SL, the obligatory luxury car of the eighties. Knowing that Tomasz kept all three vehicles in perfect running order, Brendan retrieved the Mercedes key from a magnetized lockbox and slid behind the wheel. With a shaking hand he started the ignition.

The fifteen-minute trip took nearly triple that as Brendan inched up the Merritt Parkway, white knuckled, other cars whizzing past and more than one driver throwing him an annoyed glance. He hadn't accounted for speed, or the lack of it. At last, he pulled into the periphery of the parking lot—

quite an accomplishment, considering what it had taken to prepare for the trip: the online searches for an address and the playoff schedule; the downloading of a GPS app on his cell phone; the figuring out of how to operate the app; and the rehearsing, over and over, of what he might say once he arrived.

The automatic doors slid apart like an incision spread open by an unseen surgeon, and Brendan stepped in. Cold air and nervousness pierced him. He forced himself across the lobby to the main enclosure, leaned his elbows on the dasher boards, and peered through the acrylic shielding at a giant oval of ice.

It didn't take long to spot Zac, Number 29, bulky in his pads, blond hair fringed around a red and white helmet, playing in the twelve-year-old Peewee Hockey League. For an hour, Brendan tracked the boy around the rink, awed as he skated and checked and suddenly, masterfully, scored, a split second before the buzzer. A roar rose from the stands. On the ice, the boys threw their sticks in the air in celebration, surging toward the boards as one large lump, while over the speakers came the excited announcement saying they were the game winners.

Brendan moved toward the gate and cleared his throat. "Zachary."

Zac looked up as his teammates jostled him through the opening and onto rubber pads. Players clapped him on the back of his helmet as they rocked past on their blades. His grin faded a notch. "Oh, hey."

"Can I talk to you for a sec?"

"Um, okay." Zac stepped away from the group and unfastened his chin strap to free his sweaty curls. His rosy cheeks set off the emerald-green eyes cut just like his father's.

Brendan shoved his hands in his pockets, keenly aware of the other boys calling to his son. "That your dad, Zac?"

He was sure he heard a snicker or two. He swallowed. "I saw you. You were terrific out there."

"Thanks."

"And you… got so tall."

Zac shifted his weight from one skate to the other.

Brendan cleared his throat. "I didn't hear from you. Your mom said you'd call… it was my, uh, birthday, and I thought we—"

Behind Zac, a slim, sparkling couple appeared, both sporting jewel-toned sweaters and puffy Moncler vests. The man's chiseled jaw clenched. "Heather, what's he doing here?"

Heather shook her head. "You shouldn't have come," she said to Brendan. "Hon, your coaches are waiting in the locker room." She laid her manicured fingers on her son's shoulder.

Brendan lifted a hand. "Bye, Zac," he called as his mother steered him away. "See you soon."

"I don't think so." Heather's husband rounded on Brendan, his dark eyes glaring. "Why don't you just stay away? Zac hardly knows you."

Brendan stared at the cement floor, wishing it would swallow him up as the man shoved by. "He's my son," he mumbled, keeping his head down.

"Freak," the man muttered as he pushed past.

At home that night, Brendan reached for his cell phone. He thought for a long time before retrieving the number and making the call.

"Shawn," he whispered when the call connected. "It's Brendan."

Brendan sat down in the psychiatrist's office the following Wednesday. Before Dr. Aldrich even looked up from his notes, he blurted, "I'm going through with it. The lawsuit."

The doctor kept his expression neutral. "What made you change your mind?"

"Time is running out, and I'm going through with it," Brandon repeated more firmly, in a voice a notch above a whisper.

"I see." Dr. Aldrich paused. "It's a prudent decision. You know, you have progressed nicely in these last few weeks. You're not as fragile as you once were. Have you thought it through... all that a lawsuit entails?"

"I have."

Dr. Aldrich kept his face composed, but inwardly, he was elated. The last time he'd checked, expert medical testimony had topped six hundred dollars per hour. A trial requiring his services would dramatically improve his dismal financial situation.

"I support your decision, Brendan. One hundred percent. You're sure to get justice."

Justice. In his office that night, Brendan mulled it over yet again. Justice. Wasn't it an impossible notion? Philosophy books said that justice meant an equal portion of what a man merited—his just desserts—and the good and bad things that befell or were allotted to him. But Brendan knew that in practice, the concept fell apart. Did hanging a dozen Nazis at Nuremberg provide justice for six million Jews murdered? Where was the justice for the innocent lives lost in the terrorist attacks of September 11th, 2001?

Had there been justice post-Cambodia, Croatia, Rwanda? Justice was no match for evil, at least not on Earth. Maybe it existed in a Marvel comic, but how could the concept of justice exist in a world unjust by nature, where so few had so much, and so many had so little?

The futility of it had prevented him from pursuing a lawsuit all this time. But in locking himself away in his Summer's Pond prison, he'd become a laughingstock. Brendan saw the derision in his ex-wife's eyes, and in his son's.

So yes, Brendan would finally submit to the distress of a public trial, if it meant they would respect him for it. But for now, he'd return to the kind of justice he'd pursued on his own. He opened his laptop and scoured the message boards.

Ah. DevBoys1969 was online. They'd been chatting together for nearly two years in The Playground, one of tens of thousands of pedophile chat rooms operating on the Internet and just one community into which Brendan had insinuated himself, using the handle "Youngblood." Brendan suspected that DevBoys—short for Deviant Boys—was the fourth, and most abhorrent, brand of predator: a User-and-Abuser, a predator who acted offline to produce and distribute his own photographs and movies. He was known to have a prolific collection of images that showcased his own deviant interests, including stuff he filmed, and appeared in, himself.

Besides being odious, DevBoys1969 was crafty and careful. But Brendan had already gained his trust. Patience, he reminded himself. DevBoys1969 would trip up eventually.

"Come in."

Dr. Aldrich pushed open the door across the hall from his own study and stood aside to let Brendan shuffle by. With the psychiatrist's encouragement, here they were just a few weeks later, at ten o'clock on a sunny Monday morning near the end of May, a soft, breezy day in which the cloudless sky unrolled like a bolt of azure fabric to billow above the treetops.

Brendan glanced uncertainly around the room. Its layout mirrored Dr. Aldrich's office but looked lighter and airier. Its matching bay window opened not to the busy street but to a small stone patio and fenced yard. Spare furnishings contrasted sharply with the dark, studded leather he was used to. Diplomas and certificates dotted the wall to his left, the paper in the framed glass crisply white. The names of the institutions and degrees were different from those he'd memorized across the hall. In the hearth of the fireplace stood candles of varying heights in place of the customary cords of dried wood and, unlike the filled-to-overflowing shelves in Dr. Aldrich's study, these were half empty, artfully arranged with a few legal books interspersed with framed photos.

"Brendan, this is Attorney Dylan James," Dr. Aldrich said of the willowy figure rising to come around the desk. Her faint perfume preceded her: a scent of gardenia over something else, something spicy and fresh, like a pine forest after a rain.

"It's so nice to finally meet you, Brendan." The young woman offered her hand, outstretched and earnest.

Brendan teetered back a step.

Dr. Aldrich gave an almost imperceptible shake of his head, and she dropped her arm and clasped her hands together. "Ugh! Dr. Aldrich told me you don't like to be touched, and I forgot," she said, smiling apologetically. "Sorry 'bout that."

Years ago, Irma, without thinking, had laid a hand on Brendan's forearm while wishing him a merry Christmas, forgetting momentarily how much he hated being touched. He'd recoiled as if scorched by boiling oil and fled to his suite. The holiday came and went, Brendan's nominal presents remaining unopened until Tomasz dropped them all off at the local Salvation Army in mid-January.

"Yes," Brendan murmured now, feeling something in his chest loosen. Though he'd heard the lawyer's voice before—Dr. Aldrich had put her on speaker during Brendan's recent sessions as a way of gradually introducing her—today marked their first official meeting. Perhaps it was her straightforward manner. Or perhaps it was the nut-brown hair curling past her shoulders, framing an exquisite face sheathed in mocha skin. Or perhaps it was her enormous doe eyes, radiating the same warmth and understanding he'd gleaned from her picture. Whatever it was, Brendan felt himself release some of the breath he'd been holding.

"Why don't we sit?" Dylan suggested, gliding toward the grouping of armchairs arranged around a glass coffee table. "Would anyone like coffee, or a cold drink?" Dr. Aldrich and Brendan shook their heads, and Dylan listened as Dr. Aldrich turned to Brendan and reiterated what sounded like instructions he'd offered several times.

"Remember, today is just an introduction," Dr. Aldrich said. "If you feel this will be too difficult you won't have to continue. Do your breathing. And if you need me, I'll be right next door." He hesitated a moment. "Are you sure you don't want me to stay?"

Brendan shook his head. His straggly hair fanned his cheeks.

"All right." Frowning, Dr. Aldrich paused with his hand on the doorknob. "I'm proud of you, Brendan. You've been preparing for this moment a long time. I know it's not easy."

The door closed. Brendan dropped into a chair, and Dylan sat opposite him, crossing her legs. In the sunlit office, the only sounds were the hum of the air conditioner and the muted notes of birdsong outside the window.

They sat quietly for a minute, regarding each other.

Dylan took a deep breath to steady herself. She felt like a fraud, using all these new phrases she'd rehearsed. "As you know," she said slowly, "we're here to discuss my representing you in an action against your former school. Your therapist, Dr. Aldrich, thinks you're ready. In fact, he suggested I rent his office space. This arrangement, with me based here in Greenwich, close to both you and him, works out well."

"Have you..." Brendan cleared his throat, trying to force out sound above a whisper. "Have you worked on a case like this before?"

"Not exactly. But I've helped people who've been hurt."

Brendan looked down at his hands. "So you know...?"

She spoke sympathetically. "Dr. Aldrich didn't tell me anything specific. I mean, nothing that would've breached doctor-patient confidentiality. We spoke in general terms."

"Maybe I'll wait a while."

Dylan paused. "I understand why you'd want to. It's just that time is running out. There is a statute of limitations to file. Despite legislation extending it, Connecticut law allows victims of some childhood abuse to file lawsuits only up to their forty-eighth birthday." *Sadly, some victims feel too ashamed to reveal their abuse at all,* Dylan thought to herself. Aloud, she added, "Still, everyone has a different inner timetable for when they're ready to tell their story. A different reason for coming forward. Dr. Aldrich says you're a very strong person."

Dylan waited patiently and, when it seemed like there were no more questions, she spoke again. "I want to be clear. Part of the process of litigating means dredging up trauma from the past. It means... digging up things that've been long buried. You may feel, at times, like you're reliving them. You understand?"

Brendan nodded.

"But... and this is critical... I don't want to be presumptive. This may never get to trial. A settlement is more likely. And the school will have significant legal resources."

"I guess... I guess... we try."

"You should know my fee structure up front. I'll take this case on contingency, but I'll still require a retainer to cover my expenses. It will be a significant amount." She stared at Brendan without blinking. "In a case like this, with lengthy preparations, one hundred thousand dollars for the initial retainer is standard, plus another one hundred thousand if we go to trial. And one-third of any damages."

Brendan exhaled. This was the easy part. "That's fine."

"All right, then." She rose and walked to her desk, leaning over to look at her calendar. "Brendan, we have a lot of work ahead of us. Can you come again on Wednesday?"

"I see Dr. Aldrich on Wednesdays," he said, as if the appointment took the whole day.

"How about Thursday?"

"Yes."

"Good." Dylan stood by the door. "I'm glad we met today, Brendan. I can't imagine how hard it was for you and the other boys to go through what you did. I'm going to do my best to help you, okay?"

"Yes." Brendan paused by the door. "How did Dr. Aldrich find you?"

The question she'd been waiting for. She arranged a small smile. "We had a few sessions together a while back. I came to him after my mother passed away." Her head tilted. "We can all use a little help now and then, can't we?"

"Yes."

For a second, Dylan thought he might shake her hand, but of course he didn't. He just turned and left.

The following Thursday, Brendan found himself seated once more in Attorney Dylan James' pretty office across the hall from Dr. Aldrich's. Once again, he was struck by the warmth in her brown eyes, the keen intelligence behind them, and her laser focus on his words. He forced himself to listen to hers.

She offered cookies, indicating the platter on the table between them. "To fortify us," she explained, smiling. "I can't go a day without oatmeal raisin."

He knew she was trying to put him at ease, but he passed.

"Okay," Dylan said. "Please keep in mind, this isn't a deposition. Just like I explained on the phone. Today you're just starting your story, as little or as much as you feel comfortable with. For now, it will be completely confidential. Do you consent to a recording, just for my own notes?"

Brendan agreed.

Dylan set her cellphone on the table beside the cookies and smiled reassuringly. "We can start whenever you're ready, from the beginning."

"I'm ready," Brendan said, the words little more than a breath.

PART TWO

1982

CHAPTER THREE

Even though the trip had taken less than three hours so far, it felt to Brendan like they'd been driving for an eternity. In fact, he felt as if on this day—Sunday, September 5th, 1982—time had stopped entirely. He stared out the window from the back seat of the Cadillac sedan as the miles of pastoral Connecticut countryside whipped past in a palette of greens and blues.

Litchfield County, in the Berkshire-Taconic region of the state's northwest corner, looked like farmland, a far cry from the cosmopolitan avenues abutting Brendan's coastal home in the village of Summer's Pond, but he didn't care. He didn't care about the grazing cows or the mossy stone fences or the charming New England churches with white steeples disappearing into clouds that scuttled across the sky. He just wanted to get there, already.

"We'll make a pit stop at this coffee shop for your mother," Brendan's father said over his shoulder. He sighed and slowed down. "We're almost there. Just another ten minutes."

Brendan rolled his eyes in the rearview mirror as the car pulled off the road and braked to a stop. "Come on, Mom, can't you hold it in? I'm pretty sure they have bathrooms there."

"Don't be crude. Anyhow, I just want to freshen up. We may bump into people we know when we arrive. I'll be right back."

Minutes later, Brendan's mother stepped gracefully back into the car and tucked a lipstick and compact back into her Gucci purse. Her red lips now matched her hair. "See? I wasn't long at all."

Brendan rolled his eyes again and shrugged. His mother acted as if she'd stepped out of one of her glossy magazines, like a movie star or something. It hadn't always been like that. Their family finances seemed to bounce around. Currently they were on an upswing. Way up. His parents' nonstop bickering over money had stopped.

In any case, Brendan wouldn't have to worry much about them for the next few years, not where he was going. He smiled to himself and glanced over at the maroon blazer laid out neatly on the seat beside him, taking in for the millionth time the gold buttons and navy-blue crest on the lapel with the letters T and H stitched in gold thread.

Torburton Hall Academy for Boys in the village of Calvert, Connecticut would be his home for the next four years, and Brendan itched to get them started. The elite boarding school had churned out generations of accomplished alumni since its inception in 1899, from Nobel laureates to Pulitzer Prize winners hailing from Dallas to Dublin, men with two last names like Johnson Deloitte and Porter Smith, politicians and journalists and kingpins of industry. His own father, Kenneth Cortland, had attended a prestigious boarding school and continued on to Princeton, his Ivy dream. He'd transferred that dream to his only child along with his pen set that rested in a monogrammed pouch in the new leather briefcase at Brendan's feet.

In the trunk were two large suitcases of clothes, white shirts and crested maroon vests and sweaters to be worn with khaki or navy-blue trousers. Plus dress shoes, running shoes, leisure shoes, shower shoes. And a full range of athletic wear. Brendan would play lacrosse for the Torburton Tridents, of that he had no doubt, but he also excelled at tennis and couldn't decide if he wanted to try out for the swim team. And what about track and field? Maybe he wouldn't have to choose just yet. Over four years, he could try a little of everything.

The athletic director, Terence Dunlop, had met with his family last spring. He'd heard rumors of the golden boy registered for the fall of 1982. With a cigarette dangling from his lips, he'd taken the Cortlands on a personal tour of the sprawling sports complex. They'd walked the circumference of The Winners' Circle—the circular antechamber connecting the hallways from gymnasium to Olympic-sized pool, lined all the way around with glass cabinets displaying championship cups and plaques and decades' worth of team photographs of the school's award-winning athletes. Brendan could already picture the row of Torburton trophies lining his top shelf.

There'd be more. Ribbons and badges for exemplary academics or science projects. Interesting academic excursions relating to his classes and, since money seemed to be flowing, he'd go on them all. Madrid. London. Rome. Plus trips to visit some of the international students in summer, maybe, and that wasn't counting the new friends who'd be clamoring to invite him for holidays to their family chalet in Aspen for Christmas or on a spring break junket to Bermuda. Social life would be no problem. He'd accumulated gobs of hangers-on at his previous school. Ever since the blockbuster success of Kenneth Cortland's recent film and the avalanche of press he'd received as director, when people heard Brendan's last name, they tripped all over themselves trying to befriend him. Why wouldn't it be the same at this place?

At first, Brendan had sulked when he learned some of his classmates were headed to Phillips Exeter in New Hampshire, or Hotchkiss, Taft, or Choate Rosemary closer to home. He alone in his eighth-grade class had been destined for Torburton Hall, now that they could afford it. Over time, though, he'd fallen in love with the idea. He'd take the place by storm. Heck, in four years he'd be voted president of his senior class. It would look great on his application to Princeton.

Not that there wouldn't be girls along the way, he thought. Sure, he'd marry Heather one day, but he was too young to think about that now... besides, she was staying home this year to attend a private girls' academy in New Canaan, and then she'd be sent abroad. In her absence, there'd be pretty girls from boarding schools all over New England, smart, rich, pretty girls he'd meet at debates and Valentine's Day mixers and field hockey tournaments. Cute younger sisters of his new buddies. They'd be falling all over him.

He smiled to himself. He had it all planned out.

At last they pulled in through the high, wrought iron gates, their Cadillac joining a train of cars before coming to a halt beneath the legendary Great Oak, the towering crown of which was depicted in all the school brochures. Brendan jumped from the back seat and shrugged into his blazer, taking in the sight of similarly-dressed boys hopping from luxurious back seats, carrying suitcases and books and disappearing through the grand wooden doors of Torburton Hall's main building, the Commons.

Kenneth unlocked the trunk and stood the suitcases and a duffel bag beside the car. "I think we can do this in one trip," he said. He turned to his wife as she stepped from the car to smooth her skirt and matching bolero jacket. "Eliza, would you mind taking this bag? It's not too heavy."

Eliza frowned at her feet. The high-heeled pumps made her legs look like sharpened pencils. "I don't think I can manage in these—" Her sentence was cut short by a loud gasp behind her.

"Eliza, darling, is that you?" An attractive brunette wearing a cloud of taffeta enfolded Eliza in a brief embrace and then held her at arm's length to look her over. "It's so good to see you."

"Maxine, it's been forever." Eliza smiled. "You remember Kenneth?"

"Kenneth, you're looking well," Maxine purred. "Congratulations on all your successes! I loved *A Candle for Cassandra*. I've seen it twice now. Your directing is inspired." A silver-haired man joined her, tying a mint-green sweater over the shoulders of his pink Polo shirt.

"Mitch, good to see you," Kenneth said. The two men shook hands.

"And this must be Brendan. My goodness," Maxine stared for a few moments. "What a handsome boy."

"I don't know where our Scott has disappeared to," Mitch said to Brendan. "You'll probably meet him soon, though. He's a junior, so he can show you the ropes."

Brendan shifted restlessly, waiting for the all-too-familiar scene to wrap up. These days it happened wherever they went—people stopped to greet his parents, or rather people stopped to *meet* his parents, and invariably he'd be forgotten. He waited for the inevitable.

"Hey, son," Kenneth began. Right on cue. "You go ahead and find your room. We'll be right there."

"We just want to catch up with the Williams for a minute," Eliza added. She clutched her husband's elbow and turned to the couple with a wide smile.

Slinging the duffel strap over one shoulder, Brendan picked up the smaller suitcase in one hand and his lacrosse stick and the leather briefcase in the other. He tossed his head to flick the long, blond bangs from his eyes. Whatever. He wouldn't let anything spoil the excitement of this day.

The reception area of the Commons, adorned with a "Welcome Students" banner stretched across the entrance way, smelled of cigars and aftershave, much like his father's study in their new house. It looked like it, too: velvet love seats and plush wing chairs grouped in threes, coffee tables stacked with magazines and school leaflets, heavy drapes, and faded rugs worn bare by generations of eager leather soles.

Brendan stood for a moment, breathing it all in, watching boys of every size and shape stream past, flanked by proud parents. He made his way to the registration desk.

"Hello, son!" A short, portly; mustached man smiled up at him. The name tag pinned to his lapel read *Mr. Greer, Assistant Headmaster*. "Your name, please?"

"Brendan Cortland."

The man traced a stubby finger down the list on his clipboard. "Here we are," he said, handing Brendan a large manila envelope. "Glad to have you with us, Mr. Cortland. You're in room 266 in Mariner Block. Take care not to lose your key or you'll be charged for it. There's all your important information inside the envelope: your schedule, the words to the Torburton song, rules of conduct, and so on. Study it carefully. The welcome banquet begins at six o'clock sharp in the dining room. You'll get your seat assignment then."

"Okay." Brendan nodded, looking around. "Uh... "

"And Hank here will show you the way to your dormitory."

A very thin, very gangly boy with hair the color of Cheetos looked up. Brendan stared. He'd never seen so many freckles, as if the Cheetos had exploded, leaving crumbs all over the place. He picked up his things and trailed through the crowd after the bobbing orange head, down a long hallway and out rear doors that opened onto the Quad—a grassy courtyard crisscrossed by cobbled paths that led from one stately brick building to the next in a compass rose. They veered right.

Hank stopped in front of the entrance to Mariner, stepping aside with a polite smile for an older couple who must have been someone's grandparents. Then he rounded on Brendan. "Okay, Freshie," he growled, his courtesy dissolving, "our rules aren't in that envelope but you better learn them quick. Me and the other upperclassmen are in charge. Whatever we say goes, and don't get any ideas about complaining to the staff cuz we don't take kindly to squealers."

Brendan thought back to a conversation the week before with his best buddies, Michael Harrington and Ian Prescott. They were sitting by Ian's pool with Ian's older brother, Don, who attended Exeter. "You gotta set the ground rules as soon as you get there. Right off the bat. No weakness. Don't let anyone see you're scared, even if you are," Don had advised, drizzling tanning oil on his wide shoulders. "Not that anyone'll push you around, kid… not once they hear your name," he added with a grin.

Now, with Cheetos here staring him down, Brendan lifted his chin and tried out his new trick. "Listen, Ronald McDonald, do you know who I am? Brendan Cortland." His heart beat harder as he waited for the dawn of recognition on the spotty face, and the hasty apology.

But Hank only sneered. "I don't care if you're John fucking Travolta. We're the generals. We call the shots. Get it? And you better watch out. Cuz now you pissed me off."

Brendan flipped his bangs out of his eyes, doing his best to look nonchalant. Every school had its hierarchy, its cabal of bullies. He may be a lowly freshman for today, or even for a few days, but according to Ian's brother, that would change soon enough. As soon as these jerks figured out who his father was, they'd change their tune. Plus his athletic prowess, his quick wit, his good looks... Brendan resolved not to show his nervousness. "Sir, yes sir," he saluted, pushing past Hank and entering Mariner to find his dorm.

Room 266 straddled the elbow of the L-shaped floor plan. Brendan had been inside for about twenty minutes when his parents showed up, all smiles, clucking over the spacious corner suite with its scuffed hardwood and floor-to-ceiling windows. Two narrow beds were tucked into the corners, tightly fitted with navy-blue Torburton sheets and blankets. Two wooden desks with two wooden chairs sat under the windows, and two highboy dressers and built-in armoires faced each other. Across the room from Brendan, someone had already moved in. On the desk stood stacks of paper, a jar of pens and pencils, and a framed family photograph snapped at Kennedy Space Center. A Tridents pennant was tacked above the bed. Inside the armoire hung a row of jackets, shirts, and slacks on hangers separated by a half inch each. A row of shoes neatly lined the bottom shelf. Brendan pictured the tee-shirts, underwear, and socks, folded perfectly inside the dresser drawers.

"Have you unpacked anything?" Eliza asked, entering.

Brendan shrugged. "Waiting for you, Mom."

Kenneth set down the larger suitcase. "Well, let's get started. Your mother and I are invited for cocktails, so we can't stay long."

Eliza took a breath and sized up the room, then pointed to each of the shelves where her son should store his various belongings. She arranged a few items herself: his toiletry caddy and fluffy new monogrammed hand towels, a framed photo of herself and her husband on the nightstand. Glancing at his watch, Kenneth tossed the remainder of the contents onto the bed. He zipped the empty smaller case inside the larger one and hefted them up on top of the armoire.

"Well, son, you've got your afternoon cut out for you." He looked around, nodding wistfully. "Looks just like my old room. I bet the Monday Meatloaf tastes the same, too." He chuckled and clapped Brendan on the shoulder. "Study hard and make sure you remember to eat. You'll need some bulk on those bones if you want to be captain of the lacrosse team. We'll expect letters from you every other week. Let the headmaster know if you need anything and I can wire money over. We'll see you for Thanksgiving."

Brendan chewed his lip. "What about Parents' Weekend in October?" Back in public school, his parents hadn't missed a single event.

"I have to scout some locations for my next movie, and it's a chance for your mother and me to do a little traveling," Kenneth said.

"But if we're back in time, of course we'll come by," Eliza added, patting her bob in the armoire mirror. Then she folded her son into an embrace. "Wear your scarf on windy days, you don't want to catch a cold. I'll miss you, dear."

Inwardly, Brendan wondered if she would. She had so much else to think about these days. He gave her a dutiful peck on the cheek.

After his parents left, the room suddenly felt big and silent. Brendan put away a few of his more important possessions. He set a silver boom box on the desk and put the pen set beside some school supplies and a stack of cassette tapes. He shoved the duffel bag, stocked with bottles of Coke and tubes of Pringles, under the bed and leaned his lacrosse stick against the dresser. The pile of clothes from the suitcase—the carefully ironed collars and pants—went into a heap at the bottom of the armoire. He picked up the framed photo from the nightstand. It depicted his parents at their new villa in Italy, his father in a crisp white shirt and his mother in a sarong and wide sunhat. Brendan draped his knitted Torburton scarf over the window latch.

Finally, he unrolled his favorite posters: a corn-rowed Bo Derek in her nearly transparent tan swimsuit and Farrah Fawcett in her red one. In the months they'd hung in his bedroom at home, his mother had never lingered long enough to notice Farrah's nipple or Bo's hint of pubic hair. Brendan tacked the posters above his bed. There, that was better.

He looked around. This would be the longest he'd be away from home, the longest he'd ever been on his own. Not that he'd be homesick or anything, he told himself.

He slid his favorite mixed tape into the deck and pressed the PLAY button. The last few bars of Juice Newton's song, "Angel of the Morning," filled the room, followed by his favorite Bruce Springsteen track. "Everybody's got a hungry heart," he sang under his breath. That reminded him. He reached into the front pocket of his jacket, pulled out a crumpled letter, and smoothed it against his leg.

Heather's neat handwriting covered the yellow paper, the same pale lemony color as her hair. Last night, she'd passed it to him under the table of the fancy restaurant where their two families had gone for a goodbye dinner. *I'll miss beating you at everything*, she wrote. She ended the note with a fancy B + H surrounded by a pink heart, and decorated the margins with more hearts shot through with arrows. Brendan grinned. Besides the fact that their parents acted as if they were already engaged, he really liked Heather. She was cool without trying to be, and one of the few kids who could best him at games and sports: solve a Rubik's cube faster, jump her horse higher. They were a good match.

"Just imagine our grandchildren," Heather's mother, Joan, had said to Eliza for the hundredth time the previous morning. They'd gone for a jog together and were sitting in the kitchen sipping glasses of SlimFast when Brendan came in.

"Beautiful," Eliza agreed.

"And super-achievers," Joan added. "Isn't that right, Brendan honey?"

Voices in the doorway interrupted Brendan's thoughts. A boy walked in with two giggling, pigtailed girls, followed by a set of parents: the man slight, white, sandy-haired, and bespectacled, his tweed jacket over his arm; the tiny Asian woman—five feet tall if that—sporting a cap of black hair cut in a precise pageboy. The three children were perfect blends of both, with glossy black hair and glasses over sparkling eyes that tilted ever so slightly. All ten eyes seemed to linger on the posters above Brendan's bed.

The parents shifted their attention from Farrah and Bo to greet Brendan. They shook his hand before turning to their son, taking long turns hugging and kissing him. The two identical sisters clutched each of their brother's legs, giggling as he dragged them toward the door and shook them off. He closed the door behind them and flopped down on his bed.

"Hi, my name's Jack," he said, lying on his side and propping his head in his hand, his glasses askew.

"I'm Brendan."

"Where you from?"

"Connecticut. Summer's Pond."

"I'm from Massachusetts. Did you meet anyone yet?"

Brendan cracked a grin. "Just one of the, er, generals. You?"

Jack rolled his eyes to the ceiling. "Yeah, some muscular dude who looked like Popeye. He could probably beat me up with his hands tied behind his back. I have a feeling I'm gonna be in trouble."

Privately, Brendan agreed, but he spoke with swagger. "They're just showing off. Trying to scare us."

"Well, it's working," Jack said. "I'm dead meat at a place like this."

"What do you mean?"

"Seriously? Look at me. Half Chinese, half Jewish. I stick out like a sore thumb. My last name's *Abromovitch*, for Christ's sake. I practically have a target on my forehead."

This kid was funny. "They wouldn't dare touch us," Brendan said, raking his mane with his fingers.

"Easy for you to say," Jack moaned, taking in Brendan's long, blond hair and bright green eyes under dark brows. "You're the All American Boy. You look like Andy Gibb. I bet you're real athletic, too," he added, tipping his chin toward the lacrosse stick at the end of the bed.

Brendan shrugged with one shoulder. He could be humble. "You play any sports?"

"I'm the regional chess champion in my age group." Jack sighed. "Both of my parents are doctors. I inherited their nerdy genes."

"So, how did you end up here? I'm guessing you're not a legacy."

"Nope. They just wanted to fast track me to Harvard Medical School."

Brendan wanted to laugh but rolled his eyes instead. *Ground rules,* he reminded himself, remembering Don's advice. *Be cool. Set the tone.* "By the way," he said, stretching, "just so we're clear: you'll be doing the cleaning up around here. You can start by hanging up my clothes."

The dining room, tucked into the east wing of the Commons, was surrounded on three sides by leaded glass windows, outside of which were glorious views of the rolling green hills hulking in the distance. Looking through a window from the Quad, Brendan saw that the hall held five long, white-clothed tables that seated thirty on each side.

All parents were required to leave the campus by five o'clock and now, at a quarter of six, hordes of boys gathered outside the twin doors of the building. Upperclassmen, recognizable by their size, stubble, and easy camaraderie, buzzed in front of the door, bees awaiting entrance to the hive. Younger boys spread out around them in concentric rings, with baby-faced freshmen hovering uncertainly.

Puniest of all was a pale waif who looked barely grammar school age. His eyes were enormous as he gazed up at muscular young men towering above him. After a while he caught the attention of Hank, who'd been joking with friends nearby. Hank jerked a thumb at him. The clutch of upperclassmen laughed as Hank ground the knuckles of one freckled fist into the child's scalp. "Noogie! Noogie!" he exclaimed. When he stopped, the boy teetered dizzily onto his butt.

Brendan and Jack, standing just a few feet away, saw it happen. Brendan bit his lip uncertainly, but Jack stepped over to where the boy sat rubbing his head.

"Hey," he said, reaching down to help the kid to his feet. Hank and the others sniggered. "I'm Jack, and this is Brendan. What's your name?"

"Shawn Unger." He dusted off the seat of his pants. "Thanks."

Hank folded his arms and stuck his tongue into his cheek. "Awww, aren't they adorable," he crooned. "A pretty boy, a shrimp, and... I don't know... some sort of mutt."

"We're gonna have fun with these three," another upperclassman said with a wink.

Before Brendan could form a retort, the double doors parted, held open by two older boys. Mr. Greer appeared and clapped his hands for attention. "We're forming two lines, gentlemen," he called. "Quickly and quietly. There will, of course, be no pushing as you enter the dining hall. The faster we assign your seats, the faster you will be served."

All talking stopped as the boys fell into place and filed through the doors. Teachers posted at the archway to the dining room stood with clipboards, pointing out table assignments.

Each table of sixty had been organized by year, so that Brendan, Jack, and Shawn were seated together at Table Four. The fifth table was for teachers.

Jack whistled under his breath. "Holy cow. I wonder how long it takes them to set these tables?"

Brendan glanced around at the three hundred place settings of a flat white charger etched with T.H. in the center, surrounded by seven pieces of silverware each and vases of fresh flowers placed at regular intervals. He shrugged. He'd stopped taking notice of the labor that went into orchestrating his pleasant existence.

With everyone seated, Mr. Greer closed the dining room doors and clapped again. "Please take note of where you are sitting, as your table assignment is non-negotiable for the remainder of this academic year," he boomed. "At each meal you will take your seats, quickly and quietly, and we will begin serving the meal once everyone is in attendance. Of course, we will expect you to conduct yourselves with decorum as befits this institution. Let's bow our heads."

After grace, which consisted of several phrases of gratitude and a pledge of good behavior, the staff stood up and, a few minutes later, Mr. Greer nodded toward the front table to his left. "Table One, you may get your dinner."

At the side of the room, seniors picked up trays and flowed past women in hair nets wielding spatulas and ladles, as if on a conveyor belt for meal assemblage. The aroma of grilled meat wafted throughout the room and Brendan's stomach rumbled as he waited for his table's turn, the last to be called. He returned with a loaded tray—ribeye, tossed salad, baked potato, and cherry pie—and immediately began carving a piece of juicy steak off the bone.

"This looks great," Shawn said in his thin voice. "You think dinner will be like this all the time, or just for tonight's welcome banquet?"

Beside him, Jack tucked into his dinner with relish. "My dad predicted they'd make the leftovers into a stew. He said enjoy it while you can." Just as he lifted the fork to his mouth, a hip shoved against his elbow and sent peas rolling across the white tablecloth.

"You're pretty clumsy, Mutt," a stocky kid smirked over his shoulder, his cleft chin jutting sideways as he walked from the restroom to his table of eleventh-graders.

Brendan fished a pea out of his water glass. "Let me guess," he said to Jack. "That was Popeye."

Jack nodded morosely. "I told you."

Brendan laughed. But all the same, he couldn't help feeling a whisper of doubt. Maybe things wouldn't be quite as pleasant as he'd planned.

At eight o'clock that evening, the entire student body reported to the auditorium for the first official program of the school year. Once again, Brendan sat down with Jack on one side and Shawn on the other. Around them were the same boys from Table Four. The newbie ninth-graders were already beginning to feel more at ease as they met and befriended their classmates, joking and talking and twisting in their seats as they waited for the assembly to start.

When music began to play, a hush fell over the cavernous room. As the curtains opened, two students carrying an American flag and a flag printed with the Torburton crest marched onto the stage and stood at attention with exaggerated pomp and circumstance. Then two dozen male teachers, dressed in maroon Torburton jackets and bow ties, emerged from the wings and filled the rows of chairs flanking a podium.

Finally, after a hushed lull, a man strode across the stage to the podium in the center. He seemed young, perhaps in his late thirties. The students applauded and the man held up his arms for silence. His manner was so confident, so at ease, that he reminded Brendan of the game show hosts he saw on television.

"Gentlemen." The man smiled, showing an overbite that somehow added to his charm. "Good evening. It is my great pleasure to welcome you as we commence a new school year here at Torburton Hall Academy for Boys. I am your headmaster, Edward Galloway." More applause. Once again he held up a hand. "To those of you who are returning from summers spent with your families, or from abroad, welcome back. To our seniors—the Class of 1983—this is your year! To our returning juniors and sophomores, I hope you will not underestimate the importance of this year for your academic careers.

"To our newest students, welcome to Torburton. May you feel at home and think of us"—here, he swept an arm from left to right, indicating the staff and students alike— "as your new family. This is a place of hard work, yes, but also brotherly love." He flashed a big smile. "You will find us tough but fair, demanding yet endearing. What you give to this school, you will get back in spades. With effort and dedication, you will rise to every occasion. I expect you will follow the rules, and exemplify our values, both inside and outside of the classroom." The student body clapped enthusiastically.

"Here, you are all brothers united," said Galloway, holding up two crossed fingers. "No matter your talents or interests, your career plans, whether you are short or tall, big or small, you are taking this journey together, the timeless journey of growing up and maturing. You come here as boys, but you will leave as men, men with strength of character and integrity.

"Together," Galloway said, his voice rising over the microphone in a heartfelt crescendo as thundering applause overtook him, "we will make memories that will last a lifetime!"

CHAPTER FOUR

When the applause died down, Edward Galloway smiled at the students. "Gentlemen, I will now introduce the exceptional Torburton Hall staff of the 1982 academic year. First, we have Dr. Lawrence Nevin, head of the science department. Dr. Nevin earned his doctorate in chemistry at Yale and spent over a decade at British Petroleum. This is his sixth year at Torburton." He inclined his head as the round-bellied man to his right stood up and gave a slight bow to the audience. "Next, we have Anthony Ducati, head of mathematics, and Morris Phelps, head of English and author of three very detailed books on grammar, all of which you will be reading." The boys groaned. Galloway then introduced the remaining two dozen staff members, mentioning the high points of each résumé. "It's my pleasure to give you our esteemed athletic director."

"That's Mr. Dunlop," Brendan said to the boys around him, clapping eagerly for the muscular man who'd met with his family last spring. "He promised me a spot on the lacrosse team and said I'd be playing varsity in no time."

After a glowing report on the athletics department, Galloway introduced the support staff who kept the school operating, all the while joking and charming his way through introductions like the emcee of an awards show.

"And finally," Galloway said, an hour into the assembly, "it's my privilege to present to you the Chair of our Board of Trustees, Mr. Gavin Murdock." An elderly, mustached gentleman rose slowly from his place in the front row of the audience and turned to wave, hunched over and unable to straighten entirely.

Galloway extended a hand to two women farther back. "Of course, we cannot forget the two lovely ladies at our school: our nurse, Mrs. Nancy Smythe, and our school secretary, Miss Paula Franklin."

"How about the lovely lunch ladies?" Jack joked, but Brendan ignored him, still absorbed in thoughts of varsity lacrosse.

After the assembly concluded, the boys were told to return to their dormitories, and Brendan made his way toward the Quad, trailed by Jack and Shawn. He paused on the top step, taking in the twinkling lights of the dorm rooms at night. How great it all seemed: the school, the campus, the experience. Everything was perfect. Exactly the way he'd pictured it. He felt a tap on his shoulder.

"Mr. Cortland? Glad to see you again, sport." It was Terence Dunlop, the athletic director. He'd removed his bowtie and unbuttoned the top buttons of his shirt, and held his jacket hooked over his shoulder with a finger. He leaned against a pillar, casual, smoking a cigarette.

"Hi, Mr. Dunlop!"

"Oh, let's not be so formal, eh? We're going to be spending a lot of time together on the field. You can call me Coach. You know, lacrosse practice starts Thursday. I'm going to be working you real hard, get you ship-shape to be a starter, maybe even by the first game."

Brendan grinned. "Sure thing."

Dunlop reached out and squeezed Brendan's shoulder a couple times. "Atta boy. Why don't you drop by the weight room and we'll see about getting you going with some free weights? Build up these muscles a little."

"Thanks, Coach."

"You got it, sport," Dunlop said, squeezing Brendan's shoulder a few more times.

Each weekday at Torburton Hall meant a cluster of core subjects in the morning—math, science, English, American history—and later, music, art, French, and an hour in the brand new, groundbreaking computer lab that boasted rows of big, squat monitors and a jumble of white cables spilling over the desks like limp spaghetti.

The first few days of classes made Brendan's head spin. "Which way to the Jefferson building?" he asked, rushing to find his algebra class. "How do I get to the music hall?" and "Where's the library?" He and Jack and Shawn ate together at Table Four but only shared three other classes in their schedules. With all the new information, names to match to faces, and regulations to remember, the days flew by, until finally Brendan had a free hour before dinner.

He sat on his bed and felt a sudden pang of homesickness. Not for home the way it had been lately, because ever since his dad's Hollywood star had skyrocketed, his parents were busy hobnobbing with celebrities and were rarely around. No, he missed the old days when they were comfortable, wealthy but not uber-rich; when he was a little kid and Kenneth (Ken, back then) stuck to directing mid-level movies. Even with the bickering, at least he hadn't been alone.

I'll get used to it here, he told himself. *Everything is great.* He decided to visit the gym.

Dressed in a white Tridents tee-shirt and polyester Adidas shorts, Brendan jogged down the stairs toward the weight room at the far side of the gleaming gymnasium. He found himself face to face with a cadre of upperclassmen, members of the baseball team carrying bats and mitts.

Easy, he told himself, as if calming a horse. *Easy now.* He flipped his bangs and stepped through the doorway. He had no reason to be anxious, he thought. His dad probably made more money than their dads, the just-created trust fund probably bigger than all theirs put together. And anyway, Brendan had grown up thinking he was pretty okay. By age fourteen, he stood taller than some of the seventeen- and eighteen-year-olds in the room. And he was good looking, he'd heard that for years, with his California surfer vibe. Thankfully, only three or four pimples had popped up so far, but they were hidden under his blond bangs. Already his chest and shoulders were showing signs of thickening. He flipped his hair back again and walked straight to Hank and his posse, expecting admiration.

"If it isn't the pretty boy," Hank said, crossing his arms. "Or should we call you Mr. Cortland?"

"Aw, that's not necessary," Brendan said, sounding friendly. "Coach told me to come lift some weights. In preparation for being captain of the varsity lacrosse team."

Hank raised an eyebrow and grinned at his friends. "Oh, right. Dunlop said he was waiting for you. He told me to tell you to go ahead on into his office, over there." The other guys snickered.

"Cool." Brendan turned and left the weight room, doubling back to the door marked "Athletic Director" in the main corridor. He turned the knob.

For a second he froze, confused by what he was seeing: through a veil of smoke, the back of a masculine figure in the middle of the office, naked except for briefs, flexing one muscular arm and then the other. And there was Terry Dunlop, the athletic director, with a Kodak camera held to his face. *Snap, snap, snap*, the shutter went. The only other sound in the room was harsh breathing. Dunlop gestured with his hand, and as the figure began to turn around, Brendan hastily stepped backward, hoping he hadn't been spotted.

Snap.

"You okay?" Jack looked up curiously from his chair as Brendan burst into their room and leaned against the door, panting. He'd sprinted all the way across campus, taken two wrong turns, and ended up skirting the entirety of the Commons before he found the correct path back to Mariner Block. "Did Hank and Popeye chase you or something?"

"No. I'm good." Brendan's thoughts, now that he'd screeched to a stop, tumbled into his brain one on top of another. He sat down at his desk and opened his math notebook. In his peripheral vision he saw Jack stare oddly at him, then shrug and go back to his homework.

What had Brendan seen in the athletic director's office? He wasn't really sure. The boy hadn't seemed upset, exactly. He'd just looked blank. Like he was in shock, maybe? Should he ask Greer or Galloway about it? Or just speak to Coach directly? No. Probably not. *Definitely* not. After all, he wasn't certain anything bad had happened. Why ruin a great start to the year? And anyway, it was none of his business.

On Thursday afternoon, Brendan arrived right on time for the first lacrosse practice. He dropped his bag on the sidelines with the others and hurried to join his teammates loosening up on the field, stretching hamstrings and sprinting from goal to goal. He worried briefly that Dunlop could read his mind, sense the confusion lurking there, but the man never looked in his direction.

For drills, the varsity and junior varsity players warmed up along with the freshmen. The glaring disparity in their physiques, obvious in their sleeveless nylon jerseys and shorts that rode high up on their thighs, gave Brendan pause. He'd thought to try to fit in with the upperclassmen right away but quickly changed his mind and stuck close to the freshmen and sophomores instead, especially after being bumped hard two or three times by bulging biceps.

After a half hour of warm-up, Dunlop blew his whistle and waited for the boys to congregate around him. "Bend a knee," he called, hands on hips. "And take a good look around. This is your 1982 team. Your brothers. I expect you to act like brothers, on the field and off. During games you'll have each other's backs. I won't stand for any prissy prima donna behavior. There is no room for showing off, even when college scouts are watching. We don't have stars, we only have a team... the winning team... the Tridents."

Dunlop went on for another fifteen minutes to talk about his expectations of the team—showing him respect, putting in a hundred percent, being punctual—until at last he released them to stand up, their skin branded by blades of grass.

"Now we'll scrimmage," he said, dividing up the boys into squads that would play each other.

Brendan was the only freshman to start. At sports camp he'd played defense. Today, Dunlop assigned him to offense. Brendan put on his helmet and gloves, picked up his lacrosse stick, and jogged onto the field, eager to showcase his speed and agility.

They only played one twelve-minute quarter, but in that short time Brendan outran several other players. He scooped up a perfect long pass. He scored.

"Nice work, son," Dunlop said later, laying a hand on Brendan's shoulder as he packed his gym bag by the bleachers.

"Thanks."

"But I'm disappointed you didn't come to the weight room like we discussed. You need to be committed if you want to play," Dunlop continued. "Be at my office tomorrow at five o'clock. I'll get you started on a program."

Brendan slowly zipped the bag. "Yes, Coach."

"Give me a minute," Dunlop said the next day, covering the mouthpiece of his phone with a hand. "Close the door."

Brendan stepped into the hazy athletic director's office and waited.

Yes, the man was nodding, stretching the coiled phone cord as he reached for a clipboard. *Right, got it.* At last, he replaced the receiver in its cradle. He flipped through a few pages on the clipboard, crossing out sentences with swift pen strokes. Plumes of smoke rose from the dying butt in the ashtray. The coach spoke without raising his head, as if he could track Brendan's gaze. "It's a filthy habit. I'd better not catch you trying it."

"No, sir."

"Good man. Now, clothes and sneakers off."

Brendan's heart had been fluttering all day, and at this it skipped a beat. He hovered in the doorway.

Dunlop looked up for the first time. "Do you need written instructions, son?"

"No, I…"

"Then hurry it up. I have a meeting to prep for. Everything off, and step on the scale."

Brendan exhaled with relief. He hadn't noticed the mechanical scale in the corner, the kind his doctor's office used. "I'm taking off my clothes to get weighed?" he asked, unlacing his shoes.

"Well, what else?" Dunlop said. He tapped a box of Marlboros to release a fresh cigarette. "You want to pose for *Playboy* magazine?"

Brendan shrugged out of his shorts and shirt, leaving them in a pool on the floor. He stepped on the scale to be weighed.

Dunlop's sharp voice startled him. "You're not at home with a maid to clean up your mess," he barked. "Here at Torburton you are responsible for your own things. Pick up your clothes and fold them on the chair."

No one yelled at him like that at home. But aloud, Brendan heard himself say, "Yes, sir," and he bent to pick up his stuff. Then he stepped back on the scale.

"One hundred and twenty-three pounds. Wait... don't get dressed just yet."

When Brendan looked up, Dunlop was fiddling with the Kodak. "Uh, what are the pictures for, then?"

"Before and after shots," Dunlop answered gruffly. He aimed the instamatic at Brendan and looked through the viewfinder. "Stand up straight, arms by your sides."

Brendan flipped his bangs off his face and gave a lopsided grin for the picture. "Before and after what, Coach?"

"My program. I record the progress of all my promising athletes." Dunlop motioned him closer and took a few more photos, first full length and then close ups of his torso. He seemed entirely engrossed behind the camera, and after a few seconds Brendan began to feel like a specimen under a microscope.

"Turn around."

Facing the door, Brendan tried to ignore the sensation of eyes on his bare back. He heard the shutter clicking several more times, and then Dunlop coughed and cleared his throat a bit.

He put aside the camera and picked up a pen, jotting down measurements of Brendan's height and weight. Finally, the man pulled out a thick photo album of before and after shots that had been taken in freshman and senior years. The coach showed Brendan an example of a "before" image: a weak, skinny-limbed boy. Three years later, his muscular physique looked like that of a bodybuilder.

"College scouts these days are very concerned about player size, so I put you boys on a program: weights, extra carbohydrates. I can't make anyone taller, but damn it, I'll make them as strong as possible." Dunlop looked Brendan up and down. "You, boy, you're halfway there. And if you work hard, you'll excel at athletics, because you already have talent. You're a winner."

His father would love to hear that, Brendan thought, relieved. Kenneth Cortland never tolerated losing well. His mantra echoed: *"Hard work beats talent when talent doesn't work hard."* Brendan remembered Kenneth's impatience when Brendan quit basketball after being fouled by a bigger kid. "Thanks, Coach."

"Now get dressed, son, before you're late for dinner," Dunlop said. "We'll take up where we left off next time."

As Brendan turned to step into his shorts, he felt a hand on the nape of his neck that rested just a moment too long before it trailed down the vertebrae of his spine and then dropped away.

CHAPTER FIVE

As the weeks went by and September of 1982 melted into October, Brendan fell into a routine of classes, meals, homework, and sports. By now he knew the layout of the sprawling campus, having followed the various paths and explored most of the buildings. Patches of red and gold bloomed in the distant Litchfield hills, and the warm fall sunshine lit the mature trees lining the roads. Great Oak turned a dazzling orange.

The rigorousness of Torburton Hall's academics surprised him. Until now, he'd gotten straight As with minimal effort. After he got a C+ on his first English essay, though, he found himself suddenly needing to study, something he'd never done before with any seriousness.

"C'mon, I'll *pay* you to write it for me. Name your price," Brendan tried to cajole Jack. But even after being threatened with bodily harm, his roommate flatly refused to cheat, and in the end, Brendan handed in a few sloppy paragraphs. The next day, after class, Morris Phelps returned the paper covered in red marker, told him he was on notice, and lectured him roundly about Torburton's work ethic. Reluctantly, Brendan resigned himself to spending hours at his desk beside his roommate, cramming for tests and quizzes.

On the lacrosse field, though, Brendan shone. Ever since his visit to the athletic director's office, Dunlop had been peculiarly attentive, taking extra pains to encourage him during practice and congratulate him after games. He'd assigned the assistant hockey coach to supervise him in the weight room, and while Brendan couldn't see much difference in his triceps or quads, he felt like he could run faster with all the extra cardio training.

One Sunday, he and another boy were lobbing some balls on the tennis courts. Brendan felt his speed increase, and he returned the ball harder than ever before. From the corner of his eye he saw Dunlop come over the hill and stop to watch. The following week, the tennis coach suggested that Brendan start coming to tennis practices on Saturday mornings.

Between school and sports, the freshmen found time for camaraderie at meals and on weekends. Groups of boys, neatly dressed in their maroon blazers with books in their arms, striding down paths or comparing notes in hallways or sitting in groups on grassy slopes made idyllic pictures, dioramas sprung straight from the school brochure.

Only one problem niggled at Brendan in those first weeks: the social strata of the school. After everything he'd been told, he'd expected to rise to the top rungs of his ninth-grade peers in a seamless continuum of his former impressive standing. That's what Ian Prescott's brother had promised. Brendan worked hard to be cool, but his assurance quickly dwindled. No one here thought he was special. There were many kids at Torburton who were just as good-looking, just as rich as him. Many much more so. There was an actual *sheik*, for Pete's sake!

Eventually, fed up with his cockiness, Jack and Shawn stopped following Brendan around like puppies. For three days, Brendan tried to shrug off the queer sensation of being an outcast. *They're just jealous*, he told himself, trying to take pleasure from it. But he was miserable. He decided to forget everything Don Prescott had told him and apologize to his friends.

Meanwhile, the upperclassmen made it clear that they wouldn't associate with the "children," as they called them, and the majority of them ignored the freshmen. That is, except for Hank and his crew, who seemed to take a real interest in Brendan, Jack, and Shawn.

The older boys pushed them into lockers as they passed outside classrooms, spilled water from paper cups onto their homework in study hall, stepped on their pencils.

In the dining room, Brendan didn't see the foot that tripped him and sent his tray clattering to the floor, leaving a goopy puddle of oatmeal to be mopped into a bucket. Jack, who didn't eat pork—having been raised with his father's Jewish beliefs—found that bacon mysteriously appeared on his plate and, once, in his book bag, so that its grease stained his notebooks and for the next week the smell nauseated him every time he opened the pocket. And poor Shawn took a swig of Kool-Aid only to discover that someone had poured hot sauce into his drink, and the burning in his throat turned his pale face bright red as he doubled over in a fit of coughing.

The bullying brought the freshman boys closer together. As autumn rode in from the distance, Brendan, Jack, and Shawn became inseparable.

One night after orchestra practice, the trio cut through the hedging behind the John Adams Music Hall. They happened upon the older boys crouched down in the dark beside a giant elm tree. All of them wore the Tridents hats and jerseys of the baseball team. The younger boys stopped and turned back, intending to dodge away through the bushes.

"Not so fast, kids," said Popeye in a low voice. "What are you doing out here behind the JAM? Can't you read? No Trespassing."

"S-s-sorry," said Shawn, looking for the non-existent sign. "We were just taking a shortcut."

Brendan glanced around. An empty vodka bottle lay on the ground. "Don't worry, we didn't see anything."

"Like this?" asked Hank, stepping forward and nudging the bottle with the toe of his cleat. "You want some?"

Jack put up his palms. "No, thanks."

Hank smiled, his eyes glinting in the light of the moon. "I think you do." He tipped his chin toward the others. "I think you should party with us. We don't mind sharing, right, guys?"

"Right," one of the boys agreed. "It's rude to refuse such a nice invitation."

Before they could react, the freshmen found themselves grabbed from behind with their arms pinned to their sides and their trumpet cases kicked aside. Hank turned to the elm behind him, the trunk of which gaped with a large hole. From its hollow, he pulled a full bottle and nodded to the others. Brendan, Jack, and Shawn felt arms grasp them from behind to tip their heads back and force their mouths open. Hank began to pour.

Sputtering, with rivulets of liquid running down their cheeks and necks, the boys swallowed as fast as they could so they wouldn't choke.

"Chug, chug," the upperclassmen chanted in a whisper, huddled around in a circle. At last, Hank stepped back with satisfaction, tossing the empty bottle aside.

"I think I'm going to puke," moaned Jack.

"Not on me, Mutt," one of the guys said, letting go of Brendan's arms and moving to stand beside Hank.

Hank wagged a finger and put on a voice like Galloway's. "Now, don't you gentlemen even *think* about telling anyone. We want to impress upon you how much we hate squealers."

"Fuckin' right," said the guy beside him, winding up and punching Brendan in the stomach. Brendan doubled over. Then the kid turned and did the same to Jack and

Shawn, and all three folded to the ground like collapsible lawn chairs. "Well, that was fun."

"Nice one, Scott, way to go," Hank and Popeye congratulated him, clapping him on the back. The upperclassmen filed out through the hedges, just as the retching began.

"Don't forget to clean up your mess," Hank instructed, before his orange head disappeared above the hedges. "We wouldn't want anyone to find you here and see that you've been drinking."

Muted laughter floated back to the clearing. It wasn't until hours later that Brendan wondered if he'd just met Scott Williams, the son of his parents' friends.

"Straighten your elbow on that follow-through," the tennis coach called, jogging over to Brendan's side of the court to demonstrate. Brendan returned balls until the coach nodded with satisfaction. "Good job," he said. "Hit the showers."

Brendan peeled off his headband, the one like Björn Borg had worn in the 1981 French Open a year earlier, and swung his long, damp bangs out of his eyes. He knew he'd played well in the last few practices and wondered if he'd be offered a spot on the junior varsity team.

"Hey." Brendan looked up from his bag to see Jack climbing the hill toward the courts. He took a swig from his water bottle and let himself out the wire gate. "What are you doing up here? Come walk me to the locker room."

The two boys headed back toward the athletic center, skirting the football and baseball fields along the way. It was a gorgeous Saturday in October. By now, they'd learned their way around campus, become acclimatized enough to take shortcuts like the one they'd taken after orchestra rehearsal a week earlier... the one that had landed them in trouble with the upperclassmen.

"Hurry up in the shower," Jack said. "Some of us are meeting in half an hour."

"I didn't hear about any meeting," Brendan said. He rinsed off while his roommate waited, changed into a fresh Adidas tracksuit, and followed him back to room 104 in Mariner Block. Shawn's room. Besides Shawn and his gigantic roommate Davey, an aspiring football player, five other freshmen were already inside. Brendan and Jack squeezed in.

"We've called this emergency meeting to talk about the upperclassmen," a curly-haired kid said, sitting cross-legged on one of the beds. "We need to unite if we're going to survive here."

All nine started talking at once, clamoring to describe incidents over the first few weeks of starting school. The curly-haired boy whistled. "One at a time. I'll start. Last week, someone put glue in my shampoo bottle."

"A bunch of the freshmen found gum in their dress shoes!"

"By the way"—the curly-haired boy tipped his chin in Brendan's direction, looking pointedly at the plastic bottle in his hand—"I wouldn't drink that if you filled it up from the water cooler in the freshman locker room. I heard they spit in it all the time."

Brendan made a gagging sound and tossed the bottle aside.

Davey spoke from under his bushy hair. "I saw the upperclassmen buttering Glen Wagner."

"What the heck is buttering?" Jack asked.

"I didn't know until I saw for myself. I was way in the corner of the gym behind the dumbbells, so I guess they didn't see me, but I saw them. Three upperclassmen. They blindfolded Glen and told him to lie down on a mat to do sit-ups. Then I saw one of the guys take off his shorts and squat over Glen, spreading his butt-cheeks. When Glen did his first sit-up, his face landed smack in the guy's arse."

"Ewww!" The boys in the room grimaced.

"The upperclassmen thought it was pretty hysterical," Davey added. "The question is, what can we do about all this?"

"How about short sheeting their beds?" Shawn piped up.

"Dude, we already told you that's not gonna work," a chorus of boys replied.

Brendan spoke up. He turned to the others. "We've been trying to come up with a plan, but our ideas aren't good enough. Stealing sneakers, ripping out pages of their homework... all that crap won't scare them, it'll just get them more riled up."

Jack, the stickler for rules, nodded. "And anyway, what if we get caught? I don't want to get in trouble."

"So we just let them push us around for the rest of the year? A sophomore told me they dunked his head in a toilet last year," Davey said. His meaty hand smoothed his frizzy hair.

"You're *ginormous*. You don't have to worry about that." Shawn gave his football-player roommate a once over. It was just his luck to be paired with The Hulk. Beside him, Shawn looked even more miniscule.

"And don't forget what happened to us last week behind the JAM." Jack looked morose. "The upperclassmen get away with murder around here."

Another boy spoke up. "Doesn't Mr. Galloway care about what's happening?"

"Maybe Mr. Galloway needs a new athletic field or a new wing for the library." The curly-haired boy snorted. "Parents pay for screw ups."

Jack objected, sounding indignant. "My parents would never do that."

Not long after, the meeting ended. They'd meet again in a few weeks, they decided. They agreed the best thing they could do was try to be invisible, try not to draw attention to themselves. They'd avoid being too successful at anything—*or* too unsuccessful, if possible.

"It's like that thing, a catch twenty-two my dad calls it," Brendan grumbled, as he and Jack headed to dinner. "We're supposed to excel here at Torburton. But if we're smart or talented or athletic, we're showing off, and they'll beat us up for it."

"Yeah, and if we're dumb or we have zits or spaz out in sports, we're losers," Jack sighed. "We get picked on either way."

Over the next weeks, Brendan and the rest of the freshmen boys were on high alert for upperclassmen pranks. They whispered warnings to each other in the hallways and in the dining room, in addition to holding formal meetings.

Their preoccupation with the upperclassmen made them oblivious to the subtleties of the staff's questionable conduct... until it became impossible to ignore.

Morris Phelps, the English teacher, stood at his blackboard talking about expository essays: an introduction, three paragraphs detailing the main idea, and a conclusion.

"This essay is worth twenty percent of your semester grade," he announced. "The theme this year is about your first time with a girl." He winked and grinned at the class.

A few weeks later, the results of a particularly brutal math test were posted. The curly-haired boy, a math whiz named Simon, scored a perfect one hundred. Anthony Ducati, the head of the math department, flagged him down after school that Friday. "Come on," he said, holding open the passenger door of his souped-up Chevrolet Camaro. "Let's go for a ride. You earned it."

And on the sidelines before the big football opener, some upperclassmen were overheard talking about Trish "The Dish" Galloway, the headmaster's wife.

"Hey, guys! Guess who just gave me some good luck in the locker room?" the quarterback boasted to his teammates.

"Lemme guess," a lineman said. "Was she drunk?"

"Oh, yeah," the quarterback replied with a smirk. "And let's just say she's the real 'headmaster' around here."

By then Brendan felt more at ease with Terence Dunlop, with the haze of cigarette smoke when he opened his office door, with his strong fingers gripping Brendan's shoulder in greeting. As part of his program, Dunlop demanded that Brendan come to see him at least once a month to strip off his clothes, to get weighed and photographed. He got used to that, too.

Brendan, Jack, and Shawn fantasized about all the ways they would get back at the upperclassmen. What kind of trick could they play? They ruled out any actual vandalism, like spray painting nasty messages in the locker room, because they were afraid of getting caught. It consumed their conversations. Many autumn nights, Brendan and Jack fell asleep plotting revenge.

But even during those conversations in the dark, Brendan didn't repeat the newest insult he'd begun hearing from Hank and his crew. "Smells like new money," Hank scoffed, wrinkling his nose. "Weren't you poor, like, yesterday?"

One afternoon, on his way back to Mariner Block, Brendan rounded the corner of the Commons's center hallway and heard Jack's voice. Jack was speaking into the only telephone students were permitted to use, its corkscrew cord dangling from the wall mount inside the school's head office. "That sounds great, Mom," he said through the open door. "Don't forget my ski jacket. And the red licorice shoelaces... the cherry ones.". He hung the receiver on the hook and caught up with Brendan. "After the assembly on Saturday morning, my folks are taking me to New York City," he said, more excited than he'd been in weeks. "Can't wait to split this popsicle stand."

Brendan shrugged. He hadn't really expected his mother and father to come back from Milan and was prepared to be alone for Parents' Weekend. But he hadn't expected he'd be so very lonely.

The month of October 1982 had an extra weekend: five Fridays, five Saturdays, and five Sundays. Jack's mother called it *"silver pockets full,"* a rare, auspicious event that legend said occurred only once every eight hundred and twenty-three years. Special month, she'd told Jack over the phone.

This year, Parents' Weekend began on the fourth Saturday, the 23rd, a gloriously crisp day with leaves that swirled about in the air and crunched underfoot. By ten o'clock in the morning, a long ribbon of cars idled at the wrought iron gates before being allowed to wrap around Great Oak.

An extravagant brunch, replete with a carving station and omelets made to order, had been planned for the families, and with the weather cooperating, many drifted outside to enjoy the view. Afterward, they congregated in the auditorium for the Fall Family Assembly. Edward Galloway stood on the stage at his charming best, welcoming the parents, reporting on the excellent start to the academic year. He'd been at the brunch, too, congratulating mothers on their fine sons and vigorously shaking hands with fathers. Especially those with deep pockets, Brendan noticed, watching him work the crowd. Some of these families had even shown up with bodyguards! Brendan wondered if Galloway would've sucked up to his parents. At his old school, the principal had practically licked Kenneth Cortland's shoes. Brendan couldn't help noticing that neither Galloway nor Greer went out of his way to greet the Drs. Abromovitch.

The crowd dissolved immediately after the assembly. As per tradition, families headed to points nearby for the weekend, Burlington or Boston or Newport. A few went home. Jack had invited Brendan to come along to Manhattan, but he declined when he learned that they weren't staying in a hotel but rather at Jack's grandparents' home in Queens.

Of the few students remaining behind at school for the weekend, most were from overseas and of those even fewer were freshmen, this year's class having drawn more regionally than internationally. By two o'clock Saturday afternoon, the campus looked like a ghost town. Brendan watched cartoons in the Commons for a while but soon tired of it. He pulled on his Torburton jacket and went outside.

Across the Quad, he recognized someone hurrying in the opposite direction: a tall kid, one of the few black students at Torburton and a gifted cellist. Brendan had seen him harassed by the upperclassmen but hadn't given much thought to the school's lack of diversity. He picked up his pace, hoping to introduce himself, but the boy disappeared into a building.

At least Hank and the other upperclassmen are gone, he thought, dejected, as he strolled the empty paths. It was small consolation when he thought about how happy Jack and his family had looked as they waved goodbye. He wondered if the staff had gone home, too, and if so, would there be anyone around to prepare dinner at night?

"Mr. Cortland." Brendan turned the corner in front of Murdock Memorial Library to see the headmaster striding toward him. "You're still here?" Galloway sounded surprised.

"My parents couldn't make it." Brendan shrugged, trying to look cavalier. He blinked hard a few times.

"Well, that happens. Not to worry. I've always enjoyed Torburton during Parents' Weekend. It's quiet, and I can actually get some thinking done. Hard to do that with two hundred and forty teenagers roaming around."

Brendan passed the back of his hand over his eyes. "Yes, sir."

"Good chance for you to catch up on some studying," Galloway said. He looked at Brendan thoughtfully. "Tell you what, Mr. Cortland. Why don't you hit the books for a couple hours? Then you can join me for dinner. A nice change from the dining room." He winked. "How does that sound?"

"Uh, well, I…"

"Good, it's settled. Be there at six o'clock." He pointed down the path that led toward the chapel and the infirmary. Farther back stood an imposing house with white clapboard walls and dark green shutters framing its many windows. The headmaster's residence. A quaint, picture-perfect New England home.

The woman who opened the door looked familiar. Brendan recognized her as a fleeting presence on the bleachers and at the staff table in the dining hall but truth be told, he'd been too wrapped up in his own activities to take much notice of her, even while the older boys had whooped and whispered and made obscene gestures in the locker rooms. Now he looked more closely. She was pretty and curvy and bouncy, in her soft pink, button-up sweater and matching pink pants. And friendly. She hugged him as he stood on the front porch.

"Hello, sweetie, I'm so glad Edward invited you to join us," she gushed, pulling him inside. "You poor thing, being left here all alone." She busied herself with helping him out of his windbreaker and showing him to the living room, slightly unsteady as she padded on bare feet.

"Now, Edward's got dinner almost ready, seeing as I'm not much of a cook. Before we eat I thought we could sit here on the sofa and chat a bit." She sank down onto the cushions, tucking a leg under her, and tugged Brendan's hand.

Brendan landed beside her, acutely aware of her closeness; he could smell the scent of her shampoo every time she tossed her big hair. "Uh... thank you for having me, Mrs. Galloway."

"Aren't you just the sweetest thing." She reached for a large martini glass and took a sip, leaving a smudge of lipstick on the rim. "You just call me Trish, honey. Would you like something to drink? A Coke?"

"I'm okay, thanks."

"Don't be shy, if you want anything," she said, her Southern twang lengthening her vowels. "Well, now. Edward tells me you play lacrosse?"

"Yes, ma'am. I mean Trish. Ma'am." Brendan cleared his throat. She was leaning so close that he could feel her warm breath on his neck and the distinct imprint of her bosom through the thin cotton of his shirt.

"How fun!" She sipped her martini. "I just love watching you boys on the field. It reminds me of my days at Ole Miss, cheering for our Rebels. Those college kids were just so big in their shoulder pads. I always worried that someone would get hurt. You've never been hurt, have you Brendan?"

"No, ma'am."

"Thank heaven for that. You freshmen are so small compared to the seniors. I'm afraid the little ones will get trampled when one of them big boys comes charging across the field, lookin' madder than a wet hen." Her chuckle floated over his face with a whiff of something fruity. She took a last sip and set the empty glass on the table.

"Some of those boys have full beards, as I live and breathe," she continued, reaching a finger to touch Brendan's face. "You just have a few little blond hairs here over your lip… not much to write home about. Oh! You're blushing. My, aren't you just cute as a button?"

"Mr. Cortland. Glad to see you, son." Edward Galloway appeared in the doorway wearing leisure pants and a loose shirt with a few buttons undone at the neck. Compared to his usual suit and tie, he looked half naked.

Brendan jumped up from the couch. "Good evening, Mr. Galloway."

"I see you met my wife." Galloway smiled, showing his overbite. Ice tinkled as he swirled some amber liquid in a tumbler. "Good. Well, I'm hungry, so let's eat." He turned toward the dining room.

"Help me up, honey." Trish giggled, grabbing Brendan's hand as she rose and took a wobbly step. "I haven't eaten a thing today and those martinis must have gone straight to my head." She swayed precariously, leaning the length of her body into Brendan for a long moment, her head falling back on her neck, before heading after her husband.

True to his word, Galloway served a dinner to savor: lamb chops, braised Brussels sprouts and porcini mushrooms, roasted fingerling potatoes. He and Trish polished off a bottle of wine, too, in between the barrage of questions they tossed at Brendan about his family and his studies. The headmaster seemed especially interested in

Brendan's take on his friends: who was popular? Who did the others dislike? Who was homesick?

Brendan wondered if he should mention Hank, Popeye, and the incidents with the seniors. But he bit his tongue. They'd made it clear how they felt about tattlers. The conversation lulled.

"Well, I guess I should get going," he began. "Thank you very much…"

Trish looked disappointed. "I made a special dessert! You can't leave yet."

Galloway led Brendan to the den, where he poured himself a large snifter of brandy. Warming the goblet in his palm, he sat back on the couch and motioned for Brendan to join him.

"Pudding Pops!" Trish appeared in the doorway, still barefoot, her pink lip gloss reapplied. "I made them myself." She handed out two and licked a third.

"Quite the gourmet, aren't you," Galloway said, with a sideways wink at Brendan.

Trish pouted. "Edward, don't be nasty," she said, wagging her Pudding Pop at her husband. "Anyway, I put a movie in for us. I'm dying to see it… my sisters told me they loved it." She powered up the new Sony Video Home System machine beside the television set, then plopped down between Brendan and her husband, shimmying her hips to make space.

Brendan sat stiffly, as close to his end of the sofa as possible, not only acutely aware of Trish's thigh and hip and arm pressed against his, but of the whole situation, as if he were spying down from above: a freshman pupil curled up in a dimly-lit den, watching a movie with the headmaster and his wife in their home, on a Saturday night with the campus around them largely deserted. There'd been no mention of this in the school brochure.

The movie began to play. *Lady Chatterley's Lover*, the title said, and Brendan tried to concentrate on the dialogue rather than on Trish lounging beside him, licking her Pudding Pop with long, slow strokes of her tongue. Soon enough, though, he found himself mesmerized by the film: Lady Chatterley nude onscreen. She and Mellors both. Nude. Intertwined.

"Interesting choice of film," Galloway observed in a matter-of-fact voice. "A comment on society. You know the book by D. H. Lawrence was the subject of a landmark obscenity trial. It's about class: the aristocracy and the peasantry. And sex, of course… love with the mind versus love with the body. Quite an educational story."

"It's not obscene, is it?" Trish glanced slyly at Brendan. "Oh my, you look as nervous as a long-tailed cat in a room full of rocking chairs. Don't worry, it's just play-acting."

They watched another scene, and after a while she twisted her torso toward her husband and leaned to nuzzle the side of his neck. Her angle now served to push her round bottom against Brendan. He tried to shut out the soft, slurping sound of kissing beside him and focus instead on the movie, but its explicit content made him increasingly uncomfortable. His breathing quickened. He tore his gaze away, his eyes darting around the room, taking in the long paisley curtains, the turntable and record albums, the wedding portrait with Edward Galloway and his young bride in her glittery tiara, the bar cart with its glassware of varying heights alongside open bottles of scotch, whiskey, bourbon, and vermouth.

Suddenly he realized that the melting chocolate had dripped down the back of his hand, and by the glow of the television he saw that he'd gotten a smear on the side of Trish's sweater.

"I'm really s-sorry, Mrs. Galloway," he stammered. "I… um… made a mess on your top…"

Trish twisted away from Galloway, bending an arm to find the stain, smiling knowingly when she noticed Brendan staring at her chest with eyes round as poker chips. On either side of the open buttons, her hardened nipples were clearly visible, straining under the tight knit. She arched her back a little. "Don't you worry, it's nothing that a little soap and water can't fix," she said. "Let's go wash those sticky fingers." She reached for his wrist and pulled him after her to the powder room off the front hall.

Brendan stood rigidly in front of the sink as Trish held his hands under the faucet. Then she wet a facecloth and raised her arm. "Would you mind?"

Swallowing, Brendan took the cloth and made a few tentative swipes at the material, trying not to see anything beyond the stain.

"Don't be shy. Like this," Trish said, covering his hand with her own to scrub at the stain in slow, widening circles. The washcloth soaked the front of her top, turning the material transparent. Brendan felt the distinct protrusion of a nipple in his palm. Dizzily, he dropped his hand to his side. Trish smiled and reached down for the washcloth, her fingers brushing the front of his bulging trousers in the process.

Jesus.

Brendan leapt from the bathroom and in a few quick strides crossed the front hall, mumbling thanks for dinner over his shoulder as he flung open the door and ran.

Trish came hurrying after him. "Honey, your jacket," she called, but by the time she'd reached the porch to flick on a light, Brendan had disappeared into the dark.

CHAPTER SIX

No one will believe me, Brendan thought over and over the next morning as he curled under his covers in humiliation, replaying the events of the previous night. He'd tossed and turned for hours, thinking of the explicit scenes from the movie, the likes of which were new to him. His breathing quickened just thinking about it. Of course, he and his buddies had looked at girlie magazines before—who hadn't?—but it seemed completely different seeing people in action. Not to mention watching it with the headmaster and his wife. *Did Galloway think it was normal, seeing that stuff with a kid in the room?* Was *it normal? And then there's* her. *Is* she *normal?* Who would possibly believe that the headmaster's wife had… had… practically in front of her husband?

Anyway, who could he tell? No one would believe him. Not even Jack. And Brendan wanted to tell Jack more than anyone else in the world.

He and Jack had forged a tight bond in the months they'd roomed together, especially after the night behind the JAM. They had each other's backs. And Brendan had come to feel protective of little Shawn Unger, too. He wouldn't risk these friendships with such an outrageous story.

He reached up to slide a tape into his boombox. Might as well get comfortable, as it promised to be a long day here alone in his room. No way would he venture outside in case he bumped into the Galloways someplace! He still had one tube of potato chips and, as requested, Jack's mom had left a couple packages of cherry licorice. That would have to sustain him until breakfast. With luck, Jack would return soon with more snacks.

He burrowed his face back under the covers and tried to concentrate on Springsteen. He didn't think he'd ever eat a Pudding Pop again.

When the knock came at his door early in the afternoon, somehow Brendan knew it would be Galloway even before it opened. The man stepped inside with Brendan's yellow windbreaker folded over one arm and a tray in his hands.

"You missed breakfast and lunch. I brought you a sandwich." He put the tray on Jack's neatly made bed and turned to peer down at Brendan. "You feeling all right, son?"

Brendan nodded, embarrassed. "Fine, sir."

"Good. I wouldn't want to think I poisoned you with my cooking." He chortled, his overbite more pronounced than ever from Brendan's perspective below. "How about hitting the shower? Adolescent boys don't smell like flowers, you know." Galloway smiled patiently. Brendan waited for him to leave, but he didn't. He just stood there. Was he waiting for Brendan to go *right now*?

Brendan slowly pushed down the covers. He wore only a pair of pajama pants and, rather than looking away, Galloway seemed to take an almost clinical interest in the sight. "Looks like you're going to be a muscular fellow. I heard Terry put you on his program. I bet the girls will be all over you. That face." He reached out a hand and smoothed Brendan's sleep-tousled hair.

Brendan stared straight ahead.

Galloway continued, "I hope this weekend wasn't too bad without your parents. You know, you can always come to me when you're lonely. Think of me as a friend. I'm on your side."

Brendan swallowed.

"I left a message on your parents' answering machine saying how well you're doing. I told them I've taken you under my wing. They'll appreciate hearing that, I'm sure. It means I think you're special." He reached out and swept Brendan's bangs back from his forehead in a fatherly gesture. "And, of course, you can tell me anything. Anything at all. We can keep things just between us men, you know. Like last night... no one needs to know that you were over for dinner or what movie we watched or that my wife and I may have had a glass too many. You understand?"

Brendan nodded briefly.

"Good. Well, go ahead and take a shower." Galloway clapped him on the back. "And you might want to crack open a window. It's pretty stuffy in here."

When his parents dropped him off on campus late that evening, Jack returned to room 266 to find his roommate huddled under his covers, with the windows wide open and an untouched bologna sandwich on his bed.

Two pivotal things happened in the week that followed, the last week of October, and they both happened on Halloween. Traditionally, Torburton Hall celebrated Halloween to the fullest with a giant outdoor carnival, weather permitting. The staff and students prepared intensively. Candy treats were distributed at large, and a two-day-long pumpkin carving contest would culminate with the winner announced before an evening horror movie. That year, Halloween would fall on a Sunday, perfect timing to enjoy an entire day of revelry.

In anticipation of the holiday, Jack had returned from Parents' Weekend with a bag of gear for himself and Brendan. Less prepared freshmen boys were forced to engineer costumes with whatever they found at hand. They wrapped themselves from head to toe with toilet paper to go as mummies, or aluminum foil for robots. Several were toga-clad Romans in white towels. The most unimaginative were the bed-sheet ghosts with their crudely cut eyeholes. One kid stuck bagels to the sides of his head and went as Princess Leah.

Early Saturday morning, Jack arrived on the Quad to enter the carving contest. He wrote "Room 266" on the sign-up sheet. He chose the plumpest pumpkin he could find in the cardboard bin and lugged it back to the dorm. But Brendan wasn't interested.

"C'mon," Jack begged, spreading newspaper on their floor. "First place prize is extra dessert for a week plus three homework passes." He set about sketching ideas. Brendan shrugged. Fine. He'd been moody ever since Parents' Weekend, and Jack had to coax him to join in. He'd go along with this for his roommate's sake.

Hours later, as they cleaned up the mess of seeds and pumpkin slime, even Brendan had to admit their pumpkin had turned out terrific. They'd decided to do Groucho Marx, and the face really resembled him! Brendan began to feel excited for Halloween after all.

On the morning of October 31st, Jack dumped out the contents of his brown paper bag, eager to show Brendan the costumes he'd kept a surprise. Laughing, they donned black sunglasses, black ties, and black hats.

In the vestibule of Mariner Block, they bumped into Shawn and his colossal roommate, Davey. The top of

Shawn's head reached Davey's ribcage. Both wore regular clothes.

"Get it?" Davey asked, standing beside his miniature friend and puffing out his chest. "We're Clifford and Ricky from *My Bodyguard.*"

Teachers appeared at breakfast dressed as pirates, clowns, and mad scientists. Terry Dunlop came as a Maytag repairman in a blue uniform and cap. Hank, Popeye, and a gang of upperclassmen had clearly planned in advance. They wore disturbingly convincing Mad Max costumes and after breakfast they ran about the campus yelling, "Watch the tongue, lovable," "What a turkey," and, "I'm a rocker, I'm a roller, I'm an out-of-controller!" There was Toecutter, and Johnny, and Immortan Joe, and Nux, and even baby Sprog. Brendan wondered, as he saw them tearing past toward the baseball field in a frenzy, why none of them dressed in the main role of Max Rockatansky?

That evening at dinner, his question was answered. For several days, anticipation had thrummed through the air of the campus, and tonight it came to a head. The upperclassmen buzzed in low voices among themselves, and even the teachers glanced toward the door as if expecting something to happen at any moment. Brendan had overheard many a conversation in the locker rooms after lacrosse practice: "He" was coming back. Brendan didn't know who "he" was.

But Shawn *did* know. Shawn was in the boys' bathroom at the far end of a rarely-used hallway in Murdock Memorial Library. He stayed quiet in his stall when he heard two juniors enter.

"Did you hear? Chad Hubert's coming back tonight," one said in a hushed voice.

"I thought they expelled him last spring."

"They did. I heard he's been in three other boarding schools over the past two months. The longest he stayed was fourteen days before he got kicked out again. His dad convinced Galloway to let him come back here starting November the first."

"Lucky us." The boy whistled.

"Shhh!"

After the boys left the restroom, Shawn scurried back to the main stacks where Brendan and Jack were researching pilgrims for their American history class. He reported his findings.

"Why would they let him come back if he was expelled last year?" Brendan asked in a whisper.

"They said Chad's father offered to build a whole new wing of the athletic center, with a new indoor baseball facility, like a bubble. They said he was going to buy a few acres of extra land, too," Shawn told them.

"He must have some serious dough," said Jack.

"But why'd he get expelled in the first place?" Brendan asked.

"I dunno," said Shawn. "They didn't say."

Now, just as everyone raised their heads from saying grace before the meal, the double doors opened to the hall. All conversation ceased at the upperclassmen's tables, and the freshmen, curious, watched wide-eyed. Brendan swiveled in his chair to see.

Quentin Greer, in full Lawrence of Arabia garb, walked through the door, followed by a young man dressed in black leather. Medium height, dark hair, straight eyebrows, an aquiline nose. He had a handsome, sculpted face, and carried himself with such tightly contained rage that he seemed to radiate as he crossed the floor to join his classmates.

From his vantage point, Brendan recognized the costume immediately: Mad Max. In fact, he looked so much the part that for a moment Brendan thought he was the real Mel Gibson. *That must be the guy they were talking about!*

Suddenly, everyone seemed to be clamoring for his attention. Hank and Popeye fairly tripped over themselves as they jumped to greet him. "Hey, Chad! Nice to have you back!" and, "We missed you, Hubert—hasn't been the same without you!" He seemed to ignore them all, surveying the room calmly. Then a senior called out a line from the movie: "Look what's turned up for Sunday dinner!" At that, everyone laughed, and the young man broke into a grin. Juniors at the table hastened to make room, and he pulled out a chair.

Jack and Shawn, like the rest of the boys, seemed mesmerized. Jack said, "He's like a celebrity around here."

Brendan tapped a finger on the table. "I wonder what his deal is."

A sophomore from Table Three leaned close. "Chad Hubert? I'll tell you what his deal is. His old man's worth billions. You never heard of John Hubert? He owns half the mineral mining rights in the world. He makes your dad look like a pauper, Cortland."

Brendan turned toward the upperclassmen once more, just as the new boy in the leather jacket looked up. For a moment their eyes locked. Trying to look nonchalant, Brendan flipped his long, blond bangs back, and then the new boy winked.

That evening, on the Quad, after the carnival games had been played, the carved pumpkins lit and displayed, and the cotton candy consumed, Jack pulled Brendan by the sleeve. "Let's go," he urged. "The movie's starting in the auditorium and they're going to announce the contest winners."

"They're showing *The Exorcist*," Shawn squeaked. "What the heck is an exorcist?"

Standing on the compass rose, Brendan turned toward Mariner Block. He said he was tired. The truth was he couldn't stomach watching another movie in the dark, under the same roof as Edward Galloway and, potentially, his wife, even if they were seated far apart.

But Jack wouldn't hear of it. He spun Brendan around and, palms to shoulder blades, gave him a shove in the direction of the auditorium. Brendan protested, digging his heels into the walkway as they rounded the corner of the library.

Along the path, on a row of tables, were the students' carved pumpkins. The judging had taken place during dinner, and ribbons for first, second, and third place had been draped over the winners. A knot of freshmen boys huddled and pointed. Jack craned to look over their shoulders.

"Damn upperclassmen," Simon said.

The blue First Place ribbon lay in a puddle of pumpkin. Orange shards had been smashed to smithereens, and Groucho Marx was nowhere to be seen. Jack and Brendan exchanged disbelieving looks from behind their sunglasses.

Onto the path stepped Hank, Popeye, and a gang of other juniors. "Boo," said Popeye, and the knot of other freshmen scattered.

"Well, well." Hank's Cheetos hair was covered by a wig with a blond streak in front. "Look at these ingenious costumes. What could they be?"

"Well, Toecutter, I'd say we have the Blues Brothers. And a little girl with them." Scott crossed his arms and blocked their way. "Where you going, children?"

Shawn said, "To the auditorium."

Popeye's chin jutted sideways as he smirked. "That sounds like fun. Although I don't think they'll be announcing the prizes for best pumpkin tonight."

"Maybe we should chaperone you to the movie, seeing as it's dark out here and all," Hank said. "Let's take the long way."

The upperclassmen split up, a few leading the way and a few behind to snare them in, so Brendan, Jack, and Shawn had no choice but to follow a far path that wound away from the cluster of academic buildings and dormitories and then sprouted off like a sucker branch toward the quaint little chapel.

"If we go this way, we'll have to walk by the graveyard," Shawn whispered.

"I know." Grimly, Jack tucked his dark glasses into the neckline of his shirt.

They walked along the dimly lit path, jostling each other and trying to mask their nerves. Behind the chapel was the old cemetery with its mossy headstones marking the eternal resting place of former teachers, parsons all, from the days in which the small chapel had administered the parish of Torburton. Shaded even in the daytime by the encroaching woods, black and creepy at night, it looked especially so, the boys thought, tonight. Halloween night.

As they skirted the chapel with its narrow steeple and white clapboard sides, the upperclassmen deliberately veered from the path and toward the cemetery, bodily forcing their de facto hostages along with them. Scott pushed open the creaking iron gate to let the group trudge through. Popeye led the way deep into the heart of the graveyard, where autumn leaves swished underfoot and faintly outlined plots were darkened by overhanging branches.

They stopped. Brendan, Jack, and Shawn shifted uneasily. The yellow glow of the path lights didn't reach this far and only moonlight sifted through the sooty darkness. Thick, heavy silence cloaked the enclosure.

Until the crunch of footsteps sounded from the woods. An outlined figure appeared and used a flashlight to light a way around the crumbling headstones. The figure took its time. It wasn't in a rush.

The beam of light paused on the ground when the figure came to a stop.

"Hello," it said in a smooth voice Brendan didn't recognize.

The figure walked in a circle around the three freshmen, training the flashlight in their eyes, faces, up and down the lengths of their bodies. Only when the light bounced off the figure's legs, illuminating shiny black leather, did Brendan realize it must be Chad, the returning junior, dressed in his Mad Max costume. "And who do we have here?"

Hank said, "Three Freshies. A pretty boy, a shrimp, and a mutt."

"I don't believe we've met," the smooth voice continued. "I'm Chad Hubert, back in my kingdom to claim my rightful throne. What's your name, pretty boy?" he asked, shining the light in Brendan's eyes.

"I'm Brendan Cortland," Brendan told him, trying to flip his bangs back but prevented from doing so by the Blues Brothers hat. "Your majesty," he added, but his voice wavered.

"Don't be a smartass." Chad gave him a long, considering look before he moved on to Jack. "And you?"

"Jack Abromovitch."

The upperclassmen snickered. "*Abromovitch?*" Chad repeated with a laugh, shining the light around Jack's face. "You a Kike?"

What an asshole, Brendan thought. He jumped to Jack's defense. "He's half Jewish, half Chinese."

"He can speak for himself... can't you?" Popeye asked, poking a finger into Jack's chest.

"Half Kike, half Chink?" Chad laughed again. "What does that make, a Kink? Ha."

"Told you he was a mutt," Hank said, giving Jack a shove.

Chad nodded and looked down at Shawn. "And what's this measly creature?"

Just like on the first day of school. Brendan remembered watching the older boys giving Shawn a noogie. This time, he took a breath and stepped in front of his friend. "Leave him alone, he's just a kid."

"Out of the way, smartass." Scott shoved Brendan aside.

Shawn cowered in the beam of light, tiny and afraid. "Sh-Shawn Unger, s-sir," he stammered.

"Sir." Chad swished the word around his mouth. "Sir. Very respectful. I like that. You may have just saved your little monkey ass, Unger." He turned back to Brendan and Jack, pointing the light in their eyes again. "You two dorks. Let's play a Halloween game," he suggested. "Trick or treat."

Even in the dark, Brendan could sense the smile playing about the corners of the hidden mouth. Neither he nor Jack answered.

"I said trick or treat," Chad repeated, his voice growing impatient. "Choose, or I'll choose for you."

"It would depend, uh, sir," Jack said, tacking on the word hastily. "What's the treat?"

Popeye stepped into the light. "I'll give you a treat, Kike." He sniggered. "A nice big one. You can suck my lollipop."

Everyone laughed at that.

Hank added, "Don't worry, it's kosher." And they cackled again.

"We're late for the movie," Shawn piped up, his voice quaking. "We should go before they come looking for us."

"Oh, I think we've got all the privacy we want out here," said Chad, poking him in the forehead with his index finger. "Back. To. Our. Game."

Brendan put an arm around Shawn's scrawny shoulders. "We're done," he said, mustering all his confidence. "Leave us alone."

Popeye rounded on him. "Shut your face, you little faggot," he hissed. "Before I shut it for you."

"Now, now, we don't want to mess up his pretty face." Chad paused. "Or do we?" He reached into his back pocket and pulled out a jackknife.

On Chad's command, Popeye and Scott, dressed as Immortan Joe and Nux, fell upon Brendan. They knocked his hat off and pinned him to the ground, while two others—Johnny and baby Sprog—dragged Jack and Shawn to the main path and back toward the Mariner Block. Chad said, "Make sure they stay put."

Hank held the flashlight as Chad knelt beside Brendan's head and brandished the knife. The steel blade glinted in the glare of the flashlight as slowly, very deliberately, Chad drew the point around each eye, down over his nose, and across his throat. Lightly, carefully, so he didn't break the skin.

At first.

CHAPTER SEVEN

Fleeing back to his dormitory in the dark, unsure if Chad and the others would follow, Brendan burst into his bedroom where Jack paced, waiting.

Jack's face paled when he saw what Chad had done. "You're... you're... bleeding," he stammered.

Brendan threw open his armoire to look in the full-length mirror tacked to the door inside. His reflection stared back at him, grisly, gory, terrified.

Trickles of blood ran down his face from the nicks where Chad had cut too deep. His eyes gaped, wide and white. Bits of leaves and sticks clung to limp locks of his hair and the black jacket and tie of his bedraggled Blues Brothers costume. He stood motionless for several minutes as if in shock.

"Don't worry," he finally said in a muffled voice. "It's no big deal." He picked up his monogrammed washcloth and dabbed his face, flinching at the stinging and at the sight of the red-stained terry. He threw the expensive facecloth in the garbage and got into bed.

Much later that night, Brendan huddled under his covers and tried to stifle the sobs that rose in his throat. He heard his roommate's shuffling approach and felt the tentative hand patting his foot through the quilt.

"You okay?" Jack asked in the dark.

"I'll... I'll get used to it."

Brendan heard the mattress squeak as Jack returned to bed.

He'd lied. He wouldn't get used to it, not for a very long time.

For on that Halloween night of 1982, in the dark of an old cemetery lit only by the beams of moonlight and flashlight, Chad Hubert had done something very calculated, very malicious, and very clearly intended to affirm his own unshakable superiority in the hierarchy of the school.

While his friends pinned the boy's arms and legs to the ground, Chad Hubert had knelt on his shoulders, taken out his jackknife, and carved off Brendan Cortland's signature blond bangs at the hairline.

The next day heralded class as usual. Brendan dragged himself from bed and dressed in his uniform, avoiding the mirror. He could feel his roommate's eyes boring into his skull, though Jack tried not to be obvious.

"Here." Gingerly, Jack perched his Blues Brothers hat on Brendan's head, angling it low over the forehead to rest on the dark eyebrows, pretending not to notice the tears beading on the thick black lashes. "Maybe no one will notice."

Brendan skipped breakfast. *Hold it together*, he told himself, but the tears kept flowing. All he wanted was to be home, in his bed, with a tray of hot soup and crackers like his mother used to bring when he was sick. But this time he wasn't sick, and he suspected that the days of his mother playing nursemaid were over anyway.

Just before the bell rang, Brendan entered the Jefferson building for math. He skirted his friends as they strode down the hallways and kept his head hidden behind his textbook as he slumped low in his seat for the first class of the day. Anthony Ducati wrote an algebra problem on the board and dusted chalk from his hands before turning to face the class. He squinted directly at Brendan.

"Hat off, Mr. Cortland," he said.

Reluctantly, Brendan reached to slide it off. A few seconds passed before Ducati let out a guffaw.

"Halloween's over," he chortled. "I would have thought twice about that costume." His comment sent heads swiveling to look at Brendan. He felt the weight of dozens of eyes. All the air seemed to have been sucked from the room in a collective inhale. Then, the giggles began.

Brendan called home that evening from the communal phone. His voice thickened as soon as he began to speak, and the story emerged between sniffles.

Kenneth Cortland chuckled. "You're reminding me of the time my friends and I found some black shoe polish and painted a curly moustache on the captain of the wrestling team as he slept. It stained his skin for a week. But it was all in good fun." Then his voice hardened. "Man up, Brendan. Life is tough. Do you think I got where I am by being overly sensitive? You hear me?"

"I hear you."

Stop acting like a girl, Brendan told himself that night. *Man up.*

And oh, how he tried the next day and the next. To man up, to swallow the lump that threatened to choke off his breath, to hold his head up. But the upperclassmen hadn't used shoe polish and he wouldn't recover in a week.

Forced to go to classes hatless, Brendan knew he looked ugly. On his bare forehead and halfway toward his crown, long, angry scabs formed where the knife had scraped too deep. The rest of his hair hung in glaring contrast to the shorn scalp.

When he arrived in the gym for phys-ed, he felt the familiar tap on his shoulder.

"Come to my office this afternoon," Terry Dunlop said.

Brendan knocked on the athletic director's door at four o'clock.

"I'm guessing you didn't do this yourself." Dunlop tipped his chin up.

"No, sir."

"Care to tell me who did?"

Brendan shrugged.

"I get it." Dunlop crossed his beefy arms across his chest. "No snitching."

Brendan remained silent, staring at the floor.

Dunlop sighed and reached into a drawer for some antibiotic ointment. He dabbed it on the wounds as he spoke. "Well, one thing is for sure, you can't stay like that. You look like rats chewed away at your face. Let's go."

After a twenty-minute ride in Dunlop's Datsun, they arrived in the village of Calvert and parked half a block from an old-fashioned barbershop with a red and white pole out front.

"Afternoon," Dunlop called over the tinkling bells as he pushed open the door. A wrinkled man in a white smock trundled in from a back room. "Wondering if you can do something for this young man."

The barber's bushy eyebrows shot up in surprise as he took in Brendan's appearance. He pointed to an empty chair. "Good Lord," he muttered, draping a plastic cape over Brendan's Torburton blazer and peering at Brendan's head from different angles. "Truth is, there's really not much I can do. My only suggestion is to shave the whole thing so it grows back evenly."

"Sounds about right," Dunlop said. He lit a cigarette and leaned against a wall to wait.

Reaching into a drawer, the barber pulled out an electric razor. A few minutes later, the floor around Brendan's chair was strewn with ropes of blond hair, the discarded remnants of a California boy persona. The barber shook out his smock.

"That's the best I can do, son," he said. "Time will do the rest."

Brendan forced his gaze to meet the mirror for the first time since they'd arrived. He barely recognized the boy who looked back at him with enormous, scared eyes.

Dunlop hummed under his breath during the drive back to Torburton Hall, glancing sideways at the passenger slumped beside him. He draped his right arm over the back of the front bench and steered with his left. Only once did he speak. "It'll even out in the end," he said, running his hand over the smooth crown of the boy's skull in what felt less like a muss and more like a caress. Brendan didn't know if the coach meant his hair would even out, or that Chad and his crew would eventually get theirs. And he didn't really care.

Several days after Halloween, Brendan and Shawn left the basketball court and filed into the locker room with the rest of their phys-ed class. The upperclassmen were on their way out. As Brendan reached for his shirt, someone snuck up behind him. A pair of hands pulled down his gym shorts, underwear and all.

"Guys, let's see if he's bald all over," an unfamiliar voice said to a chorus of guffaws.

Brendan was mortified. He grabbed for his shorts and tugged them up, hurrying toward the bathroom to barricade himself in a stall. *Assholes*, he choked, as once again he felt hot tears sear his cheeks. *Fucking assholes*.

Over the days and weeks that followed Brendan felt himself shrinking. A senior dubbed him "Kojak" and the nickname pinged around the campus. With little appetite, Brendan's face grew thinner; his cheekbones looked especially prominent under the shaved head.

"I'll have to take another 'before' shot for my binder," Dunlop said. He seemed somehow affronted that Brendan had shrunk instead of grown. He insisted on taking a new series of photos. Brendan acquiesced. He stood in the coach's office half naked and turned around meekly for the pictures.

November meant there were exams to study for, and soon Brendan became a fixture at the library and in his room, hunched over his desk with his nose buried in textbooks. The jaunty carriage of his shoulders caved in, and the habitual flip of his head now looked more like a nervous tick in the absence of hair to flick back. He shriveled into himself incrementally, the backward metamorphosis of a butterfly into its cocoon.

In his pocket calendar, Brendan numbered the days until Thanksgiving break, when he'd be allowed to go home. Twelve. Eight. Four. At last came the familiar sight: cars queued up around Great Oak to whisk the boys away. Brendan slid with relief onto the back seat of his father's Cadillac and clutched his duffel, not even caring that his parents had sent some new chauffeur rather than bother to make the trip themselves. He closed his eyes and leaned his head against the cool leather. Whatever.

At last, the town car turned onto Whelk Lane and pulled up to the porte-cochère. Brendan trudged inside. His father had locked himself in his den to escape the hive of activity in preparation for the Thanksgiving gathering. Eliza, overseeing the arrangements with an eagle eye for the most miniscule details, caught sight of Brendan in the foyer. She eyed the sides of his shorn hair, now grown into peach fuzz. But even the sight of angry red welts on his forehead couldn't hold her attention for long, as she was expecting several Hollywood moguls for dinner.

"You look older with your hair short," she remarked, giving him a hug before continuing on her way. "Although your barber seems to have been a little careless around the edges."

Suddenly a memory surfaced, so visceral Brendan could feel the soft lips pressed against his plump baby cheek, the soft arms wrapped around his sharp little shoulders. His knee stung where he'd skinned it on the shells by the water. Eliza saw it happen; she scooped him up to rock him in her lap.

How he wanted to return to that summer, that cradle of his mother's arms when she was still herself, before celebrities and parties and A-lists swept her away.

Brendan stared at himself in the foyer mirror. It wasn't just the hair that had disappeared; everything about him seemed to have collapsed inward. In just a few months, he'd become the kind of kid his father would have scorned, the kind he and Heather would have ignored at school.

Heather. Brendan pictured her long, sun-kissed hair flowing like a mane from under her riding helmet, or flying behind her as she leaned out of her Albacore, riding a wave. Together they'd looked like a pair of golden gods. Her arched brows would knit together in consternation and disgust if she were to see him like this. He knew she'd be over for Thanksgiving dinner, the third year in a row their families would celebrate together. But how could he possibly face her like this?

He kept to himself, ate little, spoke less, and with all the preparation underway, no one commented about the two days he spent in his room stroking his beloved boxer, Rufus, or kicking brown leaves down the lane as they walked. Thursday morning dawned, and he sat at the kitchen table morosely picking blueberries out of a muffin and eating them one by one. Eliza passed by with an enormous bouquet of flowers in her arms. "Hi, dear. Your dry cleaning is hanging in your closet. Did I mention Dad invited the Williams this year? Won't it be nice to have a friend from school."

Brendan dropped the muffin. Scott Williams would be here, in his house, at his table? By late afternoon, when the first guests arrived, he didn't even have to make up an excuse. He sat on his bed and listened for the sonorous melody of the doorbell.

Heather raced up to the second floor and banged on Brendan's bedroom door.

"It's me! Let me in," she sang out in a demanding, merry voice.

"I can't. I'm sick," he called weakly. Beside him, Rufus whined, recognizing Heather's voice.

The girl cajoled and pleaded and swore, but Brendan refused to open the door. He pictured her bewildered expression as she gave up and went back downstairs.

Later, though, when dinner was in full swing and the voices and music and tantalizing smells and tinkling of silverware filled the air, Brendan snuck out to the landing. From his vantage point crouched behind the railing he could see into the dining room below, where Irma scurried about serving platters of pistachio-crusted prime rib, hibiscus-scented cranberries, and glazed leeks. There was Heather, soft in the flickering candlelight. Seated next to her: Scott. He leaned over and said something into her ear, something that made her toss her head back and laugh. Seeing that made Brendan want to puke for real.

By Friday afternoon, all traces of the previous evening's festivities had been cleared away, and the mansion stood quiet and orderly and cold in the late November chill. Brendan sucked in a deep breath and knocked on the outer door of the den.

"Come in."

Brendan entered and lowered himself into a chair across from the recliner where Kenneth sat reading the paper.

A NEST OF SNAKES | 113

The room was smoky, with smoke curling from a pipe intermingling with that of a fire blazing in the hearth. Gold liquid in a tumbler on the table reflected the flames.

Kenneth looked relaxed. He folded the paper aside and for the first time that week seemed to see his son.

"Headmaster Galloway and Coach Dunlop both told me how well you're doing. I'm proud of you." He smiled.

"Dad..." Brendan wanted to pour his heart out. He'd been rehearsing it for days: *I don't know if Torburton Hall is the right place for me.* But if he said it aloud, he'd ruin the moment. So he waited, and considered, and when he opened his mouth to speak he couldn't get the sentence out. Instead, he started to cry.

Kenneth regarded him quietly from his recliner before he spoke. "Brendan, there are only two types of boys in this world. There are the losers, the weaklings who are immediately singled out and picked on, and they stay losers and weaklings and keep getting picked on right up until they graduate. And then there are the winners, the boys who walk in and from Day One everyone knows they are destined for greatness. Maybe they get picked on at the beginning, out of jealousy and resentment. But then they assert themselves. Give the other boys a good how-do-you-do. Put them in their place. And by graduation they're on top of the world. I am the second type. I always imagined you were, too."

Maybe I was the second type when I first got to Torburton, Brendan thought later, as he packed his freshly laundered clothes back into the duffel. *But not anymore.*

CHAPTER EIGHT

The month after Thanksgiving crawled by. Soon tinsel decorated door frames in the Commons, and felt stockings were hung on the fireplace. Brendan couldn't wait to return to the safety of his house and his dog, but all too soon, the Christmas holiday was over and he found himself back on campus in the new year.

"Hey!" Brendan sat up straighter, glad to see his roommate after hours of waiting in their room. "How was your vacation?"

"The usual. My grandparents took us to Florida. Monkey Jungle, Parrot World, Kennedy Space Center, and a lot of early bird dinners. How was yours?"

"You know. Pretty gnarly." Brendan thought of the solitary days spent with Rufus in the mansion in Summer's Pond, empty half the time as his parents came and went to holiday parties. Heather had come over one slushy afternoon, burst into his bedroom, and flopped onto his bed as if nothing had changed.

She didn't even bother to take off her wet Converse sneakers.

"Your hair." She snorted. "Do they make everyone get those haircuts?"

"Oh, sure," Brendan mumbled into his shirt, self-consciously running a hand over his bristly hair. With a start, he realized it was their first time seeing each other since he'd begun boarding school, since the two families had gone out for dinner together the night before he left. He remembered it wistfully: the first Saturday of September. The last day of his old life.

"What are you waiting for? Tell me about school," Heather prompted, propping her chin in her palms. "Tell me about your adventures. What are the boys like? Are the teachers strict?"

"Uh, it's… fun. Everyone's nice. The food's pretty good."

What else could he say? Certain things happening at Torburton were beyond belief. How would Heather react if Brendan told her, for instance, about the night after a lacrosse victory against Oakley Academy, with the appearance of Mr. and Mrs. Galloway in the locker rooms? Both the headmaster and his wife had been drinking. Galloway carried an open bottle of champagne to celebrate the big win against their rival school. He and Trish stumbled into the locker room to high-five the players. They entered the showers where Brendan and two of his teammates were finishing up. When the boys caught sight of the adults standing there, they spun toward the wall. Undeterred, Trish sashayed across the wet floor in her kitten heels, picked up a bar of soap, and started lathering their backs even though she was getting soaked by the spray. Galloway chugged from the champagne bottle and watched.

With a barely suppressed giggle, Trish noticed the effects of her handiwork. "Look, Eddie! What big sticks they have," she exclaimed. "I guess that's why we won tonight."

And then, just before Christmas, after months of incidents and encounters that wore him down, shriveled him into a ghost of his former self, Brendan had decided to confide in Shawn.

"You know… you know the Before and After book?" Brendan whispered as the two boys trudged toward the library through a dusting of snow.

Oh yes, Shawn knew.

"Does Dunlop still... uh... make you, you know, take off your clothes to get weighed?" Brendan blushed bright crimson.

Shawn nodded, staring down at his boots.

"And does he..." Brendan thought back to the beginning of the school year when he first saw the album kept by the coach, the pages and pages of plastic-sheathed before and after shots. "Does he, um, take measurements, too?"

At first, Brendan had thought the whole thing innocent, even if a little odd. Apparently, each year the head coach chose several students to monitor. He photographed them in their underwear. And he didn't only measure height and weight; he progressed to measuring other parts of their anatomies, from the widths of their shoulders and chests to the girths of their thighs. He demanded that those measurements be taken every few months for "accuracy."

Shawn's face puckered. "Once I walked in and he had this kid's picture and... he was, you know...touching himself."

Brendan swallowed. He knew about that, too.

How could Heather possibly understand? No, school was the last thing Brendan wanted to talk about with her. He felt awkward and uncomfortable.

"It's so different from Summer Academy. You wouldn't get it," he said, sounding short without meaning to.

Annoyed and hurt, Heather left after only half an hour.

But the Christmas holidays weren't all bad. There were two high points: the first was when Brendan awoke to a note on his bedside table, handwritten on his father's studio stationary. His son was a chip off the old block, Kenneth had said. The whole family was proud of all his wonderful accomplishments.

The second came on Christmas morning. Kenneth and Eliza were already awake when Brendan shuffled downstairs in a robe and slippers. They wished him a merry Christmas and presented him with a handsome platinum watch, one that cost a fortune and would, his father pointed out, last forever.

The staff, of course, had the day off, and after the presents were opened, Eliza disappeared into the kitchen. She returned carrying a tray holding three cups of creamy hot chocolate with marshmallows and whipped cream. Just the instant kind from a packet, but still. They sipped it in the parlor and smiled at each other for nearly an hour.

Back on campus after Christmas, Assistant Headmaster Quentin Greer called Brendan to his office.

"The results of your midterms are in, Mr. Cortland," Greer said without preamble, looking up from a folder. "You did superbly well on your exams, especially in science, and your classroom work and homework have been exemplary. After conferring with your teacher and Mr. Galloway, we've decided that you are a candidate for advanced placement. Right now, it seems that moving you up in science will not disrupt the rest of your schedule for next semester. We'll try it and see how you do. Is that agreeable to you?"

"Thank you, Mr. Greer." Brendan smiled. It had been a long time since he felt proud of himself.

"You're welcome. I'll mail a letter to your parents."

When Brendan returned to his room, a new class schedule lay in an envelope on his bed. Instead of continuing Introduction to the Earth with the freshmen, he'd now study biology in the afternoons, in a sophomore class.

"You're advancing?" Jack asked, walking into their room holding an identical envelope. "I'll be in Algebra One. Greer said I could've gone ahead in other subjects, too, but math's the only class that wouldn't screw up my whole schedule. How about you?"

"Science," Brendan said, with more enthusiasm than he'd felt since Halloween. The long break from school and the good news about his performance cheered him. "I'm really glad we both got bumped up. It would've been weird, me being ahead of you, since you're the brainiac and all."

"Duh." Jack grinned, relieved to see his roommate joking around like normal.

Brendan was the first to enter the classroom in early January. Black-topped block islands were mapped out in rows of three, and he placed his book bag on an empty stool in the third row. He didn't want to seem too eager by sitting in front.

As other students filed into the biology room and the teacher organized his notes at a desk in the corner, Brendan took the opportunity to familiarize himself with the room. The periodic table and assorted other posters plastered the walls, including the ubiquitous kitten advising, "Hang in there, baby," which seemed to adorn every building on campus.

Shelves lined the back. They held laboratory paraphernalia—flasks and beakers, Bunsen burners, and protective glasses—as well as some cages that looked to contain live animals. Peering closer, Brendan could make out an assortment of insects and reptiles.

He recognized two other freshmen at the next island. Good, he wasn't the only one who'd been bumped up. Brendan's gaze meandered until it settled on a familiar face two rows back.

Chad Hubert.

His head snapped around. Nervously, he raised a shaking hand to his hair. It had grown back two inches since that fateful Halloween night, and the scabs had healed to pink marks, but the memory remained raw. What was Chad, a junior, doing in sophomore science? He must have failed. Brendan shrank on his stool, praying he hadn't been spotted.

As if by sonar, Brendan honed in on the sound of Chad's voice over the others in the room. From his peripheral vision, he saw Chad lean forward toward the boy who seemed to be the token black student in the freshman grade.

"Hey, Kunta Kinte," Chad hissed.

The boy froze. From the way his eyes widened ever so slightly, Brendan knew he'd heard.

"Do I know you? Wait a minute, you're the gardener's kid, right?" Chad leaned back in his chair with a grin, and a few other boys snickered.

"Happy new year, gentlemen." All talking stopped as the teacher stood up in front of the class. He was short and thick-thighed, with a round pot belly protruding from between the flaps of his tweed jacket. His ruddy face shone with a patina of perspiration under the fluorescent lights. "I trust you all had a good Christmas. Time to buckle down, now. We have a busy semester ahead of us. For those of you who are new to this class, welcome and congratulations on your advanced placement. I'm Dr. Lawrence Nevin. I'll be your instructor for Bio 200. A few announcements…"

Nevin paced the front of the room with his hands clasped behind his back, straining his shirt buttons so that the white of his abdomen showed through the gaps. "First, your midterm grades will be posted by the door. Take a look on the way out. For those of you who received a C or lower, letters have been sent home. Mr. Cundill, Mr. Browning, Mr. Wagner… I'm sure your parents will not be pleased." He continued to pace, looking over the heads of his flock as was his habit; he seemed to be speaking to the air. "Second, next month we will be taking a field trip to Yale University, my alma mater, to visit the Applied Sciences Department." Nevin's weaving halted, placing him directly in front of Brendan's spot in the third row. His gaze settled on Brendan's face. "Third, the After School Science Club begins again on Tuesdays, by invitation only. Brendan and Allen, please see me after class. Now, turn to Chapter Seven, page sixty-eight. We commence our study of mitosis."

An hour and ten minutes later, Brendan stood beside the black boy in front of the teacher's desk in the corner of the room, head down, hoping Chad hadn't noticed him. *Stop being a wimp*, he told himself weakly. *He's the one that should be apologizing. Stand up to him.* But he couldn't make himself listen to the voice.

"Mr. Cortland, are you in there?" Nevin looked up from his seat, his double chin jiggling as he spoke. "Did you hear me?"

"Sorry, sir," Brendan mumbled. "Pardon?"

"I said, I would like you and Allen to attend my Science Club. I don't have all day. Sign here." He handed over a clipboard, onto which Allen and then Brendan hurriedly scrawled their names in the blank spaces at the bottoms of two official-looking documents. "We'll meet here for the first session tomorrow evening at eight o'clock. Don't be late."

"Yes, sir. Thank you, sir," they said.

Only two stools in the science lab were occupied when Brendan showed up at seven fifty-five the next evening. Three boys—this was the extent of the Science Club? Allen and one other freshman? Outside, snowflakes fell softly, and he hadn't passed another soul in the building, not even a janitor. He took a seat just as the door opened and in walked Shawn Unger. The boy grinned and climbed onto the stool next to Brendan.

"Hello, gentlemen," Nevin said as he entered the classroom from the back. "I've selected you four for my club. Consider yourselves lucky. We're going to do a lot of special learning here, learning that may put you ahead of the other students. Now, let's start by getting to know each other."

The four boys scraped their stools closer as Nevin indicated. One by one, they rhymed off their names and hobbies. Allen, the student Chad Hubert had insulted the day before, spoke three languages and played cello. Bobby hoped to join the debate team. Brendan admitted that he excelled in lacrosse and tennis. Shawn said he collected comic books, but Brendan knew he also had a flair for sketching.

"All right then. As an introduction to the club, we'll start with a film." Whistling softly, Nevin busied himself with turning on the projector. It crackled in the silence, and the action seemed choppy, as if the film had been spliced. It opened with an introduction to binary fission and an overview of single cell division and its phases—prophase, metaphase, anaphase, telophase—during which Nevin interjected, "Take note of this, boys, as we covered it extensively in first semester and you will be responsible for catching up."

The film jumped to reproduction in animals, showing examples of various species, from seahorses to birds fertilizing eggs. Nevin spoke over the crackling. His disembodied words sounded from dark corners of the room as he paced.

Two horses appeared in the next frame, whinnying, tossing their heads in the paddock. Nevin's voice, when he spoke, came from disquietingly close to Brendan's left shoulder, and Brendan glanced back to see the teacher stare at the screen. "Look at the size of him," the man joked, his voice strangely husky. The stallion began to mate with the mare, its astonishing length revealed on camera. A nervous titter rippled through the room.

Then the scene jumped again… this time, to a man and woman, graphically engaging in intercourse in a variety of positions. It seemed to go on forever.

When the film finally ended and the room was plunged into darkness, the only audible sound was Nevin's rapid, heavy breathing.

The teacher flipped the lights on, the harsh fluorescent tubes glinting off Nevin's perspiring, red face as he sauntered toward the four boys, all of whom stared straight ahead, too embarrassed to meet each other's eyes.

"Now, gentlemen," he said. "As I mentioned, some of the extra activities in Science Club may give you an edge over your friends, so rule number one is that we aren't going to talk about our club to anyone—absolutely *no one*—because we don't want them to be jealous. Understood? This club has been around for many years, and it has a long tradition of being one of the most elite secret societies on campus. You are privileged to be here… remember that. And with privilege comes responsibility, and it is your responsibility, Shawn, Allen, Bobby, and Brendan, to uphold the secrecy to which you are bound by the official contracts you each signed. Anyone in breach of that contract will face legal consequences."

Brendan felt increasingly ambivalent about Science Club. Only the introductory session took place in the classroom. From the second week onward, the four boys— Shawn, Allen, Bobby, and Brendan—were instructed to meet at Lawrence Nevin's home.

Nevin, like the other teachers at Torburton Hall, lived on campus in staff housing that collectively consisted of tiny cottages clumped together on the perimeters of sprawling athletic fields that stretched into the rolling hills of Litchfield County. The houses were tucked into groves of mature deciduous and coniferous trees, nestled under broad umbrellas of foliage in summer and shielded by overgrown shrubs all winter. Quiet, modest, unassuming, they also were sheltered and private.

It was to one of these cottages that Brendan and the others reported on Tuesday evenings. Those January and February nights were freezing and tar black, and often the boys had to trek through deep snow. Nevin had instructed them to skirt a section of woods in order to use his back door, as he didn't want them trailing mud and snow onto his front carpet—or so he said. Privately, Brendan thought it more likely there was another reason.

Nevin never shoveled the path behind his cottage. On those winter nights, he waited for them at his back door with a large towel. They were made to remove their wet boots, socks, and pants, and the teacher gave them each a vigorous rubdown before throwing their clothes into his dryer.

Then they went to the basement. He'd turned up the heat and added a space heater, so there was no use complaining they were cold even though only half-dressed. In fact, it was so warm in that basement rec room that Nevin himself often appeared in shirttails, and would become so overheated during the course of the night that he'd unbutton his own shirt, with his hairy, protruding gut only partly covered by baggy boxers.

After a few meetings, Brendan knew something was off. He listed his options. He couldn't call home again. His father would just tell him to make the best of it. He couldn't stop going… he was afraid of the legal consequences. And he was too embarrassed to tell Jack. Thank goodness Shawn was with him.

Week after week, Dr. Nevin showed them "scientific" films. He had a library of videotapes stacked on shelves in a padlocked cabinet, all labeled with his small, neat handwriting, that he slid into his VHS player. The four boys were told to sit, two on either side of him, on the L-shaped couch with its burgundy and hunter green plaid cover. (Years later, the sight of burgundy and hunter green plaid would prompt Brendan's gag reflex.)

The film he showed for that first meeting of the club was just the start, clearly spliced together to offer at least a modicum of academic legitimacy. As the weeks passed, though, that pretense faded. Beginning with what Nevin called "baby blues," the movies that he showed depicted increasingly explicit sexual acts.

Some of the films were shorter than others, and on occasion Nevin lifted his magazine collection from a shelf in the closet and had his boys study the glossy photographs together. As they passed the magazines around, Nevin commented on the women in the pictures, making crude remarks about their bodies.

"We're all men here, right?" he'd say. "And as a man, I'd like to get my hands on them. How about you?"

One night, Nevin brought out a bottle of whiskey and some paper cups, telling the boys that they were old enough to drink—despite their being only fourteen years of age. Those first burning gulps of alcohol reminded Brendan of his parents and their high-society friends sipping cocktails, and the Galloways' bar cart at home. Part of him liked feeling so sophisticated, while part of him knew it was wrong.

Before long, Nevin produced a carton of cigarettes. He said it was a secret present for his special friends because they were so mature. He was proud, he said. Again, Brendan didn't know what to think. All around him adults smoked but then warned him against the "filthy habit." The boys coughed and hacked up phlegm while trying to look cool and blow smoke rings.

Across from the plaid couch and carpet there stood a Formica table, where the boys did "science homework." An old wooden cart held random pieces of science equipment, including a stethoscope, to lend an air of credibility to the setup. Sometimes Nevin drew up test questions that he required them to answer, or anatomical illustrations to label... all lifted from the films and magazines they'd watched. Brendan could feel himself blushing as he filled in the blanks with dirty words he'd never heard spoken aloud before.

With each passing week, he dreaded Science Club more and more. Who could he talk to about it? No one. Because he couldn't even admit the awful truth to himself: some of the things they were doing, the games Nevin made them play, were... exciting. Some of it even felt good.

But every Wednesday morning, he awoke burning with shame.

At the end of the night before he released them back to their dorms, Nevin made sure to serve a snack: milk and cookies, usually Fig Newtons.

CHAPTER NINE

At the age of sixteen, Shawn's father, Beau Unger, dropped out of his rural high school in Mississippi. It was 1953, and Beau's single mother desperately needed help to pay rent and feed her five children. Beau took a job as a salesman and found, to his great surprise, that he could charm his way into any household with the power of his personality. "You could sell holy water to an atheist with that golden tongue of yours," one housewife told him as he piled her living room floor with boxes of *Encyclopedia Britannica*. Her statement sparked an idea: Beau began studying the Bible. Soon he became a licensed, and then ordained, minister with a reputation as a gifted orator. Soon, Shawn's father became one of the South's most celebrated televangelists.

Unlike the humble origins of Shawn's family, Allen's descended from a long line of British aristocracy: barristers, parliamentarians, ambassadors. Allen's father had attended Eton College before earning degrees from Oxford and the London School of Economics. He'd served in Her Majesty's Diplomatic Service, in the Foreign and Commonwealth offices in India, Nairobi, and Egypt, before being transferred to the British Embassy in New York City. Now, he was in line to become the Permanent Undersecretary of State for Foreign Affairs. He expected Allen to follow in his footsteps.

Bobby, meanwhile, had grown up in New Hampshire, a state grappling with an alarming cocaine epidemic. His mother, a second cousin to a celebrated political clan, had no problem financing her children's private school education… as well as her husband's gubernatorial campaign. As mayor of his hometown, Bobby's father ran on a ticket that promised a crackdown on the state's drug dealers and distributors.

Over the weeks, Shawn, Allen, Bobby, and Brendan got to know each other much more intimately than any of them would have liked.

In early February, on a Friday afternoon after class, Nevin stopped Brendan as the students were filing into the hallway. "Tomorrow," he said, "you're coming with me on a little field trip. Meet me at Great Oak at ten o'clock."

Damn. Jack and Brendan had planned to swim laps on Saturday afternoon, and then work on a history essay together. But Brendan dared not disobey Nevin. So, at the designated time, he belted himself into the front seat of Nevin's wood-paneled station wagon, expecting Shawn, Allen, and Bobby to appear.

They didn't.

"Where are we going?" Brendan asked uneasily. He'd spent enough time in Science Club to get the willies just from seeing the science teacher, let alone sitting in his car.

"To New York City, baby," Nevin sang out. "I love New York, it's a great sensation…" He wore a belted ski jacket that he unzipped as the car warmed up, freeing his pot belly to expand against the steering wheel.

"Why?"

Nevin glanced sideways at Brendan. "Here is another of my rules, Mr. Cortland. Don't ask 'why.' We scientists are in the business of answering 'how,' not 'why.' We're not philosophers. So just sit back and enjoy the scenery."

"Okay." Brendan clasped his hands together in his lap and stared out the window. "It's just that I have a lot of homework. And also, my roommate, Jack, doesn't know where I'm going, and he might be worried."

"I told Greer. And anyway, you'll be back before breakfast, so relax."

Breakfast?

Several hours of wintry driving almost due south landed the station wagon in Times Square. Nevin didn't seem to have much experience driving in the city, for he honked and braked and swore at the top of his lungs after a series of halting near misses. He maneuvered through the streets by jerking the car forward a few feet at a time. Finally, he lunged into a parking spot and stepped into the slush.

"Damn traffic. Let's go," he barked and slammed his door shut, hunching against the icy wind whipping snow into flurries.

Steps from their car, Nevin paused in front of a vendor's table piled with hats under a plastic tarp. He tried on a homburg and a bowler before settling on a tweed newsboy cap.

"What do you think?" he asked Brendan, squinting into a small mirror, turning this way and that. Brendan thought it made his double chin look triple, but said nothing. Nevin handed over a crumpled bill and they continued walking, Nevin's short legs taking two strides for every one of Brendan's.

Finally, Brendan couldn't contain the question any longer. "Why are we here?" he asked, blocks from the car, as they entered a seedy building off a side street that reeked of old urine despite the winter wind.

"There's that 'why' again." Nevin puffed as they climbed stairs to the fourth floor, stepping over trash and a pile of poo that may or may not have been left by a dog.

The man who opened the metal door looked as if he'd just woken up. His hair was long and greasy and tangled, his skin pale, his eyes hooded. "Oh, hey man," he slurred.

"Hello, Mitts."

Nevin pushed past him, dragging Brendan into a room filled with skinny, pale people draped over furniture and lying on the carpet.

Brendan's throat tightened as he looked around. Was that woman in the corner holding a syringe? Yes. She slapped her forearm once or twice and plunged the needle in, sinking slowly onto the floor until she was propped against the wall, with the needle still protruding from her arm. Out of sight, in another room, a baby wailed.

Nevin tipped his chin at Brendan, indicating he should come closer. "This is my new doll, Brendan," he said to Mitts.

"Nice."

Brendan looked at the swaying guy. "Why is he wearing mittens?' he whispered.

Nevin gave a knowing look. "From an, er, experiment gone wrong. He doesn't have much in the way of fingers. Right, Mitts?"

"Fuck off." Mitts scowled and walked away.

Nevins chuckled and pulled a wad of bills from his pocket. "Well, then, boys and girls, what's on the menu today?"

Immediately, several gaunt-looking men and women huddled around Nevin with various offerings of pills and powders. He seemed interested in some, not so much in others. He haggled and wheedled, and all the while, Brendan felt the appraising looks as the skeletons glanced his way. He shrank back against the door, praying Nevin would finish his transactions and leave.

But instead, Nevin sank down on the filthy couch and patted the cushion beside him. Reluctantly, Brendan sat. Nevin held out a fat blue pill. "Take it," he said. "It's an early birthday present."

"I don't—"

"*Now.*" Nevin's voice sharpened.

Slowly, he reached for the pill. The last coherent thought Brendan had before falling into a stupor was that he didn't know if Nevin had meant Brendan's birthday, or his own.

Brendan awoke slumped in the front seat of Nevin's station wagon. Outside was dark.

"What time is it?" he asked. His mouth felt dry and cottony and he had trouble forming the words. He tasted an odd saltiness and there was a faint scent of vomit that he realized was emanating from the front of his own shirt. He gagged a little.

"About six."

Six? Brendan couldn't remember anything after swallowing the blue pill. He touched his fingers to his lips. They felt swollen, and the back of his throat felt bruised, as if he'd bumped it with a spoon.

"Told you you'd be back for breakfast." Nevin reached between his plump thighs, where he'd wedged a large paper cup of coffee, and took a swig. On the seat beside him lay a plastic bag in which could be seen a handful of the blue pills and, beside that one, a smaller one heaped with red capsules. A third bag contained greenish, hay-like twigs, not unlike the stuff lining the bottom of a hamster cage.

"Six in the *morning?*" Brendan felt panic rise in his chest. "Was I asleep all this time?"

"Just take another nap. I'll wake you when we're back at school, and you can go take a shower." Nevin glanced over. "Don't worry, you're still a virgin, for all intents and purposes."

Brendan stared at the shadowy profile of Nevin's face under the newsboy cap, watching it alternately lighten and darken as they passed under highway lights, until he felt his eyes close despite himself.

At the next meeting of the Science Club, Nevin produced a little packet of white papers and proceeded to teach the boys a very scientific skill: how to roll joints and, of course, how to smoke them.

But even with everything Nevin did, everything he'd made the boys do, nothing over the past weeks could have prepared Brendan for what happened at the next few meetings.

Nevin told Shawn, Allen, Bobby, and Brendan to sit on the couch. As usual, the dryer thrummed in the furnace room next door, spinning their wet pants and socks. On the table in front of them sat a Polaroid camera. Nevin seemed more agitated than usual, his face moist, his chins waggling.

"A special night, boys," he said. He carried with him a tall, black tripod and opened it a few feet to the side of the sofa, then busied himself with setting the Polaroid onto its carriage. "A special night, indeed."

"Good. Very good." Nevin adjusted the viewfinder and aimed the lens toward the couch. Satisfied, he stood with folded arms. "Now, here's what we're going to learn tonight. Smile, my little dolls."

From his pocket, he took out the plastic bag of blue pills and handed one to each boy.

Hours later, Brendan awoke, nauseous and sweating, on the couch. The palms of his hands were sticky. The rec room was stuffy and hot and almost silent, the only sound the rhythmic thump of the dryer drum. He, Allen, Bobby, and Shawn were naked. And so was Lawrence Nevin.

Nevin carefully labeled and dated and tucked the Polaroids into a manila envelope. He slid the envelope into a large cardboard box in his padlocked cabinet, the key to which he kept on a chain around his neck.

"Just imagine," Nevin said to the boys, a razor edge to his words. "Just imagine what your fathers would say if they saw these. Imagine how horrified your mothers would be. How could they love you after seeing these?"

As spring of 1983 descended on Torburton Hall, so did an outbreak of impetigo, particularly among the boys who played contact sports. The bacterial infection was very common and very contagious, and the staff had lots of experience with it. Affected boys were told to report each day to the infirmary where the nurse, Nancy Smythe, removed the crusty scabs with hot compresses. Fortunately, a single course of oral antibiotics almost always cured the nasty condition within a couple weeks.

One Friday morning, Brendan lay on top of his covers, scratching. The rash had appeared on his arms and legs the previous evening.

"My sisters had that at camp," said Jack, eyeing the sores. "You're not supposed to scratch or it spreads. You should go to the infirmary."

"I did yesterday. It was locked." Brendan sat up. He hadn't talked to Jack much lately. Hadn't talked to anyone, really.

"Oh, right. I heard that Mrs. Smythe went to visit her daughter. Hey, I promised my mom I'd call before breakfast. See you in the dining room?"

"Sure."

Minutes after Jack left the room, a brusque rap came at the door. Edward Galloway stepped inside. "Good morning, Mr. Cortland," he said, holding up a clipboard and paper bag. "Well—you've already answered my first question. I see you found yourself a nice case of impetigo."

"I figured, sir," Brendan agreed. "I went to see Mrs. Smythe but she wasn't there."

"Yes, she'll be away for a few days. In her absence, I'll be your nurse." He crossed the room and sat down at the foot of the bed to scrawl notes on his clipboard.

From the paper bag he took out a pair of latex gloves, like a surgeon would wear, and snapped them over his hands. Then he took out a jar of honey.

"Lie back," he instructed Brendan, with a pleasant smile.

He proceeded to apply the honey liberally wherever he thought necessary, taking special care to coat every area of Brendan's body. Even where there was no rash.

As a precaution, he said.

Mrs. Smythe returned to keeping regular hours at the infirmary and, ten days later, Brendan's skin had cleared, but for some patches where the scabs had been particularly severe. The white clapboard building, situated alongside the chapel, looked like a smaller version of the headmaster's house, except rather than green, its shutters were black, and a red cross hung above the doorway, which Brendan stepped through now.

"Come in, Mr. Cortland," Mrs. Smythe muttered. The middle-aged woman's head of gray curls bobbed as she consulted her charts. "This should be your last dose. Have a seat."

Brendan sat at the edge of one of the metal-framed beds and unbuttoned his school shirt. Behind him a row of five beds fanned out, and three more stood empty in rooms that opened off the back hall should anyone need to be quarantined. Glancing over his shoulder, he saw that the bed nearest the wall was occupied; brown hair striped the pillow. Whoever lay under the covers appeared to be sleeping.

Mrs. Smythe opened the glass-fronted cabinet that took up the wall adjacent to the door. In it were rolls of gauze, adhesive bandages, gallon jugs of rubbing alcohol, Vaseline, Vick's VapoRub, ice packs, assorted medicines. The nurse returned with a pill bottle and a Dixie cup of water. After Brendan swallowed his penicillin, Mrs. Smythe donned gloves and opened a tube of ointment. She squirted a dollop of cream on her index finger, and leaned in to dab it on Brendan's arm.

"What's that smell?" She sniffed, her sharp nose quivering. "Is that honey?"

Brendan blushed deep burgundy and stared down at his lap. For the past ten days, Mr. Galloway had visited him daily with his jar of honey and questing fingers and a pleasant request for Jack to leave the room so "Brendan could have his privacy."

After his visits, Brendan would race to the shower. Today, though, he'd been late for breakfast and hadn't had a chance to wash off the evidence of the headmaster's ministrations.

Mrs. Smythe peered at Brendan over the frame of her thick, black glasses. "What in tarnation? Who in the Lord's name told you to go and smear honey all over yourself? Was it Galloway, again? Well? Speak up."

As soon as he heard the name uttered aloud, a stone began to harden in his throat and tears sprang to his eyes. He swallowed and screwed up his face.

"Yes, ma'am."

"That man." Mrs. Smythe's head bobbled with disdain. "Here I am emptying my budget with expensive medications and he goes and uses some ridiculous home remedy on a dozen of you." She dabbed at Brendan's right arm here and there, then switched to his left.

"He thinks he's Florence Nightingale," she continued under her breath. "Since when did he graduate nursing school? I guess he doesn't need me around here, seeing as he knows better. Drop your pants."

Tears escaped the corners of Brendan's eyes as he complied. The sweet scent became more pungent. The nurse pressed her lips together contemptuously as she dabbed the cream on his legs. "If I see so much as one more of you boys covered in bee piss, I will hand in my resignation. In my opinion, that man should be more concerned with discipline than medicine."

Brendan hurried to button up, swiping at his eyes as he did so. He glanced over his shoulder. The brown-haired boy, an overseas student from Spain who spoke flawless English, had turned over on the pillow in the far bed. His eyes, as he stared at Brendan from across the room, seemed eminently sad.

CHAPTER TEN

That spring of freshman year, Brendan felt events spiraling out of control. Everything with the Science Club, the impetigo, the upperclassmen—it all became too much. Moreover, his parents were away again and anyway, he'd decided he couldn't tell them about any of it.

It came to a head when Jack got involved.

Late one Friday in May, Brendan returned to room 266 on an unseasonably humid night, stumbling all the way in, tripping over his own feet, banging loudly into the armoire and waking his roommate in the process.

"What the hell," Jack mumbled, jarred from a deep sleep. "It's after midnight. Where were you?"

"Science," Brendan slurred, disoriented in the dark and knocking books off Jack's desk.

"Hey, watch it!" Jack reached up and turned on the reading lamp above his bed. He could smell the odor of alcohol emanating from Brendan, along with a sour stench. "Are you drunk or something?"

Brendan bent over the trash can and threw up.

Jack plugged his nose. "You are," he said, sitting up in bed. "Was it Chad and those guys again, behind the JAM?"

It was several seconds before Brendan could stop retching and wipe his mouth on his sleeve.

"No." Weakly, he groped his way to his bed and lay down, pulling his quilt up over his face. How could he reveal the details of Dr. Nevin's sick club, about how the boys were plied with alcohol and cigarettes? Or about the blue pills they'd been forced to swallow tonight, before another one of Nevin's disgusting games? There was nothing good about Science Club. Nothing at all.

"Where'd you get booze, then?" Jack could only assume Brendan was lying. When there was no answer, he scrambled out from under his covers and stood over the slight form under the blanket, folding his arms across his chest. "You've been weird for months. What's going on with you?"

Stifled sobs came from the pillow.

Jack looked around uncertainly, not knowing what to do to help. "Should I go get the nurse?"

"No."

"Mr. Galloway?"

"*No!*"

Jack spread his arms wide. "Should I call your parents?"

Brendan pushed the covers back a little and looked out from tear-soaked eyes. "Don't call anyone," he said in a shaky voice. "No one can know."

"Know what?"

But Brendan couldn't bring himself to explain. He started to cry again.

Jack reached out awkwardly and patted his friend's shoulder. *The upperclassmen*, he fumed silently. *They have to be stopped.*

The next morning, Jack knocked on the door of the headmaster's office.

Just as easily as the impetigo had spread, so did word of a squealer on campus.

That morning, Chad, Hank, Popeye, and the rest of the posse were marched into the headmaster's office. Brendan, too. He wanted to shrink into the floor.

"Is it true that Mr. Hubert and his friends forced you to drink alcohol last night?" Edward Galloway asked without preamble.

Brendan shook his head, more than a bit hung over.

"You didn't consumer an alcoholic beverage?"

"No, sir. I had an upset stomach from... from eating too much dinner."

"Then why would someone make up such a story?"

"An innocent mistake, sir."

When asked, the upperclassmen hotly denied having seen Brendan Cortland the previous evening. They'd been lifting weights with the team after baseball practice, almost right up to lights out. Coach Dunlop would corroborate it.

Shortly after, Galloway and Greer paid unannounced visits to the older boys' respective dorm rooms. They searched the rooms high and low for contraband and found a small pouch of drug paraphernalia in Chad's desk. But no drugs, and no alcohol. Without that evidence, and without Brendan's corroboration, the headmaster dismissed Jack's allegation, but proceeded to send a letter home to the Huberts. Their son would be suspended from the baseball team for the next three games, for being in possession of rolling papers and a roach clip. His place at Torburton would be reevaluated.

Throughout dinner that night, Chad and his friends glared at Brendan and Jack. Their eyes spoke volumes: *We know who you are, tattlers. And we're coming for you.*

The next afternoon, Brendan jogged onto the field for lacrosse practice. Within a minute of starting the scrimmage, he knew he was in trouble; the juniors and seniors seemed more intent on checking him than on scoring. He sprinted across the wing area after the ball, scooped it with his stick, and made a fast break toward the crease. Without warning a muscular kid body-checked him, knocking the wind from his lungs. Another came at him from the side. A third slashed his knee with a stick—clearly a foul, and as Brendan fell to the grass he waited for Dunlop's whistle blow and penalty call. But none came. He heard only the shouts and whoops of boys watching from the sidelines. Painfully he stood, determined to play on. Soon he had another chance to score. He caught a pass and prepared to shoot. But a shoulder caught him in the kidney and down he went again, writhing.

"Better keep your mutt on a leash," someone hissed in his ear as Brendan stumbled off the field.

After that practice, the upperclassmen seemed satisfied that Brendan had received their message loud and clear. Not so with Jack. His torture had just begun.

"Why'd you go talk to Galloway after I asked you not to tell?" Bruised and battered after lacrosse practice, Brendan clutched his roommate's shoulder for support as they crossed the Quad and headed to dinner.

"I was just trying to help you," Jack muttered, glancing around. From the moment he'd learned that the search of the upperclassmen dorms had produced nothing, he'd felt the target on his forehead triple and quadruple in size. "Why'd you deny that they got you drunk?"

"Because they didn't."

"But you were *wasted*."

"Chad had nothing to do with it."

Jack looked around nervously. "Then who did?"

A hard shove to Jack's side just then sent both him and Brendan sprawling onto the grass. Seeing it happen from a few yards away, Shawn Unger bit his lip and stared at the ground, making no move to approach.

Just as a second upperclassman veered toward the prone boys as if to kick them, Shawn's gentle giant of a roommate, Davey, blocked the way. Thinking better of it, the older kid backed away.

"Jesus Christ, Abromovitch," Davey said, eyeing Jack as he rose. "Why'd you want to mess with the upperclassmen? You have a death wish or something?" He turned and held out a hand to Brendan, who pulled himself up, slowly and stiffly.

"Apparently," Jack said.

"Well, just mind your own business. You don't have to go looking for trouble. Trouble will find you quick enough. Anyway, I got enough to worry about with him." Davey jerked his chin in Shawn's direction. The three of them watched Shawn shuffle through the door of the dining hall, eyes downcast, his slight frame radiating despair. He looked exactly like how Brendan felt inside. "I can't be bodyguarding you guys, too," Davey said.

"What's wrong with Shawn?" Jack asked, for the dozenth time since winter.

"No idea. He won't talk." Davey led them to the freshman table. Brendan limped along in silence. He knew exactly what was wrong with Shawn.

During dinner, Jack's tray "somehow" slipped from his grasp, splattering mashed potatoes onto the shoes of some angry sophomores, and a glass of grape juice "accidentally" spilled on the white tablecloth and sleeve of his Torburton shirt. Jack frantically wadded up some napkins in an attempt to blot away the purple stain, but it was futile.

"Here we go," he said.

That night, after finishing a math assignment, Jack slung a towel over his shoulder, picked up his toiletry caddy, and headed around the corner. The communal second floor bathroom was almost always empty by then. Maybe there'd even be hot water.

Only one other shower was occupied when Jack entered. He hung his towel on a peg, brushed his teeth at the sink, stripped, and stepped into the vacant stall. Shampooing his hair with the water on, he didn't hear Chad, Hank, Popeye, and Scott Williams slip into the bathroom. He didn't hear them command the other boy to get lost. He didn't hear the boy scramble out, dripping wet. When Jack finished rinsing the suds and turned off the tap, the four of them were standing there smiling, arms folded.

"Hello, Kike." Chad stepped forward. "Or is it Chink? I always forget."

"It's both. He's a mutt, remember, Hubert?" Hank took a step closer, too.

"So many names to remember," mused Chad.

Popeye cracked his knuckles as he came up alongside Hank. "How about we call him Snitch?"

"Or Bitch?" Scott spat. They all laughed.

Jack shivered, covering himself with one hand and reaching for his towel on the wall hook.

"Snitch." Chad sprang for the towel and snapped it at Jack's skinny legs. It left a red mark on his thigh.

"Snitch, bitch," the four upperclassmen hissed under their breath as they formed a semi-circle in front of Jack. "Snitch. Bitch."

"I-I-I'm really sorry, g-guys," Jack stammered, the whites of his almond eyes showing. "I made a mistake."

Chad turned to his buddies. "He's sorry!" he said, his arms spread expansively. "Well, that's good enough for me. I guess we can go." And he turned as if to leave, followed by the others.

A surge of relief coursed through Jack. He rubbed at the red mark and exhaled.

Almost immediately, Chad turned back. "Wait," he said, tilting his head to one side as if considering. "How do we know you won't make the same mistake again?"

"Once a rat, always a rat," said Hank.

"Loose lips sink ships," added Popeye.

"Yeah." Scott turned to Chad. "How do we know the bitch won't go running his mouth off again?"

Chad swaggered to a stop in front of Jack. "I'll tell you what, you little snitch. Maybe I'd better stuff that blabbermouth of yours with something to make sure you can't narc on us again." And he unzipped his fly while the others forced Jack to his knees on the wet tile floor. He pushed himself into the boy's mouth and thrust a few times. It only took him moments to climax.

As a parting gesture, as he zipped up, Chad instructed Popeye to wash Jack's mouth out with plenty of soap.

"Now you're our bitch," Popeye declared when he finished, tossing the bar of soap away and wiping his hands on Jack's towel. "For good."

Chad squatted down in front of Jack. "If you snitch on us again... like, if you tell anyone about tonight... you're dead. Understand? Not Galloway, not Greer, not your little musketeers, not your mommy and daddy. Understand? I'll. Kill. You."

They left him crumpled and gagging on the wet floor of the shower, as they slipped down the back stairs of Mariner Block and into the night.

When Jack didn't return from the showers, Brendan limped down the hall to look for him. He found him sitting on the cold tiles, huddled in his towel and hugging his knees to his chest protectively. Brendan didn't see any blood or bruises. But after living with his roommate for over eight months, he could tell something terrible had happened.

"What did they do?" he asked, afraid to hear.

Jack buried his face in his arms. The story came out garbled, between sobs that seemed to take forever to subside.

Brendan sank down on the floor next to him in silence. Neither said a word for almost an hour. Then they stood to go to bed.

On the way out, Brendan caught a glimpse of himself in the flat mirror tacked above the row of communal sinks. In the fluorescent light his face looked sickly green, but at least his hair had grown out a couple inches.

In the weeks that followed, a venomous rumor about Jack slithered down the hallways of Torburton Hall, just as quickly as news had traveled of his tattling. Word had it that Jack had a fondness for acts like the one Chad had forced him to perform. Most of the boys reacted with derision. Once or twice that month, May of 1983, Jack found himself shoved up against a locker with a forearm crushing his throat and a lewd remark leveled at his face. Obscene gestures seemed to follow him around campus. Jack figured Chad and his friends were behind the campaign of hate, fanning it among the upperclassmen.

He began getting stomachaches. He lost his appetite and pleaded with his teachers to be excused from classes. Brendan squirreled food out of the dining hall, but even that meager fare didn't tempt his friend. Jack began to frequent the infirmary, one of the few places he felt safe on campus. Eventually, Mrs. Smythe told him he had to return to his normal schedule as she couldn't find anything wrong with him, not even a fever or cough.

One afternoon, after searching for a book in the library stacks, Jack returned to his chair to find words scrawled on a page ripped from his notebook, informing him that if he told anyone about the events taking place at the school, his little sisters would be subject to what he'd gotten in the showers. A crude pencil sketch accompanied the threat. He rushed outside and threw up in the bushes.

Afterward, he begged Mrs. Smythe to let him spend the night at the infirmary. She let him lie down for an hour before telling him to leave. And she added that she expected to see him in the dining room for dinner.

A short distance from the infirmary, two shapes hovered in the trees off the path. They wore bandanas over their faces, but the bandanas did nothing to cover their signature hairstyles of brown mullets with rattails—single, skinny braids that hung down their necks. Jack recognized them as a pair of fraternal twins from the senior class, two unremarkable brothers to whom he'd never before spoken. But this evening, they introduced themselves.

"We've heard about you," one of the twins said outside the infirmary.

Jack stared at their shoes, afraid to meet their eyes. "Please let me pass." The twins had traded laces so that each wore one white sneaker with a blue lace and one with orange.

"What's your hurry?"

"Just leave me alone," he begged, but leaving him alone was the last thing the brothers had in mind.

They forced Jack off the footpath and into the woods, where they made him take off all his clothes. One of the boys pinned him against a tree, which wasn't hard, as Jack was weak as a kitten from fright and from days of not eating. The bark scratched Jack's cheek as one boy's arm leaned into him while his twin reached into a pocket. Jack squeezed his eyes shut, remembering Chad's knife in the graveyard and what he'd done to Brendan.

He heard the brothers confer with each other, alternating between whispers and hoots of laughter. He didn't see that the object wasn't a knife but a black magic marker.

Across Jack's back, the boy holding the marker wrote two big words: FUCK HERE, with a long, black arrow pointing to his buttocks. They flipped him around so he was facing them, and the brother with the marker wrote two nearly identical words across his chest: SUCK HERE, with another arrow pointing downward.

And as a *pièce de résistance* he wrote a last, short word across Jack's forehead. Then they grabbed Jack's clothes and ran.

Jack knelt down, sobbing long after they'd gone. He had a good idea of what they'd written; his twin sisters loved to "draw" letters on his back with their fingers, making him decipher their words. Eventually, he stood. He only had his school bag for cover. It wasn't even getting dark—though it was almost dinnertime, the late spring sunshine gave no hint of waning. He had no choice but to try to sneak back to his room unnoticed.

Thick shrubbery grew between the trees along the periphery of the grassy campus, lots of it prickly burrs. Before long, Jack's arms and legs were scratched up and the tears filling his eyes made it hard to see. He stumbled on anyway. As he reached the parking lot he had no choice but to leave the cover of woods. Even if he zigzagged behind buildings, at some point he had to cross the Quad to reach Mariner Block. He made a run for it.

When he rounded the corner of the Commons, the first whoops reached his ears. He'd been spotted as he ran, in full view of the boys in the dining room. He kept going, head down, clutching the school bag to his belly, almost barreling into a man standing on the green.

"Mr. Abromovitch," came the booming voice of Quentin Greer, "perhaps you'd like to explain?"

"Sir." Jack bit his lip at the stern, shocked face of the assistant headmaster. Over his shoulder, Jack could see students crowding the open windows of the dining room, jostling to get a look. "Please, I just need to get to my room."

"Yes, that would be the prudent thing to do. Go take a shower and wash that vile writing off your body. And then come and see me in my office."

"Yes, sir." Jack lowered his head again and ran, but the laughter that trailed after him told him that all three messages had been read and received.

At least the other boys were at dinner; chances were, the bathroom would be empty. He stepped into a stall and started to scrub. Nothing—not soap, or shampoo, or the hottest water he could stand—removed the marker entirely. He leaned against the tile under the spray, feeling like the sobs would never subside, thinking of all that had befallen him since that hateful night in this very shower. When he got back to the room, Brendan was there pacing.

He froze when he read the words. "Did Chad...?"

Jack shook his head. He dressed slowly. His clothes covered the graffiti on his body, but nothing could hide the glaring word on his forehead. The derision rang in his ears, and fresh tears flooded his eyes. "The Kingsley brothers."

"Oh, shit." Brendan's voice was hollow. "You can't tell on them. Who knows what the upperclassmen would do?"

"I know. That's why I'm leaving. I hate it here. I'm calling my parents to pick me up."

Brendan chewed his lip. He couldn't imagine this place without Jack. And if anyone had cause to hate Torburton, it was Brendan, but it had never occurred to him he could leave. "Won't they be mad?"

"Not after I tell them everything."

Brendan wondered what would happen if he confided everything *he'd* been through. Kenneth would be angry and scornful. Eliza wouldn't want to deal with the reality.

"I'll come with you to call."

They set out for the Commons. They rounded the corner in the evening shade of Great Oak, in full bloom now, and slid through the wooden doors, greeted by the smell of cigars and aftershave and the sight of wing chairs, velvet love seats, threadbare carpet. How often had they crisscrossed this hall over the last nine months? At first it had felt as cozily familiar to Brendan as his dad's study at home. Now it seemed cold and forbidding.

Down the hall, the office door stood ajar.

"Good evening, Mr. Abromovitch, I've been waiting for you." Quentin Greer stood behind a polished desk, organizing papers.

"Could I use the phone, sir?"

"Phone hours are over." He rounded the desk to stand in front of Jack. "As for the incident this afternoon, exactly who was responsible, pray tell?"

"No one," Brendan interjected.

"Mr. Cortland." Greer frowned at Brendan. "As far as I know, Mr. Abromovitch is not a contortionist capable of writing on his own back. But he is capable of answering for himself. Please don't interrupt again."

Brendan shook his head with an imperceptible movement. *Don't,* he commanded Jack silently.

Jack shrugged. "What does it matter if I tell at this point?" he said to Brendan. "I'm leaving tomorrow. My parents are going to come and get me."

Greer looked surprised. "Who gave you that idea?" he chided. "Mr. Galloway spoke with your father moments ago, after I brought this... turn of events... to his attention. He advised, and your parents agreed, that the best thing would be for you to deal with this situation head on, promptly and maturely. This is a growing experience."

The blood drained from Jack's face. "N-no. I have to talk to them. They don't know all of it. After I tell them what happened, they'll come and get me—"

"That's not how this works, Mr. Abromovitch. Here at Torburton Hall, we don't go running away at the drop of a hat. We are not raising a crop of quitters. Things may seem challenging now but I expect you will look back and be glad you showed strength of character. Now, kindly tell me who is responsible for that"—he winced at the word, still glaring on Jack's forehead—"distasteful prank."

Jack's whole body jerked like a fish on a hook. His dark eyes, when he sought Brendan through his glasses, were desperate.

"I did it." Brendan lifted his chin, making a concerted effort to summon some of the bravado that had accompanied him to Torburton in September, bravado he hadn't felt in months. "For a joke."

"Is that so? An impressive accomplishment, considering I saw you in the dining room with the other boys, and before that, on the steps in line, and before *that*, talking with Shawn Unger on the Quad. Now, Mr. Cortland, kindly return to your room immediately and write me an expository essay on the perils of dishonesty, while Mr. Abromovitch and I get to the bottom of this. Good night, Mr. Cortland."

Reluctantly, Brendan turned to leave, shooting a last glance at Jack. *Sorry, I tried.*

Jack returned to their room a half hour later and, with an oddly robotic movement, sank onto the edge of his bed.

Brendan jumped up from his desk, cringing at the sight of the word still visible on his friend's forehead. "Did you tell?"

Jack seemed shell-shocked, as if all the events of the past few weeks—the brutality of Chad Hubert and his posse in the showers, the nasty rumors, the violence in the hallways, the threatening notes in the library, and tonight, the attack by the twin brothers—had come to a head, a volcano spilling over with ugliness. His expression… of shock, defeat, and utter terror… was answer enough.

"Don't worry," Brendan said, pacing. "We'll figure a way out of this."

But Jack crawled into his bed and pulled the quilt over his ears.

Eventually, Brendan went to bed, too.

A few hours later, they awakened to thuds crackling their window. Brendan groped for his lamp. From the inky dark of the quad below, someone lobbed another egg. Broken shell and yolk splattered against the leaded glass.

How did they find out? Brendan wondered groggily.

Under his covers, Jack began to shake.

The following morning, his stomach hurt worse than ever. He lay silent and huddled, facing the wall.

"I have to hand in my geography assignment first period, but I'll swing back and bring you some breakfast," Brendan promised. He shrugged into his Torburton blazer and paused, fingering the gold-stitched T and H on the crest at his lapel. How excited he'd been at the prospect of wearing this jacket a year ago. Now, not so much.

The front door of Mariner Block swung open just as he reached it. "Mr. Galloway." The headmaster stepped over the threshold.

"Good morning, Mr. Cortland," the man said, his overbite widening into a smile, charming as ever. "Is your roommate still inside?"

"Yes…" Brendan hesitated, loathe to leave Jack alone with Galloway. "But he's not feeling well."

"Then it's a good thing I'm checking on him."

Brendan shifted his weight. "Can I, uh, come with you, sir?"

"Go to breakfast, son." Galloway held the door open for him, and once again, Brendan had no choice but to leave.

It was over an hour before Brendan had a chance to return to his room with two slices of toast wrapped in a napkin, an apple, and four packets of orange marmalade in the pocket of his navy-blue trousers. Shawn accompanied him, carrying a carton of milk stuck with a straw and a blueberry muffin.

Jack's bed was empty. "His notebooks are still here." Shawn pointed. "Maybe he's in the bathroom."

The two boys rounded the corner and pushed open the door to the bathroom.

And froze in their tracks.

The carton of milk slipped from Shawn's grasp and hit the floor with a splash. A white puddle seeped across the tiles.

From the green-painted water pipes suspended from the ceiling hung a taut rope made of three maroon Torburton Hall ties, knotted together.

And from the end of the makeshift rope dangled Jack Abromovitch, the word FAG printed on his forehead slowly rotating into view.

CHAPTER ELEVEN

Two mornings after Jack's suicide, Galloway spoke at a school assembly. The flag bearers accompanied him onto the stage. He looked out at the student body with a somber overbite.

Brendan couldn't believe his phony words. "At moments like this, we take comfort in one another," he proclaimed. "Outsiders—that is, our family and friends outside of Torburton—will never understand what this loss means to us. We are a band of brothers suffering a very private grief. Let us maintain the private dignity of that grief by not sharing it aloud. If you must speak about it, be assured that the staff is here for you if you need us."

The hour-long assembly featured a song by the Torburton Tridents Choir, "Where Have All the Flowers Gone," and a solo performance by a senior who played "Danny Boy" on bagpipes. The math chair, Anthony Ducati, ended the assembly with general announcements, including a reminder of upcoming events.

When Brendan returned to his room, he opened the door and, to his disbelief, saw that Jack's belongings had been removed during the assembly. The armoire, desk, and drawers were empty. The bed had been stripped. Brendan stared at the bare mattress where his best friend had slept just a couple nights earlier and swallowed. All reminders of Jack had disappeared. Did the administrators think they could wipe him away so easily? They hadn't even canceled the annual spring mixer. They wanted to finish the year as normally as possible.

Slowly, he felt his mind turning red. His thoughts congealed in anger. *I hate them all!*

For a few weeks, it seemed to Brendan that he was living in suspended animation, that the outward routine on the Torburton campus continued with meals and classes and sports as usual, but that physiologically, he'd shut down inside. And it wasn't just him. Sometimes he noticed other boys staring off into space, unmoving, like the entire student body was playing a giant game of freeze tag.

This world has gone crazy, Brendan thought. *Everything about it sucks. No one cares about anyone else, no one does anything to stop horrible things from happening. It's like being trapped in a place where the humans act the opposite of how they're supposed to. A bad episode of the Twilight Zone.*

At least the upperclassmen seemed uncharacteristically cordial. In particular, Chad and his friends seemed to be staying out of sight. Keeping their heads down.

There were only two weeks left in the semester and, therefore, only two more Tuesdays. At the next meeting of the Science Club, Nevin said he felt too "down in the dumps" to have fun and sent them all away. A week later, though, he behaved as if nothing had happened.

On that last Tuesday of freshman year, Nevin tapped Brendan on the shoulder outside the classroom. "Tonight's the closing session of Science Club for the year. Make sure you attend," he said.

That night, Brendan dragged himself to Nevin's basement lair.

"Gather round, boys," the teacher said, his breathing coming faster as it always did when they were about to embark on a new game. "I saved the very best for last. Hold out your hands."

Listlessly, the boys circled around the Formica table in the basement. Nevin placed two small, blue pills into their palms. He unscrewed the cap from a bottle of cheap rum and took a long swig, then passed it to Bobby on his right.

Bobby grimaced. He knew, as they all did, that there was no point in refusing. Screwing up his pudgy face, he laid a pill on the back of his tongue and swallowed it down with a gulp of rum. The amber liquid scorched his throat. He passed the bottle to Shawn, and it continued to Allen and finally Brendan. Around the circle it went until the pills were gone and the bottle was half empty.

"Okay, my little dolls," Nevin said, his voice unsteady. "Let's play doctor. Which one of you will be our first patient? Brendan, lie down on the table for your examination."

With a queasy feeling of equal parts revulsion and helplessness, Brendan lay on the Formica table and closed his eyes against the sight of the teacher holding the instamatic camera, and the three boys standing around the table.

Usually, Brendan had a trick to surviving the hours spent in Nevin's basement: he lost himself in the past. He forced himself to focus on a particular happy day he'd enjoyed, and submerged himself in the memory so completely that the rest of his body went on autopilot.

His favorite memory involved a summer trip he'd taken with Heather a month before he arrived at Torburton, in August of 1982. Their two families were relaxing on her father's boat, the *Over Yonder*, anchored just off the shore of East Hampton.

"I dare you to jump off the high deck," Brendan had teased.

Heather had shrugged and climbed the ladder onto the roof of the uppermost cabin. She stood above him for a moment like a young goddess, blocking the light with her slender form, the sun sparking off her hair. Then she stepped off.

Brendan wanted to hold onto that millisecond—of her hovering in space, before she sliced into the sea—forever.

But now, try as he might, he couldn't conjure the image. All he could think about was finding Jack in the bathroom.

Nevin's raspy voice instructed them on what to do. Brendan barely heard it. Still, a shudder ran through him as he felt the first touch. And then the drugs started to work their magic.

The sky, the sea, the pills... everything went blue.

Even the horror of Jack's death wasn't enough to stop time. The months passed on schedule and another summer glided by. A two-week trip to the south of France, where Kenneth was shooting his newest film, did nothing to lift Brendan's spirits, and the rest of vacation he spent lingering alone in his room.

Then sophomore year began. It was September of 1983, and classes were back in session. To Brendan's dismay, he'd been assigned once again to science with Dr. Lawrence Nevin, and Nevin wasted no time in communicating to him, Shawn, Allen, and Bobby that they were expected to participate in the After School Science Club.

The only upside, if he could call it that, was that Brendan didn't have to work very hard. He received top marks in science and even though he barely studied, a big red A+ appeared at the top corner of his tests and homework assignments, circled with a flourish. Nevin handed them back with a wink.

"Welcome back, my little dolls. I hope you missed me over vacation," the teacher said as the boys filed into his basement. He sauntered out of the room as they sat glumly on the red and green plaid couch and waited. Nevin returned carrying a box and opened it with a flourish.

"Look what I bought." He brandished a new camcorder. "Isn't she a beauty! Who's going to be a movie star? Bobby... you're up."

He held the video camera with his left hand and flicked the power button with a soft *snick*. The red light and buzzing meant it was recording. Bobby sank into the cushions of the sofa as if hoping to disappear, but Nevin wouldn't be dissuaded.

"C'mon, it'll be fun," he cajoled. Then his voice sharpened. "Do we need to discuss consequences again?"

Eventually, he made Bobby do what he wanted... and he caught it all on film.

And so it went over the weeks. Brendan tried his best to look away as Nevin pointed the camera for several weeks at Bobby, before transitioning over to Allen. For a long while Brendan and Shawn were spared, but Brendan suspected it wouldn't be long before they all would be "movie stars."

Over those weeks, Brendan went from feeling violated and depressed to angry and spiteful. He thought about vengeance in a way he hadn't before—not like the silly pranks he and the freshmen had imagined last year as revenge against the upperclassmen. His thoughts became violent.

Back at Mariner Block one night, as they finished washing up, Bobby confided in Brendan. "I'm never going back," he whispered.

"Huh?"

"You know... Science Club." Bobby planted his chubby legs firmly and waved his toothbrush. "I quit."

"You can't." Brendan frowned. "What about the Polaroids, the movies? Nevin will show your parents."

"I don't care anymore."

"He'll fail you. And Dartmouth won't let you in with an F in science! You're gonna let Nevin ruin Dartmouth for you?"

Bobby shrugged.

Brendan wasn't sure why he'd started feeling desperate. "But the paper we signed… it's, like, legally binding. It says our participation is mandatory. You can't break an official contract!"

"Watch me."

True to his word, Bobby quit the club for good.

Can I do that too? Brendan wondered. *Just stop showing up?* He waited to see what would happen.

Nevin made his fury known in school. "I've decided that instead of our scheduled chapter on the periodic table, we're going to do a little work on nutrition." He stopped beside Bobby's stool and looked at him pointedly. "Because some of you need a lesson on calories. Like Bobby here. He looks like a beached whale."

"That was really mean of Dr. Nevin," Shawn said to Brendan afterward. "He made Bobby cry in front of the whole class."

"It's probably only the beginning," Brendan predicted.

He was right. For the rest of the semester, Nevin proceeded to make life hell for Bobby. He ridiculed the boy relentlessly, calling him "Fatso" in front of the other boys, teasing him about his weight and his poor marks. Bobby had always excelled in science but that year Nevin gave him a failing grade.

"Bobby's dropping out of Torburton," Allen told Brendan when they returned from Christmas holidays. "Now that his chances for an Ivy League college are ruined, there's no reason for him to stay and anyway, he's humiliated."

Brendan pictured his parents' faces if he ruined his own chances for Princeton: his father's rage, his mother's disappointment. "At least what Nevin does to *us* is a secret."

One night in March of 1984, Nevin did the most shocking thing of all. He was drunker than usual, his language even more vile. He even smelled ranker. Perhaps he was angry about Bobby, but whatever the reason, he lost control.

Until then, he'd been satisfied with what he called "fooling around" games. That night, though, he flicked on the camera on its tripod, grabbed Allen, and pushed him face down on the couch. And then he did something horrifying.

Brendan knew it wouldn't be long before Nevin turned to him and uttered the dreaded words: *Your turn.*

PART THREE

2015

CHAPTER TWELVE

Dylan James closed the recording app on her phone and sank back in her armchair. She stared at the ink-filled pages on her lap.

"I'm so very sorry," she said finally, blinking away the tears that had sprung to her eyes for the dozenth time in the weeks since her client had been coming to her office. His memories had erupted in fits and starts, and while she'd tried to maintain her composure, her emotions as she listened had ranged from disbelief to indignation to pure horror. "I can't imagine… no child should ever have to go through anything like that."

Brendan didn't answer. He seemed to be in a stupor of sorts.

"Brendan?" Dylan leaned forward across the glass table to peer at him. She wondered if she should run across the hall and fetch Dr. Aldrich. "Brendan, can you hear me?"

Brendan blinked and sat up in his chair. "I hear you," he whispered.

"Let's take a break, we could both use one. Here." Dylan stood up, poured them glasses of water, and handed one to Brendan.

"Thanks." Brendan's hand was trembling so hard the liquid sloshed around as he brought the cup to his mouth. He took several long gulps.

Dylan settled back in her chair. This had been a particularly brutal session. The shell of a man who sat opposite her bore little resemblance to the boy he described as first arriving at Torburton Hall in 1982. He seemed so fragile, yet Dylan knew from her parents' clients that it took enormous strength and determination to disclose abuse. As her mother used to say, victims had a story that needed to be told. If Dylan were to obtain any justice at all for Brendan, she'd have to listen, no matter how difficult for him to tell, or for her to hear.

Dylan picked up the yellow legal pad on which she'd jotted paragraphs of notes, points that needed clarification. "Let's recap: Starting from the very first day on campus, you experienced unease in that the upperclassmen tried to intimidate the freshmen right off the bat. Your roommate confided his fears that he might be targeted, and that came to pass at dinnertime the first evening. You also witnessed another child being handled roughly. There was no supervision, no one to intervene."

"Yes."

"You were plunked into an environment where you were vulnerable at every turn, with the upperclassmen and later, with the staff," she mused. "What I'm trying to understand is where the other teachers were during all of this. They must have, at some point, witnessed bullying, for instance?"

Brendan nodded, his voice becoming stronger with his outrage. "They did, all the time. And their response was to hold an assembly and lecture us about behaving like gentlemen."

"So, collective punishment, and watered-down at that. The individual perpetrators weren't reprimanded? There were no direct consequences, for instance, if someone tripped you in the dining hall or spat in the water cooler?"

"Not that I ever saw."

"When boys were shoved in the hallways?"

Brendan shrugged.

"And... after Chad cut off your hair?"

"No."

Dylan flipped back an inch worth of pages. "Except the time Galloway and Greer suspended Chad Hubert from baseball for being in possession of drug paraphernalia. Did they do that to make a point about drugs on campus?"

Brendan gave a little snort. "When Coach Dunlop heard about the punishment, he immediately stepped in... he wanted to go undefeated on the diamond that spring and he needed his star pitcher. In the end, nothing happened to Chad."

Gritting her teeth, Dylan continued. "Did you ever tell anyone what they did to Jack in the shower room?"

Brendan looked away. "I didn't. I was afraid of what they'd do to me. Maybe if I hadn't been such a coward, things would've been different."

"Oh, Brendan... you can't think that. None of this was your fault." She shook her head. "Did you have any sense of why this phenomenon of abuse was allowed to take place at Torburton?"

"I've given it a lot of thought, obviously," Brendan answered. "I think there was, and maybe still is, this macho hierarchy of separating the weak from the strong. I'm pretty sure my dad bought into that, too. He seemed to think like Galloway, that it was all in good fun."

Good fun? Dylan wondered. Even putting the actual child molesters aside, had the bullying happened in the present day, the repercussions for the tormentors would have been severe. They would have been suspended, expelled, charged with assault and battery, and more.

She tried to relax her clenched jaw and leaned her neck over her chair back to stare at the ceiling. She felt a wash of pity for this man. After hours of listening to his painful narrative, her heart hurt for the boy who'd been thrust into such an untenable situation. She'd pursue justice for the hurt child he'd been and the tormented man he was.

"About your father. You mentioned that his attitude seemed to be 'man up.' Did you ever in later years disclose the bullying or abuse to him, or to your mother?"

"They weren't really the kind of people who dealt well with adversity. They'd finally made it in life and didn't want anything to bring them down. It was better for me to focus on the positive—my awards and trophies and accolades. The stuff that reflected well on them."

Great parenting, Dylan thought, rubbing her sore neck.

A few weeks later, Dylan sat at the kitchen table that doubled as her desk at home and leafed through the piles of papers spread around her laptop. She and her client had had several sessions together. She'd scrawled copious notes and downloaded Brendan's voice recordings into a file on her computer. She'd researched similar cases ad nauseam, in the United States, England, Ireland, France, astonished to discover the long history of abuse at elite private schools and angered by the selective media reporting of cases, disproportionally few of which had gone to trial.

Some men hadn't kept their abuse secret, and had been fairly open about it in their adult lives. Brendan, for the most part, hid his. Although the abuse had taken place over thirty years earlier, he had a remarkable memory for detail. Dylan suspected that he shared that capacity with many other victims.

After three decades of silence, he wanted to come forward. He was ready to share. The major problem Dylan foresaw in taking this case to trial wasn't the plaintiff's ability or willingness to recall or describe the events of the past but rather the very real likelihood that many of his abusers were dead. As a solo practitioner, it would be her challenge to track down any remaining witnesses. And… convince them to testify, too. For justice.

Maybe this time she'd get it right.

Dylan gathered up her notes, walked a block to the parking garage, and drove to Greenwich, glad to leave the claustrophobic space of her urban apartment for her light-filled office. The comfortable Lexus in which she sped along belonged to her father, but it had been nearly a year since he'd seen well enough to drive it, and it sure beat the train.

On route, she lowered the window and rested an arm outside, feeling the sun beat down on her skin. She drove under quaint stone bridges and around tree-shaded bends. She hummed along with her favorite tunes. The morning was glorious, and she breathed in the serenity.

She knew this peace would leach away when Brendan darkened the day with his story.

Because everything he'd told her over these weeks had been building to a final, terrible assault. That much was clear. All the heinous abuse by the upperclassmen, the athletic director, the headmaster, his wife, and worst of all, Nevin… She feared she hadn't heard the worst of it.

One of these summer Thursday mornings, Brendan would have to disclose what happened after Nevin said, "Your turn."

Brendan arrived for their meeting minutes later, on a July morning so clear, so lovely, that Dylan suggested they sit outside in the yard behind the house. They strolled side by side in silence, admiring the lilies and climbing roses and other flowers Leslie Aldrich cultivated along the privacy fence.

Dylan cleared her throat.

"I think it's time we talk about the trial," she said, gauging Brendan's reaction. "We'll have to put your statements on record, with all the rest that you haven't yet told me. I think we have a very strong case."

Brendan lowered himself into one of the garden chairs, a heavy, intricately-scrolled piece of iron warmed by the sun. He didn't speak. In fact, he stayed quiet for so long that Dylan wondered if his terror had overtaken him, if all of his willingness to speak had braked to an abrupt halt. She sat on the chair across from him, folded her hands on the round table between them, and waited.

The powering down of a nearby lawnmower left a sudden silence broken only by the sounds of birds and an occasional car. On Brendan's worn face emotions sparred— fear, fatigue, uncertainty. Pain. He mumbled, "Tell me what it would look like, all of it."

"Okay." Dylan nodded. "I'll file suit against the current entity that is Torburton Hall as well as any individuals who were associated with the school back when you were a student—teachers, staff, board members—for both compensatory and punitive damages. If it went to trial, you'd testify to the abuse, and of course I'd try to identify as many other witnesses as possible to support your claim. As I mentioned when we first met, there's a very good possibility that the school would want to settle out of court."

"You think it might not go to trial?"

"There's that chance. But we prepare anyway."

"And if I do have to testify in court, what if I… what if I break down? What if I cry?"

Oh, Brendan… you're so fragile, Dylan thought. *If only you realized you're not the only one.* Aloud she said, "That would be perfectly normal. Anyone in your situation would cry. And be really, really angry." She took off her sunglasses and laid them on the table. Her eyes sought Brendan's. "I know the thought of a trial is scary. But from the way you've been able to talk about your memories... I feel like you are stronger than you know."

Her words were eerily reminiscent of Dr. Aldrich's. Brendan chewed his lip. "And it will be public record, yes? It might make the news?"

"Maybe. But just think... if someone reads about you, someone who went through something similar... maybe he, or she, would take courage from you. You might inspire people to come forward. Help others who'd been abused."

A long pause ensued. "And I... might have to face them... some of them... again?"

"From my preliminary research I've found that some of the teachers and officials have passed away. But there is the possibility of facing people you knew, yes."

Brendan nodded slowly. Then he stood up and walked out of the garden, around the corner of the house, and back to where Tomasz waited in the town car.

Dr. Aldrich paced in his office, wearing a path in the carpet, staring at the alarming numbers on his gambling app. He'd been losing, losing, losing, on a streak like never before. Leslie had no idea how precariously low their retirement fund had sunk or how much he'd dipped into Maddy's college savings. The phone dinged again, with yet another sad face indicating a loss. "Who is it?" he snapped as a knock sounded at his door.

"It's Dylan. Do you have a second?"

Dr. Aldrich smoothed a hand over his disheveled hair before opening his door. "I have a patient due shortly," he fibbed. "What can I do for you?"

"I was hoping to talk to you about Brendan. I feel like he may be changing his mind about the lawsuit, and I wanted your advice. Without breaching attorney-client privilege, of course. But if it's not a good time..."

It's a really bad goddamn time, Dr. Aldrich thought. He forced his voice to stay even. "Brendan has made incredible progress very quickly, relatively speaking," he said between clenched teeth. "I would say we would have to expect some backward steps along the way."

Dylan looked hopeful. "You think it's just a temporary setback? He'll come around?"

"I'll make sure of it."

Before Dylan could thank him, the door had closed.

CHAPTER THIRTEEN

Irma prepared a lunch of salted herring with a cucumber salad in vinegar and set it on the quartz island. She never knew when Brendan would be home to eat these days, as he spent hours with his attorney, an activity that disrupted a routine spanning years. How could he have changed so much in such a short time? He was becoming a different person, now that this lawyer of his had appeared.

For years, she'd been reading long passages of the journals he left on his bedside table while he showered. Some of it didn't seem to make sense. There were entire pages with just a single word, "HELL," underlined so many times that the pages had shredded. There were doodles of eerie faces. The sketches of Kenneth and Eliza Cortland, Irma recognized. And she identified the pretty lawyer from the brochure Brendan kept under his pillow. But there were long, rambling, familiar entries that read like memories from the past, with names Irma assumed dated back to Brendan's youth. Those passages infuriated Irma. The men were devils, the kind she well knew, it sounded like from Brendan's writings.

Her employer was damaged, that was certain. But Irma was there to look after him. She would do her job as always: keep the house spotless, despite the clutter; cook the meals; and take care of all the tasks that fell to her as a result of her employer's eccentricities. Even the unpleasant ones. In exchange, she would continue to live in the little guesthouse tucked away in a far corner of the property, ringed with high hedges and trees, almost a quarter mile from the main house. She and her brute of a son, Tomasz, who was himself even less verbal and more limited than her employer. If she had to choose between the two... well.

She arranged a nice platter of crackers and cubed some cheese. Mr. Brendan would like that.

Irma clucked with irritation when the doorbell rang. On the doorstep stood a young man, mousy, gangly, nondescript. She opened the door a crack.

"Yes?"

"I'm looking for Brendan Cortland, please."

"Mr. Brendan not here."

The man pushed his glasses up with an index finger uncertainly. "I'm Jon O'Malley." He held out a business card to Irma. "Can you please tell him I was here?"

Irma took the card and shut the door. This man seemed harmless, but with Tomasz nowhere in sight, she'd be careful. Better to be safe.

She clucked again, thinking back to the Old Country, to her teenage years, to Tomasz.

A magical Christmas had just come and gone. The year 1955 was winding down, and at midnight her family celebrated Shepherds' Mass in the Catholic Church crowning the main square. Fifteen-year-old Irma and her twelve-year-old sister Gosia wore the new dresses their mother Maja had sewn, and thick new stockings she'd knitted warmed their legs as they shared the traditional carp-and-cabbage dinner with the other villagers. And potatoes. Of course, there were potatoes.

The Czaryi menfolk had farmed potatoes almost since King John III Sobieski first introduced them to his countrymen centuries earlier, in the mid-1600s. But while Polish farmers in other villages and far-flung regions found success sowing barley, oats, wheat, and sugar beets on their lands, Jan Czaryi and his younger brother Zarek were stubborn. They would stick to potatoes, tilling the rocky, hard soil the old way of dragging their father's wooden till behind an ox. Later, they upgraded to an iron till and a set of workhorses. The work was backbreaking. But at least their families were well fed, and the brothers made a decent living. Over many seasons, their tuber crops became so plentiful they expanded their fields, cutting down swaths of towering pines in their way.

Another typical frigid and snowy winter gripped the region, and Irma cherished the rare days following *wigilia*, the Christmas Vigil, when school was closed and her parents weren't working, days she spent embroidering in the toasty warmth emanating from the wood stove, her mother and sister alongside her while her father, in his rocker, puffed contentedly on a pipe and read books.

And then the serenity was shattered. Zarek came banging on the door, yelling for Jan to come quickly. Half a mile away, their warehouse was on fire, where not only tons of canvas-bagged potatoes were stored but the new tractors, drills, and harvesters were kept, along with the horses in winter.

The Czaryi family sped toward the warehouse in their old-fashioned Zuk van, and gaped in horror at the sight of flames illuminating the night. One side of the building had already collapsed. The air carried the stench of burning wood and metal and potatoes and the frantic, terrified whinnying and stamping of the horses.

"The horses! Save the horses!" Jan and Zarek raced forward but were quickly repelled by the heat and towering flames. They had no way to save the building or its contents. Jan and Zarek stood rooted to the spot, watching their life's work burn to the ground, as the women covered their ears and sobbed.

Cowering near the van in the ghostly light of the flames, Irma spied movement in the clearing to her left: a group of Belarusian men from just over the border, where skirmishes were frequent. She cried out and pointed, but it was too late. The men fell upon her father and uncle, beating them not for any noble political purpose or out of loyalty to Mother Russia, but simply for what they saw as a land grab. In between drunken obscenities, they shouted that the vast potato fields had encroached onto their territory.

Maja yelled for her daughters to flee. *"Biegać!"* she shrieked. Run!

Irma sprinted toward the road, gasping as her breath tore from her chest in the freezing night air, running without stopping, urging Gosia to hurry. She groped for her sister's hand. But Gosia wasn't there. In the orange-lit clearing behind her, men roughly shoved Maja and Gosia onto the bed of their rusted truck while her father and uncle lay crumpled on the ground nearby. A cry rose from Irma's throat before she could clamp it down, and suddenly a pair of strong arms pinned her down in the snow, hands roughly shoving up her dress and ripping her new stockings from her thighs.

No, a childhood filled with laughter and love wasn't what lingered in her memory. Fifty years later, all Irma could recall with any clarity was the foul breath that reeked of potato vodka, the black hair and moles on the man's face as he grunted and rooted deep inside her, and the sharp pain that tore into her—the same pain as when Tomasz tore his way out of her nine months later.

That, and the screaming of dying horses.

Brendan appeared in the stone archway of the kitchen. The time he spent outdoors each day had added color to his face, painting over the perpetual pallor. He made eye contact. He looked a little less like the bloated jellyfish he'd been for so long.

Irma noted the changes, keeping her face neutral as always. "You had visitor." She tipped her chin toward the card beside his plate.

The card, and the lunch, went unnoticed. Brendan slid onto a stool and stared out the window. "Do you remember Rufus?"

The boxer had been a part of the Cortland family for many years, passing away the summer Brendan turned eighteen. He'd been a solid, comforting presence at the end of the bed.

"I might like another pet."

"You have pet already. Maurice."

"I meant a dog."

"Does doctor say it is good idea?"

Brendan hadn't asked, but the realization came to him that he was capable of making this decision for himself, a thought that evoked a small, droll smile, because he was, in fact, a man in his forties.

That afternoon, Tomasz drove him to the local shelter. Of course, Brendan could have had his pick of dog, pure-bred, from any location he desired, as cost didn't matter. Without blinking, he could slap down thousands of dollars for a truffle-sniffing, water-loving Lagotto Romagnolo shipped direct from Italy. Or he could commission a breeder in Hungary for a corded Komondor with fur like dreadlocks. If he felt like it, he could fly to the Netherlands for a rare Kooikerhondje, the small spaniel of Dutch ancestry seen in paintings by Rembrandt that, almost extinct after World War II, had been carefully bred back to existence. If he wanted to, he could bring home a Thai Ridgeback, even though the animals were rarely found outside of Thailand.

The idea occurred to Brendan that he could give a home to a soul as broken as his own. A boxer, like the one he'd had as a child, that's what he had in mind. He arrived at the flat brick building and asked Tomasz to wait while he went inside. He eased through the door and approached the front desk.

"Hi there." A young woman glanced up from her cell phone. "What can I do for you?"

"I'm here for, that is, I think I would like a, uh, dog," Brendan stammered, painfully aware that after Dylan, this stranger would be the second with whom he'd interacted in years.

The girl beamed. "That's terrific," she said, holding out a sheaf of papers and a pen, her many silver bracelets jingling. "If you could just fill out these forms, we can get started." Had he ever owned a pet before? the questionnaire asked. Did he have one now? House or apartment? Who lived in the home? Did he rent or own? How many square feet? Was there a fenced-in yard, and what were its approximate dimensions? What was the average household income?

And why did he want to adopt a dog? His hand hovered over that last question.

Nearly a half hour passed by the time Brendan filled in all the information and handed the paperwork back. The girl leafed through, skimming his answers, and then stared up at Brendan, the little silver studs in her soaring eyebrows glinting in the overhead fluorescents.

"Whoa," she breathed, reading the parts about square footage and household income. She wrote Brendan's name on a fresh folder and slid the forms inside. "I'll be right back." She disappeared, no doubt to confer with a supervisor.

She returned with a grin. "Good news... you're approved! We don't have any boxers, like you wanted. We hardly ever do. But would you like to see who's available now?" She motioned for him to follow, her long, blond ponytail swinging back and forth with every step.

Brendan stood up, fighting a moment of anxiety. *One,* he breathed, but before he could get any further, he found himself trailing the girl down a depressing, cement-floored walkway lined on both sides by cages. Inside, dogs of all shapes and sizes and colors stirred and sat up on their newspaper as she entered.

"This is Lucille Ball." The girl pointed to a ratty-looking orange terrier. "Over here is Donny and that's his sister Marie. Stop howling, Celine! We name all our animals after celebrities, as you can probably guess. That cutie over there is Keanu."

Brendan shuffled down the row and looked at each dismal cage in turn. A few animals were small and scruffy, others long-legged and so thin their ribs were distended. All of them had sad eyes that lit up with hope as Brendan neared, even the ones with the growliest barks. The light faded as the humans passed them by.

At the very back wall, Brendan stopped and stared into a cage. Only a nose poked out from under a tattered blanket in the farthest corner of the enclosure. The whole heap seemed to be trembling. "Who's that?" he asked.

"Elvis," the girl told him. "Because he has black hair and he shakes a lot. He's going to be hard to place, poor guy… someone found him on the side of the road, probably left for dead. He's been treated really badly."

"Can I see him?"

Lifting the latch, she reached back, cooing softly as she scooped the bundle into her arms. She pushed back the blanket to reveal a shaggy black face under drooping ears. Several patches of skin showed where the fur was missing, and a line of raw stitches traced across the shaved back. Brendan reached out a hand to pat him, and the dog whimpered. "It's okay," the girl soothed, holding him close to her chest. She calmed him for several seconds.

Brendan forgot his own anxiety as he stroked the fur softly. "I like him."

The girl hesitated. "He does better with women, actually. He's pretty scared of dudes. It might be a while before he begins to trust a new owner."

"That's okay. I can wait," said Brendan.

"He has a prescription. He'll need to follow up with a veterinarian often."

"Of course."

"He really could use another bath."

"He'll have his own bathroom."

"He's on a special diet right now until he gets stronger. And he may have accidents around the house, especially if he's nervous. He'll need a lot of care."

"I'll give him everything he could ever need."

The girl stood at the front window of the reception area waving as Brendan walked across the parking lot with the quivering bundle in his arms. She noted how tenderly he coaxed the pup onto the back seat of the town car, then jogged around the back and slid in the other side. *What a strange man,* she thought to herself. But something told her the poor dog had found his forever home. She felt a flash of gratification, a sharp, unexplainable stab of joy. Sometimes there was no predicting which animal someone would fall in love with, or how they would treat them once they got home. But somehow, she knew this man and this sad little pup were meant for each other. Especially considering how he'd answered that last question on the form, the one about why he wanted to adopt a dog.

Brendan had scrawled: *To save me.*

On the way home from the shelter, Brendan all but cleared out the local pet store, enlisting a stockboy to help him gather together anything and everything a pup might need. The older woman at the cash register hooted as he piled the conveyor belt with top-brand foods and treats, the most expensive collar, leash, shampoos, bowls, and enough toys to last several doggie lifetimes. Tomasz helped him carry a few bags into the house. Then Brendan sent him out again.

The girl at the front desk of the shelter noticed the town car pull up and her heart sank. The dumpy man had returned. It happened all the time. People realized that the neglected animals needed more care than they thought, so they brought them back like a piece of unwanted merchandise to a mall. "Changed our minds," they'd say, sailing out the door. "Maybe next time." She'd gotten her hopes up for Elvis, though.

But now the front door opened and a burly man with black hair and lots of black moles entered. He looked like a bear, with a face that jutted right out of his shoulders— no neck to speak of. She'd have been alarmed had she not noticed what he was carrying: bags and bags of treats and toys, medicines, and cushiony dog beds. He heaped them on the floor by her desk.

"It's from Mr. Cortland," the man said, his tone gruff. "Mr. Cortland says to call him if you need anything else."

In his office, Brendan logged onto YouTube to watch videos about training rescues. Each of them recommended crate training. Rufus used to have a crate, he remembered. He made his way to the kitchen and opened the door to the cellar.

"Mr. Brendan?" Irma appeared, wiping her hands on her apron. "You need something?"

"I'm looking for the dog crate." Brendan flicked on a light and descended a long staircase.

He hadn't been down here in years. Along the wall to his right, unopened packages were piled. He looked at the labels—all things he'd ordered online over the years but had no use for and didn't even remember buying.

A section of the main space was furnished with a sofa and flat screen television. An empty beer can stood on a coffee table. *Tomasz probably comes down here to relax,* thought Brendan, continuing past an enormous Salvador Dali. A separate room held expensive furniture that had been moved to make room for the larger Internet purchases. Another held old golf clubs, skis, sailing equipment, and what Brendan recognized as other dated possessions of his father's. A third held stacks of bins labeled "Brendan's baby clothes," "Brendan's albums," and "Brendan's schoolwork."

Doubling back, he returned to the storage areas to take a closer look. There, folded against the wall, he found the wire crate he remembered and carried it up to the second floor, panting all the way.

Brendan unfolded the crate in the corner of his bedroom and draped it with blankets. The YouTube videos said to create a cozy den to make the dog feel secure in the space. He watched a few more videos to make sure he got everything right.

That week, for perhaps the fifth time in decades, Brendan missed an appointment with Dr. Aldrich. He'd been so absorbed in Elvis that he hadn't wanted to leave him alone, even for an hour or two. From the moment he awoke in the morning he lavished attention on the pup, speaking softly to him, trying to entice him from the fleecy dog bed he'd set inside the crate.

Brendan left the cage door open, hoping to see the nose emerge on its own. It didn't. Every few hours, he clipped a lead onto Elvis's new leather collar and led him down to the kitchen where his food and water lay, but the dog ate only a few nuggets of kibble. Then they went outside and around the grounds, the distance of their walk limited by Brendan's shortness of breath. He hadn't exercised this much in years. Elvis submitted meekly to all of it. He whined when hands reached toward him. He shook violently through his baths and when Brendan spread the prescription ointment from the vet over the sutures on his back. Leashed, he followed dejectedly at Brendan's heels, taking no interest in the grass and gardens and sand. They ventured off the property and across the road, but when strangers approached, he cowered and left a puddle. *You and me both,* Brendan thought.

"He is not eat enough. Is not get stronger," Irma observed. She set about boiling some chicken breast and plain white rice.

"Can you give it to him please?" Brendan asked. Elvis seemed to tolerate Irma more than anyone else. Just like the girl at the shelter had said... the dog didn't like dudes.

"*Nie.*" She shook her head. "Dog should eat from your hand. He is learn trust that way."

Brendan sat on the kitchen floor offering the food she'd prepared, patiently waiting. Finally, that evening, Elvis took a few tentative steps closer, inching his way out of the kitchen corner toward Brendan, until he was close enough to sniff the palm for the proffered morsels. A pink tongue appeared from the shaggy black snout, and the morsel disappeared, followed by another bit of chicken, and another. Brendan filled his palm again, and soon it was empty. When all the food had disappeared, Elvis lay down in the corner once more.

After he tucked Elvis back in his crate upstairs, Brendan fell asleep that night feeling hopeful. Maybe he'd succeeded in getting the dog to begin to trust him. The rewards would be so great, he thought, if only the little guy could get past his fear.

When Brendan woke up the next morning, Elvis lay curled up at his feet.

With August came a sweltering heat wave that baked the entire Atlantic seaboard. For almost a week, the tri-state's temperatures soared into the triple digits. Dylan lingered in her comfortably cool office until late in the evenings, loathe to return to her stifling apartment and the sound of her next-door neighbors bickering. They were a young, professional couple, and it upset Dylan to hear them... so courteous and contained in the elevator each morning... hollering at each other all night. Maybe it was the heat.

Her practice withered, too, stagnating as much as the air. She'd picked up other, menial cases—a Workers' Comp claim for a hardware store clerk with two broken toes, a minor slip-and-fall suit, and a sister suing a sister for a cat scratch wound. She continued to prep for Brendan's lawsuit even though she hadn't heard from him in weeks. She sent a couple short, no-pressure texts: *Hope you're well—I'm here when you're ready to talk again*, and *Hi Brendan, just checking in*, but had no idea if they'd been received. She wondered if she should send a letter in the mail. A chunk of the retainer money idled in escrow. Certainly, Brendan could afford it. She hoped they would move forward. *Just wait a little longer,* she told herself. *Maybe he'll come around.*

In the meantime, she read and reread her notes describing all the incidents that slashed away at Brendan's self-esteem and left him vulnerable as a shelled mollusk. All the ways that his formative years had been ripped apart.

Milk and cookies, Dylan read aloud, her voice choked with indignation and anger. The universal symbols of innocence and childhood. *Fig Newtons*.

Dylan kept coming back to a single salient point. She'd asked Brendan several times. Why did you keep going to the club? Was it because of that ridiculous contract you signed?

He'd replied, the contract, yes. And because as a teacher, Nevin was the authority figure, and we'd been beaten over the head with the importance of obeying our elders.

But there was more.

Finally, one suffocating Friday afternoon, Dylan threw her briefcase onto the back seat, programmed the address into her nav, blasted the air conditioning, and drove the short distance from the office in downtown Greenwich to the waterfront village of Summer's Pond.

Stately homes ensconced behind high stone walls lined Whelk Lane. The road meandered around points overlooking Long Island Sound, with properties sprawled across acres of manicured lawn. Here the landscape remained lush green despite the withering heat and, as she pulled the Lexus into Brendan's driveway, Dylan spied the twirling spigots of an elaborate sprinkler system.

"You must be Irma," she said to the woman who answered the doorbell.

Irma's heavily accented greeting seemed irate, suspicious, but there was recognition in her eyes. She gestured for Dylan to enter what once had been a tastefully decorated home. "Please," she grumbled, standing aside.

Curious, Dylan drew in her breath as she followed the maid into the foyer, where high-ceilinged rooms branched away. The evidence of Brendan's excessive Internet shopping stood everywhere. Dylan's eyes widened into saucers as she took in the very expensive, hoarded jungle of collectibles and gadgets of every description.

Irma stopped, allowing Dylan to survey the living room. Her eyes flitted to a hot pink chair shaped like a flower, with a price tag still on it. She gawked at all the zeroes and took a few more steps.

"A music room?" Dylan gaped at the sight of the grand piano, electric guitars, saxes and clarinets, exotic, tribal instruments and... *wow*. She let out a soft whistle. Grouped around the piano were four life-sized replicas of John, Paul, George, and Ringo, in full Sergeant Pepper regalia, looking as if they would break into song at any moment.

French doors opened to the library. Dylan's jaw dropped at the beautifully bound volumes filling shelves floor to ceiling, accessible with gleaming wooden ladders that slid along rails. Above her head were gorgeous frescoes of fawns and waterfalls, all etched around the edges with gilt. The room looked straight out of a castle.

As she gazed about, an old woman's voice croaked, "Help me... please, help me."

Dylan swiveled toward the voice.

"I need somebody," the crone said.

"Who is that? We have to do something!" Dylan exclaimed.

But Irma hadn't moved.

Dylan rushed past her in search of the dying woman. Irma trailed after her into another room, the den, as Dylan looked around helplessly.

"Hello, dolly," a voice sounded from a corner.

Dylan spun around, her eyes drawn to the depths of the room. She let out the breath she'd been holding as her eyes fell upon a gilded cage hanging from a shepherd's hook. Its occupant ducked its head and preened before looking curiously at its audience.

"Ohhh," Dylan breathed. "It sounds so real."

A hint of a smile played about Irma's thin mouth. "That is Maurice. One of Mr. Brendan's pets."

Dylan stepped closer. "Hello, Maurice."

Swinging on his perch, Maurice puffed out his bright green chest. He was an enchanting bird, with a vibrant red, orange, and black ring around his neck, and long tail feathers... nearly ten inches by Dylan's estimate.

"Stupid woman, stupid woman," Maurice told Dylan, cocking his head to one side.

Dylan giggled and turned to Irma. "He's wonderful! What kind of parrot is he?"

"Maurice is Indian ringneck parakeet. Mr. Brendan have him sent from India. He is holy bird." In broken English, Irma shared what she knew: that Indian ringnecks had long been admired for their incredible speaking abilities and had been kept as royal pets for centuries. Monks believed they were divine creatures as they were often observed in temple gardens, repeating the prayers they overheard being recited each day.

"Brendan teach him Broadway songs. I teach him Polish," Irma said proudly.

As if on cue, Maurice said, "*Pachniesz jak spleśniały ser.*"

Dylan asked, "What does that mean?"

Irma put a fist to her lips. She told Dylan the phrase meant "How are you" rather than the truth: "You smell like moldy cheese."

The two continued through the dining room and into a magnificent kitchen of sparkling quartz countertops, cathedral ceilings, and a massive stone fireplace. Sliding doors opened onto the back patio. Dylan stood behind the glass in wonderment, the strange rooms and conversational bird all but forgotten. Suddenly the opulence of the entranceway, lit by the brilliant mid-century crystal chandelier, and the bizarre contents of the cavernous rooms paled in comparison to the sight in the backyard.

"Amazing," she whispered. "Just look at him!"

Irma's broad forehead creased in a frown. It was one thing to admire the décor and the parakeet. It was something else entirely to fawn over her employer. Who was this stranger who'd trespassed into Brendan's insular world? Irma followed Dylan's gaze.

Manicured flower beds blooming with riotous colors surrounded the patio around a turquoise pool. Off to one side stood a gazebo. On the other, a garden shed. But it was the pool that held Dylan's attention.

In the shallows, Brendan stood—and *grinned!*—as he played with a soaking wet, black dog that seemed to be enjoying the frolic every bit as much as he. The thing looked like a giant mop as it trotted up the steps of the pool, raced around to the deep end, and caught the ball that Brendan tossed into the air before splashing into the water again.

Dylan marveled at the sight. Kissed by a suntan, significantly less bloated, and infused with new vitality that came from daily exercise in the form of morning jogs with his dog, the man before her barely resembled the ghost she'd first heard about from Dr. Aldrich. She slid open the door and stepped outside into a furnace-like blast of hot, oppressive humidity.

As Brendan caught sight of Dylan crossing the patio, a curtain closed over his face. His grin dissolved and he lowered his arm abruptly, the tennis ball still clutched in his fist. Elvis dog paddled toward him, keeping one watchful eye on the stranger as she approached and another on the coveted ball.

"Hi, Brendan." Dylan kept her voice upbeat. "Sorry to interrupt. You looked like you were having fun."

"It's okay." Brendan sought his reflection in the pool, inordinately embarrassed to be caught in swim trunks in his attorney's presence. He forced himself to meet her eyes. "I was going to get in touch with you."

For a moment, Dylan chided herself for showing up unannounced. She turned and gestured around the yard. "Your home is… incredible. Especially out here, with the gardens and the pool. It's like an oasis."

"Thank you."

"It must be so great on a hot day like this." Dylan blew a few errant hairs away from her face, wishing she'd pinned her heavy tresses up off her neck before venturing outside. It felt more humid than ever, and already she felt sticky in her tailored dress. "Who's this?"

"He's Elvis." Brendan hoisted himself out of the pool to drip on the flagstone. As if in response to his name, Elvis immediately padded up the steps and joined his master, giving his shaggy, wet coat a vigorous shake and sending out an arc of spray. A sheath of water landed on Dylan.

"I'm sorry!" Brendan looked mortified as he hastened to grab a towel and hand it to Dylan, who laughed as she patted her face dry.

"No worries! Actually, I'm so hot, it felt good."

Brendan ran a hand threw his damp hair. "You're welcome to come for a swim," he mumbled. "There's some, uh, ladies' clothing in the house… maybe I can find a bathing suit."

Dylan was tempted—she couldn't remember the last time she'd been in a swimming pool, and with beads of perspiration rolling down her sides, she would have jumped in fully dressed. But she reminded herself of why she'd come. "Thanks, but no. I just wanted to let you know that I'm here if you want to move forward with the trial. And it's okay if you don't."

Brendan nodded. "Come inside. Irma made iced tea."

Ten minutes later, Dylan sat in the living room, uneasily at first, wondering if there were any other "pets" in the vicinity. Her gaze darted from object to object and settled on the windowsill, on a bronze statue she recognized as the Spanish sculptor Miguel Berrocal's *Torero*, a torso in puzzle pieces. It looked more like a robot than a bullfighter. Beyond the window were quickly darkening clouds. They churned as if the humidity had risen to a boiling point. *Finally,* she thought. *Maybe a nice hard rain will wash away the heat.*

"Sorry to keep you waiting," Brendan murmured as he entered the room, Elvis at his heels. He'd dried off and changed into a golf shirt and shorts. Once again, Dylan was struck by the subtle shift in his manner, and a not-so-subtle change in appearance. He sat down on a purple stool across from her. Outside, a rumble of thunder sounded in the distance.

"You know, Brendan, I meant what I said... it's okay if you don't want to go through with the trial. I understand, really."

"But I do." Brendan rested his elbows on his knees and leaned forward. "That's what I planned to tell you."

Dylan let out her breath with a whoosh. "Okay then. On my end, I'll prepare the complaint." She gave a little start as another boom of thunder sounded, much closer this time, and the first fat drops of rain hit the window. On the couch, her cell lit up with a weather alert: heavy rains expected with possible flooding. "Looks like we're in for a storm. I'd better get going." She perched her glass on a coaster and stood up. "Thank you, Brendan."

Brendan saw her to the front door, inhaling the lingering scent of her pine and gardenia.

Her hand hovered uncertainly in midair. Then Dylan laughed, her warm eyes crinkling in the corners. "One of these days we'll shake hands. No rush."

"Yes." Brendan hesitated a moment. "I still have to tell you about the rest of what happened at Torburton. With Dr. Nevin." Another clap of thunder, followed by a jarring crack of lightening that lit the heavens like a camera's flash. "But you should go now."

Dylan bit her lip, torn between wanting to continue the story and beating the storm. "I need to hear, but I guess you're right. Let me know when you can come by the office again."

"I will."

From down the hall came a loud squawk, and then a gruff man's voice singing, "A lot of folks deserve to die."

Brendan and Dylan turned toward the den just as the sky above opened, draping sheets of rain over the house. Dylan would have loved to stay and hear more of Maurice's song but instead, she waved and sprinted out to her car. As she backed out of the driveway, she wondered if she should stop at her office or go straight to her apartment. Even at the highest setting her wipers couldn't clear the slosh of water on the windshield, and though her dashboard clock read three-fifteen, the day had darkened to an ominous, yellow dusk.

She inched her way down Whelk Lane. To her left, she saw the frothing waves of Long Island Sound swirling over the sand, whipped up by the howling wind. Trees swayed precariously and several branches had already snapped off, their leaves scratching at the sides of her car as she tried to skirt them on the treacherous curves.

Her pulse raced uncomfortably as she peered ahead. Suddenly she felt like she couldn't breathe, like someone was sitting on her chest. She pulled the car off to the side of the road and took deep breaths through her nose.

It took a moment or two for her to recognize the panic. There'd been a storm just like this on the day her mother died, or rather, on the day Dylan had made her mother die.

Irma pressed her lips together as she served Brendan his dinner that night, one of his favorite meals: lamb shank with mashed potatoes, garlicky and extra creamy, just as he liked them. Her lips all but disappeared when he only ate a few forkfuls. "Not too much sugar in the pudding,"

she muttered, offering her homemade tapioca for dessert— another of his favorites. But he declined, taking an apple from the fridge instead.

Brendan munched on the apple as he jogged up the stairs to his office, trailed by Elvis, and settled at his desk with the dog at his feet. Outside, the wind whipped rain against the sliding glass doors, and strobes of lightning illuminated the room.

He opened his laptop, typed in a string of commands. It'd been far too long since he'd gone hunting. He shouldn't have let Elvis, or the sessions with Dylan, or immersing himself in his memories distract him. He shouldn't shirk his responsibilities. For the first time in months, he reverted to "Youngblood."

The chatrooms were busier than ever.

CHAPTER FOURTEEN

The rain fell for three days and nights, tapering off early on a bright, calm morning, washing away the humidity and ushering in a sweep of unseasonably cool, and welcome, temperatures. Dylan spent those days toiling away at her notes, typing up a thick document that outlined what Brendan had told her to date. She'd just printed it out when Brendan knocked on her office door, punctual as always.

"Irma made muffins." He held a foiled-covered plate from which wafted a tantalizing smell. "Low fat banana walnut."

They carried the muffins outside, wiped off the wrought-iron garden chairs, and sat at the little table eating in silence for a few minutes, with Elvis on the grass at their feet. For every three or four of Dylan's ravenous bites, Brendan broke off one tiny piece and chewed slowly. He'd finished just a single muffin top by the time Dylan had swallowed two entire muffins. She couldn't remember the last time she'd eaten home-baked goods. These were *so* much better than the grocery store kind. Finally, she licked the last delicious crumbs from her fingers, dried them on a napkin, and pulled out her phone.

"So," she prompted, her expression turning from euphoric to serious. "Let's continue. You stopped the story when you were a sophomore."

"What would you like to know?"

Dylan brushed an errant crumb from her blouse. "Did Science Club continue in your junior and senior years?"

Brendan set his muffin on his napkin and stared at it. "No."

"Amen to that." Dylan tipped her head to one side. She couldn't make out Brendan's expression. "Did Dr. Nevin find new 'dolls'?"

"No."

Dylan raised a brow, waiting.

"He died."

Dylan was taken aback. What could she say? Certainly not "I'm sorry." "Good riddance" would be more like it, but she couldn't say that either.

Brendan blew out his breath forcefully. He'd been psyching himself for weeks to admit it out loud. He never had before, and it felt like a gut punch. *Just get it over with,* he thought.

"But not before I had my turn."

He forced himself to say more. He had trouble saying the words without breaking down. He doubled over, elbows on his lap, while his tears fell on the grass.

Dylan slid off her chair to kneel beside him, waiting quietly as he said the words.

Rape.

He'd been raped.

There. You said it. Brendan straightened. He wiped his eyes with his napkin. He nodded briefly toward Dylan, picked up the leash, and disappeared with Elvis around the corner of the house, back to the town car.

Dylan's fingers wrapped around her pen so tightly that they began to cramp. Back inside, she'd been taking notes furiously as she listened to her cell phone. But now she stopped and stared at the sentences flowing across the yellow legal pad on her lap—the ones concerning Dr. Lawrence Nevin, head of the science department at Torburton Hall, distinguished scientist who'd earned his doctorate in chemistry at Yale University and spent over a decade at British Petroleum, who'd been teaching boys at a boarding school for half a dozen years. The words were heavy and black with pain.

He was, as Brendan had said, a monster.

This teacher, this loathsome beast, had brought four vulnerable youths together in a secluded, private space, where he'd guided and intimidated and groomed them to obey. He'd plied them with alcohol, taught them to smoke cigarettes and marijuana. He'd shown them explicit and disturbing scenes of pornography. He'd encouraged them to engage in behaviors so wildly inappropriate, they were beyond imagination. And the boys complied, because they believed that the so-called "contracts" he'd tricked them into signing were legally binding.

But then he'd done worse. Starting in their freshman year, Nevin drugged them with tranquilizers so potent that by the time they woke up they had no recollection of what had happened. And while they were sedated and compliant, he photographed and later videotaped them.

To their horror, Nevin played back the videotapes for them later, Brendan had explained.

Dylan understood. It was blackmail. Nevin used the material to blackmail the boys into silence regarding his predatory abuse. The images he'd taped and photographed would be shocking and upsetting, repugnant even, to the parents. That's what the boys believed. But even more, the material could be professionally damaging for Shawn's father, a celebrated minister, and for Allen's, a high-ranking diplomat. Such material might change the trajectory of Bobby's father's political career, and undermine the standing of Kenneth Cortland in showbusiness. And their sons knew it.

Nevin had chosen these four defenseless boys especially, waiting and watching in the wings for several months before grooming the newest members of his "club." They'd be freshmen, of course, because their age and inexperience would make them the most susceptible at the school. But also, he'd selected the most vulnerable. From day one, tiny, skinny Shawn Unger had been picked on. Allen's skin color distinguished him on sight and, moreover, his British accent gave him an air of haughtiness that, though undeserved, immediately alienated him from his fellow students. The other kids teased poor, chubby Bobby relentlessly. They called him "Blubbery Bobby," eventually shortening the nickname to "Blobby." It stuck.

Brendan Cortland had been a wild card. When he'd first breezed into Torburton Hall, he'd been the kind of handsome, confident, athletic kid that Nevin coveted from afar but never would have dared mess with.

Interestingly, that changed. For some reason, Brendan had been targeted by the upperclassmen, Hank and Scott and the others and, with the unexpected return of Chad Hubert, he'd been bullied further, especially during the Halloween night incident. His parents were largely unavailable for support, Nevin knew from the files, and because of high parental expectations there would be added pressure for him to soldier on.

So Nevin waited and watched. From his expert vantage point, he saw Brendan shrivel over time, slowly losing the confidence and easy, outgoing charm, becoming scared and withdrawn and isolated, and then bullied some more.

He was the perfect prey.

Dylan eased her grip on the pen to allow blood back into her fingers. She needed to think clearly. Brendan had left over an hour ago, and she'd been lost in her thoughts of Dr. Nevin and the After School Science Club, the acronym for which didn't go unnoticed. Now she needed to put her emotions, her outrage, aside, and continue to build a case. For the thousandth time, she wondered if she could manage it alone.

The suburban town of Pelham, New York—or rather, the five villages known collectively as the Pelhams—lay in Westchester County just fourteen miles away from midtown Manhattan, but worlds away from its noise and bustle.

Twenty minutes after leaving Greenwich, Dylan turned off Split Rock Road, drove through quaint, tree-lined streets of houses old and new, and pulled up in front of a sprawling colonial dwarfing small New England-style capes on either side. The squat, shingled bungalows with center chimneys and gabled windows looked like children beside a parent.

Dylan unlocked the front door with a key from her chain. "Dad?" she called, stepping into the front hall. "Are you here?"

"Sweetheart." A slight, white-haired man came down the stairs drying his hands on a towel. His kissed her cheek warmly. "What a nice surprise. I was just about to make tea."

Dylan followed her father across the large first floor. "It's so tidy, Dad. I'm impressed," she commented, looking around the gleaming kitchen.

"The housekeeper just left. She's been coming twice a week." Dylan's father set a kettle of water to boil, peering closely at the stove knob. "Join me outside? Let's see if we can find some fresh mint."

They walked out the back door. In spring, the yard, bordered all the way around with rhododendron and lilacs, looked magical. Now, after the heavy rains and with summer waning, the first blossoms had fallen but the vibrant greens held fast, and the mums and herbs in their pots on the deck continued to thrive. It looked charming, with vines wound over the arbor and garden gnomes standing sentinel over it all.

Dylan admired the carefully-tended plantings. "Mortimer James, you've become a wiz out here. Mom would've loved what you've done."

Mortimer made his way across the deck and bent down to the pots, letting his nose guide him to the one he wanted. He tore off a few leaves and held them out for his daughter to inhale the tangy aroma. "I know. I swear I can still hear her voice, telling me what to prune. 'Snip that branch a little higher,' she tells me, or, 'Pinch those dead blooms.' After a few hours of gardening, I sit in the rocker and I can just feel her here beside me. We admire our work together."

Dylan laid her cheek on his shoulder. "I miss her, too." They stood like that until the kettle whistled. "Do you need a hand?"

"No, no. You just have a seat. I can still see my way to fix a cuppa." Mortimer took the mint inside and returned balancing two steaming mugs of tea. Dylan noticed his ginger step over the threshold.

"How's Lexi?" Mortimer sank into a blue-painted rocking chair.

"Your car's running just fine. I think she likes me," Dylan said. "If only she didn't cost an arm and a leg in parking and gas."

"Parenting is expensive."

"So you've said."

They sipped in companionable silence. "And how is your case coming along?" Mortimer asked.

"Actually, that's why I dropped by. I could use your advice."

"Oh?"

Dylan smiled at the unmistakable note of excitement in her father's voice. "Of course, I realize that the insight of a brilliant criminal attorney can be costly."

"Retired brilliant attorney." Mortimer tapped his eyebrow with a finger. "And since I'm losing the regular kind, *in*sight is just about all I have left, these days. So, tell me about the Torburton case."

Since that first call that came out of the blue—the psychiatrist asking if she'd be interested in representing his patient—Dylan had kept Mortimer abreast of her progress. Not the confidential details, of course. Just generalities. Now that the case would become public domain, she filled in the blanks.

Starting chronologically, she ran through Brendan's history of psychiatric care with Dr. Aldrich. She described the first painfully awkward meetings with Brendan and his unmistakable metamorphosis over the past months. She recounted much of his story—the physical and sexual abuse by the upperclassmen and the staff members, of him and of other freshmen. Grimacing, Dylan told her father about another aspect of the school, knowing that the appalling racism would cut Mortimer to the quick as it had her: how Brendan observed Chad and the other upperclassmen treat the token black students.

Mortimer rested his forehead against steepled fingers and closed his eyes. The prejudice he'd experienced as a black child, in law school, and even in practice over the course of a stellar career, still felt raw. He remained quiet for long minutes until finally he looked up to the sky. "Human nature never ceases to shock me... we are capable of the most heinous crimes. We have a limitless capacity for evil."

"It's so much worse than I anticipated. More perpetrators than I ever imagined," Dylan said, her face clouded with worry.

"They had opportunity. Seclusion. And collusion."

"I mean, considering the sheer trauma that poor Brendan survived, and considering what it did to his adult life, I feel like he should be guaranteed a win. Do I have what it takes to make that happen?"

"There are no guarantees in court. The fact is, as you well know, these events occurred decades ago and many of the culprits are dead now. The current administration of Torburton Hall certainly will argue that."

"Exactly my point, Dad. It's not going to be easy."

"Who said it should be? You have a chance to make a difference here. First of all, to set forth the idea that we have a cultural responsibility, not just an individual responsibility, to eradicate child abuse. That's the *first* thing. And it's high time we abolish the statute of limitations for reporting sexual abuse. Not everyone is ready to come forward on schedule! Brendan shouldn't feel pressured just because he is nearing the time limit to sue. Still, he is the perfect person to make that case, with your help."

"Dad, I don't know if I can manage this case alone." She gazed at her father's reassuring face. "Would you consider joining me?"

Ever since she'd been a little girl, her father had been her best friend, her biggest cheerleader, her co-conspirator. Sometimes, she'd felt as if her mother had two kids to contend with instead of just one. Mom was the disciplinarian, reminding them to eat the green vegetables they both hated, calling them in from building snowmen before they froze, wagging a finger as they returned from a backyard campout trailing dirty footprints across her clean floors.

Jennifer James had been a family lawyer. Throughout her childhood, Dylan often thought that her mom's clients— the battered women, neglected children, warring couples, and siblings caught in the middle of a custody firestorm—were more important than her. Dylan spent more and more time with her father, and less with her mother.

As a toddler, Dylan could chatter for hours. She had a favorite game: Dad would ask outlandish questions and she'd answer with scenarios from her imagination. *What would happen if a fairy's wings fell off?* he'd ask, pushing her on a swing. *Easy,* she'd say, swinging her little legs. *They could sew on two rose petals.* Dylan never realized that as she grew older, the questions he posed became more and more based on logical reasoning. If this, then that. Without her realizing, Dad had been prepping her for law school, teaching her to think like the lawyer her parents hoped she'd become. And she rose to the occasion brilliantly, never even considering another profession. She aced her LSAT. Helped edit the law school journal in freshman year. Graduated *magna cum laude* from Quinnipiac Law School. Her mother was astonished and thrilled when Dylan chose family law, telling everyone she couldn't wait for her only daughter to join her in practice.

Their very first case together was a particularly ugly case of domestic violence. The husband, a banker, had beaten his wife for years. One day, he threatened his wife with a gun while the children were at school. She fled at her first opportunity, fearing for her life. The husband's lawyer then claimed she'd abandoned her eight-year-old son and six-year-old daughter. Despite the wife's pleas to drop the case, Dylan succeeded in wresting custody from the man. The courts awarded sole custody to the mother and set a restraining order against the father. The next morning, he returned to his house and shot his wife before killing himself.

When Jennifer heard what had happened, she felt unwell. She was in the kitchen, on her phone scheduling an appointment with her doctor, when she had a massive aneurysm. Mortimer found her there, slumped over the table, still on hold for the receptionist.

Dylan blamed herself. She went over and over the details of the case. She should have known how unstable the husband was. She should have predicted what would happen. She should have been home with her mother instead of out with Kevin, the boyfriend she'd dated since law school. She lost herself in a haze of grief and guilt.

Kevin tried his best to be supportive and understanding. He cooked her favorite foods, set his car radio to her favorite station. And then, he broached the subject of marriage. But Dylan suspected his patience was finite, and that his grand gesture of an engagement was intended, even if subconsciously, to get things back to normal. And she was right; after she broke up with him, Kevin happily rebounded to a perky young paralegal.

It took years for the haze of sadness to lift enough for Dylan to return to the law, time she spent writing fluff pieces for a small neighborhood paper.

"Starting a solo practice is much harder than you think," Mortimer had cautioned. "And it may be more expensive than you realize. Besides rent, utilities, and office equipment, you'll be responsible for every expense, from insurance to marketing and professional memberships. Do you have a business plan that outlines the services you'll provide, your anticipated cash flow, your expenses, your long-term income projection?"

"I'm working on it."

"Well, sweetheart, you know I'll help you with capital until you get on your feet, and there is the money Mom left. But still, you have to think of the costs. Will you hire an assistant or employee, at least to manage your books?"

"Maybe I'll just use outside vendors for now." Dylan chewed her lip. "You know, things have changed so much since you started out. I won't need much space—not like your offices with the massive law library and all the file storage. Technology has changed all that."

"Yes, we dinosaurs are well aware of the changing world of law, thank you," Mortimer said drily. "And where, may I ask, are you thinking of setting up this cutting-edge shop?"

"Well… my apartment, to start. I can always meet clients in a coffee shop."

"It will be nice to have you nearby, I admit, especially now that I'm finding driving more difficult. But one day you'll need a real office, in the best location that you can afford. Everything else is secondary."

"Yes, Dad."

"Oh, and sweetheart…" Mortimer paused. "Those cases you find so trivial? Don't be surprised if you find yourself taking them on. You do have student loans to repay, if I recall."

"Coming from the man who could have been filthy rich if he hadn't taken so many cases pro bono."

Now, as his daughter waited for a response to her question—would he join her in representing a client in what could end up being a precedent-setting case?—Mortimer's face fanned into a smile. "I thought you'd never ask."

CHAPTER FIFTEEN

In the middle of the rug in the middle of her office, Dylan paced. She held the omnipresent yellow legal pad, the pages of which she flipped through intently. All around her, sheets of yellow paper lay piled like haystacks, some clustered together by session dates, highlighted and underlined with notes and comments and questions scratched in the margins. Brendan sat on the couch lost in thought, looking outside as an October breeze stirred the fiery colors in the treetops. Elvis lay at his feet, tracking Dylan back and forth.

"Brendan." Dylan stopped in front of the couch, laser-focused on connecting the dots in her notes. Brendan and Elvis turned their eyes to hers. "We have to go over something again. I know I've mentioned this before, but really, so much of the case rests on this."

Collaborating with her father had made it clear to Dylan that the original ten-page lawsuit she'd drawn up, which focused almost entirely on the abuse by the upperclassmen and negligence of the school, wouldn't suffice. Even though she'd included the incidents at Galloway's house and in Dunlop's office, she hadn't even heard about the Science Club when she wrote it. Now, she had to rewrite the whole complaint. But first, she had to ask something, something that had been on her mind since the very beginning, something she knew would be painful to her client.

"I have to ask you," she said softly, "because everyone else will. And believe me, I don't mean it to sound judgmental. But why didn't you tell someone what was happening at Torburton?"

She still doesn't understand, he thought with dismay. "Like who?"

"Well..." Dylan flipped pages. "For instance, why didn't you go to the headmaster? I know there was that time his wife acted inappropriately at his home, and the impetigo incident, but wouldn't he have protected you from Dr. Nevin?"

"I tried." Brendan stared off into space, his left hand reaching for the comfort of Elvis's warm fur. "I went to the main office after we were videotaped. Gavin Murdock, the Chair of the Board of Trustees, was there. I started to tell them about Nevin's basement, and Mr. Murdock interrupted. He wouldn't even let me talk."

"Like he knew what you were going to say?"

"Maybe. He called me a liar. He said if I caused trouble, I'd regret it."

Dylan tried another approach. "I need you to think carefully. Who else knew about the staff's... behavior... at school? Let's start with Dunlop. Who knew about him?"

"Everyone."

"Specifically?"

"For a start, everyone in his photo album. There were lots of boys. I saw them coming and going and even walked in on a couple of them. And every time, there was Dunlop, practically panting behind the camera."

"That first time Hank encouraged you to go in... it seemed like he knew what was happening. Did he or other boys ever say out loud what they knew?"

No, Brendan told her. But they all acted like they knew.

"I'm not sure that's enough. Did you ever discuss Dunlop with Shawn?"

"Just once or twice. Shawn had plenty more to worry about than Dunlop's album."

Dylan winced slightly, and made a note on her pad. She continued, "How about Trish Galloway? Did anyone else have an incident with her? Or did you ever notice her behave inappropriately with any other boys?"

"That's an understatement," Brendan scoffed. "She was always in the stands in her tight little tube tops, bouncing up and down and cheering. Half the errors in any given ball game were due to players getting distracted by her. I saw Dunlop trying not to get mad... since she was the headmaster's wife, he couldn't do much except politely ask her to sit down.

"But she showed up in the locker room a few times. Sometimes she was pretty drunk, slurring her words and tripping against the lockers. I heard that before a big football game, she told the first-string players to kiss her on the lips for luck before they took the field. Every single one of them. Most of them just gave her shy little pecks, but a few of those guys got really handsy. One of them even fondled—" Here, Brendan looked uncomfortable and dropped his eyes. "Well, she just let him do it for a while, and then giggled when Dunlop appeared. She asked if he wanted some good luck, too."

Talk about setting the women's movement back a few decades, Dylan thought. Out loud, she asked if Edward Galloway could have known about the incident.

"I'm pretty sure he knew all about her behavior."

"How do you know that?"

"Because sometimes they came into the locker rooms together." Brendan's face took on the constricted expression he wore when describing scenes from his memory in which he played a role.

Dylan pressed her lips together and tried not to overreact. "Right. The locker room." She understood, by now, how obscene, how salacious, these adults had been. But still, with every new revelation, she couldn't grasp how it could have been allowed to happen over and over again.

"So, you couldn't tell the headmaster about the abuse going on at the school, because his wife was responsible for some of it, and he let it happen."

Brendan shuddered.

Dylan added softly, "And because he was responsible for it, too."

Brendan rubbed his forehead and nodded. *The snakes.*

She continued, "And the nurse, Nancy Smythe, was aware of Galloway's daily visits to the dorms."

"As I said, everyone knew about everyone." Brendan drew a hand through his shaggy hair. "Quentin Greer knew about Galloway. Like when lacrosse season started that freshman spring. A bunch of us on the team had just finished practice and were about to shower when Galloway walks in with Greer. Galloway's holding his clipboard again. He goes, 'Let's check you for impetigo, boys.' He passes the clipboard to Greer and he makes us all strip naked so he can examine us. Then he points at Shawn's roommate, Davey. Galloway tells Greer, 'There's a vice president if I ever saw one,' and they laugh."

Dylan looked confused.

"It was 1983. The vice president at the time was George H. W. Bush." Brendan waited a beat. "He was joking about Davey's pubic hair. Anyway, Galloway finishes the examinations and they both get up to leave, like it's just another day at the office."

Dutifully, Dylan wrote it down.

Brendan glanced down at the floor. Elvis had been lying quietly at his feet throughout the whole morning. "I should probably let the dog out for a few minutes. Do you mind…?"

"Not at all. In fact, I could use some air." Glad to take a break and clear her head, Dylan set down the yellow papers she'd been clutching and followed man and beast to the door.

New England thumbed its nose at the rest of the country in autumn. Yes, some states had palm trees and beaches. Others, snow-covered ski slopes. Many boasted glittering skyscrapers. But October in New England was unrivaled for sheer grandeur, especially on those perfect blue days when sunlight shone thinly through the veil of leaves in a prism of oranges, reds, and yellows.

Elvis trotted alongside Brendan and Dylan beneath a canopy of gold, burrowing his nose under fallen branches, straining against his leash whenever he saw a squirrel, leading the way down Chatwick Road and around the corner from Dr. Aldrich's house, all the while happily swishing his plume of a tail.

A woman headed toward them from the opposite direction with a small, white poodle. With no hint of timidity, Elvis greeted the poodle, the two of them circling each other and tangling their leashes. The humans said hello, indulging the pups. The encounter lasted only a minute. How normal Elvis seemed now! He showed no hint of the broken soul he'd been. As they walked away, a small shockwave ran through Brendan. It occurred to him that to an outsider, he, Brendan, also looked normal as he walked beside Dylan. Maybe the owner of the poodle thought they were a couple.

Brendan's eyes lapped up the seasonal palettes as if they'd been parched for color, having seen only variations of gray for a decade. He enjoyed the unfamiliar pull of facial muscles lifting his lips into a smile.

He wanted so badly to put the bad memories behind him. He'd never told his story before, not to anyone. Not *fully*. Even after years of therapy, something about Aldrich made Brendan hold back. *Opening up to Dylan James feels different. Even if she doesn't win the case, even if there's no justice, just telling her has helped.* That she was a warm, caring receptacle for his story helped even more.

He needed to tell her the rest. He'd purge himself of the poisonous memories of Torburton that had festered for so long, and then he'd finally be free. He would finish telling her everything that had happened.

Well, *almost* everything.

Two more blocks, and they turned back toward Dylan's office. Her steps slowed. "Hank and the upperclassmen who bullied you... did things improve after they graduated?"

"I don't remember much after 1984. Torburton had this tradition of marking the close of every academic year with a giant bonfire. At the end of my sophomore year, a couple seniors brought out their guitars and the rest of the kids just sat cross-legged and sang, like something right out of the school brochure. Such warmth and fellowship! What a load of horseshit, pardon my language. But something that sticks out in my memory is that when everyone was walking back to the dorms, Chad passed by on the path and I thought, 'Oh crap, now what's he got in mind? Beat up on me one last time?' but he just kind of waved and said bye like we'd been friends all along."

"Did Chad graduate then?"

"Yes. Hank, Popeye... they all left. The next couple years are a blur."

Dylan paused. "And... and what became of Heather?"

Heather's letters had continued to trickle in that first year. More than anything, Brendan had longed to pour his heart out to her about his experiences at Torburton, but he didn't dare. By summer vacation, he'd managed to avoid her and anyway, she was busy getting ready to leave for boarding school abroad. One late August day, Brendan was sitting on the beach in nearby Westport, with only his Walkman for company. Suddenly Heather appeared, clustered together with four other bikini-clad girls, giggling and chatting with the others as they strolled along the surf. Brendan was surprised. He thought she'd already left for Switzerland.

Heather ran over when she spotted him, long, brown legs like a gazelle leaping across the sand, and flung herself onto his blanket. "Come with us," she urged, tugging his hand. "We're going to the snack bar."

Brendan recoiled. If anything, Heather had grown even more beautiful that year. She seemed to shine brighter than ever. He could only stutter and blush. Heather sat back on her heels and over her shoulder Brendan could see her friends, the same girls who, the previous summer, had been all flirty with him. Now they stood, hands on hips, looking at him expectantly.

"No thanks, I..." The old confidence evaporated, and what should have been an easy stream of words clotted in his throat.

Heather walked away with her friends, and Brendan knew what they were saying. He saw her backward glance and her shrug. He could practically see the contempt in her eyes.

"We didn't see each other much for a few years. It's not that she was mean or anything, but I just felt so... worthless. Like I didn't deserve her anymore."

"And she moved on?"

"No." Brendan looked up at the sky. "We got married."

Dylan tried to hide her surprise. "I... I didn't know you'd been married. Did you ever tell Heather what happened to you?"

"I couldn't bear her looking at me with… I don't know. Disdain. Disgust. So, no."

They walked in silence for a while. Finally, Dylan said, "At least you had Shawn and—" She was about to say "Jack" when she caught herself. "At least you had Shawn to confide in."

After their walk, they returned to Dylan's office and sipped tea. "Did you know," Brendan asked tentatively, "that I had a son?"

Dylan set her cup into its saucer so abruptly that some of it spilled.

"Zachary. He was two when Heather filed for divorce. I didn't contest it. I didn't even try to get shared custody. I knew I'd make a lousy father."

Dylan started to protest, but Brendan held up a hand.

"It's true. Anyway, Heather's remarried, and Zac will be thirteen next month. He's the reason I agreed to this lawsuit. I realized it was time to make some changes."

There was a short silence. "That's really great, Brendan. I admire that."

"I hope one day he'll understand why I haven't been in his life much."

CHAPTER SIXTEEN

Brendan stood in a towel in front of the medicine cabinet, combing his stringy, just-washed hair, thinking of all he'd rehashed for Dylan earlier that day, of bullies and predators. The helpless feeling of being pinned to the ground when Chad produced his knife that Halloween night. The even more helpless feeling of being victimized by Nevin.

He booted up the laptop and took a deep breath. It'd been too long since his last contact with DevBoys1969. Brendan knew he needed to take a next step, even though he found the task revolting. It had to be done. He scrolled through the thousands of images and videos he'd saved. Even after all this time, he gagged at the lewd images, wanting to cry at the terrified expressions on the little faces that pleaded for rescue.

He entered The Playground.

Haven't seen you in a while, Youngblood, said DevBoys1969 immediately.

Brendan messaged back. *Glad to be here. Need to relax and enjoy.*

DevBoys1969 answered. *Busy week?*

U have no idea. Winky face, winky face, winky face.

Do tell!

Look at this, Brendan typed on the message board to DevBoys1969. *Got it from a friend.*

DevBoys1969 took the bait: *??*

Swallowing, Brendan sent a file. He waited for several minutes. No response. *U like?* he asked at last.

DevBoys1969 replied: *She's old news. Me and every other guy in New Jersey jerked off to that puss.*

Sorry. What a rip off!

Don't worry, Youngblood. I'll look after you. Here's some new SYS. Just produced.

By now, Brendan knew the lingo: Sweet Young Stuff. *Interested,* he typed, as he felt bile rise to his throat. Not only did he risk getting arrested himself when he went "undercover"—after all, an investigation might reveal a cornucopia of pornography in his possession—but the worse part was that these men... these predators... thought he was one of them.

On the other hand, he'd discovered that DevBoys lived in New Jersey.

Brendan opened the file from DevBoys1969, sitting back in his chair so that he wouldn't have to see up close. It was a video. He hit PLAY. The footage, jumpy and unsteady, showed a man in what looked to be the back of a van. With a child. Brendan steeled himself. As he'd taught himself to do, he watched the film over and over, blocking out the images of the child and scouring the frames for clues. What did the man look like? Did he have any defining features, like a tattoo? Was there dialogue? Brendan squeezed his eyes shut and listened, trying to hear beyond the whimpers of the little boy to what the man was saying, the sound of his voice, an accent, anything.

Brendan scoured the images for days. At last he saw it, just visible outside the dirty rear window of the van: a blurry name stamped on the corrugated metal of a large, industrial-looking garage. He captured a screenshot from the footage and inserted it into a new program to clean up the image, which took several minutes. But when it was finished, the image came back clear as day. A quick Google search of the area code in the phone number pictured under the logo told him everything else he needed to know.

Sure, the guy could have driven a long way to park, even across state lines, to bring his victim to a random, empty lot. But that wouldn't explain the cup in the cupholder in the front seat of the van, the one with the same logo as the garage: Pocuddy Brothers Heating and Cooling Systems.

Quickly, Brendan transferred the video to his air-gapped computer. Then he sent a traceless email to the Nebraska State Police Department.

Brendan smiled to himself. *Gotcha.*

One brief online article in the local Panhandle news site a few days later detailed the arrest of one Danvers Pocuddy for endangering a minor. Police said they were tipped off by an anonymous source. Pocuddy would face a sentence of five to twenty-five years if convicted, the article said.

The news made Brendan more determined than ever to put these men away for good. Over the next days, thoughts of DevBoys1969 churned incessantly in his head. The shadow world seeped into the daytime.

Three nights after the article posted, DevBoys1969 appeared in The Playground, in a generous mood.

Hey Youngblood... made some new acquisitions, he posted. *Since you seem to like the old stuff. You know. Vintage goods.*

Brendan typed slowly, *Willing to share a sample? Here's a freebie.*

A file dropped. Brendan held his breath as always and clicked open the jpegs.

A strangled cry escaped his throat.

He was staring at a teenaged photo of himself.

Revealing the identity of DevBoys1969 took on a new urgency. Brendan needed to find him and find out where he'd gotten the latest images. For a week, he barricaded himself in his office, cancelling appointments and emerging only to take Elvis for a quick jog here and there. He acquired the most sophisticated computer programs used by the FBI to help him along, and dove deeper into the underbelly of the child pornography industry than ever before.

It didn't matter who the supplier turned out to be, or where in the world he lived... Whoever he was, Brendan figured, they would communicate in a language everyone understood.

Money.

At last, he succeeded in tracing the transaction that had resulted in a series of decades-old, lewd photos arriving in the hands of DevBoys1969.

And through that single transaction, Brendan finally discovered the identity of DevBoys1969.

The imposing entrance to the High Tide Grand Hotel loomed above him as Brendan entered on wobbling legs, still jittery after a nerve-wracking drive in the Mercedes, from the Henry Hudson across the George Washington Bridge and down the Garden State Parkway.

Inside the posh lobby, he caught sight of a mirror. He rarely looked at his own reflection, but tonight he paused, hardly recognizing the man looking back at him. How he'd changed over these last months! His face had thinned, highlighting the beautiful eyes and squared jawline. He'd pulled back his long hair into a ponytail that, coupled with his tuxedo, made him actually look trendy. He'd blend in perfectly with this crowd.

The same impulse that had spurred him to step onto his balcony last April now propelled him into the glittering ballroom for High Tide's 2015 Fall Gala. His gaze flitted around the room in search of DevBoys1969.

What would he do when he spotted him? Brendan had fantasized about this moment for days, imagining how it would play out. They'd lock eyes and Brendan would feel a surge of ruthlessness. He'd take charge. He'd say, "This is revenge for everything that happened at Torburton." He'd pull out his Bren Ten semi-automatic.

The sleek Dornaus & Dixon pistol, made famous on *Miami Vice*, dated back to the mid-eighties. In its heyday the gun had combined the best features of a revolver and an automatic, with its stainless-steel frame, greater ammunition capacity, and faster reloads than others on the market. Brendan's father had ordered one as soon as he saw Sonny Crockett carrying it on television but soon after, the manufacturer went bankrupt. In all the years since then, it had sat unloaded in the Summer's Pond safe alongside extra magazines, never fired. Tonight, Brendan would aim it between the eyes.

He imagined DevBoys1969 sinking to his knees with remorse, begging for forgiveness.

But truth be told, DevBoys1969 wasn't responsible for anything that had happened at Torburton. He was just a sick fuck.

And of course, Brendan hadn't even brought the gun. He hovered at the edge of the room, accepted a flute of champagne from a waiter, just to have something to hold, and darted his glance around the room.

"Hello." A woman appeared next to him, smiling. "Do we know each other?"

Brendan blinked. He took in the dark hair framing a pleasant face, the oversized glasses behind which crow's feet and laugh lines belied her age. He'd never seen her before.

"Well, I must be mistaken. I'm Bette," she continued.

Brendan stood frozen to the spot. It hadn't occurred to him that he'd have to speak to any other strangers, let alone women, let alone one standing as close as this Bette, in her sleeveless black dress and dangling earrings that grazed slim shoulders. He forced himself to nod once or twice as she chattered amiably about the importance of the fundraiser that evening.

"You are a man of few words, aren't you?" Bette said with a little laugh.

Brendan arranged his lips in a smile and let her words trickle over him as he stared into his champagne.

"Were you involved in my husband's campaign?"

Brendan's head snapped up. This was Mrs. Atkins? Wife to the mayor of High Tide, New Jersey? Over her shoulder, Brendan spotted an easel holding a sign with a welcome message from Mayor Timothy and Bette Atkins. Yes, it was her.

She said, "And here's Tim, now."

Brendan looked in the direction of her gaze to a middle-aged man wearing a white rose boutonnière tied with red, white, and blue ribbon. Under a closely-trimmed beard he had a generous smile. His affable manner, as he made his way toward his wife, was apparent as he accepted congratulations with humor and good grace. He stopped in front of the governor and a group of councilmen to chat. A moment, two moments passed... and then he was there, beside Brendan, holding out a hand in introduction.

Brendan found himself clasping hands with DevBoys1969.

Bette waved at a couple and excused herself.

Brendan knew the moment had come. "I'd love to bend your ear privately, Mayor Atkins?" he said.

"Tim, please."

Brendan leaned in. "We... uh... we know each other. I'm Youngblood."

The man's face paled. He grasped Brendan's elbow and steered him into a quiet corner of the ballroom.

"How did you find me?" He spoke to Brendan through clenched teeth while nodding and smiling at the crowd.

"The video you sent of that lovely young boy... it was... delicious." Brendan licked his lips slowly, hoping he wasn't overdoing the act.

DevBoys1969 relaxed a notch. "What do you want?"

"I think we can do business together," Brendan told him in a low voice.

A pause. "Oh?"

"Yes. A business transaction. You have a line to items I'd like to purchase, and I'd make sure you were very well compensated. It would have to be an exclusive deal."

Atkins arched a brow. "I'm listening. What are you buying, exactly?"

"Vintage goods."

A few minutes later, an unruffled Timothy Atkins rejoined his wife without a backward glance. Brendan turned and stumbled out of the ballroom, sloshing champagne on his sleeve as he hurried out to the street still clutching the glass.

Dr. Aldrich crossed his legs and leaned back in his chair, tapping his pen on the blotter and considering the patient sitting across from his desk in the overstuffed chair. The man had slumped in that chair for over twenty years. In his lap, the same jacket he'd been wearing for the past decade. Same shaggy hair, albeit pulled back. Everything else had changed. To the psychiatrist, the transformation seemed remarkable, and it wasn't just his trimmer physique and streamlined face. He sat straighter, his eyes looked alert, and his expression showed engagement, as if the man behind the face interacted with his environment and didn't just exist passively in it. In place of the beige sweater he now wore navy blue, not a shocking statement but just enough color to set off his warmer skin tone. In short, he'd brought an abrupt halt to the endless columns of N/Cs in his file.

"You've missed a significant number of sessions," Dr. Aldrich said, peering over the top of his round glasses. "It looks like our last session was… early September. I take it you've been busy?"

"I spend a lot of time with my dog."

Well, that won't pay my goddamn bills, Dr. Aldrich thought, irritated. Aloud he said, "Very good. And with Ms. James, no? I see you arriving at her office often."

"Yes."

"How is the case coming?"

"We're moving forward. Dylan says it's a strong case. She'll be ready to file soon."

Tap, tap. The pen hit the blotter rhythmically. If the case would be filed soon, he'd be called on for his expert testimony… at least that was good news. *Huh,* Aldrich thought. *Brendan must have provided plenty of background to the attorney, plenty of information about his childhood experiences.* He wondered just how much Brendan had told her that he hadn't revealed in all these years of weekly counseling sessions with *him*. Within just a few short months of meeting Ms. Dylan James, his patient had undergone a near miracle, from his perspective.

Dr. Aldrich rhymed off his checklist, but Brendan admitted to lagging far behind in his journaling, even though he'd increased his daily exercise tenfold.

"Are you taking your meds?"

"Not for a long time," Brendan admitted.

Tap, tap, tap. Dr. Aldrich didn't like the direction things were going, not at all. *Good* mental health would put him out of business. He changed the subject. "I'd like to discuss your parents again. You talked a great deal about your father, about wanting him to be proud, about him wanting you to 'man up.' Today I'd like to go back to your feelings about your mother."

"I've spent a lot of time journaling about her over the years," Brendan said. "It took me years to figure her out, but I think it boiled down to money and the fact that she didn't come from any. The sudden glamor... She spent so much time trying to convince everyone that she belonged in that world, she didn't have much energy left for anything else, least of all me. I always wonder, did she regret having me? Was I an inconvenience? An April Fool? She liked to show me off as part of the package, the perfect Greenwich family accessory, and she didn't want anything to ruin the picture."

"You think your experiences at Torburton Hall ruined the picture?"

"I was pretty much spoiled goods by the time I graduated."

"And yet you told her about the... abuse."

"Some. I saw how it distanced her. She couldn't deal with it. She pawned me off on you, no offense. She said you were more equipped to help. Which was true, of course."

"No doubt." *Tap.* "She did attend several sessions with you, if I recall. At first."

Indeed, she'd brought Brendan to his appointments faithfully for those first few months, sitting in with them whenever Dr. Aldrich advised. And then Kenneth had his first heart attack in the mid-eighties, followed by another in 1989, which left him frail until his death of heart failure a few years later. Her son's catastrophic emotional breakdown, on top of her husband's dire health issues, became too much. Eliza appointed other caregivers in her stead and slowly but inevitably removed herself from the picture.

"After Dad died," Brendan continued, "she held it together for a while. She stayed in the house and did her best to look after me. She lasted for about a year. But I guess she wasn't cut out for it, and I wasn't the best company."

Dr. Aldrich had heard all this before, but he didn't interrupt.

"She said, 'What you need is a vacation. A change of scenery. Hot springs.' She booked a spa and off we went. But nothing changed for me emotionally, and I came back home. She didn't." The dark brows over Brendan's green eyes drew together. "She'd met a man, a very ordinary man, without much power or prestige or money. I think she was much more comfortable with him, and anyway, it was a non-issue as she had all the money Dad had left in trust."

"And she had a son." Dr. Aldrich laid his pen on the blotter and leaned forward toward his patient. "You told her you'd been traumatized, you were hurt and confused and grieving. You needed the comfort and care of a parent, not a household staff or even a physician. And yet she left."

Brendan sat still.

"That abandonment expressed itself in the late nineties as extreme paranoia over Y2K, if I recall. You had an overwhelming need for safe haven, isn't that correct?"

Brendan nodded slowly.

"Do you remember feeling angry with your mother for abandoning you when you most needed her? Do you feel angry that your mother chose money over her own son?" He'd asked this question many times, to no avail.

Brendan frowned. He'd padlocked the emotions from those days.

"In all these years, you've never expressed anger toward your mother. No rage, no fury, no resentment... not one iota of bitterness over how she could leave her only child and move to the other side of the earth, just like that. In fact, you've never expressed anger at all. Do you think you are even capable of anger?"

Brendan swallowed.

"And you left your son just like your mother left you. Were you subconsciously expressing your anger then, and taking it out on your own son?"

"No... I wanted to do what was best for him..."

"Was there something about *you* that made *her* leave, perhaps?"

Brendan looked stricken. *Did I drive my own mother away?* he wondered. *Just as surely as I drove Heather away? Because I was damaged, defective?*

He reached down a hand, feeling for Elvis's warm reassurance... but he'd left Elvis at home, because Dr. Aldrich didn't appreciate pet fur on his carpet. Brendan's demeanor changed. He shrank into the chair, pulling the air around him like a membrane. He clutched his fall jacket in his fists, his dark lashes meshed together, and his whole body started to tremble. Very slowly, he began rocking back and forth. "*One,*" he counted under his breath. "*Two. Three.*"

Dr. Aldrich watched it all, the back-pedaling into collapse, and smiled to himself.

That night, Brendan had a dream, the first he'd had since spring. The attackers came from all directions, a horde let loose to feed on him. Powerful snouts of crocodiles clamping on his limbs, gnawing through skin and muscle and sinew, spraying blood everywhere... but soon they'd evolved into clawing lions and screeching baboons, feasting... and those became a swarm of killer bees, stinging under his eyelids, in his ears, down his throat. He batted and swatted at them but they surrounded him in a black cloud, so thick he couldn't see... and the black cloud changed again, and again... until, to Brendan's horror, he realized they'd become dogs, snarling, snapping, rabid dogs, devouring him alive.

Irma came in from the guesthouse, chilled by the autumn wind, and hung her purse in the butler's pantry just in time to see Brendan's slow shuffle into the kitchen. His drab gray garb that billowed on his shrunken frame, the sadness and fear that cloaked his hunched shoulders as he sat at the counter, his disinterested shrug when she asked what he wanted for breakfast... all of it hearkened back to a demeanor she hadn't seen in months. She'd become accustomed to smiles, to the sound of Elvis's excited bark at the front door as Brendan clasped on a leash for his morning run, to fixing new and different meals each day, from fruit-filled crepes to casseroles. But today, Brendan opened the sliding door and let Elvis out to do his business alone. Irma sighed. A few steps forward, a few back. Without a word, she set about soft-boiling two eggs and toasting two slices of wheat bread.

From the corner of her eye, Irma watched Brendan sit motionless, letting the food congeal in front of him. He looked like a lost little boy. Once again, she felt the familiar twin pulls of pity and irritation. He had so much wealth, this man-child, and here he sat his whole life *jak pryszcz na nosie*, like a pimple on a nose, never lifting a finger to work, spending more money in an hour on useless purchases from the Internet than her collective family in the Polish village of Lesc earned in a year.

Still, she was the most consistent person in his life, certainly more than his dead father, his invisible mother, and his conceited wife who'd been so quick to remarry. As much as she could feel affection, she felt it for Brendan, in a way she didn't when she looked at her own ill-begotten son. It was that affection that kept her in this house, at this job. She never complained. She and her son did what was needed and were paid well for it.

Elvis scratched on the glass. Irma let him in.

"Mr. Brendan," she said, looking at the ball of black fur curled by the base of Brendan's stool. "Elvis, he very attached to you. Yesterday he sit on top of couch to look out window all afternoon until you come home. You giving him a new life." Silence. "Do you think he forgets everything that came before?"

As if on cue Elvis looked up, an ear askew.

"No one forgets," Brendan said. "Not people, not dogs."

"Yes, that is so," Irma agreed. "The past, it sitting in our brain like sharp rocks. Time making most rocks smooth, like water. Other rocks staying sharp always. Best to swim above rocks." She turned away to rinse the coffeepot, feeling his gaze on her back. "Maybe pierogi for dinner?" she asked.

Brendan didn't respond.

She didn't really expect him to.

Later that day, Brendan relented and dragged himself to the beach, with Elvis scampering alongside.

Down the shoreline, he saw the silhouette of a man, a stranger, pulling a yellow lab by its leash. As he neared, he heard the man cursing the dog for lolling behind. Impatient, the man yanked the leash hard. His dog—an old one, judging by its faded coat and grizzled muzzle—yelped.

In the two or three seconds it took Brendan to stride over to the stranger, something odd happened with his eyes. Like a television set with a broken antenna, he stopped seeing clear color images and instead perceived everything in shades of charcoal static, including the man's startled face as Brendan rounded on him.

"Hurt that dog again and I'll bash your face in," he growled in a voice he didn't recognize, one that seemed to be coming from outside his own body.

The stranger's face seemed to deflate. He took a step back and raised his palms in supplication.

Brendan nodded slowly. The man turned and scurried away, looking over his shoulder to see if he was being followed, the leash slack in his hand. The dog, too, gave a backward glance, as if to say, "Thanks."

What do you know, Brendan wrote later in his journal, when color returned to his vision. *I guess I'm capable of anger after all.*

Irma glanced at the clock as she loaded plates and cutlery into the dishwasher. She'd almost finished for the day. Good thing, because her back was aching. Outside the window she could see Tomasz in the glow of a floodlight, locking his tools in the garden shed and heading for the guesthouse. He, too, seemed tired... a middle-aged man of fifty doing all that heavy leaf clearing. Soon the two of them, she and her son, would have no choice but to wind down.

Only one more chore remained, one that she'd taken on when Brendan lost interest.

In a bowl, Irma mixed a few almonds, cashews, hazelnuts, and pistachios. She added pieces of chopped apple and banana, along with some collard greens and broccoli. *Too bad peaches aren't in season*, she thought, bringing the bowl to the den. *He likes peaches.*

Back in the butler's pantry, Irma stood in front of a large glass box. When she first saw it, she'd thought it looked like something out of a horror movie. Inside crept and flew and hung an assortment of creatures, some winged, some with long, furry legs, others tubular and squishy with hundreds of suckered feet. Plus, there were mealworms, waxworms, crickets, termites, all nutrient-rich and pesticide-free. Best to keep the whole menagerie out of sight.

Here was the tricky part. Irma picked up a pair of oversized pincers. Holding the trap door open just enough to insert the implement, she snagged the nearest insect—a caterpillar—and withdrew it quickly before slamming the top. She'd learned from experience not to grip it too tightly, lest she sever it in two. Very messy. The thing squirmed between the tweezers as she brought it to the den. In the early days, many a bug had jumped out of the tank to scurry away, but by now Irma had become very adept at this process.

"Dinner time, Maurice," Irma said, unhooking the birdcage's door and dropping the bug onto the newspaper.

"Feed me, Seymour," Maurice said, cocking his head and blinking his flat eyes. "Sticky, licky sweets I crave." He often quoted from *Little Shop of Horrors*.

Irma set the bowl in the cage, accustomed to the bird's amazing repertoire. He dined on a steady diet of fruit, vegetables, nuts, and seeds, the shells of which he pried open with his powerful beak. But, being an omnivore like all parrots, he also ate meat. Insects were his favorite treats.

Irma closed the door and watched Maurice capture his feast. He eyed the prey for a moment before moving. He jumped lightly off his perch and in one swift motion, snatched up the caterpillar in his beak as it tried frantically to wriggle away. It made a soft, slurping sound as he swallowed it.

She retrieved her purse from the pantry. Time to go home.

CHAPTER SEVENTEEN

The Central Park Zoo was surprisingly busy for a chilly November morning, and Brendan had to pull his jacket tight around his leaner frame as a light flurry began to fall.

"Did you know there's no word for a group of snow leopards?" Mayor Timothy Atkins sidled up alongside Brendan and turned up the collar of his long coat to ward off the wind. "That's right. They live primarily in the Himalayas, above the tree line, and they're very solitary and elusive cats. It's rare to see two of them together in the wild. They like to hunt alone."

Brendan continued watching the spotted cubs as they leapt and played among the heated rocks of their habitat. One of them mewled loudly, and the other chuffed in response. They'd been vocalizing for the past twenty minutes while Brendan waited. "You seem to know a lot about snow leopards."

"I do. I visit them often, whenever I can get away from the office."

Brendan glanced sideways. *What an odd request to meet here*, he thought. Granted, the location was roughly halfway between their residences in Summer's Pond, Connecticut and High Tide, New Jersey, but wouldn't it have been better to meet somewhere private?

High voices behind Brendan drew his attention. A train of brightly-coated children zigzagged by, holding hands and giggling, following a young teacher who stopped in front of the snow leopard habitat. The kids exclaimed and pointed excitedly. Suddenly, Brendan understood exactly why the perv had chosen this spot.

Atkins smiled behind his collar. "Don't you just love field trips? Too bad I went into politics. Teaching is such a noble profession," he said, staring at the group. He stooped to pick up a Pokémon cap and plop it back on the head of a little boy. His hand lingered for a moment on the child's curly hair. "Buddy, you dropped this."

"Thanks, mister."

Brendan clenched his jaw as he saw DevBoys1969 close his eyes, pass his fingers under his nostrils, and inhale. Like that day on the beach when he saw the man jerk his dog's leash, he felt anger welling up from his chest, but this time he forced himself to stay calm and play along. "I was a camp counselor for years. To a dozen nine-year-olds. I miss those humid July nights, with the cabin just too damn hot for pajamas."

"Mmm, I can imagine."

Brendan swallowed. "So, do you have something for me?"

Atkins grinned and reached into his pocket to retrieve a flash drive. "I have a feeling you're really going to enjoy these."

Once again, Brendan had to calm his anger to maintain the façade. "There's just one more thing."

"What's that?"

"I need you to reach your source and arrange a meeting."

The man held up a palm. "That's a different transaction altogether," he said.

"Not for free, of course." Glancing around to see if anyone was watching, Brendan stepped closer and handed over a check for five thousand dollars.

Atkins smiled down at the check. "Anything for a friend. I'll text you." He tucked the check into his breast pocket and strolled away toward a little girl looking at the red pandas.

At home, with Elvis on the bed beside him, Brendan stared at the flash drive in his palm, reluctant to play it, afraid of the inferno of feelings it would ignite. At last, he crossed the hall to his office and plugged it in.

Ten photographs. Scans of old Polaroids featuring Shawn, Allen, Bobby, and him.

Brendan's gut curled into itself, and he ran to the toilet to vomit, splattering the seat. His senses were filled with images of green and red plaid, the hum of the dryer, the taste of Fig Newtons. When he finally straightened, the sickness remained, but he breathed through it and willed himself to move despite the nausea. He had work to do.

Back to the computer he went to finish his investigation. Finding the transaction that led him to Timothy Atkins also had identified the sender of the file. He didn't recognize the handle or email address. He traced the profile. In the chatrooms, the guy didn't have a very long history of interactions. In fact, he'd only been logging onto the message boards for a few weeks. And his commentary didn't so much suggest an interest in others' content but rather in selling his own wares. Brendan was cautious. It would have been easy for him to contact the seller in a chatroom with an offer to buy. But he didn't want the guy to get spooked. It had taken years for Brendan to develop that kind of trust with DevBoys1969. It would be safer to wait for an introduction to give him legitimacy.

A message came the next day. *The meet is set*, it read.

The location of the meeting couldn't have had less in common with the Central Park Zoo. Atkins set the time, nine o'clock on Friday night, and the address, a bar that sounded seedy from its name alone. Brendan texted back that he'd be wearing a Miami Dolphins hat.

Through the rear window of the town car, Brendan watched as they wove through a complex of near vacant warehouses and loading docks and finally came to a stop in front of a dingy, free-standing shoebox of a building tucked between two cranes. Through a greasy window, he could see muscled bartenders slinging drinks.

Tomasz slid the car into a dark alcove, far from the front door.

"You're clear on how we're doing this?" Brendan asked.

Tomasz nodded. He slapped on a Dolphins hat, clambered out, and slammed the door shut. He strode through the front door of the bar, jutting face first and bear-like body after.

Brendan counted out a minute before pulling up his hoodie and exiting the car. He scanned the dim interior of the building, chose a stool on the opposite side of the bar with a clear sightline to Tomasz's table, and ordered a scotch.

The glass came with a lipstick smudge.

Within minutes a man entered, spotted Tomasz in the baseball cap, and slid into the seat across from him. Brendan had positioned himself to see over Tomasz's shoulder, but for some reason the guy kept looking off to his left.

From his vantagepoint over the rim of his glass, Brendan could see Tomasz talking to him. Did he remember what to say? They'd rehearsed it several times: Tomasz would tell the guy, "My employer wants to make a deal. For every original item like the ones you gave our contact, we'll pay you one hundred dollars, cash. My employer wants all of them. If you hold any back, we'll find you. And it won't be pretty."

Tomasz had instructions to negotiate, as money was no object, with the goal to obtain each and every one of the "items" in the guy's possession, even though he had no idea what the items were. He just knew Brendan wanted them. And he knew he had to intimidate the guy a little. It didn't look like he'd need to negotiate much, though.

Brendan drummed his fingers on the table, watching the man as he listened intently to Tomasz. He waited for the guy to turn toward the bar so he could get a better look. All he could see in profile was thinning dark hair, a straight nose, and a satisfied smile stretching his cheek.

It looked like they'd struck a deal. The guy stood up from their table and, as he swung his leather jacket over his shoulders and zipped it, he pivoted toward the bar before striding out the door.

Brendan felt like someone had tossed a bucket of ice water in his face. He flinched with the sudden recognition. Yes, he'd aged, and not gracefully, but there was no doubt, no doubt at all, whom he'd just seen. He started to tremble.

Brendan hadn't intended to drink at the bar that night. He picked up the tumbler of whiskey with a shaking hand, swallowed it in a few gulps, and signaled the bartender for another. Tomasz joined him at the bar and waited as Brendan downed a third scotch. Then he helped his employer back to the car, where Brendan slumped inside and let his head loll back.

"We have a deal. We're meeting back here tomorrow night," Tomasz said into the rearview mirror as he sped back to Summer's Pond. "Just like you said. All good, yeah?"

"I know that guy," Brendan told him, closing his eyes. He felt the acid rise in his throat. "Or at least, I used to."

Irma set a heaping plate of salami and eggs, with three slices of toast on the side, in front of her ogre of a son. She fixed a packet of oatmeal for herself and sat down.

The weak autumn sunshine poured through the kitchen window of the little guesthouse in which they lived. The tiny rooms—a kitchen with a round table, two bedrooms, a bathroom, and a living room with an upholstered couch and matching chair clustered around a cozy wood stove—were furnished with traditional Polish embroideries and painted dolls and printed curtains. The décor evoked mid-century Eastern Bloc, not contemporary Connecticut.

As he shoveled through breakfast, Tomasz described the previous night to his mother. When he said the name of the man in the leather jacket, Irma set down her spoon.

"What you say?"

Tomasz spoke around a mouthful of half-chewed salami.

Yes. Yes, Irma recognized that name. She pictured the pages of labeled sketches in Brendan's journal, like the one of a young boy hanging from a noose. In the margins were names of other boys written in heavy-handed pen strokes that dripped hatred.

Her gaze moved to a woven basket on the floor beside the couch that held the embroidery she worked on in the evenings. A half-finished tapestry lay folded on top, with her embroidery hook sticking out of a ball of yarn. She knew that hatred, too.

"Say again," Irma demanded softly.

Her son repeated it. Chad Hubert. The name Brendan had circled and underlined in the margins.

Tomasz returned to the seedy bar later that night, pulling the Dolphins hat low on his forehead once again. Like last time, the place was nearly empty; just some truckers watching a game, a young couple by the window looking at their phones, and a table of four tired-looking housewives escaping their prisons. He slid onto a chipped stool at the bar and waited.

It wasn't long before Chad arrived and sidled up to the bar.

"Let's go," he said to Tomasz in a low voice. "I have the goods in my car."

As instructed, Tomasz replied, "No hurry." He put out a thick hand to urge Chad to sit. "Have a drink." He signaled for beers. As instructed.

A bartender was already placing two drafts in front of them when Brendan appeared and eased onto the empty stool to Chad's left.

Chad swiveled to look at the newcomer. Languidly, he gestured with his beer mug. "You… look familiar. Do we know each other?"

Brendan blanched. Chad may have aged… his hair was thin, his face thick, his beard gray… but his voice sounded exactly the same as the night in the parish cemetery at Torburton. "We do. We… you…" Brendan swallowed and tried to compose himself. "You might recognize me better like this." He raised a shaky hand to his forehead and pushed back his scraggly bangs, revealing the bumpy white scars that remained along his hairline.

Chad laughed and slapped a palm on the bar. "God Almighty. You're one of those private school jerks, right? Remind me which school again?"

"Torburton." Brendan cleared his throat. "Brendan. Cortland."

The man grinned and shook his head. "What's it been, thirty years?" He raised the glass to his mouth.

"Something like that."

"Christ, you got old." Chad smirked and took another swig. Beside him, Tomasz set his stein down with a threatening thud. Chad glanced at him, and back at Brendan. "Oh, shit. Are you... you two know each other?" He started to laugh. He didn't wait for a reply. "Now I get it. Yeah, makes sense. No wonder you want these."

Brendan bit his lip. "How did you get them?"

"I had my ways."

"But... but why sell them?"

"Simple, I need the money." Chad shrugged. "I got myself into a wee bit of debt and, well, I needed some quick cash to pay back my... friends."

John Hubert makes your dad look poor, Brendan remembered a sophomore saying to him once. "But your family's worth a fortune. Don't you have a trust fund or something?" he blurted.

"I did." Chad laughed again. "It's amazing how you can burn through money when you're young... the yachts, the girls, the high-stakes poker games, the drugs. Good old Dad got tired of it and cut me off. It was a flash of brilliance, selling this stuff. Who would've thought? There's a market for everything under the sun."

Brendan's thoughts jumbled as he listened.

Chad rubbed his palms along his jeans. "So, about our deal..."

Opening his jacket slightly so that Chad could see the top of the thick envelope poking from his inside pocket, Brendan stood. "Finish up. I'll meet you both outside."

In the parking lot, Brendan watched from the shadows as the two men left the bar and headed toward an old-model BMW. Chad reached into the car for a large cardboard box and handed it to Tomasz. Together they walked over to the alcove.

As Brendan handed the envelope to Chad, Tomasz leaned over and whispered, "Don't you want to open the box? Make sure it's what you expected?"

Brendan shook his head. No. No, he didn't want to open it, certainly not in front of anyone. He slid onto the back seat beside it.

Chad grinned and pocketed the envelope. "Nice doing business with you," he called over his shoulder as he sauntered away.

"I don't know what's in that box, but I'm guessing it's not exactly Hallmark cards," Tomasz remarked, starting the ignition. "How did he know you weren't going to call the police?"

How indeed? "Maybe he was willing to take that risk."

The town car took the same circuitous route as the BMW out of the industrial area and past the wharf. When it came time to hop on the parkway, though, Tomasz ignored the exit and continued to trail after.

"What are you doing?" Brendan asked, looking out the window at the dark, unfamiliar neighborhood. "Why are you following him?"

The town car stayed on the tail until Chad pulled into a residential driveway. Tomasz slowed down to watch him saunter up to the front door and let himself in. "Making sure he doesn't go to the police, either."

"Good thinking."

Tomasz whistled as he pulled into the garage and brought the cardboard box inside. Brendan took it from him to carry up to his room, and Tomasz was fine with that. He said good night and paused in the shadows, hovering for a while to watch Brendan let Elvis out for one last pee. Then he headed down the path to the guest house.

He whistled as he picked up the backpack sitting by the front door.

He whistled as he doubled back on the path to see the lights in the mansion extinguish one by one, and waited an extra fifteen minutes just to be sure Brendan had fallen asleep. Then he waited another few minutes for his mother to appear. Together they drove off in the town car.

All the way back to Chad Hubert's house.

Brendan would never know.

The street was dark and empty when they parked under a tree. Tomasz pulled a mask from the backpack. Whistling under his breath, with his face ensconced under black nylon, he crept around the house in the shadows to peer into back windows. The galley kitchen was dark and empty. So were the small bedrooms and the tiny dining area. On the far side of the house, though, Tomasz paused, careful to stay hidden. Through the living room window he could see Chad sitting on the couch, nursing another ale, illuminated by the glow of his television. Alone.

Good. So much easier this way.

Tomasz made his way to the back door, signaling for his mother. She stayed close behind, quiet and patient. Tomasz knocked sharply. When Chad opened the door an inch, Tomasz's palm shot out, swinging the door wide and slamming the knob through the drywall as he pushed his way in. Irma followed and closed the door.

Before Chad could react, a meaty fist slammed into his gut. Air rushed from his lips and he staggered backward, but the blows kept coming, raining down on his torso and face, splitting his lip, shattering his nose.

"Wait," he gasped, spitting blood. "I can pay. I have some of the money now. I'll get more."

Another punch, this time to his jaw.

"Stop... please... I'm sorry, I'll get all of it, please stop..."

In the shadows, Irma smiled. She loved hearing them beg.

Tomasz didn't stop.

CHAPTER EIGHTEEN

Late the next morning, as Irma held her son's swollen hand under cold water from the kitchen faucet, the doorbell rang. She opened the door to a gust of November chill.

Dylan stood in front of her. "I wanted to make sure Brendan's okay?" she said. "He hasn't answered my calls."

"Pierdolić," Irma swore under her breath in Polish. Aloud, she said, "Mr. Brendan still upstairs. I get him."

As the words passed her lips, Elvis bounded down the stairs to greet Dylan. Brendan appeared on the landing, looking haggard. Hastily, he smoothed his hair when he caught sight of Dylan.

"Are you sick?" Dylan asked, bending to give Elvis a scratch behind his ears as she searched Brendan's countenance with concern. "Did you forget we were meeting today?"

"I'm sorry, I didn't sleep much last night."

"No worries." Dylan set her briefcase down in the middle of the living room carpet and shook her finger with mock sternness. "If Mohammed won't come to the mountain, then the mountain will come to Mohammed! Or something like that. Well, I'm the mountain, and I've come to hear the rest of your story. Because I'm filing this lawsuit with or without you."

Brendan nodded. He looked over at his housekeeper. "Irma, maybe you can make coffee while I wash up?"

Irma nodded blandly and returned to the kitchen. Moments later, Dylan appeared in the archway.

"Where's Maurice? I don't hear him."

Irma turned her back and shrugged as she brewed coffee. "Maybe Tomasz take him for a walk." *He sleeping, dumb woman*, she thought.

Brendan came downstairs just as the coffee finished perking, and they set steaming mugs on the living room table. Dylan referred to the notes she'd brought. "Last time, you were talking about the spring of 1983. Can you expand on that?"

Brendan chewed his lip pensively. He'd been up most of the night thinking about Chad Hubert and the box of photographs. For hours, he'd stared at the cardboard box where it sat on the floor of his bedroom, illuminated only by shafts of moonlight sliding in between the edges of the drapes. He hadn't had the guts to open it. He wasn't sure he ever would.

The silence in the living room stretched on until it became uncomfortable. Brendan seemed lost in thought, too caught in his jagged rocks to speak. They'd been discussing the case all day, had finished the sandwiches Irma made for lunch hours earlier. Giving Brendan a minute to breathe, Dylan left to fetch more coffee before they resumed.

At last, Brendan stirred. "Jack was right to worry," he said. "Chad and the upperclassmen weren't about to take it lightly, the fact that he'd informed on them. Even if he was mistaken and even if they didn't end up getting in trouble."

Brendan crumpled until he was folded almost double, his face in his hands. Dylan dropped to her knees on the carpet beside the Edra chair, reaching out a tentative hand to Brendan's shoulder, and then withdrawing it quickly. He gave no indication that he felt her touch or even that he was aware of her presence there beside him. When he looked up, all his emotions were etched in his expression: guilt, horror, sadness. He passed a shaking hand over his face. "Jack was so good. There was no beast in him, but they hurt him so badly. And, oh my God, he died. He died."

And then a startling sound erupted from Brendan's throat—a harsh bark, almost, repeating itself every few seconds, accompanied by convulsions of his torso. Elvis sat up and whimpered. Dylan hurried to the kitchen for help.

"What you do to him?" Irma dropped the icepack she was holding. Tomasz, on a kitchen stool, moved his arm behind his back to hide the purple knuckles.

"I didn't do anything…"

"Mr. Brendan?" Irma bent over him and looked up accusingly. "I never seeing him cry before."

The guttural sobs, if indeed that's what they were, sounded like an animal trying to regurgitate something rotten. Irma made shushing sounds and slowly the barking subsided. Brendan's body eased.

Dylan sank again to the floor. "Hey," she said softly, searching Brendan's pain-contorted face.

"I'm sorry," Brendan apologized, taking deep breaths and looking from his attorney to his maid.

Shaken by the sight of Brendan's outburst, Dylan recalled overhearing her parents discussing cases of abuse victims and the long term damage they'd sustained. "Do you… do you want to get some air?"

Irma nodded firmly. "Yes, good to go outside. Nice long walk before supper."

Taking the path past the pool, Dylan watched Brendan pick up a stick and toss it for Elvis to fetch. His face looked pasty but his eyes were dry.

"How can a young boy be so desperate that he takes his own life?" Brendan wondered aloud, stopping to stare off into the distance. His words were carried off by the wind to another yard, dispersed like old ash. "I think Galloway did something to Jack that last morning when they were alone. Maybe it was the final straw, the trigger. Jack kept getting it from all sides and he couldn't cope anymore."

"You were getting it from all sides, too."

"Yes, but I was..." He stopped.

"You were what? Stronger than Jack?"

A strange look passed over Brendan's face. "I never thought of that."

Dylan nodded and they walked in silence. At last she spoke. "I can't imagine how hard this has been for you. But do you think... do you think describing your memories of Jack has been cathartic in some way?"

"Maybe." Brendan shoved his hands into his coat pockets and squinted toward the sinking sun. "I'm sorry for that, back there. A grown man, bawling like a baby. But I... um... feel better, talking to you. There's something... I don't know, safe about you."

"Thank you for trusting me." Dylan reached out. How lonely, to exist without touching and being touched, without the reassuring contact that softens the desolate human condition? Slowly, gingerly, she laid her hand on his shoulder.

Under her palm, Dylan felt his body tense. When he turned toward her his chin came into contact with her skin, and she felt a shudder course through him. She dropped her hand.

Brendan took a shaky step back. "I know you and Dr. Aldrich are doing your best to help."

"That's true." There were so many questions Dylan wanted to ask, but she wouldn't push. She'd let Brendan disclose more details at his own pace.

By now, they'd walked so far they couldn't see the main house in the dimming light. They were nearly at the farthest point of the property, the back quadrant that continued beyond the footpath and behind a grove of tall conifers.

Following the path as it curved around a bend, they came upon a tumbled stone cottage, half hidden, glowing with light from windows on which sash bars divided the glazed glass into diagonals. Hansel and Gretel wouldn't have seemed out of place.

"How charming! What is this place?" she exclaimed.

"The guesthouse. Irma and Tomasz live here." As if scripted, the arched front door opened and a bear of a man stepped outside. The overhead porch light illuminated his many black moles and his startled expression as he caught sight of Brendan and Dylan heading in his direction. Ducking his head, he managed a grunt in greeting before loping away.

Dylan's neck prickled as she watched him disappear into the shadows. On the walk back, she coddled a question, loathe to upset Brendan further, until finally she asked it.

"What did you mean, 'there was no beast in him'?"

"Just that most people have an evil side. They have the capacity to be monsters who do horrible things. Jack didn't, though."

They returned to the main house. Irma opened the door and announced that dinner would be ready soon. As they stepped inside, she added, albeit with tight lips, "I cook too much corned beef. Maybe Mr. Brendan's friend like to stay?"

Dylan looked delighted at the offer, the first overture the woman had ever made. "I'd love to."

Brendan lit up. "We'll eat in the dining room tonight, Irma. On the good dishes."

Dylan said, "I could use a drink. How about you?"

"Dr. Aldrich says..." Brendan's voice tapered off. "You know what? Yes." A glass-shelved bar gleamed in an alcove between the den and the dining room, fully stocked. Many of its bottles were unopened, but instead of going there Brendan beckoned for Dylan to follow as he opened a door. A stone staircase spiraled down to a self-contained wine cellar. He flipped on a light and rows upon rows of corked bottles came into view, lining the walls of the sweet-smelling room.

"Oh, my." Dylan drew in her breath and circled in place. "I didn't know you were a wine aficionado."

"I'm not, really. This was one of my father's passions. I've done some research, added to his collection over the years, but I haven't opened one in a very long time. Go ahead, pick anything you like."

Dylan reached for a random bottle and passed it to him.

"Domaine Leroy Latricières-Chambertin Grand Cru, Côte de Nuits, France," he read from the label, his perfect pronunciation a result of superior education. "You have good taste. That one's worth about twenty-four hundred dollars."

She started to slide it back into place with a low chuckle. "How about a vodka martini instead?"

"Absolutely not. The pinot noir one you selected will be perfect with dinner."

Dylan smiled to herself. Those words, coming from Brendan, sounded so peculiar. She wondered if he'd heard himself.

Irma served the beef with cabbage and freshly baked bread. Brendan opened the wine, poured them each a glass, and sat back. Once again, he felt overcome by the same surreal feeling he'd had walking the dog a month earlier… that this scene appeared, from the outside, to be utterly ordinary. Enviable, in fact. Here he was, dining with a gorgeous woman, enjoying a fabulous bottle of wine, in the dining room of what was once a magnificent home. Completely ordinary, if you overlooked the more bizarre things like his earlier outburst, or the fact that upstairs stood a box of his nude photographs.

Brendan wanted to be normal. So badly.

Dylan lifted her glass. "To Jack," she said softly.

Mortimer James was appalled at the extent of the tragedy that had occurred. "This elite private school," he said the next morning, squinting to turn off the burner under the kettle. "This school charged parents thousands upon thousands of dollars for the privilege of attendance, for residing on its grand campus, for membership to its exclusive club of alumni. It assumed responsibility for these children. It was supposed to protect them and keep them safe."

At the table, his daughter scrawled a note on a napkin. "I might borrow that for my opening statement," Dylan said. "I mean, I am opening, right?"

"Of course you are. When are we filing?"

"I'm aiming for next week. I have some material to add but overall, the lawsuit is almost written. Assuming he doesn't surprise me with another abuser crawling out of the woodwork."

Mortimer set two mugs on the placemats: *See You Later, Litigator* for him, *Let's Assume I'm Right* for her. "How did the school respond to Jack's death?"

"According to Brendan, they scrambled to mitigate the damage. By the time Jack's parents made it to the hospital from where they lived in Massachusetts, the school had already convened an emergency board meeting."

"It would be good to know what they discussed."

"I'll subpoena all the minutes that remain. If there are any." Dylan reached into her leather messenger bag and pulled out her omnipresent legal pad, half-filled with black and purple scrawling. "Listen to what Brendan told me last night over dinner. He said Galloway and Greer packed up all of Jack's things and had them delivered to the Abromovitch house. They didn't let the parents come to the school. Who knows what they were told, that poor couple."

"Did Brendan ever speak to the family again?"

"Never. He said that after Jack's death, there was a school-wide assembly in the auditorium. Galloway got up and made a tribute to Jack, talking about how disturbed a young man he'd always been, and how sometimes 'despite people's best efforts to help, the darkness wins out.' And he made a point of saying how it would be best for Jack's family to be left alone in their grief. Not to be reminded of their loss."

"Despicable." Mortimer stood up to rinse the mugs. Dylan noticed how he ran his fingertips toward the sink to orient himself. "Do you need a hand?" she asked.

"No, dear." He looked thoughtful as he leaned against the counter to face her, drying his cup with a small towel. "And Jack's parents never reached out to Brendan?"

"Brendan has a hunch that the school administrators told them not to, using the same sort of perverse logic: that the boys were traumatized, were undergoing counseling, and were better off left alone."

"You're saying it's quite possible that they never learned of the circumstances that caused Jack to take his own life?"

"I suppose. I don't know which would be worse— learning that your son took his own life or learning how culpable the people around him were."

Shaking his head, Mortimer muttered, "Shameful, shameful."

"Right? Sometimes I think I'm becoming so invested in Brendan that I'm not being objective."

"That big heart of yours. You brought home every stray you found."

"But their behavior really is shameful, isn't it? By any standard?"

"Inexcusable. But, Counselor, remember your job is not to prove that their behavior was shameful, or immoral, or disgusting. Your job is to prove that they broke the law. That they caused harm, and knew, or should have known, that they caused harm."

"You can't get more harmed than dead."

In mid-December, Dylan told her father the suit was ready to file in United States District Court.

Mortimer advised against it. "Let's wait," he said, "until after the holidays. We're going to want some press around the filing. Newspapers... what's left of them... are on a skeleton staff now, and too many readers are away. Better to aim for January."

So Dylan did something she hadn't in months, since she'd opened an office in Dr. Aldrich's house on Chatwick Road, actually. She took time off.

She couldn't remember the last time she'd spent an afternoon with her grandmother, or gone out for dinner, or had drinks with the girls. How many invitations had she declined, choosing instead to sit hunched over a keyboard, surrounded by a field of yellow? She texted her three best friends, sorority sisters from college, and arranged a day in Manhattan beginning with Sunday brunch at Earthbound, the trendiest eatery in the Village, the one where vines and trellises grew along the walls and moss covered the entire floor.

Afterward, the foursome spent the afternoon at a spa.

"I needed this," Dylan groaned, face down on a slab as a masseuse worked the kinks out of her shoulders. "I didn't realize how tense I'd gotten these last few months."

"You think discovery was stressful? Just wait until the trial starts," her friend Lacey, an environmental lawyer, mumbled.

"It's just so emotional." Dylan winced as the strong fingers kneaded her spine.

"Speaking of which, are you going to the memorial this year?" Lacey didn't have to specify further. Memes of the catastrophic bus accident in Connecticut three years earlier had been posted and reposted on social media for weeks. The entire state still reeled in grief. Major television networks aired gut-wrenching footage of a school bus skidding sideways off a snow-covered bridge and plunging into an icy river below. But Dylan needed no reminder: the images were branded behind her eyes.

"I'm drained. I have to take a step back from all the sadness."

Lacey propped herself up on her elbows. "Don't. Hold onto that emotion. Your outrage and your empathy for your client will be clear to the jury. Remember who you are."

Dylan lay silent under the sheet. Who was she, actually? Smart and driven, enough to overcome the hurdles of law school, as a woman and a mixed race one at that. Still, a neophyte, mired in debt, trying to make a go of a brand-new solo practice in a field that was traditionally male-dominated and sometimes held patriarchal echoes of the old boys' club it once was.

How often had she felt the pressure of needing to live up to her parents' reputations in the legal community? The responsibility of making her father proud, of honoring her mother's memory? And now, the added weight of wanting to do right by Brendan. Could she? Sometimes she felt paralyzed by self-doubt. Like a motherless waif.

Dylan's thoughts settled on Brendan. She'd never met anyone like him—so fragile, so raw, but with a seedling of determination that spontaneously sprang from the wasteland of his existence. He had strength he wasn't aware of. Each day she saw the changes in him. Not just the slimmer face and physique but the straighter posture, the firmer voice, the way he'd begun not only to sustain eye contact but to search her face as if looking into her soul.

For the next half hour, she closed her lids and worked hard to relax. She would take these next few days to reconnect with her family, to rest, to celebrate the holidays, and then she would dive back in.

The following day, Dylan bought a bouquet of flowers and headed to Winter Garden, the nursing home where her grandmother lived.

"Nana!" she exclaimed, awash with regret for neglecting to visit the frail lady sitting by the window. She set the bouquet on a table and enveloped her grandmother in a gentle hug. "I've missed you so much. I'm sorry I haven't been by."

"My sweet girl," Nana said, her papery face opening into delight. "Let me look at you. Come sit beside me and tell me about your life."

Dylan perched at the edge of the bed, beside her grandmother's walker. "I've been working on a big lawsuit, Nana, and it's taken all my time and energy. That's no excuse, though. I shouldn't have waited so long to see you. I promise it won't happen again."

Nana reached out a shaky hand to pat her granddaughter's. "No, dear, don't apologize. I know how much work goes into these cases; I watched your father at it his whole life. You are so much like him, aren't you? And like your poor mother. Toiling away for justice."

"One very broken man deserves it, Nana."

"You'll find it, my dear. You will."

CHAPTER NINETEEN

Yuletide hardened Irma's already rough edges. Not a year had gone by that she hadn't spent lost in thoughts of that fateful December night five decades earlier. The crunch of ice, the cold, the smell of winterfire smoke in the air… all of it brought back the sight of her father and uncle unmoving on the ground, and the helpless feeling of seeing the brutes throw her mother and sister into their truck. Of being pinned on her back in the snow. The defining event of her youth returned in vivid flashes every Christmas.

A search party had found Maja's corpse the day after the attack, in the lower fields that her husband and his brother had begun clearing the previous autumn. Beside her was Gosia, icy blue and barely clinging to life. It was several days before the villagers could dig deep enough into the frozen ground to bury the three bodies of Maja, Jan, and Zarek. Gosia, they sent to a facility far away in Warsaw, rundown and dirty, to live out her days. She'd never be the same again.

All these Christmases later, Irma still wondered why she hadn't died with her parents. Even after she had Tomasz, she often regretted her escape—how her flailing hand had come across the embroidery hook still in her dress pocket, how she'd grasped it and plunged it deep into the eye of her drunken assailant like a pin into a balloon. How she'd scrambled up and disappeared into the tall, dry grasses as he screamed and spurted blood onto the snow behind her.

Upstairs, in a bedroom in the house on Whelk Lane, a cardboard box stood unopened. Brendan still hadn't looked inside. He knew he should tell Dylan about it but he prevaricated; it occupied his thoughts. Plus, he still had DevBoys1969 to deal with. And then there was the business of that visitor... someone named Jon O'Malley, who'd returned a second time but who Brendan had patently ignored. He'd left another card—it read *Barnaby Partners*. Probably wanting to peddle some new investment.

As the December days became colder, Brendan went through his daily routine immersed in thought. One day, he asked Tomasz to cut down an evergreen. Tomasz found the perfect tree on the far corner of the property and in mid-month, up it went in the den. Brendan retrieved the long-unused Cortland family heirlooms from the basement: glittering ornaments, crystal baubles, glass figurines, and twinkling lights stored in wooden crates. He hung the decorations late one night, lost in his memories of a comfortable childhood, before the huge success of Kenneth's last few pictures, culminating in the worldwide phenomenon, *A Candle for Cassandra*, that sent Brendan to Torburton.

The week before Christmas, Irma asked what Brendan might like to eat for his holiday dinner. She'd make whatever he wanted, she offered, as she did every year. But this year Brendan surprised her.

"Let's go to the store together and see what there is," he said.

Irma grunted, then took her coat and purse from the hook in the butler's pantry, wrapped a scarf around her square head, and followed him out to the town car with

Tomasz. They went at dinnertime, when the store would be less crowded.

Brendan pushed the grocery cart—another first in decades—up and down the aisles of the upscale market in town, considering all the options.

"Would you like goose, Mr. Brendan? Or maybe I make leg of lamb?" Irma offered. Cooking remained one of the few pleasures in her life.

Brendan strolled along, looking at the array of foods. "What's your favorite?" he asked.

Irma gave the smallest shrug. "Tomasz like sausage and onions." She added a few ingredients to the cart. In the cereal aisle, she reached for a container of store brand instant oats. "I bring to guesthouse." she explained.

"Irma," Brendan mused, as if the thought just occurred to him. "You get paid enough, right?"

"Yes, Mr. Brendan." The accountants had set up direct deposit years ago.

"How much do I pay you?"

A pause. "You are... generous. Tomasz and I, we are fine. I send money to sister every month, in nursing home." Irma didn't mention that long ago, Gosia had been transferred to an expensive facility outside Vienna. Once a tuberculosis sanitorium, Karlzdorf Baden now served a rich clientele with long-term medical needs in a beautiful and discreet setting.

Brendan nodded slowly. They continued walking the aisles together, with Brendan filling the cart to heaping. Irma glanced at the cart, at his hand pulling items from the shelves, the caviar and imported cheese and expensive cuts of meat. She remembered the endless meals of potatoes and cabbages her mother had served so long ago.

Out for a walk with Elvis that evening, blanketed in the silence of a fresh snowfall, Brendan basked in the splendor of his village. The residents had festooned their front doors with wreaths, wound fairy lights around their trees, set single beacons in each windowsill in New England tradition. The houses looked festive and inviting, as if happy families lived inside, ready to celebrate the warmth of the season.

Brendan watched his dog, a shadow of black in the glow of moonlight, leaping through drifts and over branches encrusted with ice. He'd taken to letting Elvis off his leash now that he could be trusted to come bounding back when summoned. He called and Elvis materialized, with a snout covered in frost and tail a-wagging. Brendan smiled to himself at the antics. This animal had brought him so much joy. He wanted to share it.

Dylan listened to the message for the third time. On the line, Brendan's voice was deep and calm, so different from the first time she'd heard him speak in that thin, reedy voice. It was becoming a masculine voice, even an attractive one. Inviting her for Christmas dinner.

She called back and left a message of her own, apologizing profusely and explaining that she, her father, and her grandmother celebrated together.

Moments later she received a text: *Please bring them. I would be honored.*

Dylan accepted as, after all, she didn't want to disappoint Brendan. The four of them could have a festive little dinner. And then the thought occurred to her… might she have been disappointed, too?

Tomasz parked at the base of Greenwich Avenue, a broad boulevard lined on both sides with boutiques of high-end brands and designers, dotted with antique shops and restaurants, anchored by an imposing Roman Catholic church. Brendan got out. Even though they were just a few miles from home, and even though he could see it from the window of Dr. Aldrich's office, the last time he'd stepped foot on this street had been when he was still married to Heather.

Steeling himself, Brendan shopped alongside the holiday crowds, trying not to bump others. Soon, though, he felt something unexpected—he began to enjoy himself. He found it was enough to nod in return to the pleasant greetings of salespeople and the smiles of other customers. The curious stares and prying questions he'd imagined didn't materialize. Instead, he took his time browsing through the merchandise, familiarizing himself with the latest fashions, admiring art and décor. He became adept at tapping and inserting the credit card he'd only used online. He savored the boyish exhilaration of being able to have anything he wanted. He could buy and buy and buy and none of it would dent his bank account. It took a couple hours, but Brendan eventually emerged victorious, his arms laden with bags and packages.

Back at the house, he took his haul into the den and laid everything on the rug in front of the tree. He surveyed the spread of treasures with satisfaction, picturing the looks on everyone's faces as they tore open the wrapping. He'd have so much to write afterward, he might need to buy a new journal.

Tomasz had been the easiest to shop for. For him, Brendan had purchased a tan leather coat lined with wool, expensive sunglasses, and a pair of buttery soft driving gloves for winter.

Irma had been more difficult. It was harder to know what to get her, the gruff woman who took care of others:

his house and him, her son, and the sister and village she'd left in Poland. In the end, Brendan picked up a Balenciaga bag, a Bvlgari watch, a Swarovski crystal swan... some trinkets to accompany a hefty bonus.

For Dr. Aldrich, Brendan found a designer briefcase to replace the psychiatrist's dog-eared one. Inside, he put a rare first edition of Sigmund Freud's *Interpretation of Dreams*.

And then there was Zac. Last year, Brendan had given him a hockey stick signed by Alex Ovechkin and tickets to an NHL game in Los Angeles. This year, he wanted to do something more impressive. He thought about getting a set of dirt bikes for his friends and him, or a sailboat to moor in the sound. But then he wondered if the extravagant gifts made him look even more freakish. He decided on something conservative. He invested his son in shares of blue chip stocks, enough to make the boy a very wealthy man if he let them mature into his adulthood.

Brendan had picked up a few more odds and ends, which left only one more gift on his list. He turned down a side street to find himself in front of a small jewelry store with bushels of poinsettias in front and holly on the lintel. Bells jingled as he opened the door.

"May I help you?" A manicured, older woman with trendy lavender hair stood near the entrance.

Brendan cleared his throat and avoided the woman's eyes. "I'm looking for a gift."

"For your wife?"

"No, for my, uh, attorney. Well, she is more like a friend." He coughed. "I want to... thank her for her help. Not like a ring or anything."

The woman donned a pair of glasses and smiled knowingly. "Something tasteful yet significant. Nothing overtly romantic, but valuable enough to express your... appreciation."

"Yes!" Brendan exclaimed, relieved. "Exactly." The shopkeeper had captured the essence of what he wanted...

a gift to strike the delicate balance between professional advisor and confidante that Dylan had become. Just one gift. Something that said everything.

"Something like this?" She unlocked a display case and set a box on top of the glass.

Brendan stepped closer. The bracelet, resting on its velvet cushion, sparkled. A slim rope of diamond baguettes studded with exquisite diamond solitaires. He could picture it glinting from underneath Dylan's sleeve, catching prisms of light as it rested against her dusky skin.

"That's it!" he said breathlessly. He paid with a credit card, tucked the package into his coat pocket, and kept his hand on it all the way back to where Tomasz waited.

Brendan set the beautifully wrapped parcel under the tree. It would be a wonderful holiday.

Christmas Eve at the Cortland mansion wasn't at all what Dylan had expected. She turned into the driveway, the tires crackling over hardened snow amid the glow of garden lights. The double doors, hung with fragrant wreaths, opened, and Brendan came outside. He greeted Mortimer James and helped the man's mother negotiate her walker up to the landing and inside. Dylan followed her father, carrying dessert.

Inside, chandeliers glowed and Sinatra's croon filled the spaces between human voices. Brendan ushered them inside.

To Dylan's surprise, much of the junk heaped along the walls had been cleared away, leaving behind only the best décor. The double doors had been thrown open and the den twinkled with a beautifully decorated tree. Elvis lay on the carpet in front of the roaring fire. "I can't believe the transformation," she said, glancing around the room and at Brendan, who hovered nearby, half hidden by branches.

Irma entered, carrying a tray of champagne flutes, and behind her came Tomasz, looking like an immensely uncomfortable circus bear in a suit, dwarfing a platter of delicate puff pastries filled with gruyere cheese and crabmeat. For Dylan, who remembered the man's odd demeanor on the porch of the guesthouse, the sight was discomfiting. Nevertheless, she thrust out a hand, then turned and introduced her father and grandmother to his mother and him.

Irma and Tomasz muttered hellos.

With everyone together in the den, Brendan doled out gifts. On Mortimer and his elderly mother, he bestowed two giant, overwrapped Christmas baskets containing imported crackers and cheeses, cookies, and fruit cakes, festooned with giant red bows. A thick, handmade throw would keep Dylan's grandmother warm, and her father received a bamboo chest of imported English tea.

Irma accepted the expensive purse, watch, and crystal swan with faint confusion, a "what am I supposed to do with this?" face. But the fat envelope of cash, that drew a smile.

Finally, only one small present remained under the tree, which Brendan had to work up his courage to give. At last he handed it to Dylan.

She peeled back the wrapping and lifted out the velvet box. For one brief moment, her heart stopped.

Lifting the lid, she drew in a sharp breath and held open the box so her father and grandmother, beside her, could see. "I don't know what to say. It's the most gorgeous thing I've ever seen."

"You can wear it in court. For good luck," Brendan said. He nodded toward Mortimer, who lifted the bracelet from its bed and clasped it around his daughter's wrist.

"I can't! I can't accept this... it's too much."

"No one will notice it under your sleeve," Mortimer told her.

"Please, it would make me happy. In the spirit of friendship. I wanted to thank you for listening to my story." Brendan turned to the rest of his room. "I wanted to thank all of you for helping me celebrate tonight. Merry Christmas."

At dinner, they toasted Mortimer James, the newest member of Dylan's legal team. Port accompanied a selection of rich cakes and tarts, and when only crumbs were left and everyone had grown full and sleepy, the guests said their goodnights.

The house lay empty and silent once Brendan shooed Irma and Tomasz back to their cottage. He eyed the half-empty bottle of port and brought it to the den. The fire had long since died, and he sat alone in the moonlight, drinking. Maybe it was that feeling of being drunk. Or maybe it was the still-fresh image of Chad at the bar that brought it back. Or the unopened cardboard box he'd pushed to the back of his closet. Whatever the trigger, as soon as Brendan closed his eyes in the early hours of that Christmas Day, his mind plunged back to a spring night in 1983. It was the night he'd stumbled back to his dorm room and been sick, which had set into motion the events that led to Jack's death. The memories gushed forth as if from an open wound.

In his mind, the picture seemed dark and grainy, an old daguerreotype. Sensory details accompanied the image—the feeling of the humidity through which he'd dragged himself to Science Club. The blink of the fluorescent light on the basement ceiling and music playing in the background. The darting, reluctant eyes of Shawn, Bobby, and Allen above him. The sound of Nevin's raspy breathing when he told Brendan to lie back on the Formica table for the "experiment," and Nevin's sour smell when he unbuttoned his lab coat and took off his shirt.

In the days following Christmas, Dylan didn't hear from Brendan, even though she'd called to thank him for the lovely dinner and gift.

"Hi, Nana! You look nice and cozy," she said now, leaning down to kiss her grandmother where she sat, wrapped snugly in the afghan Brendan had gifted her two weeks earlier. "Aren't you going to open your basket?"

"It's so pretty, I'm enjoying looking at it." Nana smiled at her granddaughter, her face crinkling. "And at you."

A cold January wind howled outside Winter Garden as Dylan tucked the edge of the blanket around her grandmother's frail shoulders. "You look pretty too, Nana. You sure you don't want to try some of those delicious cookies? I'll keep the bow on."

"I suppose I should, before they get stale."

Dylan parted the cellophane overwrap in the back of the basket and deftly slipped out a box of expensive, pastel-colored macarons. "We filed the lawsuit yesterday," she said, opening the lid of the box and helping herself to a pink confection.

Nana chose a yellow one.

Chewing quietly, Dylan reached into her bag and pulled out a folded copy of the *Connecticut Daily Dawn*. She shook it out and turned the page. Across the top, the bold headline read: "Private School Accused of Rampant Sexual Abuse," with the byline Sandy Davidson. "Dad called the reporter to give him a heads up that I was filing." She perused the article thoughtfully. "I'm sure this is just the first of the coverage. Especially if it goes to trial."

"What does it say, dear? I don't have my glasses on."

Dylan read aloud, "A lawsuit was filed in Connecticut Superior Court today accusing an elite private school of allowing rampant physical and sexual abuse dating back to the 1980s. Brendan Cortland, of Summer's Pond, Conn., alleged he was abused at Torburton Hall Academy for Boys, the boarding school he attended in Calvert, Conn., from 1982 to 1986. 'From the day he arrived on campus as an innocent fourteen-year-old child, Brendan found himself submersed in a culture of unrelenting sexual and physical abuse by various members of the staff as well as by the older students,' said Dylan M. James, Mr. Cortland's attorney. 'Rather than provide an environment where pupils could excel academically and spiritually, Torburton Hall was a hive of molestation, where pedophiles roamed freely, forcing young boys to participate in sexual acts with each other and with adults. Physical assaults were commonplace. Because of the abuse he endured, my client has been scarred for life.' "

Dylan looked up to see her grandmother's eyes wide with horror. "I'm sorry, Nana, I'll stop reading. I didn't mean to upset you."

"That poor man," Nana said. "So kind, so generous, but of course I could tell right away that he carries a terrible weight on his shoulders. At Christmas dinner he seemed very fragile. It's a wonder that he found the strength to come forward and talk about these things."

"It took an enormous amount of courage," Dylan agreed. "I haven't spoken to him yet. I'm not sure if he saw the article and, if he did, how he feels about it." She glanced down at the newspaper again. A photo had run alongside the article. "The reporter did a good job quoting me exactly. And the way he ended it could be especially helpful to the case. He asks that anyone with knowledge of the events get in touch with me."

"Do you think they will?" Nana asked.

"It happened a long time ago, but I guess it's a possibility."

A half hour later, Dylan stood up to leave, promising to come back the following week. She stepped from the room and paused to let aides pushing lunch trolleys and social workers with clipboards bustle past. A stooped, elderly resident shuffled toward her as he made his way down the hall. As he passed, he glanced up at Dylan and nodded, then went back to the immensely tiring task of moving his brittle body forward one step at a time.

Dylan leaned against the wall and pulled out the newspaper once more. She stared at the photograph for several minutes, under a bright wall sconce.

Three rows of lacrosse players stood dressed in maroon and gold Torburton Tridents jerseys in a team photo dated 1984.

The tall, blond boy in the back row of the class picture was immediately recognizable as a young Brendan Cortland, his face youthful and tanned and handsome. But something was off. Something that marred the good looks. As Dylan stared, she realized what it was.

His eyes. They looked worn and world-weary. Brendan Cortland had the eyes of an old man.

CHAPTER TWENTY

Dr. Aldrich passed the document to Brendan and leaned back in his chair, only the thrum of the radiator breaking the silence. "As we expected, I've been asked to testify," he said at last, crossing his legs as he watched his patient skim the single sheet of paper. "Which, of course, I will do."

"Thank you."

"I just want to make sure you're prepared for the tide of feelings that this lawsuit is likely to cause."

"Yes."

"Because look how far you have come. Clinically speaking, you have made excellent progress. And I wouldn't want anything to jeopardize that. Here you are, in your red sweater and blue jeans, looking fit and trim and dare I say even a little... confident? At the thought of a courtroom victory, maybe? But the trauma of telling your story, in public, in front of strangers, is likely to have consequences."

Brendan remained silent.

Dr. Aldrich drummed his fingers on the armrests of his chair. *Diddle um, diddle um.* "I want you to be forewarned. You understand that you will, in all likelihood, have to air your dirty laundry in public? And speak about all the awful, shameful things?" He tried to block out the faint sound of his phone vibrating in his top drawer where he'd stashed it, hoping to avoid the alarming notifications that popped up insistently.

"It will probably be in all the newspapers, a sensational story like this," he continued. "Greenwich Millionaire Claims Sexual Abuse. Probably on television, too, and all over the Internet, of course. You should be prepared for that."

Brendan pushed the paper across the desk. "I am."

Dr. Aldrich returned the form to a manilla envelope in his lap. "People will wonder if you are... Well. Twisting the truth."

"I wouldn't lie about—"

"Of course not. But this is something we should be discussing. Each week. You need to resume your weekly sessions, Brendan." *Diddle um.* "Tell me, have you had any more dreams lately?"

Brendan turned to look out the big picture window, at the murky January sky and slush and crusts of snow lining the curbs along Greenwich Avenue. A few stragglers braved the scouring wind but for the most part, the wide street lay empty.

He frowned. Yes, he'd had a new dream just the other night.

Even though Brendan didn't seem to be in distress, Dr. Aldrich turned on the cloying tinkling which had, for many years, soothed some of his patient's most fearful moments.

Rather than help him relax, the sound provoked a Pavlovian response: when Brendan heard it, he felt his heart constrict, and the dream came flooding back. As if he associated fear and shame and horror with wind chimes.

The sun hung low in the cloudless Italian sky, suspended behind a curtain of shimmering heat that reflected off the rippling waves and the hull of the yacht as it bobbed in the Tyrrhenian Sea.

Brendan lay on the gleaming white deck, the uppermost of three, listening to the faint sounds around him: the low purr of submerged motors, the occasional cry of circling gulls, the soft squelch of the rubber-soled boat shoes worn by the uniformed crew as they approached. Another limoncello, Mr. Cortland? A dry towel, sir? More ice?

Farther away, the clang of bells and rhythmic bumps of boats against the docks caught his attention. Lazily, he roused himself enough to prop up on his elbows. The vista was magnificent. Over his shoulders and behind the ship, a stretch of sapphire-blue water as far as he could see. In front of him, the rugged Lattari Mountains of the Amalfi Coast, hulking above the tiny, secluded village of Vetri Maré. Brendan could almost smell the tangy fragrance emanating from the groves of lemon trees that grew along the rock face, alongside steep paths that wended upward into the cliffs, the summits of which offered glorious views of the Mediterranean beyond.

The hamlet nestled in a verdant valley. On a strip of white sand stood the town's iconic lighthouse, carved from rock eons ago but more recently inlaid with glass mosaic tiles in the shapes of mermaids. Two jutting outcroppings of land bracketed a beach dotted with umbrellas beside dazzling, terraced hotels. Above them, pastel-hued villas spilled from the mountains. In one of those tumbled villas lived Brendan's mother.

A day earlier, when the yacht had arrived in Vetri's bay, Eliza Cortland had appeared on the pier, clutching her wide sun hat with one hand and waving a greeting with the other. Brendan putt-putted to shore in a small skiff manned by one of his crew. His loose, white linen shirt flapped in the wind as he stepped onto the dock to gaze at his mother. Her ageless face above her sarong looked as supple and unlined as when he was a boy. She folded him into an embrace.

"My darling," Eliza exclaimed, kissing her son's cheek. "I've missed you so much." They walked arm in arm along the surf, chatting easily, as if no time had passed since their last meeting.

Still, Eliza slowed and hung her head. "Darling, I'm so sorry for how I behaved. I've been so selfish, and it's been my biggest regret that I disappeared from your life to come and live here. I hope you can forgive me. I want nothing more than to be here for you."

Brendan's heart bloomed, overjoyed at the words he'd waited so long to hear. He and Eliza climbed arm in arm to the Cristallo Café, situated below a centuries-old monastery hewn into the mountainside, and sat near a stone wall that cradled tables against the cliffs.

"How long will you stay?" Eliza sipped her espresso.

Brendan shrugged lightly. "No particular plans. I wanted to see you, and beyond that, I'm in no hurry to leave Amalfi."

"It is breathtaking, isn't it?" Eliza's oversized sunglasses turned toward the sea. "Tomorrow, you must go to Erchie, the fishing village just beyond the point. They have a marvelous pastry tasting."

"I'll do that."

Sundrenched hours flew by as they chatted easily and lunched on local, fresh-caught seafood. Afterward, Eliza suggested they browse the downtown artists' quarter, a charming, cobbled maze of shops boasting cases and cases of sparkling glassware. The famed artisans of Vetri Maré, Glass by the Sea in English, had broken away from the Venetian tradition of glassblowing in the sixteenth century, leaving the Murano islands of northern Italy for the tiny port village in the south. Their delicate works were said to be even finer than the Murano multi-colored *millefiori*, its enameled *smalto*, or its milky *lattimo*.

In a shop tucked into a narrow alleyway Eliza greeted an elderly couple, her neighbors, who sat on low stools fanning themselves in the heat. She bought Brendan an exquisite violet bowl of *aventurine*, glass threaded with gold etching, and to display inside, three glass pomegranates that caught the light in a deep garnet shimmer.

Much later, carrying the bowl and pomegranates wrapped snugly in cocoons of Italian-printed newspaper, Brendan followed his mother up the steep stone stairs to her villa. Eliza served dinner on her terrace, shaded by a veil of bougainvillea and clusters of citrus trees gravid with fruit. Eliza patted Brendan's cheek, kissed his forehead. At sunset, Brendan took his leave, promising to visit again the next day. Eliza stood at her open door, waving goodbye as her son descended the stairs to return to his yacht in the bay for the night.

Now, he lay propped on his elbows on the deck of the yacht, gazing off into the distance, remembering the previous day with his mother. He thought, *How happy am I. I never expected this gift.*

"Honey?"

Brendan turned his head toward the low voice.

"I think I'm burning. Can you put some more lotion on my back?"

Brendan complied gladly. He sat up to face the sleek, bronze body of the woman stretched beside him on the deck with her head pillowed on her forearm, the rope of Christmas diamonds sparkling on her wrist, her face half hidden under a tangled cascade of dark hair. He reached over her for the tube of sunscreen, squeezed some onto his palm and, ever so gently, began to smooth it over the expanse of her sun-warmed skin. His fingers took a well-traveled path: above the twin peaks of shoulder blades, down into the dips between ridges of ribs, and down, down, over the bony line of vertebrae, until he encountered the unforgiving boundary of a bikini bottom.

Dylan let out a soft sigh. "Ummm."

The sound spurred him to continue. He squirted another dollop of lotion between his palms and laid both hands on her shoulders to work the kinks from the damp nape of her neck. In profile, her eyes fluttered shut and a smile played about her lips. He massaged the muscles of her upper arms and from there trailed an inch or two down her sides. His fingertips brushed lightly, so lightly, over the swells of her breasts where they escaped the confines of her bikini top, then slid an inch under the thin fabric.

Another sigh escaped her lips, and almost of their own accord, Brendan's fingers glided along the silky skin, down her sides and back up again, each time slipping a little deeper under the red triangles of her bikini top, until at last she raised her torso to give him full access. He pulled the string on her back and slid his hands under her, groaning aloud as her breasts filled his palms.

Her top fell away as she rose onto her knees and leaned her back into his chest, reaching' up to glide her fingers through his hair. As he continued to caress her hardening nipples, she rocked against his lap, her arms still above her head. Then she caught one of his hands and guided it over the plains of her stomach, into the wet valley below.

Purring like a cat, she fell forward onto her elbows, arching her spine, raising her backside enticingly. He'd grown achingly hard, his erection straining upward. He hooked a finger into the red bow at her hip, yanked open the ties, and tossed aside the piece of fabric. Knelt between his wife's knees to enter her.

Just then, she swung her head sideways, twisting to meet his gaze.

An anguished cry tore from his throat.

In his dream the face morphed, mutated—until the one staring back at him belonged to Shawn Unger.

The sound of wind chimes gradually penetrated the ringing in his ears, and Brendan surfaced from his thoughts to find himself still seated across from Dr. Aldrich. He became embarrassingly aware of the heat reddening his cheeks.

"We only have another few minutes if you want to tell me about the dream. What kind of predator this time?"

Me, thought Brendan, as he stood up and shrugged into his coat, brushing the tears away with a sleeve. He let himself out of the office quietly, aware of Dr. Aldrich's perplexed expression as he left.

Brendan knew he'd changed and clearly, so had his dreams. Instead of forcing him to face monsters, his dreams now seemed to be forcing him to face himself.

And he knew something else, too. This would be his last session with Dr. Aldrich and his wind chimes.

Dr. Aldrich tapped a finger against his pursed lips as the door closed behind his patient. Absently, he reached for the vibrating phone in his drawer. He pushed down the taste of bile as news of yet another stinging loss, this time at Santa Anita Park in Arcadia, California, appeared on his screen. Almost immediately, though, the phone jangled and the screen changed to read, "Leslie." *Goddammit.* The last thing he needed right now was his wife calling to nag. He declined the call but just moments later, another call came through, this time from an unknown number. "William Aldrich," he snapped. The unfamiliar voice on the other end started to speak. As Dr. Aldrich listened, the beginnings of a smile appeared above his goatee.

"Thanks for coming by on such short notice. I wanted to talk to you in person," Dylan said, sitting beside Brendan on her couch. He was quiet today, more than usual, and flustered; even Elvis, laying at their feet, kept one eye on his master. "I've been trying to find others who can substantiate the allegations. Anyone who might come forward with information."

Brendan couldn't meet her eyes. His cheeks flamed with snippets of his dreams, dreams of her that had been recurring, in one form or another, for weeks. "Like who?"

Dylan waited a beat before speaking. "Bobby."

Brendan paled.

"I sent him a link to the article about the lawsuit." Dylan reached for a folder from the table in front of her, and set it on her lap. "He lives in Maine now."

"Maine?"

"Yes, in Brunswick. He's been a college professor for the past nine years." Seconds
icked by in silence.

"A professor," Brendan said at last. "What does he teach?"

"Macroeconomics."

"Is he married?"

Dylan nodded and anticipated the next question, adding, "With three teenaged children." She opened the folder and slid out a holiday portrait: Bobby and his family. She passed it to Brendan, who stared at it silently.

Poor Brendan, Dylan thought, her heart twisting. His childhood friend, who'd survived similar abuse, had gone on to lead a seemingly normal life. *It must be torture for him, to know how much he's missed.*

"Good. Good for Bobby." Brendan looked up from the portrait and stared out the window at a February snowfall. "Did he agree to testify?"

"Well... no, he didn't. He said he wants to leave the past in the past. He said he'd never told his wife or kids about private school, and it sounds like he was anxious to keep them from knowing."

"I can't blame him."

"So, not a great development for us. Our case would be so much stronger if more witnesses came forward. I've been trying to subpoena some of the others. Unfortunately, I haven't had much luck." Dylan handed over the next photograph, a candid shot. It showed a distinguished-looking black gentleman in a suit, trench coat, and hat, standing in front of an arched door and tall, wrought iron gates. There were armed guards on both sides of it.

"Allen graduated from Torburton Hall and went on to university in Cambridge. He has remained in the United Kingdom ever since, as a career civil servant on Downing Street. He's called a Spad—that is, he's acted in various special advisory positions. Allen is personally close to the sitting prime minister. His aide made it clear it wouldn't be in Allen's best interests to be 'caught up in a scandal' like this. Apparently, he's in line to be chief of staff."

Brendan nodded, unsurprised. "I always pictured Allen doing something like that. He was so smart, so elegant, even back when we were young. Thank goodness Torburton didn't manage to steal that from him."

"And I left a message for Shawn."

"You did?"

"Yes. As you probably know, Shawn runs a number of companies in Silicon Valley. Another one of his startups is going through an IPO."

"I'm happy for him, that he's been so successful."

"I'm hoping he'll agree to be deposed."

Dylan stood up from the couch and paced back and forth. "The defense will have lots of witnesses. They'll certainly call Torburton's current headmaster—actually, headmistress. A woman named Margaret Maynard who will, of course, explain how different and wonderful the school is these days. They'll find current students who will rave about the place, who will testify to never having experienced or even seen abuse. Members of the board will explain their strict codes of conduct and reporting requirements. Teachers will talk as if they're present-day saints.

"I want you to know that I placed a call," Dylan added slowly, "to Jack's parents."

Brendan's head snapped up. "You'd put them on the stand? That would be terrible for them, wouldn't it?"

"I know testifying would be painful. But don't you think they might want retribution for their son's death? I know I would."

"Isn't there anyone else we can count on?"

"Galloway passed away a long time ago or I would've compelled him to testify. Greer suffered a series of strokes; he's too far gone to help. And there's the upperclassmen. The boy you called Popeye, I traced him to New Zealand, where he's been living."

"How about Hank?"

"I called. Whoever I spoke to said he couldn't take the phone. I'll keep trying." Dylan paused by the couch. "Then there's Chad Hubert, who is… um, technically… still living in the area. But there's one snag: he's in prison."

"What?" Since their meeting a few months earlier, there'd been no word from Chad. Brendan worried that he might reach out, try to get more money from him. Or that the police would get wind of the transaction. But no. And the cardboard box was still taped shut in his bedroom. "Why?"

"It appears he broke into his parents' house and tried to crack their safe. A silent alarm went off and the police caught him in the act."

Brendan shook his head. At the bar, Chad admitted to burning through his trust and needing money. But this? *Jail?*

Dylan continued. "There is Scott Williams, who I believe is still local, and I'm calling tomorr—"

"Absolutely not."

"I'm sorry?"

Under no circumstances would they ask Scott to testify, Brendan said emphatically.

Dylan seemed confused, but Brendan remained adamant: Scott was a minor player in the cast and wouldn't be of value, he said.

But he was a witness to what happened, Dylan argued.

Brendan refused again. When he stood, he swayed, and Dylan reflexively put out a hand to steady him.

"I'm fine." He felt the heat of her touch in a slow burn and shoved his fingers—the ones she'd brushed against—deep into the pocket of his jeans. "Let me know if there's any more news."

As Tomasz eased the car over patches of ice in the driveway, Brendan cursed himself. *Idiot,* he later wrote in his journal. *You and your stupid, impossible dreams. Your family is lost. Not even a mother. No one to love, no one to love you back. No job with coworkers who say good morning good night have a good weekend see you Monday. No cheering at hockey games or prom pictures of a pretty daughter. Never a normal life.*

And especially, you will never have Dylan James. She might be your lawyer, your advocate, even your friend.

But you will never have her in the way you want.

CHAPTER TWENTY-ONE

Over the next few weeks, as snow piled over Summer's Pond and the fierce Atlantic winds ripped through bare branches, Brendan thought about the life he'd once had, long ago, before he'd stepped foot on Torburton soil. The loss permeated him. He thought about other boys at other institutions. Many had been victimized, had experienced trauma like he had, but they'd gone on to live rich and meaningful lives. Why hadn't he? Was he the exception? Why did the events of youth dictate adulthood for some but not others?

Brendan resolved to focus on the upcoming court case. And he filled himself with dogged determination to heal. He vowed to stoke the spark that had brought him this far, from an empty shell of a person to a functioning, feeling man. He would do it for Zac.

Each day, he devoted several hours to feeling better. He bundled Elvis into warm, doggie tartan and trudged around his village to explore new neighborhoods. He converted an unused bedroom into a home gym, purchased weights and cardio equipment, and hired a trainer to come weekly. He tried meditation and yoga. He listened to self-help podcasts and read stories of recovery. With sheer force of will, he toughened that part of his constitution that had softened from confident boy into Jell-O.

One afternoon, Tomasz skidded over a patch of black ice, nearly smashing into an oncoming car before sliding off the road into a snowbank.

"That was close," Brendan gasped from the back seat. "This car isn't safe. We should be driving a four-by-four with better traction. I'd feel terrible if something happened to you or your mother." The next afternoon, he went to the local dealership. When he left, the salesman stood happily waving after him, all smiles.

Meanwhile, Brendan's dreams of reuniting with his mother continued. And so did his dreams of holding Dylan in his arms.

Over that same timeframe, Dylan doggedly handled her lawyerly tasks. One day, in early March of 2016, she clicked on her inbox, filled with the usual messages: A couple communications regarding the Workers' Comp claim; an invitation to attend a law society luncheon; a petition demanding a ban on assault rifles, to which she added her name; a thirty percent-off coupon for Macy's spring sale. And then she saw it: an email from Connecticut Superior Court. Notification of an electronic filing. Dylan opened the docket shakily, quelling the tiny voice that begged her to cancel the whole thing.

A date had been assigned: Monday, June 6th, just over three months away. The long series of pleadings and motions filed by both sides had led to this moment: the court deemed the case eligible for trial. Dylan picked up her cell phone, intending to call Brendan but dialing a different number instead.

"Dad," she said, hearing the quake in her voice when he answered. "We have a date for trial."

A flurry of activity ensued between the arrival of the notification in Dylan's inbox and the beginning of the trial. While Dylan and Brendan had been prepping for this all along, Dylan now brought her client to the modern building in Stamford with its signature circular sculpture in front and showed him around, familiarizing him with the courtroom setting.

She launched into the trial prep phase of the case in earnest, compiling detailed documents. Emailed questions and answers flew back and forth from a bevy of witnesses she'd collected and, of course, from Brendan. According to the results of those writings, she summarized depositions.

Who was on staff at Torburton Hall at the time Brendan attended? Besides his, were there any other allegations of abuse? She subpoenaed logs from the infirmary. Complaints to the administration. Minutes from board meetings. She peered anywhere and everywhere for evidence of wrongdoing.

Investigative work kept the computer glowing long into the nights, until words on the screen blurred and Dylan's bleary eyes stung. Each new witness she identified, every individual connected to the case who could corroborate her client's stories and support his claims, left her exhilarated. And every roadblock filled her with frustration.

The strategy she'd been plotting in her mind began to take shape on paper. How would she present her case? She wrote and whittled and polished her opening remarks. She planned the order of witnesses. She even coordinated her outfits, mixing and matching what she'd wear each day, down to her lipstick and shoes. She'd leave nothing to chance.

Still, as spring beat back the gray of winter and erupted in triumphant colors, Dylan spent many sleepless nights staring into the dark and listening to the whir of her ceiling fan. On the other side of her paper-thin wall, the couple from the neighboring apartment continued to bicker relentlessly, hurling insults. "Son of a bitch," the wife shrieked. "Whore," the husband spat. Little grenades lobbed back and forth that exploded in Dylan's ears.

You never knew what people were capable of, she thought. *Until you did.*

Mortimer and Dylan rocked side by side on the deck, surrounded by a profusion of blossoms—lilacs, azaleas, and rhododendrons—all in full bloom. The garden looked fairy-tale charming and smelled sweet. Over tea, they discussed the case.

"But why haven't they offered to settle yet?" Dylan fretted. "Do they think they have an airtight case?"

"Remember, it's a big firm with lots of resources at their disposal," Mortimer said.

The jangle of a cell phone interrupted the quiet. A Connecticut number appeared on Dylan's screen. "It's them," she said, reading the name on display.

"Don't be surprised if they throw out an obscenely low number."

Dylan's fingers shook as she connected the call. Mortimer set down his cup and peered at his daughter, listening to the one-sided conversation until she disconnected.

"It's just as you said. They offered five hundred thousand."

"Laughable."

"And conditional on non-disclosure."

Mortimer scoffed. "Brendan will never go for that. Even if the settlement was substantial, he wouldn't agree. It's never been about the money for him—he wants the perpetrators punished and their crimes brought to light."

"I know. I'll have to present the offer to him anyway."

Mortimer resumed his rocking. "So. Who's hearing the case?"

"Aberdeen."

Mortimer slowed.

"What is it?" Dylan frowned. "Is there something I should know about Judge Aberdeen?"

Mortimer measured his words. "Fred's fair-minded but sharp-tongued, known for his impatience with inexperienced attorneys and his particular dislike of the female ones. Nothing overt. Nothing that could label him biased, certainly. But his dismissive tone and hint of contempt speaks volumes about his subtle disdain for women in law."

Dylan let out a groan. "Terrific. We got a misogynist. How old is this guy?"

"Early seventies, probably."

"Not that much older than you." Dylan poked her dad playfully. "But light years less evolved."

Mortimer laughed. "We can't all be Mortimer James." Father and daughter grinned at each other, until the moment of levity passed. "I think Fred despises anything he perceives as weakness."

Great, Dylan thought. *How's he going to feel about me... or Brendan?*

PART FOUR

2016

CHAPTER TWENTY-TWO

As expected, her client rejected the settlement offer. Now, after months of late nights and sleepless weekends, the morning of June 6th dawned, a day carefully chosen by the courts so that if all went well, the entirety of the trial could take place without any intervening holidays.

Dylan dressed in her navy suit and nude heels, gathered her hair into a low bun at her nape, and clasped the bracelet onto her wrist. She raised her cuff and stared at the diamonds in the mirror, watched them glitter with the slightest wave of her hand, saw them throw shards of white. She breathed in their light and imagined them as a source of strength before tugging down her sleeve. There. She looked capable. She looked like the kind of attorney who knew what she was doing. In fact, she looked a lot like her mom. She imagined her mom gazing down at the proceedings and vowed to make her proud.

Arriving early at the courthouse, Dylan laid out her belongings as she passed through security. Brendan wouldn't be present for this morning's proceedings and, as she climbed the stairs, Dylan didn't recognize a single colleague or acquaintance. She rounded a corner. Her father, standing in the hallway, smiling and dapper, was a welcome sight. "Hey!" she exclaimed. "How did you get here so fast?"

"I am familiar with the train," he told her wryly, kissing her cheek. "Did you think I'd be late on this important day?"

"Thanks, Daddy," she murmured. His solid presence gave her an immediate boost. *Like a dose of Five-Hour Confidence*, she thought. Too bad he couldn't bottle the stuff.

Twenty minutes later, they filed into the courtroom.

Showtime.

Approaching her chair, Dylan scoped out the defense team from the Hartford-based law firm Sabato, Warwick, and Kohn, widely known as bulldogs in their field. The principals were flanked by young associates whose names she didn't know, and what looked to be a row of underlings seated behind. So many of them! She glanced over her shoulder toward her father, where he stood chatting with another attorney. Mortimer nodded and quietly moved to the empty chair beside her.

The bailiff called everyone to order. "All rise." Everyone stood as the judge swept in, prominent bald spot shining under the lights, black robe swirling around his legs. The bailiff waited for the judge to settle himself in his seat on the raised dais before he continued. "Superior Court is now in session, the Honorable Frederick Aberdeen presiding. Please be seated."

Fred Aberdeen cleared his throat and bowed his chin to his chest, making the pink patch of skin atop his head clearly visible. It looked like a Cyclops eye surrounded by coarse lashes.

Aberdeen was the last judge Dylan would have chosen to try her case, but now he cleared his throat one last time. "Good morning, ladies and gentlemen. Calling the case of Brendan Rainier Cortland versus Torburton Hall Academy for Boys. Counselors, you may state your appearance for the record."

Dylan stood tall. "Dylan James and Mortimer James, representing the plaintiff," she said, before sitting straight-backed.

Warwick rose lazily. "Vincent Sabato, Sidney Kohn, and Robert Warwick for the defense, Your Honor."

"I whooped your butt back in the day, isn't that right, Bob?" Aberdeen said affably, sharing a low chuckle with the men.

"The tobacco case." Warwick shrugged helplessly toward the bench. "You've never let me live it down, Your Honor."

"And never will." Aberdeen wagged a playful finger, then turned to Dylan. His genial manner cooled a degree. "Are you ready to proceed with voir dire, Miss James?"

Dylan swallowed her irritation. Who used "Miss" anymore? "Yes, Your Honor."

"Proceed."

The bailiff opened a door to an anteroom, and the pool of potential jurors filed into the room. Male and female, old and young, various ethnicities. From this pool, the two sets of attorneys were to choose six impartial men and women and a couple alternates in case someone dropped out. Hours passed as the candidates took the stand and were questioned one by one. The lawyers probed to see who might have an innate bias that would prejudice against one side or the other. The final selection was vital to both the plaintiff's and defendant's cases. At this point, it was anyone's guess what the jury box might look like.

Dylan appraised the assortment of middle-aged white men who, she suspected, might be more sympathetic to the school administrators. She used one of her allotted peremptory challenges to reject one without identifying why. Were any of the candidates teachers? There were two. One was a gym teacher, whom Dylan thought might be a problem... would he identify, on some level, with Terence Dunlop? The other, a young woman, taught history. Dylan thought she might be more sympathetic toward Brendan. Maybe women would be more sympathetic to the plight of the victims in general? Critical thinking, she reminded herself, pushing her mind back to the lessons of law school. She rejected the gym teacher and accepted the historian. On and on the selection went, with both sides asking carefully constructed questions. Dylan knew enough to suspect that there would be one difficult juror, one hold out. Even if the profile of the final jury looked perfect on paper, it wouldn't necessarily work that way in real life.

After two days of voir dire, the jury was selected: three women, two men, and one person by the name of Lem, whose gender seemed to be fluid. Dylan imagined that Lem might have been bullied in school and would empathize with the victims in this case. Secretly, she pinned her hopes on Lem.

The next day, Wednesday, Dylan arrived early in court. Brendan was supposed to meet her in the lobby, but he was nowhere in sight. Her heart raced as she passed through security. Her knees quaked under her skirt as she climbed the stairs. Her palms felt clammy, and she headed straight for the ladies' room to wash. For a moment, she leaned on the sink to breathe.

Today, it began in earnest.

And Brendan was late. She sent him yet another text. *Almost here?* she typed.

No answer.

For the hundredth time, she wondered if he'd changed his mind. If, after all these months, his terror and dread had won. Maybe the shards of his spirit couldn't be glued together. She had no way to assess the situation. She hadn't seen him, actually, for days.

We have to go into the courtroom, she added. *Come as fast as you can.*

Minutes later, Brendan still hadn't shown up. Reluctantly, after letting everyone else from the hallway precede her, Dylan slipped through the door and slid onto her seat at the wooden table with her father.

"Where is he?" Mortimer asked in a low voice. The empty chair between them gaped like an open mouth.

The bailiff stepped up to call the courtroom to order and ask everyone to rise. Just then, the door opened and a man entered. Dylan blinked.

It was Brendan. Or rather, a new version of him. His hair had been stylishly cut. The distinguished silver at his temples matched the silvery sheen of the expensive, pinstriped suit tailored to fit his newly trim form. His light tan contrasted with the frosty white shirt at his neck and the platinum of an expensive watch on his wrist, the one his father had given him so many years ago. He strode into the room and stood behind the empty chair at Dylan's side.

"You look…" Dylan felt flustered. Then annoyed. "But you're late. We thought you weren't going to show."

Judge Aberdeen cleared his throat, his Cyclops eye surveying the courtroom until he raised his chin. "Are both sides ready?"

"Yes, Your Honor," the attorneys said in chorus.

With a curt nod, Aberdeen turned his stern expression to address the members of the jury. He instructed them not to discuss the case with friends, family, or each other. He instructed them not to read media reports. He instructed them not to talk at all, in fact, until they were sequestered in the jury room.

Then Aberdeen asked the clerk to swear in the jury. A pale, thin man came forward. "Will the members of the jury please stand and raise your right hand?" he said in a high voice. "Do each of you swear that you will fairly try the case before this court, and that you will return a true verdict according to the evidence and the instructions of the Court, so help you God? Please say 'I do.'" He waited for the collective agreement. "You may be seated."

Aberdeen raised his eyebrows toward Dylan. "Well then, Miss James. You may proceed with your opening statement."

CHAPTER TWENTY-THREE

The moment Dylan had prepared for these many months had arrived. Her heart stuttered, and she stood up clumsily, bumping against the edge of the table in her haste. *Breathe*, she told herself, catching her hands behind her back to hide her trembling fingers, surprised by her own nervousness.

In front of her the jury sat in its box, six sets of eyes trained expectantly on her. For a moment, black spots swam in her field of vision and her mind went blank. She couldn't do this. Why had she ever thought she could?

"Miss James?" An impatient voice came from the bench.

Dylan swallowed and forced a sound from a throat clamped shut. "Your Honor, m-members of the Court, ladies and gentlemen of the jury... thank you for c-coming today," she began, hearing the stumbles. The words spilled out fast, and her voice sounded mechanical in her own ears. She thought briefly of her father behind her and her mother above. She glanced at the barely-visible glitter on her wrist. She would *not* fail the people counting on her.

The sentences she'd memorized and rehearsed all spring slowly emerged.

"Over the next days and weeks, you will hear stories of events that date back to the 1980s, stories about monsters, stories that are so horrifying you will have trouble believing they are true. But they *are* true." Her voice steadied, warming to the subject. "These are stories of abuse that occurred at Torburton Hall Academy for Boys, an exclusive and very expensive private school located in Calvert, Connecticut, an institution that charged thousands upon thousands of dollars for the privilege of attendance. This school had a fiduciary duty—not to mention a moral obligation—to protect its students.

"But monsters roamed the halls of Torburton... monsters disguised as older students, teachers, administrators, even the headmaster himself. The children who entered Torburton were just fourteen or fifteen years of age, innocent and vulnerable to physical assaults by the older students. And they were easy prey for pedophiles. When you hear of the horrors inflicted on these children—horrors such as forced drug and alcohol use, sodomy and fellatio, group masturbation, and yes, rape—you will think it impossible.

"You will think to yourselves, there's no way this evil could have happened. Surely someone in a prestigious school like Torburton would have intervened, would have protected these defenseless children. But you would be wrong. I will show you how no one came to the rescue of these boys—not the staff, not the administration, not even the Board of Trustees. Even though all of them... down to the very last one... knew about what the monsters were doing. *And not one of them did anything to stop it!*"

Dylan paused. She'd become so thoroughly wrapped up in her own indignation that she found herself bracing her hands on the jury box and almost shouting. The courtroom echoed with her sudden silence. Now, she straightened. Very deliberately, she raised an arm, the arm that glinted with the diamond rope, to gesture toward the plaintiff's table. She lowered her voice, almost to a whisper. The six members of the jury leaned forward to hear.

"Over there sits Brendan Cortland, a victim of this ongoing, relentless abuse. As a child, he suffered rampant serial molestations and assaults that you and I can't begin to fathom. Because of that abuse, Brendan Cortland is a broken man." Dylan followed the jury's gaze over her shoulder, to see what the jury saw. To Brendan.

With a start, she realized Brendan didn't look broken. Not anymore. She looked with new eyes to see him as the jury did: a strikingly handsome, wealthy man.

Preternaturally still, yes, but what she knew to be extraordinary shyness and reticence could very well be interpreted as quiet confidence. A powerful and self-contained man.

Suddenly, Dylan realized that nothing about him resembled the fragile husk who'd crept into her office a year ago. His yearlong "makeover" had improved his looks, yes. But she wasn't fooled. He might look polished on the outside, but inside he was as fragile as ever.

She wished the jury could have seen him then. Her eyes shifted to her father, seated at her table. Mortimer gave her a meaningful look. What was he trying to tell her? She swallowed down a moment of panic. She hadn't accounted for this. She needed to improvise. She needed to make the jury see beyond the polish.

"The man you see before you looks very normal, doesn't he? Well-dressed, well-groomed, handsome." From the corner of her eye, Dylan saw that all the members of the jury were appraising her client. "Well, let me tell you about Brendan. Last summer, a ghost of this man shuffled into my office, so terrified, so anxious, that he couldn't even look me in the eye. He was a mess. He spoke in a whisper. He hadn't been outside of his home, except to go to his psychiatrist, in years. That's right. *Years.* Physically, he was overweight and pudgy. His wife divorced him years ago and he is estranged from his only son. *All* of which was a result of his childhood abuse. You see, he closed himself off, tried to protect himself from a world he considered dangerous and predatory. Brendan Cortland was so broken that he couldn't stand to be touched by another human being. In fact, in the eleven months we've worked together, we have *never even shaken hands.*"

Dylan glanced at the jury. Some looked at Brendan with overt sympathy, others reserved judgment for the moment. It was hard to decipher the expression on Lem's face. Dylan raised her palms.

"So, even though the man you see here may look whole, he is far from it. He is shattered. As fragile as ever. It's not always easy for outsiders to see the turmoil inside a person, no matter how calm, how put-together they may appear." This last part she uttered standing in front of Lem. "I hold Torburton Hall accountable for all of it. The one thing, the only thing, that will help put Brendan back together again is justice. For him, and for all the other innocent boys who were victimized at that school.

"For him to know that the crimes he suffered will be exposed and brought out into the light, and the cloak of secrecy will be thrown open... that is justice. When the perpetrators—the child molesters and batterers and bystanders—are punished in a court of law... *that* is justice."

Mortimer gave her a single nod that brimmed with approval as she slid back into her chair. Dylan felt flushed and warm, triumphant... especially after hearing Brendan's all-but-inaudibly whispered, "Thank you."

A few feet away, Bob Warwick slowly stood up, his suit jacket straining over his immense torso. He leisurely straightened a few papers on his desk, as if the Court had all the time in the world to wait. *He looks like a giant sloth*, Dylan thought, what with his bushy eyebrows over droopy eyes and almost lazy movements intended to impart an air of repose. Watching him made her want to curl up in a hammock to snooze away the afternoon.

Warwick's indolent manner, cultivated over years at trial, lulled witnesses into such a relaxed state that he often caught them unawares. Now, he moved to stand in front of the jury with practiced ease, and sleepily blinked at each man and woman in turn.

"Well." He shook his head with a harrumph. "That was something, wasn't it? A story of devils and demons. Of a man in pieces, a Humpty Dumpty who needs to be put back together again… by you. But even Ms. James expects that you won't believe this story. She said so herself. Perhaps that's because it's not entirely true." Warwick paced slowly, measuring his thoughts as if they'd just occurred to him. "Now, don't get me wrong. The last thing in the world these fine educators at Torburton Hall would want is for a boy to be hurt. *Any* boy. And they take these allegations very, very seriously. But, ladies and gentlemen, consider these points."

Warwick held up an index finger. "First, the alleged abuse dates back to 1982. That is over *three decades ago.* No one, not a single person, from the administration or staff or Board of Directors from the 1980s still works at or is attached to Torburton Hall. Not even a lunch lady. The Torburton Hall of today is a vastly different legal, financial, and governance entity than it was thirty years ago. The alleged abusers aren't there anymore. The people who *are* there are innocents." Now he held up two fingers. "Second, why would Mr. Cortland—why would anyone—wait so long to come forward? Waiting, in fact, almost until the statute of limitations ran out? Perhaps because this was a very calculated decision on the part of a not-so-broken man." He unfurled another finger. "Third, what does he stand to gain from this lawsuit? Ask yourselves, why is it that this wealthy man would pursue this kind of monetary action? He may insist that he doesn't need the money and is just looking for justice. A noble cause, right? That's what Ms. James would have you believe. However, I submit to you that there is another reason for this eleventh-hour lawsuit: Mr. Cortland is not as wealthy as they may want you to think. In fact, he's nearing the brink of bankruptcy, and a simple review of his financials will substantiate that."

A ripple ran through the length of the courtroom. Dylan's neck prickled. She allowed herself a sideways peek at her client. He looked stricken.

Warwick waited several seconds for the murmurs to subside and shook his head sadly. "Abuse is a terrible thing. We cannot, and do not, condone any word or deed that diminishes or harms a child in any way. But our legal system itself is jeopardized when unsubstantiated claims are allowed to fester. We have a responsibility to the courts and to our nation to ensure that bogus claims do not overshadow real ones." He gave a little bow and returned to his seat.

On the bench, Aberdeen nodded curtly. His expression was hard to read, but Dylan suspected that he'd enjoyed Warwick's opening remarks.

She called her first witness.

Irma and Tomasz sat on a bench in the hallway and stared ahead at the wall. They'd talked about the trial, after Brendan's attorney had first told them they'd have to testify. Irma turned to look at her son in his tight-fitting suit, wondering what he was thinking, wondering if he was *ever* thinking. This was her son, a silent, hulking presence in her life for over fifty years, who spoke English without an accent when he chose to speak at all, whose words were emotionless. He did whatever his mother asked of him but had revealed nothing of himself to her. He'd been like this from the very beginning, she thought, from that terrifying night in the snow in Lesc when millions of mole-faced sperm had coursed through her with their heads jutting out of their microscopic bodies.

A bailiff poked his head into the hallway and called her name.

Irma stood and entered the courtroom, her coarse hair in its customary braid, her features expressionless, as if she were standing at the sink washing dishes rather than testifying in a court of law. She stepped into the witness box, laid her hand on a Bible, and swore not to lie.

Dylan approached. "Good morning, Ms. Czaryi," she said. "Thank you for coming. I'd like to ask you a few questions regarding your employment in the Cortland household."

Irma nodded.

"What is your position?"

"Housekeeper. Cooking and cleaning, grocery shopping."

"Can you please tell us how long you have known Mr. Cortland, and how long you have worked for the family?"

"I know Mr. Brendan since he is boy. Mrs. Eliza hire me when I come to America."

"Was Kenneth Cortland, Brendan's father, alive when you started?"

"Yes."

"And you brought your son, Tomasz, to America?"

"He fifteen when I start to work in the house. He already strong. They hire him too. Pay him to work outside. Landscape, wash windows, shovel snow."

"What was Brendan like as a youngster?"

Irma softened. "Very sweet child. Happy and smart," she said. "In school he in the middle of attention. They start to call him prince of school. And he look like prince, too. Face like angel. And so good at sports! Mr. Brendan, he everything. *Everything.* Until he go to boarding school."

"What do you mean?"

"Even after just few months, at first Thanksgiving, he come home different." Irma shrugged.

"How so?"

"Nervous. Sad. And haircut... he look like he been in accident."

Dylan asked, "And after that first Thanksgiving, did things get better?"

Irma shook her head. "No. He quieter every time he come home. He... disappearing. Like a bucket with crack. All the life leaking out of him."

"Did you ever ask him what was wrong?"

"Not my place," Irma said. "Something bad, something terrible happen to him at that school. It change him. But I try to cheer him up. I cook him all favorite foods. Doesn't help. By the time he graduate he almost stop talking. He hardly ever go outside. He never see friends. No interest in nothing."

"But he got married?"

He married Heather, Irma told the Court with a sour expression. She thought he would be happy at last, but they divorced. She kept the house they'd bought together, and Brendan moved back home.

After a few more questions, Dylan thanked Irma and returned to her seat, indicating to Warwick that it was his turn. Warwick slouched in front of the witness box, hands in his pockets.

"Ms. Czaryi, you like your job?"

"Yes." Irma tilted her big chin toward Brendan. "Very much. Mr. Brendan quiet. Tomasz feel good there. I enjoy to cook."

"Very commendable, Ms. Czaryi. Do your friends—the other housekeepers in the neighborhood, I mean—do they feel the same way about their employers?"

"I not talk much with others," Irma said, wagging a finger. "They like chickens, always complaining. I am lucky one. Mr. Brendan not need much."

"Do your friends complain about money?"

"Yes," Irma said. Sometimes their checks were late, or they worked extra hours or weekends without pay, or the families made a big mess in their homes. Lots of complaining, she said.

"And how much does Mr. Brendan pay you?"

At this, Irma looked startled. "I… uh… not sure. Paycheck go straight to bank account. I think same as other housekeepers?"

Across the room, Dylan frowned, mentally urging Irma to remember what she'd been coached: *Only answer the question that is asked.*

"You just stated that you and your friends discuss money and paychecks, didn't you? Isn't it odd that you don't know your own salary?" Warwick pressed. "Well, let me tell you. You cleared one hundred and sixty-five thousand dollars last year. That is at least *double* what other maids earn, even in the most affluent neighborhoods. Does that surprise you?"

"Mr. Brendan very kind."

Across the room, Dylan bit her lip. Why hadn't she thought to ask about this?

"He is, isn't he?" Warwick smiled. "Can you please tell the jury how kind he was this past Christmas?"

Irma looked blank.

"For instance, did he give you anything?"

Irma licked her lips. "He give gifts."

"What gifts?"

Irma named them.

"Anything else?" Warwick probed.

Irma shifted uncomfortably in her seat. Aberdeen interjected. "Answer the question, please, Ms. Czaryi."

"He give bonus. I send for my sister. Ten thousand dollars." Her voice dropped.

"Ten thousand dollars." Warwick turned his back to Irma but continued to address her while facing the jury. "How generous. Would you say that is typical? I mean, do most maids you know receive that kind of money as a bonus?"

Irma dropped her chin to her chest. "I don't know."

Warwick looked confused, like he was trying to figure it all out in his head. "So... after years of silence, suddenly Brendan Cortland is your best friend? He gives you a huge sum of money just a few months before his trial is set to begin?"

"For Christmas..."

"An employer who pays you an excessive salary, with yearly raises and bonuses, and buys you exorbitant gifts... anyone would be crazy to jeopardize a job like that, isn't that right?"

"I don't know..."

"I mean, it would be in your best interests to keep that employer happy. For instance, to say things that might help him in a lawsuit?"

Dylan jumped to her feet to object, and Warwick withdrew the question. He said, "That's all for now, Ms. Czaryi."

Irma's too-large forehead creased into a frown.

Aberdeen glanced at Dylan. "Redirect?"

"Yes, Your Honor." Dylan returned to her spot in front of the maid, and requested that she tell the Court what Brendan had been like over the past year.

Irma's forehead smoothed. "After he begin meeting you, he change. He start going outside more. He talk, he smile, he watch what he eat. He adopt dog, they walk for miles together. They swim, they play. He getting better."

"Getting better?" Dylan echoed.

"Maybe telling you about bad men help him," Irma said. "He seem... lighter. Like cake rising in oven."

"How do you know there were bad men? And that he's been telling me about his past?"

Irma clamped her mouth shut.

"Mrs. Czaryi... please answer. You're under oath."

The woman glanced at the judge and collected her sweater around her shoulders. "From writing in journals. Mr. Brendan leave open. I read while clean."

"Ah." Dylan hadn't known this. She moved closer to the jury. "So you're telling us that since Brendan has been talking about the bad men, revealing the horrors of his past, he has been healing himself. That he has become healthier since he released some of the poison he's been carry—"

"The witness said no such thing," Warwick objected. "All we know for sure is that she snooped in his diary. The rest is conjecture."

Dylan said she had no more questions.

Irma frowned again. "I not lying."

Aberdeen looked down at her levelly. "Step down, ma'am. You are finished for now."

Dylan watched Irma make her way out of the witness box and across the room, avoiding looking in Brendan's direction. Aberdeen instructed Dylan to call her next witness.

Tomasz Czaryi entered the courtroom, looking stiff and unnatural in the suit and tie he'd worn at Christmas. He took Irma's place on the stand and was sworn in. Dylan couldn't help feeling a chill as he turned to her, just like the time outside the guesthouse. He was an intimidating man.

She forced her mind back to the present and began to ask questions. In answer, Tomasz testified to Brendan's isolation, his terror of the outside world and his cocoon-like existence. At least he was predisposed to giving one-word answers, which was a good thing, Dylan thought.

"And what do you do for Mr. Cortland?"

"Outdoor work. Driving. Errands," Tomasz said tersely.

Determined not to be caught off guard with this witness as she'd been with Irma, Dylan made it a point to ask Tomasz about compensation and the Christmas gifts he'd received from his employer. She thanked him and returned to her seat, and Warwick approached the hulk on the stand.

"I have a few questions, if you don't mind," he said, his tone friendly.

"Okay."

"Mr. Czaryi, tell me again… what is your annual salary?"

Tomasz stated the amount: ninety thousand dollars.

"Wow!" Warwick feigned surprise, turning to the jury. "Just for doing a few chores, and driving a guy to a psychiatrist once a week?"

Tomasz shrugged.

"And what kind of car have you been driving Mr. Cortland in?"

"Range Rover."

"Not a town car?" Warwick prompted, his droopy eyes nearly closed.

"He had a town car before. But it was slippery on the ice. He bought himself a Range Rover."

Warwick gestured with a hand. "Is that so? He bought just *one* Range Rover? Only one, for himself?"

A shadow passed over Tomasz's face, and his normal growl dropped even lower. "He bought… two."

Judge Aberdeen leaned forward. "Mr. Czaryi, please speak louder so the Court can hear."

Tomasz cleared his throat. "Two. One for him and one for me. Said he wanted me and my ma to be safe."

"And what did you think to yourself when Mr. Cortland bought you this extravagant gift?"

"Nothing. He's rich. He can do what he wants."

"Sounds like you've got a pretty good thing going with Mr. Cortland. If I had a cushy set-up like that, I'd sure want to keep it. Wouldn't you?"

"I guess."

"So whatever Mr. Cortland needs you to say, you'll say. Right, Mr. Czaryi? Withdrawn." Warwick smiled and sat down.

Dylan sprang up to face Tomasz. "Let's talk about your cushy set-up. Do you shovel snow all winter?"

"Yes."

"When did the household acquire a motorized snow blower?"

Tomasz estimated it was about five to ten years earlier.

"When I visited, it seemed to me there was an exceptionally long driveway in addition to a number of walkways and very, very long paths around the property. Did you shovel all that by hand up until five to ten years ago?"

"Yes."

"And the leaves... you raked them by hand before you had a leaf blower?"

"Yes."

"Lawn mowing?"

"Yes."

"Weeding and gardening?"

"Yes."

"Do you wash windows?"

"Three stories' worth. And I clean the chimneys, chop the wood, paint the exterior every few years, do the general repairs, and all exterior and interior maintenance."

Dylan turned to the jury. "Doesn't sound so cushy to me. No more questions."

CHAPTER TWENTY-FOUR

"Shit, shit, *shit*," Dylan cursed her reflection in the ladies' room. Her first two witnesses may have failed to advance her cause. But it wasn't their fault, it was hers. All hers. Why hadn't she recognized that Warwick would ask about how much Irma and Tomasz were paid, how much they'd been given? Of *course* Warwick would frame Brendan's generosity, and the Czaryis' loyalty, in a different light.

But what he'd said about Brendan being broke... well, even if it were true, it doesn't change the fact that I have to win this one. For him. I can't afford to let anything go wrong.

Even if she'd gotten off to a rocky start, this trial had only just begun. She'd have many opportunities to prove her case. Maybe she'd ask Irma and Tomasz to return. Dylan wet some paper towels with cold water and dabbed the back of her neck. She straightened her jacket and walked back down the hall to the courtroom, glancing at her diamond bracelet as she opened the door, as if to fortify herself.

"I know it seems a little bumpy right now," Dylan said, back in her office. "But I'm confident more people will come through." She chose her next words carefully. "I did put someone on the witness list who agreed early on to come, but she stopped returning my calls."

"Who?" Brendan stared out the window overlooking the back garden of the Chatwick house. "I thought no one wanted to."

"Your mother. I'm still hoping she'll make it."

Brendan digested that, picturing what it would be like to see her again. He was immediately struck by a scent memory of Houbigant's Quelques Fleurs, top notes of citrus, jasmine, lily of the valley, and rose, which Eliza had assumed as her signature perfume after the Princess of Wales wore it to wed Prince Charles.

"I doubt she'll come all this way for me. I doubt anyone else will testify, actually," he said dismally.

"That's where you're wrong." Dylan smiled. "Someone else did agree to testify: Nancy Smythe."

"*Nurse* Smythe?"

Dylan nodded. "She's alive and well, living in a retirement community in Oxford."

"Well, she definitely knew what was happening, at least with Galloway." Brendan spat the words out. "She knew, but she did nothing."

"Yes. Her inaction supports our claim of negligence and negligent infliction of emotional distress."

At the age of eighty-three, Nancy Smythe looked very much like she had at age fifty-three: the same gray curls, the same squint of her blue eyes behind thick, black glasses, the same bony hands that gripped the front of the witness box in which she sat.

"Tell us about the kinds of things you treated at Torburton Hall," Dylan said.

The woman's head bobbled slightly. "I have to think back," she said. "It's been many years. But if I remember correctly, it was mainly colds, stomach bugs, minor sports injuries... sprained ankles, concussions. You know how boys are. They play rough."

"Sometimes." Dylan continued, choosing her words carefully. "Any other injuries you can think of?"

"Well, I did bandage up quite a few cuts. And one night stands out in my mind: some seniors came banging on my door at midnight. They brought a poor freshman to the infirmary covered in bee stings. Fortunately, he wasn't allergic." Her head bobbled as she clucked her tongue sympathetically.

Dylan looked at her curiously. "There was a curfew. Why would they be out so late at night?"

"I don't rightly know. But his friends, those older boys, they looked right spooked. It's a wonder none of the others got stung."

"Did they say what happened?"

"Just that the little boy had been playing with a hive."

"Did you suspect that perhaps the older boys had a hand in the accident?"

Mrs. Smythe looked baffled.

Dylan continued. "You mentioned colds and bugs. Any other kinds of contagious conditions?"

"Well, you stir a couple hundred boys together in a pot like a boarding school, and like as not they're bound to catch everything under the sun."

"Such as?"

The nurse listed a few diseases: chicken pox, measles, the flu.

"How about impetigo?"

Mrs. Smythe nodded. "That one was a given. We had an outbreak almost every year."

"And what was the common treatment for impetigo?"

"Impetigo is an infection, so I administered antibiotics like amoxicillin or penicillin."

"By mouth?"

"That's right."

Asked if any medications were used topically, Mrs. Smythe said she used ointments to help heal the scabs.

Dylan crossed her arms in front of the witness box. "How about home remedies? Like honey?"

Mrs. Smythe clucked, her wattle wobbling like that of an old, indignant hen. "Yes, that one's been used for a hundred years. My own mother used to spread it on me and my brothers as children."

"But why would honey be used at Torburton Hall if oral antibiotics were available?" Dylan continued, drilling down.

"Some people didn't put too much stock in modern medicine, I guess." Mrs. Smythe shrugged. "It's hard to break with superstition."

"Do you recall anyone in particular who stuck with that tradition of using honey to treat impetigo?"

"Not that I recall."

"How about Headmaster Edward Galloway?"

Cluck, cluck. "Ah, that's right, now that you mention it. Ed Galloway, he used to slather the boys in the stuff. They'd come in, a sticky mess."

"And did you ever think it odd that Mr. Galloway spread honey, specifically, on the boys' genitalia?"

Mrs. Smythe shifted uncomfortably. "Well, now, I suppose he wanted to prevent the scabs from spreading."

"But you were administering oral antibiotics, you said, to treat the boys. Why would he want to go by an old wives' tale *in addition* to your treatment?"

No answer.

"Do you think that perhaps Edward Galloway enjoyed touching the boys at his school, and that's why he employed that particular remedy?"

A bony hand covered the old woman's mouth. "Good heavens," she said, her face etched in shock. "I'm sure he thought he was doing right by those boys. Even if he was misguided."

"Misguided? I'd say that touching their genitals was more than misguided." Dylan pursed her lips. She tried another tack. "Besides sports injuries, were there any other more serious injuries that you noticed at the infirmary? Specifically, any of a sexual nature?"

"I don't follow you."

Yes, you do, Dylan wanted to admonish. They'd gone over her testimony at length. The nurse had assured her she wouldn't be embarrassed on the stand.

"Mrs. Smythe, did you ever, while working at Torburton Hall, treat any child for an injury that appeared to be the result of a sexual assault?" Dylan asked.

"Well... over the years... but as I said before, they could be rough... and they were curious, you know..."

"Boys will be boys?"

The woman looked relieved. "*Exactly.*"

"Can you be specific, please?"

"Well, there was this boy from Spain, if I recall... he came in with his bottom, er, a bit bloody. His English wasn't very good so he couldn't explain it fully."

Dylan returned to her table, opened a folder, and quickly flipped through a few pages. "According to school records, there was a single boy from Spain who attended Torburton Hall, for one year in 1982. The records indicate that his English was, in fact, excellent. Would you like to rephrase your answer, perhaps?"

"Well... maybe it wasn't the language barrier then. I don't know how the accident happened if he didn't tell me."

"So, as the school nurse, you witnessed children—how old, fourteen? fifteen?—come in with injuries of a sexual nature. Injuries that you chalked up to 'curiosity' between boys. Did you ever report any of those injuries to the authorities? Did you ever call state child services, or send any of the boys to the hospital to be looked at by a doctor?"

Dylan's question was greeted by a short, heavy silence, then, "No."

"But you were aware, as a medical nurse, that by Connecticut law, you were legally bound to report such incidents? And by not reporting them, you were not only breaking the law, you were aiding and abetting child molesters?"

The woman sat back in her chair, as if to move as far from Dylan as possible. For the first time since she'd taken the stand, she looked uncertain. Frightened, even. "Edward always handled such matters."

"You discussed this issue with him?"

"At staff meetings, it may have been mentioned."

"Again, I ask you to be specific, please."

"Ed talked about the boys. Which ones were good looking, which ones were going through puberty, that sort of thing. He and Trish loved those boys."

"So I heard." Dylan glanced at the jury, hoping they could read her expression of irony. "And at these staff meetings, was the behavior of other teachers discussed? Dr. Nevin, for instance?"

On the stand, the witness flinched. "Yes, well, everyone knew Lawrence to be eccentric."

"By eccentric, you mean a rapist and pedophile?"

"Objection," put in Warwick.

"I'll rephrase. Knowing Dr. Nevin's predilections, was any attempt made by you or anyone else on staff to report or curtail his activities? To prevent him from being alone with the boys in his apartment?"

"Ed may have spoken to him once or twice, but Dr. Nevin was an excellent teacher. They were friends."

"Mrs. Smythe, did you ever have reason to believe that Brendan Cortland was being abused at Torburton Hall?"

She swept her arm to indicate Brendan, who sat motionless, eyes closed.

Nancy Smythe squinted in his direction from behind her black glasses, seeming to notice him for the first time. "If I remember correctly, he was a sad youngster. I never considered that he was being abused. I suppose it... wouldn't be impossible."

When it was Warwick's turn to question her, he simply rose heavily from his chair and held his heft behind his table, as if he knew he wouldn't be standing for long. He asked just one simple question.

"Mrs. Smythe, in the years that you acted in the capacity of nurse at Torburton Hall, did any student ever come to you saying he'd been raped or molested?"

Her answer, under oath, was a resounding, "Good Lord! No."

But she added, just after he sat down: "It was just horseplay. I'm sure that kind of thing went on at every such school."

CHAPTER TWENTY-FIVE

"Sweetheart. You're doing so well up there." Mortimer put an arm around his daughter's shoulders, enveloping her into a fatherly hug before she'd even stepped through the front door.

Dylan let herself be congratulated. "I admit, it's getting better." She burrowed in his shirt and breathed the familiar aftershave. "Even though Warwick shot down Irma and Tomasz. But Nancy Smythe seemed like she was questioning protocol. It may be the first solid point we scored since the beginning of the trial."

"I think you scored a few."

"It's so stressful, Dad. I'm… scared."

Mortimer didn't need to see his daughter's expression; he knew it well. He hooked a finger under her chin and tilted her face up to his. "Stop. Stop blaming yourself. What happened wasn't your fault. You did everything right."

"Mom died because of that trial."

"Mom died because she was sick. She'd started having headaches days earlier."

Dylan shook her head. Her narrative was ingrained.

"Listen to me," her father said. "Focus on the now. You are coming across as proficient, eloquent, sympathetic… and those are invaluable qualities in an attorney. Warwick may be more adept at manipulating the witnesses, but think how many more years of experience he has."

A long sigh escaped Dylan's throat. "But in the end, it's the witnesses who will convince the jury, not me."

Mortimer took Dylan's hand and led her down the hall and into the kitchen, where they sat down in their usual chairs, the ones in which they'd had more heart-to-heart talks than either could remember. "Don't underestimate yourself. And don't forget, you haven't even called our key witnesses yet... Dr. Aldrich has yet to testify. And, of course, so does Brendan. And nothing Warwick can say will dilute the effect of his truth."

Dylan rubbed her temples. "I hope you're right. I really, really hope so." Her cell phone dinged with a notification. She picked it up and scrolled through her emails. Suddenly, she stiffened. "Dad, you'll never believe this!" she exclaimed. "It's from Eliza Cortland. She's flying in!" She texted Brendan immediately. *I have news. Please call.*

"No response?" Mortimer asked after a while.

"No. I'll try again in a bit." Dylan stared at her phone. "Brendan disappeared from the courtroom so quickly yesterday that I didn't have a chance to speak with him, and my calls went to voicemail. I think Nurse Smythe's testimony upset him. Either that, or he's just disappointed in how I've handled the case so far."

"But hearing that his mother is coming to testify should cheer him up."

"I hope so."

In his office, Brendan yanked open drawer after drawer and pulled out unopened mail, anything postmarked from a bank or financial institution... everything he'd ignored for so long.

Barnaby Partners looked after all of it. They had for years. They paid the bills, and it all came from his inheritance, so that even after all the monthly expenses and the sizable cost of maintaining the waterfront mansion and grounds, the principal was substantial. His spending wouldn't make a dent. Or at least, that's what Brendan had always assumed. Unless, of course, Barnaby's investments had tanked?

His mind ticked off the most recent purchases: cars, diamonds, large cash withdrawals. They were just the tip of the iceberg. He'd never wondered about that particular iceberg before.

Was it true, what Warwick had said in his opening speech? Brendan jogged down the stairs to the kitchen. The counter was still bare. He turned, raced down the hall, flung open the front door and jogged over to the mailbox. Inside were several envelopes. He rifled through and tore one open, gaping at the numbers printed on the statement. His stomach clenched as the reality hit him. Impossible. No, no, *no*.

Fred Aberdeen sat in his chambers, a cramped affair of law books stacked on sagging shelves, too much furniture on a threadbare rug, yellow pollen collecting on the windowsill. It hadn't changed in decades, except for the grudging additions of a computer and printer on his old desk. He was feeling his age, that was certain... his joints were particularly arthritic in this blasted, humid June weather, from his aching knees up to his gnarled fingers. And to top it all off, his gout had flared up, making it hard to walk. Goddamn, he hated getting old... each day his body found new ways to flout him.

He turned his attention to the trial at hand and frowned. All these so-called victims parading through his courtroom... it boggled the mind, this political correctness gone haywire. Never mind that there were actual murderers and rapists and thieves out there who'd committed *real* crimes. These days, everyone was a victim of something. A single, misdirected joke at the water cooler and a perfectly good manager got fired for sexual harassment. Someone's sensitive little feelings were offended and suddenly it was a hate crime. And these entitled kids who didn't know how to stand up for themselves? They'd sue for this newfangled cyberbullying or some such crap and pocket a million dollars or more. Not like when he was growing up as an army brat, moving from base to base: he'd learned mighty quick that a swift kick in the nuts was the best defense.

And now this bullshit about emotional distress at a private school *thirty years ago*. A complete waste, as Warwick had pointed out, of judicial resources. Aberdeen looked at the witness list. It figured. That whiny little lawyer with a man's name would be calling a shrink to the stand to rattle off a few hours' worth of medical mumbo-jumbo.

God help him. Aberdeen stooped to the bottom shelf of his bookcase, reached for a bottle of scotch and a glass, and poured.

Leslie Aldrich leaned toward the bathroom mirror to apply a coat of eye shadow, her face immobile, barely acknowledging her husband's perfunctory kiss goodbye. She'd been furious when she found out about their drained retirement account and Maddy's depleted college fund, and after a solid week of screeching at her husband like a crazed owl, she hadn't bitten off more than a few words for months.

Never mind, William thought, straightening his bow tie. She wouldn't be angry for long. Things were getting better. He'd won his last few bets. And now, of course, he'd be paid for his expert testimony. Handsomely. He picked up his trench coat and briefcase and descended the stairs of the house on Chatwick Road.

Despite the downpour, Dylan's steps were determined as she entered the courthouse and shook the rain off her umbrella. Today would be a good day, she'd make sure of it. As she laid her wet belongings on a tray to be x-rayed and walked through the metal detector at the entrance of the building, she thought about this morning's proceedings. Today's witness, Dr. Aldrich, would mark a turning point in the testimony. She'd spent many an hour in the psychiatrist's office, discussing Brendan's history of pathology. The medical findings were rock solid.

On the stand, with his nearly-white goatee and close-cropped white hair—a blatant nod to Freud, Dylan thought—Dr. William Aldrich looked every bit the seasoned psychiatrist, right down to the round spectacles. She wondered if they were prescription or if he just wore them for effect.

"Please state your name and profession," she began, once he'd been sworn in.

He did, and rhymed off his credentials to boot—University of Virginia, Columbia and Johns Hopkins Hospital, Maryland. He said he'd been practicing psychiatry for nearly four decades and threw in a few awards, too.

"Can you tell the Court what sorts of problems people have come to you with?"

Dr. Aldrich leaned back, crossed his legs, and settled in. "In my career, I have treated a breadth of psychiatric conditions, from the most mundane to the most complex. Over the years, I've seen patients with compulsive disorders and attention deficits, anorexia nervosa, even amnesia. Many a dissociative personality has visited my office... pardon the pun." He smiled at his own humor. "I treated a paranoid schizophrenic who killed and cannibalized a homeless man. Another who insisted on mutilating himself and succeeded in cutting out his own tongue. Mothers with postpartum depression, one of whom tossed her baby off her balcony. A teen who'd learned how to build a bomb on the Internet and detonated it on his first day of high school, killing five classmates. The grieving parents of four of those classmates."

Aldrich paused to let his words sink into the jury before continuing. "Children who exhibited psychosis in the primary grades. Alcoholics. Addictions of all sorts. Heroin, food, sex, gambling." His eyelid twitched as he thought about a horse race the day before.

"That is quite a list."

"Just the tip of the iceberg."

"Is it fair to say that you're an expert in recognizing mental illness and in treating it?"

"Without question," the doctor said, trying to look humble.

Dylan turned to Aberdeen. "Your Honor, at this time I tender this witness as an expert in the field of psychiatry."

"You have the Court's permission to proceed."

"Thank you, Your Honor." Dylan returned to Aldrich. "Can you describe, please, what Brendan Cortland was like when you first met him?"

"Brendan first came to see me in 1990 as a young man of about twenty years of age. A common age for the onset of schizophrenia."

"What?" Dylan looked up from her notes. "Did you... did you diagnose him as schizophrenic?"

"At the time I did not. He presented with severe anxiety and depression, with all the associated symptoms."

"And why, exactly, did you believe that Brendan was so severely distraught?"

"His father had taken quite ill the year before Brendan started therapy."

Dylan frowned. Wrong answer. "Anything else, Doctor?"

"He was quite paranoid about Y2K, if I recall correctly. He thought the world would come to an end."

What the hell is he talking about? She tried again. "Would you say his condition was severe, and deteriorated rapidly?"

Aldrich nodded. "Yes, Kenneth Cortland had a heart attack that left him quite frail. In fact, he passed away soon after."

Dylan held up a palm. "No... Dr. Aldrich, I am asking about Brendan, not his father... whether *Brendan's* condition deteriorated."

"Ah... well, yes, of course Brendan was hit hard by the death of his father."

"But..." Dylan stopped in front of the stand and shook her head. "But besides the death of his father, why *else* did you think Brendan had come to see you?"

"The origins of his condition were not apparent at first. It was especially difficult in that as a young man Brendan was not communicative."

Dylan glanced at the jury. To her dismay, some of them seemed slightly bored. "Dr. Aldrich, are you familiar with the major motion picture called *Awakenings*, starring Robin

Williams and Robert De Niro? It came out some years ago." The jury seemed to perk up at a reference to popular culture.

"Yes, of course. That movie was set in a New York hospital in 1969 and depicted patients who'd survived the 1917-1928 epidemic of *encephalitis lethargic* and become catatonic as a result."

"And Brendan's condition became eerily similar to that of the patients in the movie?"

"Well, no, actually. As a product of Hollywood, that movie took many liberties with what happened, medically speaking. And, of course, Brendan had had no such infection. In fact, he was nothing like the patients portrayed in that film."

Dylan stopped her pacing and looked up at the witness box, frowning. "That's right... of course," she said haltingly. "Brendan didn't have encephalitis. But his condition was similar?"

"No, actually. Catatonia—the kind depicted in that movie—is much more severe than anything Brendan displayed. Those patients displayed muscular rigidity and mental stupor. They were unresponsive to stimuli."

When they'd rehearsed his testimony, it had been Dr. Aldrich's idea to equate Brendan's condition with the mainstream movie, to describe it in a way the jury could understand. Why was he going off script? Dylan tried to get him back on track. "But there were *some* similarities between Brendan and the patients in the movie?"

"No. They were brain-damaged, whereas Brendan functions quite normally."

"N-Normally?" Dylan sputtered.

"Yes, normally, within the confines of his own home in that he is perfectly capable of self-care, as is obvious. He reads books, he watches television. He's quite adept on the computer. He fathered a child and continues to support him."

"But… but… he didn't go outside for years. Except to see you."

Dr. Aldrich gestured toward Brendan, patiently explaining for the jury. "That's quite true. Agoraphobia— the fear of leaving one's home—is quite common."

This was not at all what they'd discussed. Dylan returned to the defense table, keenly aware of Brendan's penetrating stare boring into the side of her head as she stood beside him. She flipped through pages of notes, knowing she was keeping everyone waiting but trying desperately to find the section she and the doctor had discussed just last week.

On the bench, Aberdeen seemed to be getting impatient. "Miss James, if you are not prepared to question your own witness, I suggest you excuse him rather than keeping us all in suspense," he said.

"It's not necessary, Your Honor, I'm ready." Dylan crossed back to Aldrich holding up a page. "You recalled that Brendan showed, and I quote, '*echolalia, perseveration, and verbigeration.*' Can you please explain those words for the Court?"

"Those are medical terms that simply mean the repeating or echoing of words or nonsense syllables." Aldrich shrugged. "Not at all uncommon. And I specified that Brendan exhibited only *traces* of that symptomatology early on and that they disappeared very quickly."

"But what about what you called his flattened affect?"

"A common side effect of depression, Ms. James. You certainly don't smile much when you are down in the dumps, do you?"

Down in the dumps? It was all Dylan could do not to scream. Why would Aldrich use such a weak idiom? Before she could recover herself, Aldrich continued.

"Yes, Brendan seemed to me to have chronic depression, a condition that affects many of us, and even perhaps most of us, at some point in our lives. The World Health Organization estimates that three hundred million people globally suffer from depression. Here in the United States, one out of every six people experiences it, especially with the stressors in our modern society, like divorce."

Dylan bit her lip. She glanced back at Brendan, and then up at the judge. As she hesitated, Aldrich continued.

"Brendan's condition was characterized by feelings of sadness and worthlessness. Feelings which you yourself, I'm sure, have experienced. And I'm quite certain that if I were to poll the courtroom here today, most of us would admit to having had at some point in their lives."

For his part, up on the bench, Aberdeen was following along the testimony, and Miss James' reactions, closely. This morning's proceedings had taken an interesting turn.

"Your Honor," Dylan said. "I'd like to request a recess after all."

"We'll adjourn for lunch," Aberdeen said. Too bad. The morning had become more entertaining than he'd have guessed.

"In my opinion, I think you should hand him over to Warwick." Mortimer kept his voice low and murmured into Dylan's ear.

"What? How can I? He hasn't answered any of what we discussed." Dylan wrung her hands, looking up and down the hallway.

"And I don't think he will. The charts we subpoenaed don't date all the way back to Brendan's initial visits, and we gave Aldrich leeway on his notes because we assumed he'd support us. But in the meantime, I would suggest you let Warwick have a go at him so you'll know where you stand. Then you can resume with some clarity. Right now, he's a wild card."

Dylan bit her lip to keep it from trembling. Once again, her father was sure of how to navigate, able to see the correct way forward. Clarity? All she could see ahead of her was the murky darkness of dread.

Mortimer made his way through the rainstorm, stomach growling. He could have gone to a diner or deli or any of the pizza counters closer to the courthouse, the ones that were hopping at lunchtime on a weekday, with the suit-and-tie crowd streaming in from the courthouse district to grab a quick bite. But he'd been a stalwart at this hole-in-the-wall Asian place, where the owner's wife prepared Kung Pao chicken extra spicy, just for him. Mortimer chatted with the owner while he paid.

As he turned to pick up plastic cutlery, a familiar-looking head of white hair caught his attention. Mortimer squinted to focus his eyesight. The man turned, bringing his white goatee and round spectacles into view. Yes, there sat Dr. Aldrich at a table, enjoying a plate of noodles. Mortimer felt a visceral dislike for the man. He turned to leave the restaurant and nearly collided with Vincent Sabato on his way in. They nodded courteously at each other, and Mortimer headed back to the courthouse.

CHAPTER TWENTY-SIX

In his high voice, the courtroom clerk reminded William Aldrich that he was still under oath, and Warwick roused himself enough to amble over to the witness stand for the cross examination.

"Good afternoon, Dr. Aldrich." Warwick's droopy eyes were nearly closed, his eyebrows like centipedes resting on a shelf above them. "You told the Court this morning that Brendan Cortland first came to you during an unhappy and unfortunate time in his life. Is that correct?"

"I think his mother, Eliza Cortland, initially sought help for Brendan. But yes, it was during the illness and subsequent death of his father."

"Ah. My mistake." Warwick's brows rose, pulling his eyes open. "In your experience, would that turmoil alone, though, have been enough to propel Brendan into decades of weekly therapy, for what his counsel has attempted to characterize in court documents as severe mental illness?"

"Everyone grieves differently, of course." Aldrich stroked his goatee thoughtfully. "There are those, certainly, who become stuck in grief, who cannot process the death of a loved one—a child, a parent, a spouse, in rare cases even a pet—and move forward in a healthy manner."

"And is that what you really believed happened with Brendan Cortland?"

"No."

"What did you think, then, was the cause of his... er... problems?"

"The study of psychiatry is unique in the world of medicine," Aldrich said. He could have been giving a Psych 101 lecture. "A psychiatrist is not like a pathologist, say, who is able to look under a microscope at abnormal cells that cause a disease, or a radiologist who can read an MRI or CAT scan and identify tumors that cause certain symptoms. Or an allergist who can pinpoint the cause of anaphylactic shock. In my line of study, we don't always find out the causes of illness because they are often experiential as much as organic."

"So, in other words, you think Brendan had a bad experience that caused his illness?"

"Possibly."

Warwick spread his big arms a few inches from his sides, as if he didn't have the energy to lift them higher. "Like... abuse, for instance?"

"I considered it."

"Did Brendan ever say to you he had been hurt?"

"He told me about being bullied."

"And sexual abuse?"

"He alluded to it but never in detail, no."

Warwick stopped and faced the members of the jury open-mouthed, as if he'd unexpectedly stumbled upon a pivotal point. Their collective gaze shifted from him to the witness and back again. "Do you mean to say that in all your years of weekly therapy sessions, Brendan Cortland *never* described the alleged sexual abuse he suffered at Torburton Hall Academy for Boys?"

"Under hypnosis he admitted to some... er, uncomfortable situations... but he never actually described them while conscious."

Warwick continued. "He never mentioned the word 'abuse' with regards to that school?"

"That's correct." Aldrich crossed his legs. "Nonetheless, I did suspect early trauma. I worked from a few hypotheses."

"Those being?"

"Well one, of course, was that Brendan Cortland was a neglected child. His family's finances changed dramatically when he was about eleven years old, after his father's string of film successes. He'd become a world-renowned movie director. Suddenly, Brendan had all the material comforts anyone could want or imagine, but his parents became largely absent. His father traveled for work, and his mother reinvented herself as a socialite, too busy with social obligations and maintaining her new celebrity standing to properly care for her son, leaving him instead with the newly hired household staff. Brendan felt acutely the pain and trauma of being ignored by his own parents. A rejection, if you will. His emotional experience very closely paralleled that of a child left at an orphanage. In his mind, his parents metaphorically discarded him. Later, that feeling was magnified when they shipped him off to boarding school."

"Are you saying that all children of wealthy families, who happen to have a maid or chauffeur or butler, and who then go to boarding school, are destined to become mentally unstable adults?"

Aldrich chuckled and shook his head. "Of course not. Which led to my second hypothesis: that Brendan had a congenital defect, or at the very least a predisposition toward extreme anxiety and depression. But I ended up treating him on the basis of my third hypothesis, which was simply a combination of the first two."

"Meaning?"

"In other words, a person who has a tendency toward a certain disorder, when exposed to the right set of circumstances, or external stimuli, will develop that disorder."

Warwick slow-blinked in understanding. "So, in Brendan's case, he was predisposed to being sick, and later rejection brought on that sickness?"

"And let us not forget one more critical factor: his very literal abandonment by his mother, the only parental figure in his life. Eliza Cortland left Summer's Pond and moved to Europe immediately following her husband's death."

"Let me make sure I have this straight." Warwick leaned in closer. "Mr. Cortland was never sexually abused at Torburton Hall?"

"I have no direct knowledge of it."

"And if he was abused at that school, wouldn't he have disclosed it a long, long time ago?"

"One would think so."

"Did Mr. Cortland ever explain what motivated him to file this suit?"

Aldrich smiled. "He mentioned something about a girl in pink boots." And shrugged as if to say, *Never mind. Too silly to pursue.*

"But if Mr. Cortland didn't tell you about the alleged abuse, how did you know about it?"

A shadow passed over William Aldrich's face then. His lips, between the white bristles of his goatee, flattened into a thin line. "He told his attorney."

"Is that common—for a psychiatric patient to reveal such an intimate secret to a person he'd just met, rather than the therapist who'd been treating him for many years?"

"Brendan told Ms. James a story. Why he chose her, I don't know."

"Unless perhaps Mr. Cortland and Ms. James have a relationship beyond attorney and client." Warwick glanced at Dylan. "Lovely bracelet, by the way, Ms. James."

Dylan sprang up. How could he know? "Objection! Move to strike!"

Judge Aberdeen said, "The jury will disregard the last remarks. Mr. Warwick, do you have a question?"

"Did Mr. Cortland tell Ms. James the truth?"

"Whether the story is true, I also don't know. But it could be that he *believes* it is true, subconsciously."

"Doctor, one last question: Why would Brendan Cortland go to all the trouble and expense of this lawsuit, and accuse innocent people who'd never actually hurt him?"

"Blaming a dead teacher or a faceless institution for the hurt feelings Brendan experienced as a child is much easier than confronting the one person who is still alive and is in actuality responsible for that hurt: his mother. Any other motivations, such as the financial ones you suggested, may be true, too."

Warwick gave him a little bow and turned to Dylan. "Your witness."

Dylan strode over to face Aldrich head-on. "Dr. Aldrich," she said, from between clenched teeth. "Yes or no: Is it possible that Brendan confided in me simply because he trusts me more than he trusts you?"

Aldrich's eyes narrowed and his lips pressed into a thin line. "Well, I would highly doubt—"

"Please answer yes or no. The symptoms Brendan exhibited over the course of the twenty-eight years you've treated him, the same symptoms you noted in your professional medical charts, include agoraphobia so severe that Brendan has been largely unable to leave his home or hold a job?"

"He didn't want a job. But yes."

"And his symptoms such as exaggerated fear response to being touched, inability to form or maintain intimate relationships, and terror of strangers, are consistent with abuse?"

"Well, clinically speaking, yes, but—"

"And isn't it true that the vast majority of cases of childhood abuse are reported not when the victims are children, but *much* later, when they are adults?" Dylan's eyes bored into Aldrich's.

"Yes."

"Isn't it also true that adults can develop post-traumatic stress disorder, or PTSD, *long* after the abuse occurred?"

"Yes."

"And that PTSD manifests in substance abuse, loss of interest in everyday activities, failed relationships, panic attacks, flashbacks, nightmares and night terrors, *all* of which Brendan experienced?"

Aldrich concurred, albeit reluctantly.

"*Dr. Aldrich*," Dylan almost hissed, "I ask again. Is it possible that Brendan Cortland's damage resulted from being abused at Torburton Hall?"

"Again, I have no evid—"

"Yes or no."

"Yes, I suppose it is possible."

Asshole, Dylan thought as she turned on a heel, shooting Aldrich a withering look. "No more questions."

The doorbell rang. Gah, another visitor. Soon they'd have to hire a doorman.

"You have company," Irma announced shortly, returning to the kitchen to clear away Brendan's dinner plates.

Puzzled, Brendan stood up. The familiar figure hovering in the foyer straightened as he approached. He stopped short.

"Heather."

"Hello. I hope I'm not disturbing you. I was in the neighborhood."

"Please, um, come in."

"Thanks, but no. The girls are in the car. We just had dinner with my parents." Heather's bright smile seemed painted on her smooth face. "You look good, Bren. I think I saw you walking a dog a few times, and… anyway, you're looking really good."

"Thank you. You as well."

She nodded, looking down at her sandals peeking from under a flowing summer dress. "I've been asked to testify."

Brendan looked startled.

"I didn't even know what happened until I read about it in the news. I just came to say how shocked and sorry I am for what they did to you. I couldn't make sense of how you… how everything… had changed. I wish I had."

"You couldn't have known."

"Why didn't you tell me?"

Brendan looked at the floor, the chandelier, the beveled glass panels beside the front door. Everywhere but in her eyes. When he finally spoke, it was to tell her the truth. He'd been too ashamed. He'd been afraid of losing her.

Heather's face flooded with remorse. "Was I that heartless?" She blinked back tears. "I'm so sorry."

The hall echoed with silence for a moment.

"Anyway, maybe you could call Zac and take him out for lunch one day? If you want to."

"I'd love that."

Outside, a car horn tooted. "I'd better go," she said, and handed Brendan a small square of paper. His son's name, with a phone number below.

He stared out after her. As she opened the door to slide into her SUV, the overhead lamp came on, briefly illuminating two heads of glinting blond hair in the back seat before fading away to black.

The house on Whelk Lane loomed over the dark yard. The only movement seemed to be the dance of fireflies over the grass, a ballet of lights that leapt and pirouetted and then stilled.

Inside, Brendan avoided the medicine cabinet mirror as he washed. At his feet in bed, Elvis snored rhythmically. For an hour, Brendan stared into the darkness. Finally, he sat up and took a page from his nightstand—the printout of Heather's family. Zac, his two younger sisters, and her. And Heather's new husband.

Had Brendan pushed Heather away? Would she have understood if he'd just given her a chance? At this point, he didn't know what was true anymore.

Images exploded in his head like a trail of fireworks, bursting and then vanishing so that he wasn't sure they'd been there at all, leaving black holes where memories had hung before. The testimony of his trusted therapist on the stand... what was true and what wasn't? Brendan couldn't tell. Was the dysfunction in his mind the result of abuse, or had it been dormant since birth, just waiting to appear? Had his parents been responsible for it? And what about the nightmares? Had they symbolized the horrors he'd endured, or had they simply been a byproduct of his sickness?

For the first time in many, many months, Brendan dreamt that night of stumbling into a nest of snakes. Their long, thick lengths slithered around his body to squeeze the breath from his lungs, killing him over and over and over again.

CHAPTER TWENTY-SEVEN

Once again, Brendan wasn't answering Dylan's texts. Normally, she would have jumped into her car and headed out to Summer's Pond to tell him in person, but she didn't have time, not now. The news couldn't wait, so she dialed his number, though it was only six o'clock in the morning.

It rang and rang. Finally, Brendan answered, with a gravely, jarred-awake voice.

"It's me," Dylan said. "Sorry to wake you, but you need to know... I'm on the way to the airport to pick up your mother."

And she floored the gas and sped toward the pale sun rising over the East River.

The Alitalia flight landed ten minutes before schedule and deposited its two hundred-person contents safely on the ground at LaGuardia. Passengers disembarked from the Airbus 330 and wheeled expensive Italian suitcases across the climate-controlled airport before joining the throngs of travelers spilling into the oppressive heat of New York City.

Eliza Cortland, traveling with an aide, exited the arrival hall and stepped carefully around the puddles on the concrete, followed by a porter pushing a cart of luggage.

Fashionably dressed, impeccably manicured, and carrying her seventy years with straight-backed aplomb, she slid on a pair of black Prada sunglasses and prepared to wait.

Dylan picked her out immediately and pulled up alongside the curb, waving. The porter loaded luggage into the trunk, helped the woman into the passenger seat and the aide into the back.

"It's a pleasure to meet you," Dylan said as they drove up the Grand Central Parkway. "I'm so thankful you could make the trip."

"Of course, dear," the woman said pleasantly, looking out the window at the passing scenery.

Brendan very nearly didn't come to Court that morning, what with a sleepless night before and then the stunning phone call that woke him just as he'd dozed off. The feeling of unreality persisted into the light of day. Everything Warwick had suggested, what Dr. Aldrich had said… how sick was he? His cheeks burned with humiliation at the thought of being dissected in front of a room full of strangers. What would today bring, and could he bear it? Would his mother really show up, and if so, what would *that* be like?

Irma pursed her lips in irritation and scraped the breakfast she'd prepared into the trash. All Brendan wanted was black coffee.

Tomasz frowned at Brendan's reflection in the rearview mirror as he backed out of the driveway.

Brendan nodded agreement. "I feel like crap." Pulling up to the courthouse late, he arrived just in time for a clerk to close the courtroom door behind him. He settled himself into his seat as Dylan called her first witness.

"Darling," Eliza Cortland murmured as she passed in front of him, helped by her aide to the witness box.

Though he was expecting it, the shock of seeing his mother after a prolonged absence made Brendan miss the first minutes of her being sworn in. Seeing her there on the other side of the room had a dreamlike quality. She'd aged so much! Had she sent an understudy to play her role because she—the real mother with the flawless skin and deep red hair he remembered—couldn't make the show? Finally, he clamped down the shock enough to hear what she was saying.

In answer to Dylan's query, she described for the Court what a wonderful child Brendan had been, so curious and sweet, with a face like a cherub. "I was forever sweeping his bangs from his eyes," she said. "At bedtime he just wanted to snuggle, with a book or a song. But during the day he was always in a hurry to get out of the house, always rushing to play outside with his friends or jump in the pool." Eliza's manner, as she spoke, was measured, self-contained. She patted the faded beige hair caught in a bun.

"Would you say Brendan was well adjusted in the primary grades?"

"Oh, yes. He was very smart. He learned to read young. He did very well in school, too. He received top grades and honors. His room was filled with certificates and trophies. He had lots of friends, always very popular and outgoing."

"And what happened at the end of eighth grade?"

Eliza seemed not to hear the question. Dylan repeated it.

"Well, of course, since we had the money, we enrolled Brendan in the best academy, Torburton Hall, in the tenth grade—did I say tenth? I meant ninth. Yes, ninth. Just as his father had. And grandfather, as I recall. He was very excited about it."

"And he got off to a good start?" Another pause. "Mrs. Cortland? I asked if Brendan got off to a good start?"

"Yes, dear. We dropped him off in July and he just settled right in."

Dylan peered at Eliza. "You mean September, right? Not July."

"Oh... we visited in July." Eliza touched her forehead. "Yes, September. That would be right."

Dylan worded the next question carefully. "And how did Brendan seem to you when he came home to visit after his first few months at Torburton Hall? Did he seem the same as always, or different?"

"He..." Eliza's frowned and pressed her fingertips to her temples. "He'd gotten quieter, more withdrawn. Nervous. Not at all himself."

"And do you have any idea what triggered that change, Mrs. Cortland?"

Eliza closed her eyes. Several moments passed, and still she didn't answer.

"Mrs. Cortland?"

Eliza opened her eyes a crack.

Dylan took a step forward, raised her voice a notch. "Mrs. Cortland, you said Brendan became nervous and withdrawn. I asked if you knew why that happened."

"I... I'm sorry...I..." Eliza faltered.

"Did Brendan act differently after starting Torburton Hall?"

"Objection," Warwick drawled. "Leading."

"Withdrawn. Mrs. Cortland, can you tell us what else you remember about Brendan when he was in his early teenage years? In grades nine and ten?"

Eliza squinted around the courtroom. "Gianna? Gianna, my pills?"

Her aide stood up at the back.

"Mrs. Cortland?" Dylan felt her stomach twist as she watched Brendan's mother fall apart.

Judge Aberdeen spoke. "Mrs. Cortland, do you need a moment?"

"I'm sorry. It's one of my... spells... coming on. Oh..."

Aberdeen excused her from the stand, and Gianna hurried over to the witness box. Eliza's hands fluttered like butterflies as she was led from the room.

The judge told the counselors to approach. He frowned at Dylan.

"From now on, please ensure that your witnesses are capable of testifying, Miss James," Aberdeen said acidly. "I am not a fan of ineptitude. Kindly keep it to a minimum."

Dylan stood helplessly, wondering if a key witness had just slipped through her fingers.

"I didn't know she's been having trouble, or that traveling would be so hard on her. I never would have asked her to come, or put her on the stand."

"How could you have known?" Brendan sank down on the couch in his living room, all of them back at his house after their day in court. There were many unknowns associated with the case. Once again, he agonized over the thought of the photos he'd obtained. *Give the box to Dylan,* he told himself for the millionth time, *and let her present whatever's inside as evidence.* He just couldn't bring himself to do it. "It's not your fault."

"It really is." Dylan faced him. "Anyway, if your mother is able to return to the stand, after I finish with her, Warwick will have the opportunity to cross. He'll ask for specifics of what happened after your father's film success—about your grades, your favorite activities, your best friends, stuff like that. She won't be able to answer."

Brendan didn't respond.

"Because she didn't pay much attention to you after that point," Dylan continued. "Right? And that will support Dr. Aldrich's claim that she neglected you and that's why you got... sick."

"I loved her," Brendan said softly. "Until I hated her. I grew to hate her and my dad so much, because they sent me to that school and they didn't save me. And then they both disappeared when I needed them most."

"You can't really blame your dad, can you? I mean, he *died*. He didn't really have a choice. And your mom, well, maybe she felt she didn't have much of a choice either. Maybe she just lost the capacity to be... present."

Brendan said nothing.

"But she came back. She's trying to be what you need now."

"A little ironic, after all these years."

Dylan laid a hand on Brendan's forearm, noticing that he didn't flinch away. "Maybe she realizes she doesn't have much time. This might be her last chance to connect with you. So, we need to prepare the responses to every one of these points."

Voices at the top of the landing halted their conversation. Eliza, with Gianna at her elbow, made her way down. "Darling," she said to Brendan, holding Gianna's arm.

"Hello," Brendan said, rising. "How do you feel?"

"A little tired. I think I may have overdone it these last few days." She looked around the room, taking in the mismatched furniture, the eclectic art on the walls, and the remaining collectibles still on display. "The house looks rather different. I suppose I have been gone for quite a long time."

"Would you like some tea? Irma can bring it to us in your library."

"That would be lovely." Eliza turned to Dylan. "I'm sorry, dear, if I wasn't helpful in court this morning. Gianna says my episodes are becoming worse."

"Not to worry," Dylan assured her. "Let's see how you feel tomorrow. You'll have a chance to testify again if you're up to it."

"Perhaps after a good night's sleep."

"Please make sure to let Brendan know what you decide. Brendan, text me as early as possible. See you in the morning." She let herself out.

Brendan accompanied his mother to the library, studying her as she perched in her favorite chair and asked Gianna, in Italian, to bring her a sweater from upstairs.

"How is Rafael?" he asked.

"Sadly, he passed away, darling. But I had already been seeing Sebastian by then."

"Sebastian?"

"Another friend. He and I went our separate ways."

Brendan gave her a sad smile. "I suppose we have a lot of catching up to do."

"That's true, dear. But between the two of us, it looks like the developments on your end are the more exciting ones."

Upstairs, Elvis sat by the door to Brendan's office with his black ears cocked. At the desk a few feet away, Brendan's fingers made the rhythmic clicking sound Elvis had become used to. Tonight, though, new sounds in the house had filled the darkness. The old human, who'd arrived this afternoon, had been restless, wandering from room to room upstairs, sometimes argumentative with the other human—one who clearly didn't like dogs, as she'd used her toe to push him away. Now, in the big room down the hall he could hear the soft snoring of the old one and the other one humming in the shower. The human with the gardenia and pine scent had visited earlier, but she'd disappeared. Elvis liked that one.

One floor below, there was commotion in the bird cage, which signaled that the feathered creature with the loud voice was hunting insects as they scurried about on the newspaper.

Finally, Brendan said, "Bedtime, buddy."

Elvis understood. He could comprehend a wide range of words, especially with added pitch and context—the energetic, promising tone of, "Wanna go for a walk?" as Brendan put on sneakers for their morning jog; Brendan's enticing voice when he filled a bowl with food or opened a bag of treats; and this, his quiet nighttime manner, the one that meant they'd lie down and sleep.

Miles away from Summer's Pond, Dylan wiped off her makeup with angry swipes of a cotton swab. She'd just finished going through the subpoenaed charts from Dr. Aldrich. Two folders worth of paper... and eighty percent of the notations were useless, documenting only a lack of improvement to his symptoms. The charts dated back to 2008. There must have been earlier ones. She and Mortimer would obtain them somehow.

In the meantime, she'd return Eliza to the stand and get the responses she needed. A few more witnesses and it would be Brendan's turn to speak.

She had the bases covered. She would *not* screw this up.

Gale Perth, the prune-faced overseer for the State Board of Education's newly opened Inspectorate General, took the stand. Dylan questioned him judiciously, fully aware that his testimony could help Warwick's case to some degree. She'd have to steer with caution.

"Mr. Perth, is there a difference in how a state oversees private and public schools?" Dylan asked.

"Yes, there are many differences," the old man said eagerly, "and they vary from state to state, but there are commonalities. Since private and parochial schools generally don't receive federal funding but instead charge tuition to attend, they also are exempt from some of the federal regulations. For instance, they can set their own curriculum, focusing their teachings on areas they consider important. The state doesn't dictate the curriculum to them. However, this doesn't mean private schools aren't inspected regularly. They are. And that's heavily regulated by the state." He certainly liked to talk.

"Any other differences?"

"Private schools are generally operated by religious institutions and organizations and aren't necessarily overseen by public boards. They operate on contract law. That is, the relationship between the school and the students and their families, whereas public schools provide constitutional rights. And private schools don't actually have to license their educators."

"Can you please explain that?" Dylan looked at the jury with a puzzled expression. "Are you saying that a teacher at a private school isn't necessarily a teacher at all?"

"In the sense that he or she doesn't have to be state licensed, that's correct. The obligatory qualification is only an 'ability to teach,' which is highly subjective, of course. On the other hand, in public schools, teachers must be licensed and are overseen by a licensing agency."

Dylan asked if the governance of schools had changed much over the last three or four decades.

Perth said no, not much.

"Mr. Perth, I'm assuming you are aware of the *Boston Globe's* investigative report of prolific abuse in private schools?"

Yes, he'd seen it, he said. Everyone had. The paper's Spotlight team, the same research arm that had unearthed the Catholic Church abuse scandal, had recently run the explosive story detailing over two hundred claims of abuse at sixty-seven private schools in New England alone. Perth looked affronted that the lawyer had even mentioned it.

Dylan said, "The report is shocking in that, in the past, so many school administrators knew of abuse but ignored it. In one case, a headmaster told a victim he had a 'vivid imagination.' In another case, a teacher who had molested a child was deemed to have 'poor judgment.' What are your thoughts about that?"

"Obviously, schools know more now than they did then. Back then, they wanted to… er, respect the privacy of those involved."

"Would that be the victim's privacy, or the perpetrator's?"

Perth hesitated before he admitted the answer was both. "But there was pragmatism in that approach. Allegations, after all, couldn't always be proved. And school administrations wanted to be very careful about ruining someone's career."

"The classic cover-up?"

"An abundance of caution."

"Mr. Perth, can you think of any *financial* reason a school would be motivated to hush up allegations of abuse?"

The expression on the witness's face looked strained, as if he were reminding himself that he was under oath.

Finally, he explained that parents often view private schools as a refuge from what they consider the 'risky behaviors' at public schools. Who would send their children to, and pay tens of thousands of dollars in tuition for, a school that had a reputation for sexual misconduct? Who would fund an endowment at a school that employed pedophiles?

Dylan nodded. What was Perth's knowledge, she asked, of accused pedophiles moving from one school to the next? How easy was it?

"It's true that the leadership of schools sometimes allowed abuse to remain secret. And because there was often no record of sexual impropriety, it was very easy for teachers or administrators to hop from one school to another. They may even have carried letters of reference when they left."

"And new schools weren't always alerted of the allegations?"

"Unfortunately, that's correct."

"What I'm hearing," Dylan said slowly, "is that there was a system of largely self-regulating entities, where privacy was valued and transparency wasn't required. A system that existed well before social media and other mass communications platforms, and before public declarations of abuse became commonplace. One like the system of the Catholic Church to move abusive priests from one parish to another. And that's the system in which Brendan Cortland found himself in the early to mid-eighties. Does all of this sound about right?"

"More or less."

Dylan thanked him. She had no more questions.

Brendan didn't recognize the name.

He sat with Dylan in his gazebo, watching Elvis chase a rabbit through the flower beds. Another grueling week of trial, and here they were on a Saturday, prepping for the week to come. "Beverly Spitz? I have no idea. A friend of my parents, maybe? Let me Google her."

"You won't find much."

Brendan lifted his sunglasses. "I'm sorry. It doesn't ring a bell."

Monday morning, Dylan arrived in court pumped with caffeine and optimism. Brendan's bemused expression as the session convened told her he had no idea what to expect. From the bench, Aberdeen permitted Dylan to call her first witness of the day.

The door opened, and into the courtroom walked—or rather, waddled—an obese woman with long, graying hair, a loud, chevron-printed dress and chunky, mismatched jewelry. She stepped up to the witness box with some difficulty, panting from the exertion as she was sworn in. Her "I do" came out in a huff.

Dylan waited patiently for her to breathe. "Ms. Spitz, what is your profession?"

"I'm a school bus driver."

In his chair, Brendan stiffened. Now that she'd caught her breath, he recognized the voice immediately. It was a beautiful voice, actually—mellow and rich. Not a voice one would expect from seeing her. Dylan turned to search his profile, but he wouldn't meet her eyes.

"That's a very commendable job," she said. "Though I can't imagine it pays very much."

"It doesn't."

"I'm guessing you may need to supplement that income. Isn't that right, Ms. Spitz?"

"Yes."

"Is it through another line of work that you know Mr. Cortland?" Dylan indicated Brendan at the plaintiff's table.

The woman gave him an appraising look, as if putting face to name for the first time. "Yes."

"And can you please tell the Court in what capacity you know him?"

Bev Spitz nodded, her double chin jiggling. "After hours, I'm a phone sex operator. Brendan—uh, Mr. Cortland—was my best client for many years. He knew me by my professional name, Kitty Knightly." She smiled broadly.

"A phone sex operator." Dylan's eyes widened. "In case anyone is unclear, what exactly does that entail?"

"I serve my clients by creating scenarios over the telephone. Sexual ones. Fantasies that my clients find arousing."

"And when did you serve Mr. Cortland in this way?"

Bev's grin faded a notch. "He stopped calling about a year ago."

"Ms. Spitz, if you would, can you describe some of the common... er, scenarios... that your clients request?"

"Oh, all kinds of things. I have clients who like to be the teacher and I'm the naughty student, or I'm the naughty babysitter, or the naughty flight attendant. I've done every naughty girl there is, which is fun. They have great imaginations when it comes to this stuff. The handyman is a common one: they come to my house to fix the cable or read the water meter, and I'm the naughty housewife and I seduce them." Bev had warmed to her subject, and was speaking animatedly, gesturing with her chubby hands. "You name it, I've heard them all. Dominatrix themes are more popular than ever. And I have one guy who used to be a marine or something, and he has a whole fantasy about an enemy squadron that kidnaps him during Desert Storm and keeps him as a sex slave. Very detailed. Like, how does he think of this stuff? It's a little freaky, but whatever. He's paying for it."

"Could you describe for the court the themes of your telephone sessions with Mr. Cortland?"

A NEST OF SNAKES | 333

A pause. "Well… there was really only one theme. The same story every time."

"And that was?"

A puzzled expression flitted across Bev's face. "It was sort of a fairytale. Or rather, a mishmash of fairytales, like how a child tells it. He's a prince, I'm his princess with long, blond hair. He rescues me from a castle with a terrifying dragon. He sneaks in and carries me off to get married."

In Dylan's peripheral vision, Brendan remained frozen, staring straight ahead. Dylan urged Bev to continue.

Bev's expression softened, as if it brought to mind fond memories. "We get to our wedding night in his castle and the dragon bursts in. Every phone session, Brendan described a different way he slayed the dragon. In detail. It got pretty gory."

"And then in the fantasy, you had sex?"

"Well, no. We never really got to the sex part. It was killing the dragon and saving me that turned him on."

Nodding, Dylan asked, "And what did you make of all this?"

Bev looked puzzled. "I don't understand."

"I mean, what were your impressions of Brendan Cortland throughout these sessions? Based on his fantasy, did you ever get the feeling he was emotionally damaged in some way?"

"Objection," Warwick drawled. "The witness is not a psychologist or therapist and her opinion of Mr. Cortland's psyche has no merit." Beside him, Vincent Sabato and Sidney Kohn chuckled.

The judge agreed. "I'll allow it. Ask a different question, Miss James."

"Ms. Spitz, did Mr. Cortland ever *say* anything to you that suggested he'd been abused in any way?"

"No…"

Dylan walked across the courtroom, thinking. "Ms. Spitz, this imagery that Mr. Cortland asked you to play out... you said it was like a fairytale. Didn't you ever think it was strange that he paid you to live out such a juvenile scenario, one that never even culminated in actual sex? Didn't you think there was something wrong with a full-grown man who was so childlike in his fantasies?"

"If you put it that way, I guess it's pretty weird."

"Thank you. No more questions," Dylan said.

Judge Aberdeen turned to the defense team. "Mr. Warwick?"

Warwick sat with his eyes closed. "Ms. Spitz, do you think it's weird that some men fantasize about sex with young girls?"

"It's pretty common. I hear it all the time."

"And do you think it's strange that some men might find it arousing to fantasize about bondage or sado-masochism? Or rape?"

"I mean, they're just harmless fantasies. There's some real sickos out there who do more than fantasize."

"Agreed." Warwick raised his caterpillar brows. "So, wouldn't you say that there is a whole range of harmless fantasies, that one is as normal as the next?"

"I guess." Bev shrugged, her chins jiggling.

"Then you agree that Brendan Cortland's fantasies are a product of a mind that is no more or no less damaged than that of the next guy."

"Objection!" Dylan sprang to her feet, waving a hand. "*Objection.*"

Aberdeen turned toward her. "So you said, Miss James. No need to repeat yourself. What is your objection, exactly?"

Dylan parroted, "The witness is not a psychologist or therapist and her opinion of Mr. Cortland's psyche has no merit."

The judge pursed his lips and agreed. "Mr. Warwick, what's good for the goose is good for the gander."

"No more questions at this time," Warwick conceded.

In her seat, Dylan gave herself a little high five.

As if drawn by magnets, every pair of eyes in the courtroom was trained on Heather as she sat down in the witness box. She seemed not to notice the attention. The years had done little to diminish her beauty; if anything, her maturity highlighted an unexpected radiance. Only faint webbing around her eyes marked her age. Her skin and hair glowed under the dull fluorescent lights, and the pale blue of her irises shone as she spoke in a strong, composed voice.

"I suppose I was in some sort of denial," Heather was saying, in answer to Dylan's question. "I didn't want to admit how much the Brendan I'd known had changed."

"Yet you agreed to marry him."

"You have to understand, our parents had primed us for it. My mother, his mother… they'd planned it out for years. We were a given. We'd live this fabulous life. We were the golden couple, everyone said so."

"But were you?"

"Well, everything happened so fast when I came back from college. I just assumed he was nervous or something, and once we were married he'd go back to normal."

"Did he?"

"Not at all. He was like a shadow of his former self. I'm outgoing, so I socialized for the both of us. Brendan just sort of faded into the background. I kept myself busy… with the wedding plans, the new house, parties, trips with my girlfriends. All that. He was… he was a small price to pay for the lifestyle."

Dylan clasped her hands, quelling the urge to slap Heather. "And later, your marital relations seemed normal?"

Heather looked down at her lap. "Not at all. We barely had a physical relationship. It was a miracle when Zac was conceived." She shook her head. "And everything got worse once he was born. Brendan seemed terrified of him. He never wanted to hold him or be left alone with him, like he was afraid he had something contagious the baby could catch. We made it through the first two years, but ultimately, I just...you know. I needed more from a husband, more than Brendan could give."

"What did you make of all this, of Brendan's strange behavior? You were his wife. Didn't you ever ask him if something was wrong?"

"I may have. But like I said, I was in denial. I don't think I truly wanted the answer because it would've shattered the illusion of our perfect life."

Dylan asked, "Mrs. Williams, can you pinpoint a time in Brendan's youth when everything changed?"

"Absolutely." Heather nodded with assurance toward Warwick and his team. "Looking back, it seems as clear as day. Brendan was completely fine until he went away to boarding school. Something happened to him at Torburton. I mean, my husband didn't seem to have had any problems there. But then, Scott didn't talk about his childhood much. Anyway, I didn't put two and two together until I read about Brendan's lawsuit in the paper."

Dylan stopped in her tracks, the next question forgotten. Heather's last few words were drowned out by the low buzzing in her ears. How had she missed it? She'd never connected the names. Heather Williams' new husband was Scott, as in Scott Williams, one of Brendan's tormentors. It was a common name, yes, but somehow Dylan had never made the connection. She spun around toward the audience and pinpointed a handsome man sitting off to one side. She couldn't have known for certain, but somehow, she felt sure it was him. So lost was she in her thoughts that she didn't hear Warwick's objections to Heather's statements, or Judge Aberdeen's "sustained."

Slowly, Dylan turned back to the stand. "Mrs. Williams, did your husband ever mention if he'd known Brendan Cortland at Torburton?"

"As I said, Scott didn't talk about the past much, but I know they overlapped by two years. His parents and Brendan's were quite friendly. I imagined the boys were friends, too."

From the plaintiff's table came a loud cough. Dylan glanced at Brendan, who was shaking his head. *"No,"* he mouthed.

"Uh… your witness," Dylan said.

Warwick cross-examined Heather. He only had a couple questions. "I just want to clarify something," he said. "You told the Court that Brendan 'changed' "—he used air quotes with his thick fingers—"when he was about fourteen years old?"

"That's correct. Before that, he was… normal."

"But before that he was just a child. Doesn't every child change at puberty, Mrs. Williams? Didn't you? In fact, isn't that the very definition of puberty… that a child *changes* into an adult?"

"Well, I suppose, but Brendan was different. It's not like he got muscular or grew a beard or his voice dropped lower. His whole *personality* changed."

"You're saying you would expect a grown man of twenty-five, or thirty-five, to have the same personality he had as a child of twelve?"

Heather's brows knit together. "Maybe not. But something happened to him that took away every ounce of self-esteem he had as a kid. He should have grown up to be a confident, capable, successful man like his dad. But he didn't."

"I think, Mrs. Williams, that Brendan Cortland is exactly the adult he was meant to be. The youthful idea of him you cling to is simply that: an idea. There was no trauma, no cataclysmic event. He just grew up." Warwick shambled back to his table. "No more questions."

In the hallway near the courtroom, Heather emerged from the ladies' room to join her husband. They bumped into Brendan and Dylan as they rounded a corner.

"Goodbye, Bren," Heather said. "We'll talk about plans with Zac soon."

Scott took Heather's elbow to steer her forward rather than wait for a reply. As soon as they were out of earshot, Dylan turned to Brendan, understanding.

"You didn't want Heather to know that Scott was a bully back then," she said slowly. "You're trying to protect her."

Brendan didn't need to respond. His sad eyes, as he tracked his ex-wife down the hallway, said it all.

The call from Shawn Unger came as a surprise. He'd agreed to a videotaped deposition, but the initial public offering of his newest venture soaked up his every waking moment. Now, with the IPO signed on the west coast and the trial underway in the east, he told Dylan he'd be on the next flight from San Francisco. Dylan tried to contain her delight.

Shawn arrived in town that Thursday. He and Brendan embraced outside the court building, clapping each other on the back, happy to be in each other's presence before ugly memories had a chance to tarnish the reunion. Brendan stared at the man: compact and wiry, with the lean, hard body of the avid cyclist he was, looking the picture of California health and success.

"Thanks," Brendan said. "Thanks for doing this."

"Hey, you're the brave one. You came forward."

When Dylan called him to the witness stand, Shawn stood with feet planted firmly to be sworn in, nodding grimly. Brendan pictured the little boy he'd been the first time they met, sitting on the ground and rubbing his head. Tiny, pale, and so innocent.

In answer to Dylan's litany of questions, asked as she paced deliberately in front of the jurors, Shawn spoke matter-of-factly, as if recounting the plot of a movie he'd once seen. A movie he and Brendan had starred in. A horror movie.

Shawn described the bullying by the upperclassmen, not just the relentless teasing, or the incidents where Brendan had been present, but things he'd never told anyone, like the weekend they locked him in a broom closet for an entire day and laughed when he soiled himself, or the time they forced him to wear a diaper and crawl around like a baby.

Soon the testimony segued to the teachers. Shawn described his encounters with Terence Dunlop. Being made to undress, being measured, being photographed. How he'd once walked into the coach's office to find him masturbating to the photos.

Dylan paused here to let the jurors absorb Shawn's words. Then she asked, "Who knew about the Before and After book?"

"All the students."

"Terence Dunlop continued coaching until he died a few years ago. To your knowledge, was he ever disciplined for his misconduct?"

Shawn frowned. "Not while I was there, no."

"Let's talk about the Science Club," Dylan suggested, steering Shawn's testimony to the abuse by the science teacher.

Shawn described the afterschool meetings in Nevin's basement and his own role as a "doll." There were no disparities, Dylan noted, between his and Brendan's accounts of the events. His words were sparing and emotionless. Perhaps because of their simplicity, his stories held so much weight.

"Lawrence Nevin was a pedophile," Shawn said. "He hardly tried to keep it a secret. Everyone at the school knew, from Gavin Murdock, the Chair, right down to the school secretary, Paula Franklin, who sorted the mail. His pornography magazines came every month."

"Do you know what happened to all the photographs and videotapes Nevin kept under lock and key? Or Dunlop's Before and After book?"

"No. I wish I did. I'd burn it all."

"This level of tolerance," Dylan mused, "of Dr. Nevin and all the others... how do you explain it?"

A silence ensued as Shawn weighed his words. "There was a highly sexualized atmosphere at the school," he said finally. "Obviously, there is a certain sexual element among normal, developing boys stuck in any cloistered environment, but this was different. It crossed into abuse, and it went all the way up the ladder. Abuse became a part of Torburton culture. It was accepted and condoned in every generation of new boys who came in. I had an inkling early on, and of course at a certain point I became quite sure of it, that the upperclassmen, the bullies who tortured us, like Chad and Hank and their friends, they'd been sexually abused themselves."

Across the room, Brendan's head snapped up. He sat wide-eyed as he assimilated information he'd never considered before.

"At what point were you sure?"

When they targeted Jack, Shawn replied. "With Jack, their bullying became so malicious. Like the rage was just leaching out of them. That, and the sexual nature of their assaults."

Dylan tipped her head to one side. "Mr. Unger, I know you only have a day or two before you have to leave. Why did you volunteer to fly across the country and testify?"

Shawn nodded toward Brendan. "To give a voice for those who can't. To tell the stories when no one else will. To support Brendan. And for our friend Jack, who can no longer speak for himself."

Warwick had no questions.

Back at her office, Dylan smiled to herself. Shawn had done well, very well.

Her phone rang. She knew without looking what it would be: another settlement offer. She listened to the proposal, one million dollars this time, still contingent on non-disclosure. She said a polite thank you, knowing her client would reject it anyway.

She scanned her inbox. Her early subpoena for Torburton Hall Academy for Boys to produce the Before and After book had yielded nothing. The current administration reported through their attorneys in an email that they'd thoroughly searched the premises but had come up empty-handed.

One step forward, one step back.

The next morning, Gale Perth returned to the stand. Dylan wanted to talk about Finland. "Finland's education system used to be a combination of private, public, and grammar schools," she said. "In the 1970s, the Finish government decided to abolish private schools, because they created too much segregation, too much divisiveness."

"Kindly stop pontificating," Aberdeen said, "and ask a question if you have one?"

"Sorry, Your Honor. I was getting to it."

"Now, please."

"Yes, sir." Dylan's mouth was tight as she turned to the stand. "Mr. Perth, as recently as 2015, just *last year,* there was a case of a teacher in a private school here in Connecticut alleged to have assaulted a girl in her dormitory. The girl went to her headmistress, who said, and I quote, 'Young lady, go back to your classroom. Stop causing trouble.' The girl had the courage to reveal the lewd and obscene behavior in a social media post. Do you know what happened, Mr. Perth?"

"The teacher left the school."

"The teacher disappeared the next day," Dylan clarified. "No police involvement, no formal charges, no media, no explanation, and certainly no apology. Is that correct?"

"As far as I know."

"Do you know how it's possible that not in 1982 but in 2015 a school could get away with that?"

"I don't have an answer," Perth admitted.

Dylan stood outside the courtroom during a brief recess. She shook Gale Perth's hand and thanked him for his testimony. A tap on her shoulder interrupted the conversation, and she turned around. "Mrs. Cortland!"

"Hello, dear," Eliza said. "I'm sorry to disturb. Do you have a moment?"

"Of course."

"I'd like to continue what I started, if I may. I'm feeling much more myself today. These two days of rest have helped tremendously. And hearing what's been said up there on the witness stand... well, I have more to add."

Eliza Cortland took the stand.

Aberdeen peered at her, and at Dylan. "Miss James, you are satisfied that your witness is capable of testifying today?"

"I certainly am, Your Honor," Eliza said before Dylan could reply. She sounded utterly lucid, and indignant.

The judge shot her a warning look.

Dylan put in, "I am."

"Proceed."

"Mrs. Cortland, last time you were here you testified that just a few months after starting ninth grade, Brendan became nervous and withdrawn. I asked if you had any idea why?" Dylan began.

"Well, of course," said Eliza. "Immediately I assumed someone at Torburton Hall had assaulted my son. I should know."

"But then... as a mother... why didn't you act on your instincts?"

"I most certainly did." Eliza leaned forward. "I called the school several times. The assistant headmaster, Quentin Greer, finally returned my messages sometime between

Thanksgiving and Christmas of Brendan's freshman year. I said to him point blank, 'I believe someone there hurt my son.'"

"And what did Mr. Greer answer?"

"He said, 'Things like that don't happen at our school.' He managed to sound quite outraged, actually. Clearly, avoiding scandal was more important to him than the safety of the students."

Dylan wondered why Eliza hadn't spoken to the headmaster himself rather than his assistant.

"It was the 1980s," Eliza said, arching a brow. "If Brendan's *father* had called, no doubt Edward Galloway would have taken the call. I was just the mother. Regardless, I doubt Mr. Galloway's response would have been much different from Mr. Greer's."

"You dropped the matter?"

"No. I discussed it with my husband. He assured me he'd have a word with Brendan. And I am embarrassed to say I let myself be convinced that he would handle it, that everything would be fine. Kenneth told me that he, too, felt awkward and introverted at Brendan's age, that it was just part of maturing."

"And the haircut?"

Eliza looked down. "Yes. I should have paid closer attention to that, but I was caught up in holiday preparations. I did ask Mr. Greer if army-style haircuts were mandatory at the school and if so, why it hadn't been mentioned earlier. He said haircuts were optional."

"You didn't follow your instincts."

"No." Eliza looked at Brendan, her face awash in regret. "And then we received this wonderful letter from Mr. Greer telling us of Brendan's success at the school, and how they wanted to fast-track him. I let myself be swept away by the praise.

"I'm so sorry. I botched my job as a parent. I didn't protect my son. I knew something was wrong, but I didn't fight for him. I wanted so badly to believe that everything was fine, that such an expensive school had to be fine. But of course, it wasn't. Nothing was good at that school."

Dylan gave her head a little shake. "And what about Heather? Surely you noticed that Brendan and Heather had stopped speaking to each other."

"Yes, well, temporarily. But they did marry in the end... although it took some doing on Kenneth's part to make it happen."

"Can you explain?"

Eliza looked over to Brendan, her face a mask of pity. "Heather's parents weren't quite as well off as they'd let on. Heather had everything to gain by marrying Brendan. Even then, Kenneth had to draw up a contract. If, after their union produced an heir, Heather wished to leave, she would be entitled to a certain sum of money."

Across the room, Brendan made a soft, strangled sound.

"I'm sorry, darling," Eliza said to him. "You weren't meant to know that. But it was necessary."

"Necessary?" Dylan echoed.

Eliza looked pained. "Because Heather never would have married Brendan otherwise. He'd deteriorated so much by the time they married in 2001. He wasn't the same person he'd been."

"Thank you, Mrs. Cortland."

It was Warwick's turn to question Eliza. He stood in front of the jury with his sharp intellect camouflaged behind sleepy eyes. "Mrs. Cortland, you said you thought Brendan might have been bullied."

"Yes."

"Do you happen to recall the names Michael Harrington or Ian Prescott?"

"They were classmates of his in Summer's Pond, if I recall."

Warwick lifted a lazy hand to gesture toward Brendan. "Yes, they were friends of his... eventually. Do you recall speaking with their parents at any point?"

"No."

"Both Michael and Ian said that Brendan and a group of boys bullied them in sixth grade so often they went home from school crying. Mrs. Harrington and Mrs. Prescott both complained to you *repeatedly* about your son's behavior."

"I don't think so. I would remember that."

Warwick continued. "Maybe you were busy with other things. In any case, when we interviewed them separately, Michael and Ian had remarkably similar accounts of the bullying they were subjected to. Brendan was the ringleader."

Dylan objected. Warwick hadn't asked a question.

Warwick turned to Judge Aberdeen with a little shrug. "I'm just pointing out that sometimes the question of who is a bully and who isn't is not as clear cut as we might think. But I do have a question, Mrs. Cortland: And that is, how is it you don't remember these incidents? Is it because you were not the caring, concerned parent you would have us believe? Were you not absent from Brendan's life?"

Eliza bristled. "I wasn't absent. I was just busy. My husband became a very important man, a respected Hollywood director. I had to entertain, to travel with him..."

"Mrs. Cortland, did you love your son?"

"Of course, I did. I may have made some mistakes, but Brendan knew I loved him."

Warwick nodded and turned as if to sit down, but then thought better of it. "Oh... one more thing... after your husband passed, you left the country. Some would say you abandoned Brendan. Is that love?"

"I..." Eliza's eyes filled. "I couldn't stand to look at him. He was so broken by Torburton. If we'd been better parents, maybe we could have saved him."

Dylan felt a tiny rush of adrenaline, a moment of hope that the trial was turning in their favor and they might actually win. She tasted the faintest sweetness of victory on her tongue. Eliza had come through.

And Brendan? Brendan had been tested more than any man should be, by sitting through all the testimony of other witnesses. And tomorrow, she'd demand that he give of himself again, at great personal cost. Tomorrow, she'd demand again that he uncover his memories. She prayed it would all be worth it.

CHAPTER TWENTY-EIGHT

Brendan Rainier Cortland surveyed the courtroom. Off to his left were the members of the jury, all turned to him curiously, expectantly. Above his right shoulder sat the judge peering down like a bald eagle from his perch. In front of him, the defenders of Torburton Hall waited for their turn to launch an assault. But before they could, he would talk to Dylan. And there she came across the floor, her face radiating the deep empathy she'd had for him all along. As they'd rehearsed, he would focus on her, on her warm eyes, to the exclusion of everyone else in the room. He wouldn't disappoint her.

Brendan vowed to tell the truth, but after he sat down, he didn't know if he could. Seconds ticked by.

"Brendan," Dylan repeated.

"Mr. Cortland, are you unable or unwilling to testify this morning?" Aberdeen frowned at him.

Brendan looked around again, at the judge, the jury, Warwick and his cohort. So mocking, all of them. Suddenly, he felt the wash of helplessness, the familiar terror of being stalked. All he had to stave them off with was his story.

It would be so much easier if he could just show the pictures.

He sought Shawn's eyes, then Dylan's, and nodded.

Dylan let out the breath she'd been holding. "I'm going to ask you to start at the beginning, from your earliest memories of arriving at Torburton Hall in 1982 and the incidents involving upperclassmen."

A year earlier, Brendan had whispered the story. Now he began it again, talking first about the upperclassmen, about Hank and Popeye and Chad. He described those earliest weeks of walking around campus with the other freshmen, and the clusters of juniors and seniors who lurked along the paths, waiting for opportunities to harass and haze them.

Within moments, he'd sunk back into his memories.

On the stand, Brendan shook his head. "Poor Jack and Shawn. They had no idea, not even an inkling of how bad things were going to get for them that year. They suffered unbelievable abuse."

"Objection!" Warwick held up a hand. "Hearsay. We are discussing Mr. Cortland's life at Torburton Hall. Not the lives of his friends."

"Your Honor, it speaks to Brendan's experience of how the school tolerated the very worst behaviors by the adults and students, and also to his emotional state after witnessing what happened to the other boys."

Aberdeen nodded. "I'll allow it. Continue."

Brendan launched back into his story, arriving, finally, at that fatal spring night, the juncture when Jack Abromovitch decided to intervene, to tell on the upperclassmen for supposedly getting Brendan drunk. Clearly, the upperclassmen had decided to teach him a vicious lesson, and their bullying spiraled.

The violent confrontation with the Kingsley brothers marked the point of no return.

Silence engulfed the room as everyone digested the story. At the back of the courtroom, a door opened and some of the spectators filed out.

Brendan barked out a harsh sob just like the sound he'd made in his living room when first talking about Jack's suicide. But this time, to his surprise, tears rolled down his cheeks. He wiped his eyes and tried to compose himself. "There was a *Lord of the Flies* culture at Torburton," he said thickly. "Either you were a bully or you were being bullied. And boys learned very quickly to keep quiet; snitching was the worst possible offense and anyway, it wouldn't do any good. There was no one to snitch to."

Dylan's voice was quiet. "Boys were assaulted, intimidated, berated. The racism was astounding. Why couldn't you tell an adult?"

"You have to understand that everyone—*everyone*—was complicit in crimes there. The teachers knew what the students were doing to each other. But the teachers were themselves criminals. The administrators knew what the teachers were doing to the kids. But the administrators were themselves criminals. The support staff and the Board knew what the administrators were doing. There was literally nowhere to hide and no one to turn to."

Dylan shook her head. "But what about the parents?"

Brendan drew a long, shaky breath. His answer seemed to surprise the jury. "Our parents were groomed before we were," he said.

"How?"

In two ways, Brendan explained. "First, half the students were legacies. So clearly, the fathers and grandfathers and great-grandfathers had been through it all before us."

"Do you think all of *them* were bullies?"

No, not necessarily, Brendan said.

"But if they were victims, why would they want to subject their children to the same treatment?"

"Tradition... to be part of a tradition is a very powerful thing. Maybe they wanted their own sons to succeed where they couldn't, to be strong where they'd been weak. To prove something. Or, maybe their memories just faded."

Dylan paced in front of the witness box thoughtfully. "You said the parents were groomed in two ways. What was the second way?"

Brendan faced her as he answered, but it was clear to everyone in the room that he didn't really see her. "I've done so much research on private schools over the years," he mused. "Being locked in my house, the Internet was my connection to the world. And I had nothing but time on my hands. And I found it's the same with all these elite private schools, everywhere in the world. And it's always been the same. Our parents enroll us in these places because the schools promise to fulfill their dreams. The *parents'* dreams, of what their offspring will achieve in life. In the United States, these boarding schools are the fast track to the Ivy League, to attending Harvard and Yale, to becoming politicians and heads of industry and the most prominent leaders of the community. They're the networking field for some of the world's most powerful people.

"The glossy photos in these school catalogues scream it out. 'Send your children to our expensive, exclusive school, and they will be part of an elite society. Our crest will make them worthy of praise. Come, buy status for your children and, by extension, for yourself.' Never mind that our souls were crushed in the process."

Now, Dylan whispered to herself. "Brendan, you broke your silence today, emerging after what actually has been *decades* of silence. Why?"

The pink rain boots. His son. Heather. Jack. There'd been many catalysts. "Because it's time for the truth to come out. Too many of these monsters were allowed to live out their lives without admitting to their sins. If I stayed silent, I'd be helping keep their secrets. I'd be complicit in their crimes. And in my own suffering."

"You mean at the hands of Dunlop? Or the upperclassmen?"

"That doesn't begin to cover the full scope of the abuse."

In the quiet moment that followed, Judge Aberdeen took the opportunity to interject. "This is a good time for us to recess for the day. We will reconvene tomorrow morning." A brisk tap of his gavel, and everyone rose in the room.

"Well?" Brendan stepped down from the stand, exhausted.

Dylan nodded and gave him an encouraging smile. "Perfect. You were just perfect."

In a cramped apartment above a hardware store, Lem sobbed. Holding back the tears during Brendan's testimony had been excruciating, because what had happened to Brendan and his friends had been almost a mirror image of what happened to Lem. The rough shoves and rude comments in high school hallways were a given. So were the teachers who did nothing because it was easier to ignore than to address the fact that Lem was being bullied.

But the other part, now that was unnerving. Lem remembered so clearly the pediatrician who had examined and measured and jotted down notes in a chart, month after month. Those office visits where the doctor would quietly lock the door had seemed wildly unprofessional, even to a child.

If only Lem had the courage to stand up and point a finger, like Brendan. *Maybe one day*, Lem thought. *Maybe one day*.

Brendan stood under the spray of his shower and let hot water wash over him. It'd been grueling, as he'd guessed it would be. And even more difficult days lay ahead.

Wrapping a towel around his waist, he made his way downstairs.

Irma was just leaving. She hung the key ring on the hook in the pantry and picked up her purse.

"*Dobranoc*," she said and let herself out.

Brendan caught sight of that day's issue of the *Connecticut Daily Dawn* left on a chair. Clearly, Irma had meant to bring it back to the guesthouse to read. Brendan unfolded it to a frontpage article on the Torburton case by Sandy Davidson, who'd been writing almost daily since the beginning of the trial. Reading his words, Brendan was struck by how sensitively, how accurately he'd reported the testimony, and how clearly outraged the man was by what the school had done. He hated the subject matter, but he had to admit the reporting was exceptional. Maybe he'd follow Sandy on Twitter, as the paper suggested.

Suddenly, he had an idea. An answer to something that had nagged him for many months. He fixed himself a martini and went back upstairs. He slipped into a robe and entered his office, where he opened one of his laptops and sent Sandy a detailed, anonymous, and untraceable message regarding Timothy Atkins, the mayor of High Tide, New Jersey.

After it sent, Brendan sipped his martini and waited for his other laptop to boot up.

One down.

But so many to go.

He entered The Playground and typed, *Youngblood here. Craving something sweet.*

CHAPTER TWENTY-NINE

Two weeks into the trial, Brendan returned to the stand for his most difficult day yet: the day he would begin to talk about Galloway.

Edward Galloway had been the headmaster of Torburton Hall from 1979 to 1995. Unlike his contemporaries, he wasn't an alumnus. In fact, Galloway had never attended a private school, nor did he have any experience in the field of education. Prior to his posting, he'd managed a large swimming pool supply company in Atlanta. But by marrying Patricia Fenwick, he married into a Southern family with connections. Farming him out to the top position at a remote New England school not only offered Edward some legitimacy but solved the problem of Trish, whose escapades garnered a wild reputation around town.

Galloway approached Torburton as another business to be managed. He saw parents as customers and their sons as products rather than young minds in need of guidance and nurturing. His marketing and communications skills were put to good use to recruit students and within four years of his posting, the student body had grown substantially, as had the budget for school operations. Galloway had undisputed charm. No one could fundraise like him. With a whiskey in one hand and an outstretched palm, he worked his way around a room, telling an anecdote here, an off-color joke there, and the checks practically wrote themselves.

To the boys Galloway seemed like a dream, pleasant and engaged, not at all like his strict, severe predecessor. Brendan recalled how Galloway greeted his family the day Dunlop had taken them on a summer pre-registration tour. Kenneth shook Galloway's hand vigorously when they left; Eliza gushed in the car on the way home. And Brendan felt a wash of excitement as he pledged to be the type of student Galloway described at the welcome assembly of the 1982 academic year.

"He was a very hands-on type of headmaster. In every sense." Brendan's joke fell flat. The members of the jury winced and waited, and Brendan's voice dropped once more as he launched into a detailed description of Galloway's dirty little practices, his shower inspections and dorm visits and "medication" applications, all done with his charming manner and friendly overbite. Since he was head of school, who could protest?

"So, Galloway committed crimes with impunity." Dylan turned to the jury. She opened her mouth to continue just as someone stood up near the door to the courtroom.

The man was frail, bent. He rose with difficulty and leaned on a cane for support. But when he opened his mouth to speak, the force of his words silenced the room.

"That bastard!"

Aberdeen rapped with his gavel and called for order. He told the man to sit down, to keep quiet, not to interrupt his proceedings.

The man cried out, "When does Galloway answer for his grotesque failure to protect the children in his charge? Where is the justice here?"

"Sir, if you continue to speak out, I will have a bailiff take you into custody," Aberdeen warned.

"It's high time I spoke out!" the man croaked, trying to brush away the bailiff reaching for his arm. Sitting beside him, a white-haired woman reached up, begging him to sit. "Who will speak for our son? That school killed our boy.

Where is the justice for him?" And he sat down heavily and his face crumpled.

Sobs wrenched from his chest, the bitterness of three decades of grief echoing in the silence of the courtroom. Beside him, the old woman wept silently.

The man choked out, "Who will speak for our Jack?"

For a moment, even Aberdeen was too shocked to respond.

The waitress brought six steaming cups of coffee to the booth and set them in front of Brendan, Shawn, Dylan, Mortimer, and Jack's parents. They were seated in an alcove in a small café several streets from the courthouse, hoping to be out of range of the reporters and lawyers attached to the Torburton case.

The two doctors looked frail, even more diminutive than before. Both were in their seventies, long retired, and the many painful years since Brendan had seen them last were etched on their faces.

"We were wrong not to agree to testify. We know that now," the man said. "Very wrong."

Beside him, his wife nodded. "If it's not too late, we will give a written testimony. For Jack."

"I'm so sorry for your loss, Dr. Abromovitch," Dylan said softly, laying her hand on top of the woman's. "I can't imagine what you both have been through."

"Please, call us Sol and Helen."

Helen reached into her purse and took out a small, framed photograph of Jack in his maroon blazer and tie.

Shawn reached for it tentatively. "My God. I haven't seen a picture of him since…"

"It was thirty-three years this spring." Sol reached into his pocket for a pill bottle, shook out two capsules, and swallowed them dry. "He had his whole life ahead of him. He never got to graduate. Never had a chance to go to college, get married, have children. He'd never even driven a car or learned to shave."

Helen said, "We've spent our whole lives counting the nevers."

Brendan shook his head, staring at the photo in Shawn's hand. "I feel so responsible. If I'd stayed with him that morning, if I'd been able to protect him… maybe I could've…"

"No!" Helen leaned toward Brendan. "It was not your fault, either of you. You were great friends to Jack. He was so happy to know you both."

Sol sighed. "We read about the lawsuit a few months ago. We heard your testimony. About what they did to you boys at that place."

Mortimer looked from him to his wife. "Have you been here through the whole trial?"

"Yes," Sol answered. "We weren't surprised to hear the allegations. We knew the school had been culpable in Jack's death. Not at first, of course."

"You never believed what the school told you. Did you investigate Jack's death?" Mortimer asked.

"We knew our son," Helen said. "We knew something had happened to him, as his parents and as medical professionals. But the grief was too fresh to think about bringing a lawsuit. When we finally did, Torburton persuaded us to drop the investigation."

"Oh?"

Helen stirred her coffee quietly. "Tell them, Solly."

Sol nodded. "A few years after Jack's suicide, we had another child. A little girl, born with beta thalassemia."

"Another name for Cooley's anemia," Helen added. "A life-threatening blood disorder.

She required so much care, around the clock… constant blood transfusions, a pump attached to a needle in her stomach every night for chelation therapy to prevent her from going into organ failure from iron overload… I had to leave my practice to look after her. It was a very difficult time…" Her voice trailed away into silence.

Dylan blew out her breath. "They paid you off. That's why you didn't want to testify."

Sol and Helen exchanged glances. Clearly, even after all these years, they were still questioning their actions. "The medical bills were astronomical," Sol said. "The twins were going to college. And the school pointed out that nothing would bring Jack back to us…" He shrugged.

Shawn asked how their daughter was doing.

"We had her until she finished high school," Sol said evenly, as his wife pulled another photo from her purse. The young girl looked just like the twin sisters Brendan remembered—glasses, glossy black hair. "She even went to her prom. For Cooley's, she was quite a miracle at the time."

A lump formed in Brendan's throat as he met Sol and Helen's gaze. There were no words.

That night, Brendan knelt in front of the cardboard box he'd shoved to the back of his closet in the office, behind the safe with its Bren Ten, behind a row of suits. He'd never peeled back the tape, never opened it at all, could only imagine what was inside.

He knew this: allowing Dylan to show the photos to the Court would win their case. Shawn's words echoed in his mind.

He lifted the sealed box, carried it downstairs and out the sliding glass doors off the kitchen, and set it inside the metal fire pit on the patio. He lit a match, held it to the cardboard, and watched as it caught fire. He watched as flames snaked over the paper and devoured the box and its contents. The fire burned bright-hot for long minutes, illuminating the pretty gardens, until finally it petered out to a smolder.

In the embers, a silvery moonbeam caught on a last glossy corner of a polaroid. Brendan fished it out and wiped off the ash with his thumb. A young boy's shoulder—impossible to tell whose, maybe his—with a background of burgundy and hunter green plaid. After a few seconds, he scooped some embers onto the photo and sprinkled them into the pool, in a reverse baptism signifying not a new beginning but an ending. He watched as the still water swallowed ash and paper until it was gone.

When Brendan stepped into the witness box next, he was visibly shaking. He crossed and uncrossed his legs and clasped his wrists around his knee, breathing deeply to calm down. His haggard appearance belied the excruciating process he was undergoing, all the grappling with doubt.

He looked out upon the room, the people serving on the jury because they'd been so ordered, probably resenting his disruption of their lives. There were Eliza and her aide sitting directly behind Dylan; Shawn, with a small, encouraging smile; Warwick regarding him sleepily; Dr. Aldrich, who'd sat through all the testimony following his own. In the back rows sat Sandy Davidson and the other reporters: the young kid in the Adidas jacket; the bearded Millennial type with the man-bun; and the girl who looked as if she hadn't even graduated college, all of whom no doubt waited for a titillating front-page story. And there was another regular: a splotchy-faced, bald man hunched in his seat, who had appeared every day of the trial but seemed to have no reason to be there except for morbid curiosity.

When Brendan's eyes scanned the courtroom and rested on Jack's parents, sitting quietly holding hands, he knew. Jack's death had been preventable, and Sol and Helen deserved to know the truth. More than anyone else, they were owed justice.

"Today," Dylan started, "won't be easy. But I would like you to tell the Court, to the best of your ability, about your relationship with Dr. Lawrence Nevin."

Slowly, Brendan described the genesis of his involvement in the Science Club: the way the bullying of the upperclassmen led to his increasing isolation, intensified studying, and higher marks. How ironic that the treatment at the hands of the older students led him directly into the jaws of a pedophile.

Those Tuesday evenings spent in the science lab and then in the basement of Lawrence Nevin's residence stole the innocence of Shawn, Allen, Bobby, and Brendan, and countless boys before them. They were systematically groomed for abuse.

"Nevin made attendance at the Science Club compulsory. He told us it was educational," Brendan said.

"In what way?"

"We were learning about human behavior, he said. To make it seem legitimate, we had to watch these instructional films. But they were just porn. Adults, children, adults with children... books and magazines... he had reams of it. Before the club, I'd never seen sex depicted so graphically."

Dylan asked if he ever refused to go to the club or to watch the movies.

"We had to do everything he told us to do. There were lots of punishments if we didn't. As rewards he gave us cigarettes and beer, and after a while beer became hard liquor. Then came marijuana and eventually harder drugs, cocaine," Brendan said.

Dylan asked where Nevin got the drugs.

"We took turns going with him to New York. I remember a squalid drug den in a really dirty apartment building. I think... while I was there, he drugged me."

Brendan remembered those foggy car rides that ensued. Not once, not twice, but on several occasions. The time spent in the grungy apartment ended in lost hours with no memory of the time that had passed and only physical sensations—of nausea, dizziness—as mementos of the trips.

"How did you feel when Dr. Nevin gave you drugs and alcohol?"

Brendan grimaced. "The alcohol made me sick and confused. I remember the feeling of not being able to walk straight. And the drugs made me black out. The room would be spinning. I had no control, I was powerless to stop him. It was really scary."

"And did he give all four of you the drugs at once or just one at a time?" Dylan asked.

"It depended," Brendan explained, "on what we happened to be playing. Sometimes we did group games. Other times we did things... individually."

Dylan chewed her lip, knowing she had to ask but regretting the shame Brendan would no doubt experience in the telling. The jury needed to hear. "What were the games, Brendan?"

Gripping the edge of the jury box, watching her client and listening to his testimony, Dylan felt the same wave of disbelief as she had a year ago when she first heard the stories. Her soul wept. *They were just children.* One of the jurors gasped aloud.

After a while, Dylan asked a question. "Do you know what became of all the photographs and videos?"

Thoughts of the previous evening's rite, and of DevBoys1969, washed over Brendan in a torrent. "That's the worst part. All these years I've been afraid that my pictures would end up on the Internet, on child pornography sites."

Good God, Dylan thought. She hadn't known about that, or about many of the other details he'd provided in his testimony. *Imagine searching for your own images on kiddie porn sites? The things he must have seen.*

Dylan's gentle voice sounded through the haze. "How long did the abuse go on?"

"Until… until the end of sophomore year."

"It must have been such a relief when it finally ended," Dylan murmured. "I have no more questions."

Mortimer and his daughter conferred in the hallway following Brendan's testimony. "He did well," Mortimer said in a low voice. "The jury saw him very sympathetically. But it must have been hard on him."

"I know." Dylan peered at her father. "Are you okay?"

"I'd feel better if I could punch a few of those teachers in the face. But a verdict in our favor will be a close second."

Quietly, William Aldrich let himself into his office and locked the door behind him. He sat down at his desk and pulled out his keyboard on its sliding tray. From the breast pocket of his suit jacket, he slid two slim envelopes and placed them carefully beside the keyboard.

Inside the envelopes were the checks given to him by Vincent Sabato, one after he testified for the plaintiff and one after cross examination. He'd earned enough to cover his gambling losses... enough to replenish a good chunk of Maddy's college fund. He wasn't sure why he hadn't cashed them yet. A few days earlier, he would have.

But then he'd heard Brendan's story. The testimony pulsed in his ears. That man, that poor, broken man had suffered terribly. Every agonized word that came from Brendan's mouth had pierced Aldrich through and through, injecting him with remorse. When had his practice ceased to be noble? When had he become such a low beast? He shared the blame for Brendan's sickness as much as anyone.

His fingers began moving, opening Internet Explorer, almost of their own accord.

He typed one word in the search bar: "monster."

Aldrich wanted to know what words in the English language captured the essence of a man like Nevin, so willing to gratify his own perverse needs that he would knowingly sacrifice the wellbeing of children. A few options came up: Abomination. Demon. Incubus.

For several minutes, Aldrich scanned articles. Apparently, monsters appeared in the mythology of every culture. From the Latin *monstrum*, "monsters" had come to mean something unnatural or unpleasant, a malfunction of nature. Anthropologists, Aldrich read, said the basic role of the monster was to illustrate the human fear that existed over millennia—of falling prey to terrifying predators. Of being stalked, torn apart, consumed by creatures waiting to devour and destroy.

Carl Jung postulated that mythical monsters were simply representations of the "monster within," the atavistic, animalistic impulses at the core of the human psyche. These "shadow" aspects, he wrote, lived in the deepest, darkest unconscious, the evil repository of man's most repressed desires.

For another half hour, Aldrich scrolled through search results before exiting the browser and closing his eyes. What would Freud have said? Surely he would have pointed out the snakelike nature of monsters throughout history, the phallic symbolism in them. Perhaps Freud would have suggested that the serpentine characteristics common to many monsters—the Chinese dragons, the Roman Hydra, and the six-headed serpent Scylla in Greek mythology— were not surprising at all.

Yes, Brendan Cortland had encountered monsters as a youth. They'd preyed upon him and the other innocent children at Torburton Hall.

But there were still monsters in Brendan's life, Aldrich admitted now. He dropped his face into his hands.

How could he have failed Brendan, when the man was so obviously in pain? Kept him coming to appointments just to bill him? Ignored his symptoms, which were clearly so much more pathological than anything he'd pointed to in his charts? Failed so grossly to earn his patient's trust that Brendan finally chose to pour out his story not to him, but to Dylan James?

Was he, William Aldrich, a monster too?

CHAPTER THIRTY

Back in the witness box, Brendan trembled. Sleepless nights after laying himself bare, Warwick's relentless drilling, Shawn's testimony, Heather's admissions, all made his head pound.

Added to that was the guilt that Dylan's remark prompted.

Had he felt relief in that spring of his sophomore year, when the abuse finally stopped? No. He couldn't remember feeling any relief. Mostly, he remembered the overwhelming shame. There had been anger, powerful gusts of it that threatened to blow him away. And guilt and sorrow for all that had happened, like Jack's death. But when the abuse ended, it left only shame in its wake.

And now, after what Warwick had revealed while questioning his mother, he felt even more ashamed. It was true. Suddenly, Brendan remembered just how mean he'd been to his classmates, Michael and Ian.

Had he been a bully back then, too? Maybe he'd only been a kid, as if that were an excuse. But even then, he'd had a bit of a monster inside himself, hadn't he?

He looked up through his thick lashes. Warwick was staring at him from his table. The man stayed seated for the cross.

"You've told quite a story, haven't you?" Warwick said, leaning back in his chair.

Yes, Brendan agreed.

"And yet, I'm forced to return to my original question. Why are you doing this?"

"How do you mean?"

"If you win this case, the jury might award you a lot of money. Isn't that right?"

"Objection." Across the room, Dylan willed Brendan to look at her. *Don't let Warwick get under your skin.*

"Mr. Cortland, you testified that you had sexual intercourse with Dr. Nevin in the spring of your sophomore year."

Brendan ran his fingers through his hair and felt the drench of perspiration on his scalp. His head ached. "That's right."

"At which time Dr. Nevin passed away?"

"No."

"What do you mean, no?" Warwick slung the word like a dart.

"I mean, yes... he did, um, pass away." Brendan blinked several times to rid his eyes of the salty sting of his own sweat. The room swam in his vision.

Warwick stood up and leaned forcefully on his knuckles. "You must have been relieved."

Brendan thought about the day Science Club came to a screeching halt, with Nevin never to be seen again. "No."

Suddenly, the last vestiges of Warwick's apathetic manner dissolved. The sausage fingers that usually dangled limply at the big man's side were now raised toward Brendan. "Wasn't it enough that the man you call your primary abuser had died? You were glad about that, *weren't* you?"

For a moment the courtroom tipped sideways before righting itself. "I... I don't remember."

Warwick's eyes narrowed shrewdly. "Odd. Anyone who'd *truly* been abused would have wished for their abuser to die. Wouldn't that have felt like retribution? But you say you didn't. So you must want something else. Not justice. All these years living in the lap of luxury. Big house, maid, chauffeur. You frittered away your inheritance. You need money, and this trial is your best shot. Isn't it?" For the first time since the trial began, Warwick revealed his cunning nature. His eyes bored into Brendan's as if he could see right into his skull.

In response, the ugly thing that had remained submersed all this time in Brendan's mind surfaced like a submarine: a memory festering with pus and guilt.

Yes.

He'd *wanted* the pedophile to die.

He stopped fighting and let the recollection bloom. It was time, he thought, at last. A calm settled over him and the words quietly left his mouth:

"I did want Nevin dead. And I killed him."

A collective gasp sucked all the air from the room. Brendan raised his chin. "I killed Lawrence Nevin."

CHAPTER THIRTY-ONE

Pandemonium erupted in the courtroom after Brendan's confession. There was a chaos of excited chatter, Sandy Davidson and the other reporters snapping photos and speaking into their cell phones, Warwick and his colleagues conferring urgently at the defense table. Aberdeen rapped for order and excused the jury from the courtroom. They filed out, exchanging bewildered glances.

Aberdeen's face purpled. "Counselor," he snapped at Dylan. "An unexpected development?"

"I'm sorry, Your Honor... I... I had no idea..."

"Well, why the hell *didn't* you know? It's your job to know. It's on the first page of the *Idiot's Guide to Becoming a Lawyer*." He turned to the witness stand with a sweep of his black sleeve and glared down at Brendan. "You realize you just confessed to murder, Mr. Cortland?"

Brendan looked serene. The relief of admitting his crime was etched all over his face.

"Mr. Cortland, I am advising you to retain counsel. Do you understand? I am not presiding over a murder case!" He turned back to Dylan. "Miss James, I won't allow my courtroom to become a circus. We could very well have a mistrial on our hands."

In his newsroom the same afternoon, Sandy Davidson typed furiously on his laptop. In less than an hour, the *Connecticut Daily Dawn* had posted the explosive story of Brendan Courtland's admission to murder while testifying during a civil action against Torburton Hall Academy for Boys.

The Associated Press picked up the story. And soon it was all over the country.

Hours later, Dylan entered the tiny holding room and quietly walked to a chair opposite Brendan. "You okay?" she asked.

He slumped on a low bench, ghostly pale, eyes closed. A guard hovered silently by the door.

Dylan perched on the edge of the chair. "You need to help me understand. You have to tell me everything."

"I know." His lids fluttered open and he focused on Dylan. "I know. But the trial—what's happening?"

"Warwick moved for a mistrial. I'm sorry, Brendan. This part... it's over."

"It's my fault. I didn't know what I was saying. Or rather, I didn't know I was going to say it. It sort of bubbled up. Will I go to jail?"

"There will be an investigation. You'll go home tonight, but you'll have to report back to Court tomorrow."

"Will you represent me?"

"I'm not a criminal lawyer," Dylan said. "But my dad is."

Brendan seemed to notice Mortimer, hovering in the doorway, for the first time. The older man walked across the room and sat down beside his daughter, professional and attentive and very much in his element. "Why don't you tell us what happened, Brendan?"

And so the words Brendan had kept buried for over thirty years were exhumed at last. They left his throat with the rattle of brittle bones.

Spring of 1984.

Over a year of evenings in the basement of Dr. Nevin's house on campus. Almost a year since Jack took his own life. As Brendan feared, his "turn" had come, and Nevin had raped him repeatedly. Now, Brendan showed little interest in anything or anyone around him. He did whatever he was told, handed in his assignments without enthusiasm, ate what was put in front of him. He rarely talked or reacted to anything and, for the most part, even the upperclassmen lost interest in him.

One evening in May, as he listlessly rounded the corner of Nevin's cottage for club night, he heard muffled cries. The back door was unlocked. Brendan let himself in and went down the stairs.

Nevin was undressed, and he had Shawn Unger in his grasp.

The large, sweaty man wrestled Shawn onto the couch, ignoring his protests. "Stop squirming and relax," he snarled, trying to pull off the boy's underwear.

In Bobby's absence, Allen and Brendan had taken the brunt of Nevin's abuse in that spring of sophomore year. For whatever reason, they'd submitted. But until that night, Nevin hadn't yet turned his sights on Shawn.

Brendan saw the movie camera on the tripod with its red light blinking, and all at once fury blinded him. Without thinking, he grabbed Nevin by the arm. The sheer force with which he pulled brought the man sprawling backward. Nevin crashed onto the floor at Brendan's feet, slamming his head on the corner of the coffee table with a sickening crack.

A groan escaped Nevin's lips. He flopped once, like a big, white fish, and then lay still on the carpet.

Brendan recoiled from the lifeless body at his feet.

"Is he..." Shawn whispered, coming to stand beside Brendan.

For a long moment, they stood staring.

"We have to go." Shawn jiggled Brendan's shoulder, trying to shake him out of the stupor.

Brendan didn't budge. Holy Christ, what had he done?

Shawn scooped up his clothes and headed for the door. "C'mon, Brendan, *now!*"

At last the words seemed to penetrate, and Brendan panicked. He sprinted after Shawn across the basement and up the stairs. They ran around the house and past the shrubbery along Nevin's walkway. Just as they reached the main path, they collided with a knot of upperclassmen coming from baseball practice. Chad Hubert and his gang.

"Sexy lingerie you got on there, shrimp," Popeye sniggered. "Were you two out on a date or something?"

Brendan moaned. He couldn't handle any more that night. He turned and ran all the way back to his dorm, to the room he shared with a new boy, and sank onto his bed, staring into the dark. No, he couldn't handle any more. He couldn't even cry.

He didn't feel relieved that Dr. Nevin was dead, or that his own personal nightmare had ended. He hadn't meant to kill anyone. He just wanted Shawn left alone.

Long minutes ticked by in the holding room. Mortimer sat with his eyes closed, deep in thought, while his daughter scratched notes on a pad. Her cell phone dinged with new texts, emails, and voicemails from Sandy Davidson and other reporters, all of them hungry for details.

"And then?" Dylan looked up from her pages. "What happened the next day?"

"Greer found him when he didn't show up for class, and by lunchtime everyone knew Nevin was dead. Galloway said he'd taken a fall." Brendan looked from Dylan to her father. "I saw the hearse come for his body that afternoon. I kept waiting for the police to take me away. But no one talked to me or anything."

Another pause. Dylan jotted notes in the margins of Brendan's story. Mortimer opened his eyes. "You said the camcorder was recording when you found Nevin assaulting Shawn?" he said.

"Yes. I saw the light blinking."

"Was it still on when you left?"

"I don't know. The whole tripod fell over when I pulled Nevin off the couch."

Mortimer glanced at Dylan. "So, it's possible that the videotape captured not only Nevin's assault on Shawn, but the aftermath as well." He steepled his fingers and concentrated. The silence stretched. "A battered fourteen-year-old boy musters the strength to pull a heavy, grown man off the couch with such force that he falls backward, striking his head so hard that he dies."

"That's right."

"You slayed the monster," Dylan murmured. "And you've held onto the guilt for over thirty years."

Mortimer looked at Brendan thoughtfully. "Tell it again, from the beginning."

"All the school minutes you subpoenaed during discovery. There was nothing in them about Nevin's death?" Mortimer asked, as he and Dylan strode toward the parking lot.

"Not that I caught. I'm going back to my office now to see what I missed."

"I certainly hope you find something. Because unless there is evidence to the contrary, Brendan could very well be charged with Lawrence Nevin's murder."

At her desk, Dylan rifled through folder after folder, skimming over photocopies of old letters and documents until her eyes burned.

It was well after midnight when she came across a memo signed by Gavin Murdock, Chair of the Board of Trustees, dated May of 1984. It read, in part,

By now you will have heard of the untimely passing of our friend and colleague, an esteemed member of our staff. The unfortunate circumstances surrounding his death are of a confidential and personal nature. Therefore, we expect the utmost discretion and ask you to continue to respect the privacy of all involved. As always, we act with the best interests of Torburton at heart.

No one was identified by name, but Dylan felt certain the memo referred to Nevin. There were no other documents referring to the event. No mention of a call to paramedics or police. No mention of an inquiry of any kind.

But clearly, the school administrators had known everything. They'd hushed up the death of Lawrence Nevin, Dylan suspected, to protect themselves. Because if anyone had looked further into the circumstances regarding that night, they'd have uncovered a rape in progress. Torburton Hall would have been accused of employing a pedophile.

Unfortunate circumstances, indeed.

When the phone call came a few days later, Dylan almost ignored it, thinking it might be yet another reporter. It wasn't. The voice on the other end sounded so thready she could barely make it out; nor did she recognize the name, Henry Orman. As the man started to talk, Dylan grabbed for a pen to write down every word. Rhythmic beeping in the background further prevented Dylan from hearing everything clearly. And then the voice faded altogether, long before all of her questions were answered.

Four men languished in a jail cell. One squatted against the cement block wall at the back of the small space. Three were on their beds. Of those, one was a drug dealer and one a gang member, fast asleep on their respective bottom bunks. On a top bunk, above the drug dealer, Genius George peeled off his socks, picking at his yellow toenails and humming under his breath. George had earned his moniker after an attempted robbery: masked and gloved, George had successfully escaped with the contents of the till from a busy convenience store. However, he'd greedily grabbed the customers' cellphones as they cowered in a back corner. An hour later, half a dozen "find my phone" apps pinpointed his location to the police.

George hefted himself to sitting and dangled his feet toward the floor.

"Hey, Richie Rich." He tipped his chin toward the man crouched by the back wall. "When's that hot piece of ass lawyer coming back? Ask her if she's looking for more business." He licked his lips and grinned, a gap where his front teeth should have been.

Rolling his eyes, Chad Hubert rose to standing. Richie Rich! Really? Clearly, someone had blabbed about his father's money. Chad had been given fifteen to twenty years in prison for extortion, B and E, and multiple counts of assault. He could be incarcerated for a decade.

Anyway, Chad didn't know when Dylan James, the beautiful African American attorney they'd all seen in the news, might be back, or if she would keep her word about helping with an appeal. Even if she did, the court system was clogged and hearing dates would be routinely pushed back. But the thing was... it didn't really matter.

She'd shown up here out of the blue, the first visitor Chad had had in months. A guard had summoned him from the laundry room where he worked and brought him, through a series of clanging metallic doors and clunking locks, to a visiting room. The woman sat on the other side of a plexiglass divider and told him about the phone call she'd gotten from Henry Orman. She hoped Chad could explain.

Chad was quiet for a long time. He thought about the night he sold his box of porn and the masked intruder who'd beaten him within an inch of his life. For a long moment, he thought about Jack. He'd seen the television news coverage of Brendan's admission to murder. Chad knew the truth. For once in his life, he was ready to do the right thing. He'd come clean. If he never got anything in return, so be it.

Yes, that masked man's lesson had left its mark. Chad had learned about feeling helpless. Here, in prison, that lesson served him well, as there flourished all manner of predator and prey between its walls.

The Lexus sped along the highway, through valleys and between rock walls, past verdant green fields and billboards advertising local diners off the next exit. The sun sank lower as the exits stretched farther apart. At last, the ornate sign came into view: Torburton Hall Academy for Boys. Dylan turned into the private drive, isolated by thick woods all around.

She parked under a magnificent old tree immediately recognizable as Great Oak, and let herself through the wooden doors of the Commons, where two middle-aged women stood waiting.

The older of the two extended a hand. "Ms. James, we're happy to assist in any way. I'm Margaret Maynard, the headmistress, and this is my assistant, Amarah Singh. I see you've already printed a map of the grounds. Would you like us to accompany you around the campus?"

"Thank you, Ms. Maynard, Ms. Singh. If you don't mind, I'm going to walk around alone a bit."

Following the map, Dylan left the foyer and started walking, pulling her wool coat tight against the chill of early November. Over her shoulder, the Commons loomed behind her, and in front of her the campus spread out in all its glory—stately buildings, perfectly manicured lawns crisscrossed by white paths, hills rising in the backdrop. A world of its own, secluded and sheltered. To visitors, the institution had the rarified air of elite academia, of high ideals and noble pursuits. But Dylan knew that behind its grand appearance, this place held dark secrets.

She made her way across the compass rose to stand in front of Mariner Block. She took in the sight of the weathered stones, the arched doorway, the wide moldings around the rows of leaded windows. She gazed up at the second story, wondering which room had been Brendan's, wondering if the ghost of Jack Abromovitch flitted down the dusty hallways or hovered in the trees somewhere nearby. To her, the imposing structure seemed to hold so much grief and pain, and so little of the innocence and wonder that Brendan and his childhood friends had been promised. As she stood there, a boy in a gray hoodie and a backpack pushed open the door and stepped outside. He passed her on the path and gave a little wave. She wondered, what was his story? Was he safe and happy here at present-day Torburton Hall? Was he, as Brendan had suggested, among the bullies or the bullied, or had this school's culture finally changed over the years?

Dylan continued across the campus to the sports complex. Its main doors were open, and groups of boys came and went, all in various types of uniforms and gear, jostling each other as they pointed her out. She walked around Winners' Circle, her footsteps echoing in the empty corridor, and examined the glass cases lining the walls, the dozens of trophies and pennants and team portraits. It didn't take long before she found the same team photo the *Connecticut Daily Dawn* had run last winter, with Brendan himself staring back at her through an old man's eyes.

A door stood open to the equipment storage area, and Dylan entered. She surveyed the shelves stacked with helmets and pads and the various bins of balls. She ran a finger across the row of jerseys on hangers and wondered how much, if any, of the equipment dated back to the eighties. Probably none, judging by the mint condition of it all.

Continuing toward the gym, Dylan asked a group of students where she could find the athletic director's office. They pointed to a locked door, with an unfamiliar name on the placard. The subpoena to produce a certain thick, blue binder had proved fruitless and once again, Dylan wondered if the book could possibly be on the other side of this door. No way the staff would risk spoliation, would they? Surely they knew that intentional withholding of evidence was a crime.

Outside, Dylan passed clutches of maroon-clad boys going here and there, past the Murdock Memorial Library, the chapel, the old graveyard, the headmaster's residence, now white with shutters the new headmistress had painted blue... all of the settings for Brendan's sordid stories. She remembered his whispered words and the fearful look in his eyes as he'd first uttered them. Never once, in all this time, had she doubted that they were true. It didn't matter how much he had, or didn't have, in the bank. What mattered was his story.

Finally, Dylan reached a part of the campus that was quiet, save for the whistling wind; no students to be found, not here. She stood in front of the staff residences on the far slope, off the path that led from the athletic fields past the academic buildings and back to the dormitories. She'd made an arc around the far reaches of the campus. Had come full circle.

In front of her stood a little cottage she thought could had been Nevin's, from Brendan's description of its locations and his penciled X on the map. The site of so much horror. In the fast-dimming light, Dylan squinted at the map and concentrated. Brendan needed her to figure this out. He needed to come full circle, too.

In her mind she went over it again, for the thousandth time since receiving the phone call weeks earlier. Brendan had been here, at this spot on which she now stood. He'd been running, up the stairs from Nevin's basement and out into the warm night. He must have been completely freaked out. Maybe he'd paused to lean his hands on his knees and catch his breath. Or slowed to wait for Shawn. Or maybe the sight of Chad Hubert and his buddies returning from practice had stopped Brendan in his tracks.

Dylan's cell phone rang in her purse. "I'm here," she said, turning three hundred and sixty degrees to survey her surroundings. "It's exactly the way he described."

"It hasn't changed?" her father asked.

"I don't think so. I'll call you back." She hung up.

Mortimer said a deathbed confession, even when it aligned perfectly with the information Chad Hubert provided from prison, wouldn't hold up without evidence. But suddenly, she thought she knew where she might find some.

Dinnertime on campus meant that all those boys she'd encountered were now ensconced in the dining room. Only a few minutes of dusk remained, and the lanterns by the paths switched on. Dylan hurried past a few buildings to beat the encroaching darkness, tracing her finger along the map and squinting at the paper as she went. At last, she came to a halt.

In front of her was the John Adams Music Hall, aptly shortened to the JAM, lit and unlocked to accommodate after-hours band and orchestra rehearsals as well as individual students who wanted to practice their instruments. The halogen lights blazing inside threw dim beams on the dry grass. Dylan stood in front of the main entrance and then turned to her left, hoping she'd navigated correctly.

Yes. There, off to the side of the building and angled between empty gardens, stood a long hedge, still waxy green juxtaposed with the bare brown branches above. Dylan left the path to walk the length of the hedge, disappearing behind the side of the music hall and out of its lamps' reach. She flicked on her cell phone light. Had she gone the wrong way? Her boots kicked up dried leaves, unraked in this remote corner. She reached a dead end in the form of a stone wall and doubled back.

There. She'd missed it the first time, but now she saw what she'd been looking for: a gap in the hedging, used by generations of boys who'd wanted to take a shortcut, perhaps, or take advantage of the seclusion to break a few rules. She turned sideways and squeezed through, trying not to snag herself on the sharp bristles. Her phone illuminated a small clearing, in the center of which stood an ancient elm. Taking a deep breath, Dylan stepped over the gnarled roots and circled to the back of the tree... to the gaping black hole in the trunk about four feet off the ground. She reached in a tentative hand, trying her best to quell the squeamishness, praying not to disturb any creature that happened to live inside.

Her questing fingers felt the roughness of bark, the stickiness of dried sap. She held the light with her left hand and aimed it into the hollow while standing on her tiptoes. Thrust her right arm deeper in, running her touch around the circumference of the space. A flurry of tiny legs swarmed over her skin and she suppressed a scream. Then her fingertips came upon something smooth and hard, jammed on an angle, just out of reach. She grimaced and curled her fingers around it, pulled it out. A half-empty bottle of brownish liquid. She tossed it away.

She reached back in. Forced her arm all the way in up to the shoulder. With the tips of her fingers, she felt something else. Something cool and crinkly.

Gingerly, Dylan wrapped her fingers around it and pulled. A wadded-up garbage bag. Heavy. She pocketed the phone and pulled, hand over hand, incrementally bringing out the length of green wrapping, like pulling the entrails from the belly of a beast. She forced herself to move slowly so the decaying plastic wouldn't snag or spill. At last, it was all out. She spread it on the ground, took out her phone, and shone the cell on it. It was crawling with the last bugs of the season, scurrying in a frenzy to escape the light.

Dylan sucked in her breath, and carefully shook the bag open to let the contents spill by her feet.

A baseball bat.

A video tape.

The weapon used to kill Dr. Lawrence Nevin, and the recorded evidence of a 1984 rape and murder.

CHAPTER THIRTY-TWO

"Get up, Hubert," the guard called again. "Your lawyer's here."

"Yo, Sleeping Beauty." Genius George flicked a piece of yellow toenail across the room. It landed on Chad's eyelid. "Wake up and ask her if she makes house calls."

Chad swung off his bed. He followed the guard to the visiting room and shuffled to the farthest booth. On the other side of the partition, Dylan waited impatiently.

They picked up phones.

"I found everything. Forensics is going over it. I'll need you to write a statement."

Chad nodded slowly. "Tell Brendan I'm glad."

In his living room, Brendan tried to process Dylan's shattering words: Deathbed confession. Henry Orman. No disparities. Solid evidence. Exonerated.

Brendan's brain swam with new information he needed to assimilate, information that would effectively negate everything he believed about himself. He hadn't, as he'd thought all this time, murdered Nevin. He'd lived inside that belief for over three decades. The paralyzing self-loathing and guilt that colored his whole life… he'd gotten it wrong.

Dylan's explanation took his breath away:

Nevin had bumped his head on the table, knocked silly, but not dead. The teacher had started to regain consciousness before Brendan and Shawn even made it out of the house.

Fate had intervened then, placing Brendan on the path just as the upperclassmen were returning from practice. Popeye had teased poor Shawn for being outside in his underwear. Shawn started to cry, and he and Brendan both ran away. Yes, Popeye had made cruel jibes about Shawn, but it was Hank... Hank who'd seen Brendan and Shawn running out of Lawrence Nevin's backyard... Hank who recognized their terror for what it was... Hank who assumed—correctly—that Nevin must have been molesting them, just as Nevin had been abusing Hank since his own freshman year. It was *Hank* who had snapped.

Hank waited a beat before racing around the yard in his cleats toward the basement where he'd cowered so many times, letting himself in and clattering down the stairs he knew so well. Chad Hubert followed on his heels. There was Nevin, naked and disoriented, hoisting his gross body off the floor, groping for the tripod to set his precious camcorder back on its cradle.

Hank saw the opportunity. He grabbed for the chain around Nevin's neck from which dangled the key to the padlocked cabinet. He fumbled with the lock and swung open the metal door. A large cardboard box stood inside. He hefted it into his arms and thrust it into Chad's, ignoring Nevin's weak grunts of protest behind him. "Take it to my room," Hank hissed. "Don't let anyone see you with it."

Chad, unaccustomed as he was to being given orders, only lingered for a moment before doing as he was told.

The teacher struggled to stand. Hank turned around. All the horrors he'd experienced as one of Nevin's "dolls" welled up. He picked up his baseball bat and swung, striking the man in the throat, just once. There wasn't a lot of blood. But one blow was enough to crush his larynx.

On the camcorder the light blinked. Hank turned it off and ejected the tape. At his feet, the wet gurgling sound coming from Nevin's ruined throat seemed to take forever to stop.

Dylan and Mortimer had been granted an audience in Judge Frances Wong's private chambers regarding the murder investigation. They sat alongside her broad desk in front of a portable television set on a cart. It hadn't been easy to requisition a VCR, their being obsolete, but now, Dylan slid a videotape into the slot of a machine perched on the cart and pressed PLAY. The television crackled into life.

On the screen, dark, grainy footage settled into the image of a man, his skin white and expansive. He could be seen cajoling and then struggling with a small-framed boy. About five minutes into the film, another youth entered the room and pulled the naked man off the couch. Voices rang out, and the room tipped horizontally as the tripod clattered to the linoleum. The audio continued to catch the conversation of the boys, with the lens pointed sideways at the frayed edge of plaid upholstery and a warren of dust bunnies under the sofa. Minutes ticked by in silence.

Then, hands appeared in the lens, and the man's hairy chest and face could be seen close up as he reached for the camcorder and shakily lifted it. He grunted and swore as he righted the tripod and set up the camera. Just then two more youths ran into the room, their shoes making an odd clacking sound. There was shouting and a skirmish, and then one boy, who Dylan identified as a young Chad Hubert, left with a box in his arms. The other boy, redheaded and freckled, brandished a bat.

And then came a loud, sickening crunch.

Once again, the picture went off-kilter before going black.

Dylan rose to eject the tape. She handed it to Judge Wong where she sat behind her desk.

"I think we can easily ascertain what happened from this video," the judge said. "Forensics?"

"Fingerprints and DNA didn't match any on file. However, traces of blood from the baseball bat were identified as B negative, the same type Yale University had on record as belonging to Dr. Nevin."

"It seems conclusive," Judge Wong said decisively.

"Thank you, Your Honor," Mortimer said.

Judge Wong held up a finger. "Not so fast. The box that Mr. Hubert is seen carrying away. Is it still in his possession?"

Mortimer clasped his hands in his lap. "No, Your Honor. Custody was transferred to Mr. Cortland."

"I presume it was entered into evidence during Mr. Cortland's trial?"

"No." Dylan spoke up. She glanced at her father, who nodded. She cleared her throat. "Mr. Hubert gave the box, which was presumed to contain pornographic images, to our client a year ago. Or rather, he sold it. And Brendan destroyed the whole thing. I just learned of this recently."

Mortimer hastened to add, "This would not, of course, be a case of tampering with evidence, since Mr. Cortland was the plaintiff."

The judge frowned. "I don't have to tell you both that the purchase of child pornography is a federal crime."

"Brendan had every reason to believe that he himself was depicted in the images, along with his friends. He wanted to protect them," Dylan said. "Even if it meant losing his case."

Judge Wong sighed and looked at her watch. "I'm due in court. If there's nothing else, I'd like to wrap this up. I'm closing the case. Let's let Mr. Cortland get on with his life."

In the dining room a month later, Irma ladled out generous portions of soup. The wafting steam from the pot had fogged the window so that the rain outside was hardly visible. She passed around a basket of hot crusty bread, the kind she knew Brendan liked best. She'd been serving his favorites all week in celebration of his being officially exonerated.

"A toast," Brendan said. "Come, Irma and Tomasz, have a drink with us."

Mortimer raised a glass. "To Brendan. And to putting this whole ordeal behind you."

"To Brendan, and next chapters," Dylan echoed.

Irma cleared her throat, and everyone turned curiously toward her.

"To Brendan. Good man. Long life." she said.

They clinked five glasses.

Brendan sipped the wine, dipped the bread in spiced oil. He felt weightless after prolonged worry, here with his friends at the beautifully set table of crystal goblets and fine china and flickering candles. He'd been convinced he would be found guilty of murder. Under the table, Elvis's weight on his feet was the sweetest pleasure of all.

"Thank you all, for everything," Brendan said quietly. "You've been so kind to me."

Mortimer swirled his wine. "This morning was extraordinary. The victory may not look the way you pictured it, but it's a victory, nonetheless. You told your story, and the world heard it. You've helped so many others. And you truly honored Jack's memory."

"And you've put down your burden of guilt." Dylan laid a hand on Brendan's unflinching arm. "You can put it all to rest now."

He looked down at her touch, at the diamonds sparkling on her wrist. For a moment, he lost his voice. Then he lifted his glass and offered a toast of his own, this time to Dylan's new office. "A little late, seeing as you've been there for weeks, but I wanted to congratulate you."

"It's not as nice as the one in Dr. Aldrich's house, but I couldn't stay under the same roof as that man, or continue paying him rent."

"His loss."

"Looks like he and Sabato will lose their licenses to practice," Mortimer put in. "The inquiry will take a while."

The three ate their soup and bread in silence for a few minutes. In the quiet, they could hear Irma serving her son his dinner in the kitchen.

Dylan finally asked, "What will you do now?"

Brendan shrugged. "The house is for sale, with the contents. Irma and Tomasz are moving on. I guess I'll get a job like a regular person. Maybe something in IT. Or something with animals. I don't know, but this dinner is kind of a last hurrah."

Irma reappeared carrying a platter of roast beef. When they'd eaten their fill, Brendan turned to Dylan.

"I want you to know how sorry I am. It's my fault there was no verdict or award. You took my case on contingency and I know the initial retainer wasn't enough to cover the hundreds of hours of hard work you both put in. I'll pay you over time, I promise. But for your sake, I wish I could've given you more. I wish I could've given you the win."

From the den, a voice cackled and sang out, "Diamonds are a girl's best friend…"

The evening wrapped up early, as Mortimer begged fatigue. At the front door, Brendan shifted uncertainly. They hovered over goodbyes, wondering when they'd see each other again outside the context of a legal battle. At last, Mortimer held out a hand. "Don't hesitate to call if you need anything," he said. Brendan looked at the proffered hand and, after a moment, clasped it hard.

And then it was Dylan's turn. "Take care," she said. "Okay if I...?" She reached up her arms and enfolded Brendan in the scent of gardenia and pine. The sweet shock of her embrace cascaded over him. He slid his arms around her and held her close for a long moment. She left a soft kiss on his cheek, and its heat remained on his skin long after the Lexus disappeared down the road.

In fact, it was still warm as Brendan found his cell phone and texted her the words he'd been wanting to say for so long. And smiled broadly at the reply.

Later, as he did every night, Brendan lay in bed and recounted the course of events over the past year and a half: telling Dylan his story, prepping for the trial, and how it all had gone sideways with his admission of guilt, blurted under psychological duress. How the lawsuit had come to a grinding halt in a mistrial, with the defense witnesses never called and the verdict he'd imagined for so long never to materialize. And then there were the tortuous days afterward, when he'd had to wait in purgatory for the murder investigation to sort itself out. It all seemed surreal.

The contents of the box could have won the civil suit for him. But it wasn't worth it, not if it meant having strangers see him, see Shawn, Allan, Bobby, and other boys, at their most vulnerable. For whoever saw those images, whether it be the judge or the attorneys or the jurors, those people would have the pictures emblazoned in their minds, *never* to be forgotten. No. Much better to have destroyed this part of a past that should never have been preserved.

He'd finally confessed to Dylan about the box he'd burned. She'd gazed at him with her warm brown eyes that seemed to understand.

Only a week after that conversation, a notice came. Hank had died. Hank, who'd been one of his primary tormentors at boarding school. Hank, who'd been in and out of hospital as an adult. Hank, whom Shawn rightly guessed had also been one of Nevin's "dolls."

Brendan drove Dylan in the Mercedes to the funeral, at a church in a nearby town. It was a short ceremony, attended by Hank's elderly parents, his brothers, and a few friends. The eulogies were brief: all of them were testament to the quiet life he'd lived, much of it spent fighting his illness. The photo beside the podium depicted a splotchy-faced, bald man at the end of his days. Brendan and Dylan recognized him from the courtroom.

When the service was over, the attendees accompanied the coffin from the church to the adjacent cemetery. The plot waited with the headstone already in place. "In memory of Henry Orman, 1966-2016. May he rest in peace."

In bed, Brendan thought about what had happened that very morning, the most unexpected event of all, the thing he never could have predicted.

He, Mortimer, and Dylan had appeared in court in Stamford as a formality. They'd been told to appear before Judge Wong and the state attorney to put the murder case to rest. One last hearing and it was done.

Outside, on the courthouse steps, Brendan was about to say goodbye when he stopped in his tracks.

He drew in his breath in astonishment at the incredible, startling, heart-wrenching sight. Beside him, Dylan put a hand to her mouth.

There, at the bottom of the steps beside the circular sculpture, with television cameras filming, a large crowd filled the plaza. It numbered fifty or seventy or a hundred. Grown men with sad but determined eyes, and the loved ones who supported them. All stood silently, a few holding signs with messages: "Silence Ends Now," and "End Private School Abuse," and "It Happened to Me," and "A Childhood Stolen."

Brendan stared and stared. He had no words, and the people who stood before him expected none. Everything that needed to be said had been uttered in the courtroom.

As Brendan descended the steps, the men organized themselves into a line. When he reached the bottom stair the first man held out a hand. Brendan took it hesitantly. His handshake became firmer as he made his way down the line, looking each man in the eyes, the next and the next and the next.

No, the jury verdict Brendan wanted hadn't materialized. Yet in the end he'd managed to get justice after all.

EPILOGUE

In the guesthouse, Irma lay in her narrow bed and slept a deep and guiltless sleep. She offered no apology for the things she and her son had done over their lifetime. Monstrous things.

She'd known all along what had happened years ago to Brendan at the school. She'd recognized the signs. It had been so easy to identify Brendan's abusers from his journals and track them down.

All those beatings Tomasz had doled out over the years. First Coach Terry Dunlop, in the late nineties. Irma and Tomasz had visited him together.

"You can't do this," the coach had shouted, shielding his face from the blows. "I'll call the police."

Irma had replied calmly, "No problem. And we tell police about special picture book."

That had shut the guy up. Irma knew Dunlop would never talk. He'd been the first, the trial run, and he'd taught Tomasz valuable lessons about where to land punches. To this day, the Before and After book sat in her bottom dresser drawer, not five feet away from where she slept.

And then came Popeye a few years later, identified in Brendan's journals as Wilson Vanderhof, a man with two last names. He'd made light of his behavior as a teenager.

"It was all in good fun," he protested. Tomasz showed him a different kind of fun. The smug smile evaporated before Irma's eyes.

And then there was Galloway.

In her bed, Irma turned over and stretched comfortably on the flannel sheet.

Galloway had turned on the same charm he'd possessed decades earlier as headmaster. Irma savored the time with him, and eventually the charm disappeared.

"People will be looking for you," the man had yelled until hoarse. But no, he was wrong, they wouldn't.

Of course, in her unquestioning, emotionless way, Irma simply cleaned up the mess afterward. She and her son. A team.

Since then, there'd been many others—men who did terrible things to little boys and girls. Tomasz had beaten them to a bloody pulp. Sometimes they fled without a word, but occasionally they vanished forever with the help of Tomasz and his garden tools.

How Irma wished she'd had a chance to sic Tomasz on Brendan's selfish little ex-wife and her new husband. Or Aldrich or, of course, Lawrence Nevin. Oh, how she would have enjoyed *that*.

Never mind. They'd accomplished a lot, taught many a lesson. Showed them, all of them, how it felt to be helpless and hurt.

How it could damage a person forever.

THE END

ACKNOWLEDGEMENTS

Both Brendan Cortland and the prestigious boarding school he attended in the 1980s are fictional, but I'm sad to say that the kind of abuse depicted in *A Nest of Snakes* was and is all too real.

Actual reports from the United States to the United Kingdom prompted me to write this novel. I was horrified by what the plaintiffs endured as children, and equally horrified that so many adults were complicit in the assaults and in covering them up. I thought it took extraordinary courage for individuals to come forward with their truths.

My hope is that this book will help shine a light on social issues that need illuminating. Sexual abuse of children, bullying, and the machismo culture that often proliferates in private boys' schools are just some of these harms.

I'm deeply grateful to so many people who helped bring this book to life:

Thank you first and foremost to the wonderful team at WildBlue Press including Steve Jackson, Michael Cordova, Ashley Kaesemeyer, Devyn Radke, Stephanie Johnson Lawson, Elijah Toten, and Tatiana Villa.

Huge thanks to my two editors, Leslie Schwartz and Donna Marie West, for your sharp eyes and keen insights.

For the reams of savvy legal advice, thank you to Attys. Adam Federer, Sheryle Levine, and Andy Bowman. I couldn't have written the courtroom scenes without your input.

Michelle Adelman, your expertise regarding the therapy sessions is so appreciated.

Grazie to my Amalfi Coast consultants, Louise LaRocca and Ellen Goldman.

Hats off to Larry Till, the original Princess Leah.

KJ Howe, thanks for brainstorming at the Miller Tavern... I'll need another "jolly" meetup for Book Three, please.

Pssst... thanks to my undercover agent, Gary Krebs.

To my friends and family (hubby Craig and kids Jordyn, Jake, and Coby, my beets forever; Peter and gang; Elaine and Ben; and the assorted Levisons in the GTA and beyond)—you're the best, I love you all, and I hug you in advance for telling every person you know, and every acquaintance you have yet to meet in your lifetime, to read this book.

To my father, Steve Vadas z"l, whose quiet strength and resolve I feel around me, and most of all, to my beautiful and profoundly wise mother, Veronica Vadas—I treasure your love and endless encouragement. Dad, I apologize for not inheriting even one iota of your mathematical brilliance. Mom, *köszönöm szépen* for your gift of imagination.

And to the incredible storytelling community—the supportive authors, librarians, booksellers, reviewers, bloggers, and, of course, the readers near and far, today and tomorrow—thank you for letting me tell Brendan's story.

ABOUT THE AUTHOR

Deborah Levison is an author and publicist. Her first book, THE CRATE, won seven literary awards. Reviewers described it as "heart-wrenching," "harrowing," "lyrical," and "a brilliant story." Jerusalem Post said: "Exquisite."

Originally from Canada, she now lives in Connecticut with three children, two doodles, and one husband.

Visit *www.debbielevison.com.*

For More News About Deborah Levison,
Signup For Our Newsletter:

http://wbp.bz/newsletter

Word-of-mouth is critical to an author's long-term success. If you appreciated this book please leave a review on the Amazon sales page:

http://wbp.bz/snakes

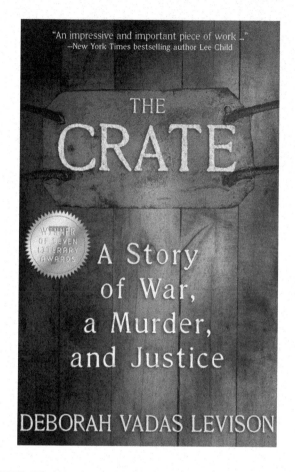

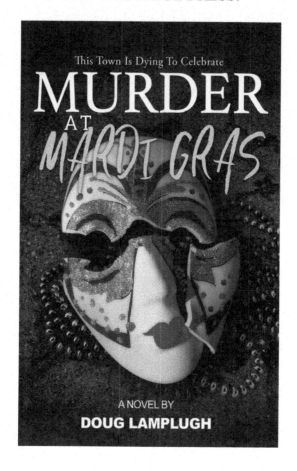

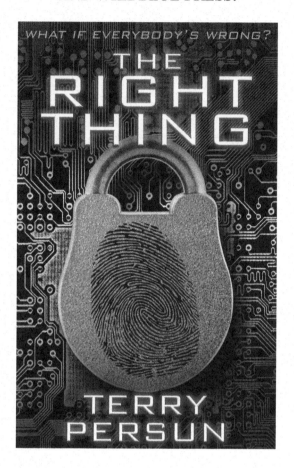

I

Made in USA - North Chelmsford, MA
1334562_9781957288390
09.27.2022 1348